Seeds Of Ascension Series:
Book Two
Gateways

I0652265

BOOK TWO: GATEWAYS

First edition. December 12, 2024.

ISBN: 978-1998052004

Written by Frank Talaber.

To the memory of all of those children and the adults that stared up into the stars on cloudless nights, staring at millions of stars, galaxies and dreaming of riding on starships going on incredible adventures.

I was one and still am.

Dedication

To the memory of all of those children and the adults that stared up into the stars on cloudless nights, staring at millions of stars, galaxies and dreaming of riding on starships going on incredible adventures.

I was one and still am.

"Come to the edge," he said.

"We can't, we're afraid!" they responded.
"Come to the edge," he said.
"We can't, We will fall!" they responded.
"Come to the edge," he said.
And so they came.
And he pushed them.
And they flew."
— Guillaume Apollinaire

Prelude

It won't be anymore.

Roger turned over in his bed, wondering if Luke had ever had days like this dealing with crazy events and crazier beings, living life behind a lightsaber.

Welcome! rang out in his head. A voice he never heard before was now calling out to him at night, every night.

Drumbeats, hearts melting. Beating like an eerie dream cast in dim light with abeyance drawn in the moonlight. Stars blinked in cascades of clouds asunder while a crow in a darkened tree spate in disbelief.

Not in disgust, but mere enjoyment of the moment. The very moment a page turns in some holy text, to begin the next chapter.

When all is silent and in the still of the night, one only hears the blades of grass that are moaning under the caress of the winds perceptive touch and the thump of a heart.

Roger awoke shaking, while somewhere in the cosmos a star began blinking in response.

"Damn!" hissed a reptilian voice from the dark side of the moon and, slamming his clawed hand on the consul, glared at the warning light blinking before him.

Chapter One

Science News
February 12, 1991

Scientists have reported a new frequency or some sort of energy radiating from the very central core of the galaxy and spreading out into its further reaches. Its source is unknown at this time, as is its nature, but it appears to be a new photonic pulse, the likes of which have never been detected before.

I closed my eyes and he was there. "So, I don't totally understand. I go to sleep at night and you arrive. Are you just a figment of my imagination? Something I created to deal with what I'm going through? I've read that the human mind uses dreams and sleep to sift through the day's events and store what it needs to remember."

"Hmm, that is logical and a justifiable position. A skeptic could rationalize away everything that is happening to them. Convince themselves that all of this is simply dreams. Rationalize until they sort order from chaos. Quiet the fear inside that exists when we confront that edge of the unknown. And in the end, the skeptic believes in nothing other conspiracies that other sceptics believe in."

I hesitate. "I call myself a skeptic, and a strong one. But with everything that has begun to happen I find myself wondering about a lot of things."

"Wondering is good, believing is better for it gives your life purpose, puts you on a path, but believers can only work on trust and love of self and of life."

"And something else I'm starting to realize."

"What?" it asked, and as it looked to me for an answer, I saw what I took to be curiosity cross its face. The first glimmer of any emotion from this being.

"Connections. I'm beginning to see connections."

"Good. That is important. You are doing well in this learning of the gateways and of journeying through the chakras."

"But you never answered any of my questions."

"You will find your own answers. Right now, you are establishing will and purpose, the foundation of the third chakra. Understanding comes later."

It gestured toward another inset tile. Deep in a cavernous pyramid, tall columns disappeared into the darkness, preventing me from seeing where the roof

9

was, or even if there was a roof. The tile was of petals surrounding a circle and inset was a crystal that began to glow as I stared at it. Below that stood a ram.

"The strong horns of will, power and internal purpose." The crystal grew even brighter until I was nearly blind, covering my eyes as the Hathor talked. "Manipura. The first two chakras are of flow downward. This one is of eruption, fire, determination and upwards flow. Internal will and purpose. Or as we just mentioned believing."

I reached out to cover the crystal and attempted to block out the blinding light. Instead of touching the glowing surface I encountered nothing. It slipped away and I fell into the tile and into darkness.

I stood up in the darkness, the crystal glow hovering behind me. I reached again for it. Glittering flashes sparkled everywhere. Blinded I chased the crystal as it weaved out of my grasp.

Every time I reached out and got close the light intensified, my fingers grew hot. Afraid, I withdrew, not wanting to burn myself. Instead, I closed up and sat down until the sun broke over my shoulder and light filled the room.

I stood up, trinkets and rattles stirred. I looked down. Hair flowed long, dirty and coarse in my face. I was a female again, but not helpless this time. Leathers of animal hides covered my body and, around my neck, bits of dried flesh strung in a necklace. A medicine pouch hung on my side. Outside seagulls squawked, air was heavy with humid salt smell of the ocean. Simple white painted buildings of the town yard glinted through the windows.

I knew what had to be done and shoved aside the two austere looking women staring at me in disgust from their black and white outfits. Nuns, they were called. It suited them, for they had 'none' connection to the Earth and even though they considered themselves pious and strongly spiritual, I knew they were missing a connection to this world and this land. But I wasn't here to save them, it was the one inside that needed my attentions.

"Begone, savage," one said as she made signs on her chest that I knew were of the cross bearing their god. "You'll harm her. She is in God's Good Hands now."

I stood over Crystal Running Water, or Mary as they called her. She had already been tainted by their ways and had denied all the teachings of our people, our ancestors. She would have been picked to be a shaman in training as she had great gifts of healing. I should not have come, but one never turns their back on their own people in need. "Not as much as the harm you've already done.

She will not live the night and you have no means of saving her," I grunt in their foreign tongue.

"No, we are praying for God to come and save her soul. She will join St. Peter and live with Jesus in heaven."

"Your God will not have her yet. Her time is not yet. Leave this room." I growl and shake my raven's rattle at her. The head nun turns and runs from the room screaming to get the men to come. I pick up Crystal, her body is hot and easily mistaken for fever-ridden but it is not fever that resides in this one. Still, it will eat her alive just the same. I open the side window, no one is around. They are guarding the front entrance. I pull myself and Crystal through the window and carry her to a sacred grove in the woods.

I deposit her body on the ground I've covered in cedar boughs and pine needles ahead of time. I quickly light smudge to burn all around us. No spirits will dare enter past these boundaries while I begin my work.

Crystal's eyes flicker open. "Grandmother, what are you doing?"

"They would let you die. You are not meant to die, you will live a long life. Some of this you will remember, most you will not," I bark in our tongue; she nods and falls unconscious again. The evil spirit inside is eating her spirit with great haste. I have not much time. Cries of alarm ring out from the village, they have discovered my doing and I have less time now."

I close my eyes and begin a slow walk around the body, knowing it is not the eyes I need to see with. Instead I see the demon twisting around inside her, it is hungry, gnawing away at her spirit. I shake the raven's rattle and the ground shakes. The creature stops and turns to look at me.

Great red eyes of hunger glare out from the shaggy fur of the grizzly looking beast. It is strong, savage like the grizzly. Teeth glint in a snarl. They want to devour Crystal's essence and perhaps mine if it could.

I pull another rattle from my belt and shake it several times until her body is frozen solid. The beast looks down and snarls. It turns to leap at me, enter me if it cannot have the girl. I shake the raven's rattle again and it staggers, dizzy. This battle is greater than it had hoped for.

"Begone, foul demon, there are others for you to devour, but she is not yours."

I hear people approaching and the voice of the mother nun yelling, as soon as it sees the face of the head nun projected from my mind's eye the beast is gone.

She is easier prey to hunt and more satisfying. I shake the rattle again and I am back.

"I am so cold now. Thank you."

"That is a good sign. You'll be okay. Know this, your son will become a powerful minister among the whites. He will be half white and will lead the missionaries to destroy the last of the old ways, the native ways. There will be no more Ska-ga shamans after me. None will follow, the old ways will die."

"Why do you save me then?"

"Because you are one of my blood, and as a healer of my people, I could not let you die knowing I have the ability to save your life. I cannot judge those I save, that is not the way of our people, nor the Ska-ga. We do what we must."

"Thank you, Grandmother."

Shouts burst from the woods as she stands up on shaky legs. I turn to leave and a crack from one of their thunder-sticks rings out. Searing pain bursts from my shoulder and I stagger backwards, blood pours into the sky. Several men burst into the glade.

The head nun points an accusing finger at me. "You should rot in hell for taking this child from us and trying to kill her with your heathen ways."

"No!" *young Crystal screams.* "Don't harm her! She has saved my life, I am cured."

The head nun feels Crystal's head. "Goodness the fever has left her. Get this girl some clothes."

They wrestle me to the ground, crushing me into the still burning smudge. It cannot protect me and keep these men from me, just as I cannot prevent what will happen in the future.

Young Crystal Running Water turns to me as they shackle my hands. "Howa, thank you, again. I shall never forget I was born native, no matter what they teach me."

Later I know she will help me escape. My time is not yet either. I am picked up and shoved forward to fall face first into the cedar boughs, with my hands bound behind me. My medicine bag is trampled and kicked aside. My blood flows back into the earth that created it from the wound inflicted of buckshot and pellets.

"You should be punished for this. But she lives, so we will take you in to attend to your wound and teach you the kindness of Jesus and begin to teach you *his ways, cleanse you of this heathenism. Someone make sure her hair is cut and she gets a bath." The head nun holds a hand over her face, as I watch a bead of sweat break her brow. The beast is already within. "Let us hurry back, this accursed glade gives me shivers."*

"We'll see just how strong your God is now." I lean into her and whisper, "forgive them, for they fear the unknown and they know not what they do."

Richmond, BC

"Main Gracious Hall is the main temple," the Buddhist guide announced to the first guests touring the grounds of the Buddhist Temple in Richmond, British Columbia, Canada that day. His traditional yellow, orange robe rippled under a gentle breeze as he walked. The smell of pungent incense filled the air in honor of Buddha. Some guests wrinkled their noses, unused to the burning aroma. Others relaxed under the calming fragrance that burned everywhere.

"Many come to visit us every day," said one of the shaved monks standing guard outside the Ksitigarbha Buddhisattva Hall, which housed the pictures of the departed ones.

"Yes," the other replied. "Many have come to see His Holiness. He is the 14th reincarnation of the Dalai Lama. Does anyone know what Dalai Lama means?"

The group stared blankly.

"It literally means the Ocean of Wisdom. The Dalai Lama knows all."

"Is he inside? The ocean?" a young boy asked his father as the tour group approached the small temple. "Does he have to pee often?"

"No son, behave. The Ocean is a man."

"Will we get to meet him, Dad? Why do they shave their heads? Dad, I have to use the bathroom now."

"The Dalai Lama was found living in a boy about your age. The name given by his parents was Lhamo Thondup." The guide continued his rehearsed monologue, trying to ignore the well intentioned, but irritating young lad pulling on his dad's hand.

The boy pulled on the robe of the tour guide as he stood behind him. "So when do we get to see the Ocean?"

"I'm sorry little one. You will probably not get to see the Dalai Lama today. He entered this temple only minutes ago to meditate for the souls of the departed. He will usually meditate for over an hour and is not to be disturbed."

The boy thought hard and looked up at his father. "Dad, I have to meditate. Can I go inside?"

"But I thought you had to pee?"

The Dalai Lama was deep in prayer, oblivious to everything until he opened his eyes looking around the temple. Had he just felt that? A subtle shaking of the ground? His dreams were disturbing earlier this morning, which for a man of his serenity was most unusual. He couldn't sleep, so he got up early and came here to pray instead.

As he closed his eyes it happened again, only stronger. That one he definitely felt. He rose to his feet, worried about being in the building should a real quake start. The tremors returned with double the intensity. The Dalai Lama grabbed hold of the counter and held on. Dust sifted down from the ornate ceiling. He clasped his hand over his mouth as the gold statue of the thousand eyes, thousand hands of Avalokitesvara Buddhisattva shook. He knew what this meant; this was no earthquake. He turned for the door.

"But Dad, you promised I'd get to see the Dalai Lama."

"I'm sorry son and I didn't promise, he is not into visitors."

"Now we move on to the adjoining temple on the other side of the main temple, which is called Thousand Buddha Hall." The guide monk commented.

The group moved on. The boy stared at the door as his dad yanked at his arm.

"But Dad! It's him!" he said. The door flew open and the Dalai Lama staggered outside. The two monks guarding turned and stared into the ashen face of their spiritual leader. He sagged into their arms, fighting to stay conscious, not looking at all like the serene being he was.

The two monks in total awe held their leader. "Your Holiness, are you all right?"

"It begins," he sobbed. "It begins."

"We will take him to his quarters."

"Yes, I must lie down. Then I will pray for us."

The two monks bustled the Dalai Lama to his quarters, leaving the tour group aghast at the happenings. One quickly called for other monks to watch him.

"What happened?" a senior monk asked, as he entered.

"The Dalai Lama said the ground started shaking beneath his feet. He said it was an omen. I don't understand."

"An omen? I felt no shaking."

"Neither did we?"

"Yes, we felt nothing. Maybe it was nothing," the second guide confirmed.

"You, guard the Dalai Lama while we investigate," the senior monk ordered.

The two ventured inside the temple. Hundreds of gold-foiled cups were strewn about, dust covering the floor. A trail of prints led out of the building.

"This is not possible. I swept in here this morning."

The senior monk thought a moment. "His Holiness had this happen once before in 1950. He felt the ground shake beneath his feet. It was taken as an omen that one way of life was ending and, after much destruction, another beginning. Two days later the Chinese began their invasion of Tibet, eventually overthrowing the Dalai Lama and forcing his evacuation." He turned and stared at the thousand-armed figure of Avalokitesvara Buddhisattva.

As he did, a young girl and her mother entered. The young girl stared at the statue. "It broke. Mom, why did it break?"

The two monks gasped and fell before the indestructible god, chanting in front of the figure, now aware of the large crack running through it.

The young Chinese boy pulled at his dad's hand. "See, Dad, we did get to see him."

In his bed the Dalai Lama broke into a sweat, muttering, feeling ill for the first time in many years. "It begins."

****

Belle Glade, Florida

"Your mama don't dance and your daddy don't rock n roll," blasted out of the boom box on the bench next to John as he reached in to tweak the air mixture adjustment one more time on the Edelbrock four barrel carb.

Pressing stop on his cell phone, he listened to the thumping purr of the over-cammed engine. "Yeah, like a hungry panther about to devour its prey."

He closed the hood. "Now, time to prowl."

John Miller slammed down the hood of his '91 Mustang and jumped behind the steering wheel. The thundering vibrations of the five-liter, three hundred cubic inch engine shook right through the seat. "Okay, time to go for a test spin." He'd just spent the last six months tearing the engine out of the car, rebuilding it along with the transmission, and was ready to try it out.

He eased the stick-shift into reverse and backed out of his parents' driveway, feathering the throttle. Johnny hated life in the small-town community of Belle Glade, Florida, as much as he hated the oppressive humidity living so close to Lake Okeechobee in the heart of the Everglades.

"I hope he gets some mufflers on that thing," his mother yelled at her husband from across the living room. The noise from the car with the open header was deafening.

His dad just shook his head and muttered to himself as he grabbed another beer and continued watching the baseball game mad since his team just gave up three hits and were now behind. "I hope he gets insurance."

John grinned as he eased the car down the street, it had taken him over a year to rebuild this car, working part time. He didn't want to make too much noise just yet, he had to get on the old interstate first and make sure the car wouldn't overheat. There usually weren't any cops on that road and it had a straight stretch about two miles long just before the swamp where he could really put his foot into it.

Sweat poured down his brow as he gripped the wheel. The lump of the racing cam shook the car at an idle due to lack of engine vacuum; maybe he'd gone too radical on valve timing. He grinned. "Go hard or go home," he'd tell his buddies, well, he wasn't going home right about now.

He was going to get insurance next week, but couldn't resist one joyride, had to test the cooling system and give the engine just one blast. He might even have to pull the timing back anyway if it's too far advanced and the engine pings under acceleration. Johnny grinned as he signaled onto the nearly deserted highway and punched it. Tires screeched in a cloud of blue smoke as his back sunk into the seat and the car shot forward. "Yeah, that's Ford power, baby."

Chapter Two

Earth Science News

A study just released by an independent think tank has concluded that the natural progression of intelligent life in the galaxy is to eventually leave the planet of birth and live in large ships in outer space. A planet's resources will become depleted, much like the yolk within an egg, so in order to survive and continue to grow the organism must break free. A planet is simply an incubator and, sooner or later, we must leave, probably never to return.

The optimum environment would be to live in very large ships in which the environment is completely controlled. These ships could travel between solar systems and produce everything needed to sustain the race.

"So where do we go from here?" Roger asked Theodore. "It would appear, at least from the tape that we sent something out there somewhere into the wild blue yonder or star system or galactic whatever." Theodore laughed slightly as they sat in their usual pizza place hangout.

Theodore stared back as the usual crowd wandered by. "My guess is that the signal we sent out will take a while to reach whoever but from my guess it has been testing us."

"Testing us for what? Pretty elaborate test. Did we get an 'A'?"

"Not sure but think about it. I mean, it's not every day you'd get initiated into the galactic community and this intelligence, maybe several, would have to be very elaborate. Possibly tens of thousands of years older than us. I think we may have just begun the Ascension of humanity."

"The galactic community? Ascension? Where do you get this crazy stuff from?"

"Okay Rog, I know you've an open mind, a little more than most, so try this on for size. What if all those alien fuzzy pictures, ships, flying saucers, little green men, the guys with the big heads, dark eyes etc. are all for real. What if all that exists and more?"

"What are you getting at?" Roger stared at Theodore as if he was from another world.

"There's a growing conspiracy theory among the Ufologists, that not only are all the sightings for real, but they are staged, planned events, getting us ready; no, making us used to the fact that life exists out there no matter how many times we are told that we are alone in this universe. Think of it like this. In our history hundreds of years ago, we thought the Earth revolved around the sun and that the sun was the center of the universe. Then we discovered that we were not as important as we thought and that our sun wasn't the center of the universe after all, but it was only one of a billion billion such stars in the galaxy. Then we discover that our galaxy was only one of a billion billion galaxies."

"And?"

"And what if we were to find out that we are not alone. What if there's many more races out there and they are kinda like a federation of races, a UN sort of affair."

Roger looked at him with a puzzled look. "Like on Star Trek or something? We going to run into a race full of Spock beings with pointy ears?" Roger kidded back.

"Yes. You do the math. We could be talking about virtually millions of worlds with life much like ours. Now, would you just open your arms to a new kid on the block? One with nuclear weapons? One that wants to wipe out his own kind. Would you not put some sort of testing program in place to see if we are ready to be let in to the grownup leagues? And, more importantly, how would you go about getting the general population ready for such an extraordinary event?"

"Well, it would cause chaos no matter what."

"True, but if you continually bombard people with flying saucers, get them used to the idea that life does exist out there, it wouldn't be such a big deal, now would it? I mean think of it, Close Encounters Of The Third Kind, Stargate, Star Wars, ET, Men in Black, etc. What if they're influencing the creative minds, writers, TV producers as well?"

"You might have a point there. The other day I saw Bill's kid slept with a stuffed ET and a big-eyed alien. To him they're cuddly toys and not the horrible meat-eating aliens we grew up with in our day, like the monster from the Black Lagoon."

"We only fear the unknown. Once it becomes the known, it becomes accepted and commonplace. Can you imagine what would have happened if the aliens had landed here in the forties or fifties? Sheer pandemonium. I mean, people jumped out of their windows when Orson Welles broadcast the War of the Worlds back in the thirties. Today a spaceship could land across the street and we'd probably give the guy a ticket for illegal parking."

"So, you think they are not only testing us, but keeping us in isolation until we've become used to them."

"In part. There's also a deeper problem. I think our governments are also keeping us in the dark. It's a known fact that the US government categorically denies anything to do with alien life. But did you know it is a life sentence for a US citizen to talk to an alien life-form? Yet they deny anything UFO-like in nature isn't real."

"Yeah, but except for a few fuzzy pictures from the moon, and shot late at night, there isn't any real evidence."

"No, do the research. I have. Now take this." He handed Roger a memory stick. "I've a couple more complete copies but I figured if anything ever happened to me you could use one too. It's all there. Our government has alien ships in their possession, they signed deals with aliens back in the fifties, and they keep covering up evidence. Evidence that proves, time and time again, that not only this world, but also our moon and Mars have proof of alien activity."

"What? Now you're blowing my mind. I thought I saw some sort of program where they said the moon landings were faked."

"Only one. I think the one after Edwin Mitchell. He's reported to have found a crystal tower nearly a mile high on the surface of the moon. There are so many things that I've studied. Like, you heard about the Roswell incident, back in 1947. The alien spaceship crashing near Roswell army base in New Mexico? It was published in newspapers around the world. The next day a press release stated that it was only a weather balloon. I visited Roswell and talked to one of the old guys that worked there. He said that there was a ship, and there were bodies pulled from it. In fact, a group of boy scouts accidentally came across it and reported the same thing. All covered up. But because of that a new base and agency formed."

"The infamous Area 51. Not heard of an agency though."

"Called MJ12. Bit like the Men In Black, I suppose. One of their jobs was to keep everything under wraps and discredit, or even silence permanently, anyone who spoke too loudly about aliens. It's all real Roger, it all exists, it's all in my notes. In fact, evidence shows also that we didn't evolve from here. That we were seeded from beings from another world or worlds."

"Are you for real? Which ones?"

"Most, if not virtually all, of the early religions and cultures, particularly the native religions, talk about gods coming from the Sirius, Orion and Pleiades systems."

"I guess I'll really believe it when I run across some Pleiadian hitchhiker someday and bring them home."

"You and me both." They both laughed.

"Ah, mom, he doesn't poo in the house and they make the neatest door stops. Can I keep him? Can I?" Roger goofed around in his little boy voice. Theodore pushed the memory stick closer to Roger. "Okay I'll take this and check them out but I think you're being awfully paranoid."

"Perhaps. But if MJ12 did get to me and "flashy thing" my brain, someone else has to continue this, or at least be aware of everything I've discovered. It's all in there, take a look."

"You really believe this stuff?" Roger turned the memory stick over in his hands.

"Really. Read and learn. I didn't until I began to study. Some days I wish I hadn't." Theodore pointed at the stick. "There are things in there that even I had a hard time believing and it gives me nightmares. The truth is, we really don't know what is out there, or what has happened in the past on our world."

Roger watched a haunted look cross Theodore's eye and swallowed hard before beginning. "Well, if it would help you any, I believe you. At least in part. I believe I've seen your alien."

"What are you talking about? What alien?"

"The one that planted the metal in us at the lake."

Theodore glared at him, lost. "I'd forgotten. You mentioned something about that before all this started."

"This is crazy, and I've never told anyone, but I see her occasionally. I call her my guardian angel. So, you think she might be an alien, and pretty good looking like something from one of those erotic comic books I used to read."

"What?"

"She's exactly as you describe. The first time I saw her is when I was in the car crash with Mike. She pulled me from the wreckage and saved my life."

Theodore looked even more puzzled.

"And hang on to your pizza slice."

Theodore picked up the ham and pineapple piece waiting to bite into it.

"You know there are some that swear pineapple should never be on a pizza. Sacrilegious!"

Theodore put the slice down. "Okay, give me the surprise before I choke on this."

"I saw her the other day at the garage where Sparky keeps getting the large bones from. I swear they could be dinosaur bones."

"Dino what?" he gasped out, before choking on the beer he'd just inhaled.

"Sparky keeps dragging bones home. Huge bones. The kids call them dinosaur bones. Old Mrs. Miller claims she never gives him any and anyway she rents the joint to some recluse. I figure he's getting them from that guy or from her husband's old taxidermy stuff that she's kept in there."

"Pretty weird! And you swear she looks like the woman from our summer camp." He bit into the pizza, hoping to wolf it down before Roger blurted out more.

"Yes, but that's not half as weird as the shit you've been telling me." They both laughed.

"True enough," Theodore grinned at Roger.

"By the way it's good to get together and even better to see you loosen up and laugh a little."

Theodore snickered. "It's been too long."

"That it has, that it has." They laughed again and swallowed down the beers before them.

****

So alone. In essence as an angel I've been alone with only my resources to fall back on. The memories of her second training assignment rang home. *Yes, didn't get much lonelier than being dead or in a state where only blackness reigns.*

Sherida found herself floating in a world of etherealness. A body but nothing with real substance.

Something grazed her cheek, a claw materialized. Her blood fell into the void. Licks of hunger rang out. She quickly shrank into herself closing everything out and cocooned into her.

Where am I? She ran through her training. This is Malefetorious. She had been told they are ghost hunters. Ghosts that live off the energy of killing, stalking ghosts, usually ones that have just died. Hot breaths rang across her back like licks from a great predatory cat relishing dinner.

They were here and they wanted her, needed her, were hungry for her.

Sherida stayed withdrawn, thinking. What draws immaterial creatures to hunt non-living beings or living ones? Unless?

To think and act like a killer is to be one. She breathed deeply, then exhaled, exuded a cool vapor that they surged through and which stopped them in puzzlement. Sherida spun herself into a mist and seeped upward, lost in a mindless place. One came swirling by, as she swirled, sniffing. She wrapped herself around it and slashed its throat. Blood of an evaporating essence spewed forth. The others like piranha leaped in, feeding on their brethren. Her essence shifted as they grew satiated, lazy, bloated on their brother. Her whistling breath struck like a python's tongue. Striking again and again until only the silence answered.

She drew back into herself, no longer one of them and waited, closing her heart, mind and soul. Knowing otherwise might attract more or others of a more vile nature than these.

To be merciless was the only way to survive here. No remorse, no thought, just kill or be killed, and then eaten. The hunt of the hunted.

She felt the white light calling her back home and smiled. She'd passed the second test.

There was another.

Inside a sneer cascaded through her. To deny she enjoyed it was lying. To open your soul to the possibility that you could kill relentlessly was one thing. To allow that black essence to also release its vileness inside and somewhat enjoy it, was another. She knew from the training that was what was inside all of us.

Now to check on Roger. I can't fail my assignment and let him be harmed. Somehow my sense is he can help.

She closed her eyes, remembering it took months of training to quell that needful hunger, and, sometimes at night, she'd still wake in a shiver. Her fingers craving that need to lick the blood from them. *Yes, once woken some evils beckon to call on your soul.*

****

Rain cascaded down in sheets outside as Roger rose from his bed. *The dog! The damn dog! I left him outside again, didn't I?* Getting up, he searched all over, knowing Sparky wasn't inside, but hoping just the same. "Crap! Double crap!"

Lightning lit up the doorway a moment as he put on his rain gear and stepped outside. After quickly checking the backyard he marched straight for Mrs. Miller's garage with his torch in hand.

"Sparky? Where are you?" he growled as he entered her backyard. A small bark from underneath the crawl space. Roger looked under the gap and saw his four-footed friend disappear inside the garage. Tomorrow, he's definitely asking her to board up the escape hatch underneath. "Then no more bones for you, buddy boy and I can stay nice and dry in my comfy bed. Not out here in the rain and cold like some godforsaken vampire."

He began to crawl towards the opening, his slicker catching on a jagged protrusion. "Damn! Well at least its dry under here." He pulled off the rain gear and kept crawling until he reached the opening and slowly stuck his head in. Sure enough, there was Sparky, just out of reach and obliviously gnawing away. "Man, it stinks in here, like ... like ...," He looked around and there were various shapes hidden under tarps. Blood seeped out from under them. "Like dead animals. I hope those are dead animals and not..." His mind went crazy thinking of some serial killer hiding bodies in this of all places. "Christ. That's it. I'm taking you and getting out of here fast before I heave and police come running or some mad slasher comes after me."

He rose up through the opening, past a small red beam. A corresponding red light began to flash on a panel behind him.

As Roger reached out to grab his dog he heard something began to quietly power up and knew he'd made a horrible mistake. A flash of brilliant light blinded him. He dropped Sparky to protect his eyes. Squinting he tried to adjust to the daylight.

"Daylight? What the hell?"

The air was humid and the ground damp, squishing under his feet. Foliage hung off the trees in green coats of incredible beauty and shapes. Heat from a full sunlit day smothered him. "Wow! It's like being in Hawaii. What is going on here?"

He spun around, searching for his dog. *One thing's for sure, I ain't home anymore. How is this possible?* He stared up at the sky and noticed the single moon hanging over the horizon. *Well at least I'm on Terra Firma but in the middle of what appears to be some godforsaken jungle.* It was apparent the garage was booby-trapped or something, he thought. *It flings you to another part of the world or some such thing. How was this possible? Who exactly was living in Mrs. Miller's garage? Maybe Theodore was right about this alien stuff and she had some version of Darth Vader or Luke Skywalker staying here. Only... where was his dog?* "Sparky!" A bark in the distance on the other side of some bushes gave away Sparky's whereabouts. He looked about and grabbed a few rocks and piled them on top of each other like an Inukshuk he'd seen in Canada on holidays one time. *If I've been moved somewhere, I'd better mark this exact spot. I guess my Boy Scout training paid off after all.* Cursing, he swept aside the sweat pouring down his brow. Roger pushed himself through a last stand of bushes until he stood on the edge of a massive sweep of plains stretching out before him.

He blinked in disbelief as thousands of animals moved over the plains, herds of beasts, and there amongst it all was Sparky barking away, chasing after a bewildered beast that looked like a rhino, only much larger. Funnily enough, it was terrified of the yappy terrier. But Roger knew that was no rhino. No, that was nothing even remotely mammalian in nature. As it snorted and turned its head toward him, Roger caught sight of the three horns on its head, surrounded by a large frill of bone. The ground thundered as it ran. "Good God!" He was staring at a full-grown beast from the science books he'd read as a child. It was nearly ten feet tall. A triceratops. Its defenses designed to keep at bay a huge predator like an Allosaurus or a T. Rex, but it seemed unsure how to deal with some pint-sized mutt.

Roger gulped as the thought hit home. He probably was home, just a few hundred million years early!

****

Great. How did an Alpha Draconis manage to get this close to me and I never got to detect it? Let alone realize it's breaking a few dozen laws of intervention and theft of ancient artifacts. Sherida had scanned the remains under the tarps and found that they were what the humans called dinosaurs. Sherida shook her head as she stood in the center of Mrs. Miller's garage, which is where she'd tracked Roger to, only there was no sign of him. She looked around the garage at the technology. Shielded, she knew the equipment wouldn't detect her, but it had detected Roger, who was now in the dim and distant past, sent via their standard time warp security device. She would have to intervene again to save him. *Probably importing those poor creatures for genetic studies of the humans' prehistory. Either that or maybe a renegade glory hunter.*

A red light began to blink on the machine. *He's coming back, probably alerted to the earlier intrusion. No time to return Roger.* She blasted the video station so at least whoever was coming would not realise who had breached his security, which is the last thing she could possibly want. She hit the magnetic alarm switch, opened up the security gate, and leaped through it.

****

Sherida skidded into tall grass screaming the flood of information that overwhelmed her. She crumpled to her knees and turned down her extra sensory facilities at the pounding volume like being front row to a Metallica or AC/DC concert.

She shook her head. Allowing the bio-circuitry to kick in and flood her mind with painkiller. Sherida snapped her laser from its place and scanned the area.

Two reptiles were just ahead of her through a stand of trees. This whole thing was beginning to get worse by the minute. She moved cautiously through the copse and stared in awe at the open plain before her. To know of the dinosaurs of Earth was one thing, to see a herd grazing was another.

The shrill beep of her scanner alerted her. She guessed, correctly, that the hunter had followed them and began to cover the ground towards Roger in a blur. Another blip appeared. "Oh no, that's no rogue alien hunter. Too large." She tore off after Roger, her speed-enhanced muscles kicking into a faster gear until she became a blur. Things had just got incredibly bad as the two very large blips began to close in on her location.

Roger stood stock still, feeling the urge to let loose his bowels double with each nano second as the lumbering triceratops Sparky was chasing ran straight at him.

Make yourself big; it works to scare off cougars and attacking dogs. Roger jumped up and down waving his arms around. The dinosaur thundered to a stop staring at him in wide-eyed shock about twenty feet away. "Well, what do you know it worked! Imagine being terrified of a little dog. Or is it the fact you never saw a human before? Is evolution that scary?" Roger suddenly realized he was the first of his species to talk to a living, breathing dinosaur! The beast stood blinking, its eyes widened in fright staring at him or...

Roger laughed until he realized the ground was still shaking and thundering. "What the..."

A piercing shrill scream from behind. He turned to see two Allosauri running towards him. The beasts thundered closer, running on their massive hind legs like chickens, only these chickens were hungry, bore a shitload of nasty teeth and capable of hitting incredible speed. Roger gulped.

Something bearing white hair slammed into him and sent the two of them tumbling over the grass. She picked him up, carried him at a run to the edge of a stand of tall bushes and dove into them just as the Allosauri slammed into the triceratops, bowling all three dinosaurs over. Carnosaurs and herbivores tumbled in a pile of flesh. Knocked off its feet the herbivore was a goner as the meat eaters tore into the soft underbelly and began to rip out hunks of meat three times the size of Roger. The triceratops screamed in pain, blood gushing everywhere, as the carnivores gorged on their living feast. Shrill victory cries shattered the humid air amongst the crunch of bone and rendering of living flesh.

Roger stared at the grim horrific scene being enacted from some Jurassic movie before him, totally forgetting about the being that had saved his life.

"Allosaurs, as you call them, are amazing beasts. Hunting in packs of two or more, they would let one of them hit their prey at full speed like a battering ram before it had time to defend itself, and the others would attack the overturned soft under side of their quarry. Deadly, but brilliant."

He turned to the direction of the voice and stared into the face of his angel. "You! You're real! My angel. The one that I've spotted time and again over the years. The one that saved me when Mike died in that car crash. You pulled me from the wreckage." He began to blather like a child mumbling before its unexpected idol and no pen to sign an autograph.

"Hey relax. First of all, I have a name, and it's Sherida. What I don't have is time to explain everything right now. You just have to trust me." A beep from her wrist stopped her. She glanced down, flipped back a fold of skin and stared at the screen.

Roger gulped as he stared. You're not an angel but a robot?"

"No this is an implant. Look, I don't have time for answers. It's here already. I must move fast. Don't move from this spot, it will be looking for you and not me." With that she clicked on one of her teeth and vanished from Roger's sight.

"Hey, wait a minute! What's looking for me?" Roger spun around. "In godforsaken two hundred million BC."

Sherida moved to a few feet from Roger and watched her screen; like she thought, the Draconion was heading straight for Roger. She had to be fast to take down the enemy. They had amazing reflexes, speed and probably were shielded.

Roger struggled to believe what was happening. One minute at home in a cost warm bed, next in God-knew-what-million BC watching dinosaurs have lunch, having chatted with his guardian angel with computer implants, or whatever they were. Theodore wouldn't believe this in a million years!

Savage growls rent the air. Roger watched mesmerized as the two Allosauri continued to tear into the flesh of the moaning triceratops. Its eyes blinked a couple of times, blood gushed from its mouth, until it died with one last gasp of breath.

The click of something metallic. A strange buzzing filled the air and he slunk down behind a log. Sherida was nowhere to be seen. *Where the hell is Sparky?* Shimmering into view about forty feet away, a being, dressed in full body armor, pulled a laser from its side and stared at a dial on its arm. Roger guessed correctly that it was the guy from Mrs. Miller's garage.

The being clicked a button and a greenish tinge swept the area. Something raced towards the being, an outline showing in brilliant red. "Sherida?" He gasped and stared down at his hands, his body. He was covered in the red glow, some sort of detection field, maybe?

Before Sherida could reach the being tracking them, it spun around and fired once in her direction, no doubt taking aim at the red glow as Sherida herself was still cloaked. She was flung backwards as the laser hit her full in the shoulder. The alien raised its weapon again. She was too slow.

"No!" Roger hollered. Distracted, the alien turned and trained its laser in his direction. Just then the small, yappy, terrier–sized, glowing red object burst from the bushes and leapt for the hunter.

The alien looked down, confused, seemingly unable to focus on the dog tearing into its leg. The being let out a scream not unlike the hunting call of the Allosaurus and dropped the laser in shock. Caught off guard, it seemed terrified of the snarling canine. It tried freeing its leg from the dog. The alien flicked a button on the back of its head and the helmet popped backwards. The greenish glow of the force field ended as it stared down at the attacking dog trying to shake itself free.

"Good God!" It wasn't human, or even mammalian in nature. It was some sort of reptilian being. It looked so similar to the Allosaurus that it could have been a smaller, more refined, more ...

... more evolved version. The alien glanced over in his direction and then stared up in the air.

Something large blocked out sunlight as it crossed Roger's path. The powerful thigh of one of the carnivores thumped past him. It had left its prey and moved to attack the alien somehow sensing it was another reptile.

The alien swatted aside the dog and reached for its weapon. Too late, as the huge reptile leaned over and snapped up the screaming being just above the knees. The Allosaurus lifted its head straight up and with one gulp swallowed the alien whole, which for the giant carnosaur was just a mere snack, gagging slightly on the metallic taste of the alien's outfit before turning to return to its main course and the screeching call from the other dining Allosaurus.

"Christ!" Roger stared at all that remained. Just shins. And blood-filled boots.

A horrible roar filled the area with the stench of decomposed meat from its breath as screeching the attacking one returned to its meal, one leg thumping down again only a few feet from Roger cowering behind the log. He watched the two dine for a moment and then slunk backwards into the brush where he remembered Sherida lying. She moaned as he picked her up and she opened her eyes. "Thank goodness you're still alive."

"What happened?" She shook her head. A yapping filled the air as Sparky ran up to his master, tail a wagging.

"Shhh..." He held his finger in front of his face admonishing the canine and checked to make sure the two carnosaurs were still tearing into their meal. "You are the most annoying, most troublesome, most incredible little dog in the universe." He smiled and hugged his little dog, looking none the worse for wear after the swatting the alien had given it.

"Sir Sparky, my hero and our rescuer, the most incredible pain-in-the-rear dog."

"The Draco?" she asked, rubbing the back of her head whilst looking over at a nearby stand of bushes.

"The what? Ah, if you mean Mr. Lizard dude, it's dead. Sparky came to my defense attacking it and bit into its leg. When it screamed out loud the Allosaurus attacked and swallowed him whole. He's no threat now; just became a Dino-snack. I don't know about you, but I don't want to end up the same, so how do we get out of here?" He smiled naively.

"My head," Sherida moaned as she flipped back a flap of her skin and glanced at her arm as she glared up at the area behind them and shook her head. "I could have sworn something was just over there. Oh, perhaps it was just my head spinning or damage to my visual cortex, cerebral circuitry."

Roger shivered. "That is just too creepy. So you say you're human, look very human, like, with added circuitry, so not an android? Or what do they call those beings from the science fiction movies with Arny; cyborgs?"

"Well, Pleiadian actually, the genealogy is closely related to human, but for the most part you're right. By Rama and Zarathustra," She glanced at her arm. "I think the blast took out some of my control system circuits."

"Do you think you can get yourself repaired?"

"Don't know. I can do some internal repairs mainly to body tissues and the like but I don't have any tools around here to work with the bio-circuitry, and unless I can get myself back on line we're stuck here, I'm afraid, forever."

Roger slunk to his knees. "What do you mean, stuck here. We get back the same way you came, surely! How was that, by the way?"

"Through his device that I activated. I synched my circuits to the controls so I could act as a remote control to take us back, but now that circuit is damaged. The only other way back is with the Draco's equipment."

"The what?"

"The Alpha Draconis. One of the few non-humanoid races out there. Normally a peaceful race, but not one of the ones known to abide by all the laws of the Federation. He was here, from what I gathered, to go hunting dinosaurs, to take home for a profit."

"Alpha Draconis? He looked like a more advanced version of a dinosaur, I mean, a reptile. There are more of them out there?"

"Yes. A planet full. Due to a meteor hit here most of the reptiles here were wiped out and the mammals took over, as was the case on many worlds. Being a cold-blooded race, as on many worlds, they don't take to severe climate change."

"Ah, many worlds?" His eyes opened wide, remembering what Theodore had said about all the planets that could be supporting other races. "How many worlds are we talking? "

"Out of the 450 billion suns in this galaxy, there are approximately two million known races. Fortunately, most are humanoid," she said, matter-of-factly.

Roger stood there in shock. "Two million? There are two million races out there?"

"Yes. And that's only in our galaxy! Not something that I really should have told you but as we may not make it out of this predicament alive I thought you might like to know." Sherida answered him with a smile. Working at her controls she managed to get her blood to stop flowing out of her arm and with another couple of clicks, skin began to grow back over the cauterized laser burn.

"Whoa, there!" Roger stood in shock, eyes bulging. "You are for real. Man, I can't take this all in. I'm flung back in time a few hundred million years by my neighbor, who just happens to be a reptilian creature, poaching of all things, his cousin dinosaurs, and who coincidentally actually is a dinosaur, or at least a distant relative. I then discover that I have, in fact, got some kind of guardian angel watching over me, as I always suspected, but never really believed in the cold light of day. However, you then materialize right before my eyes and save me yet again, only to tell me there's a bazillion others scattered out there. Have I got all of this right so far?" He wiped at the sweat on his brow.

"Yes. You are very perceptive."

"Perceptive? Am I? Great, I spit it out there, but don't understand any of this."

"There is much out there that you will eventually discover to be the truth. The universe is not as you believe it to be. I will explain later. Right now we must return to your time, and the only way to do that is with the transmitter, which our friend has with him along with a battery pack that I can use to reenergize the time shift device. Unfortunately, he just got swallowed up. I think his reptilian scream, or even his scent, must have set off the Allosauri to react in defense.

"Mr. Draco is now just an appetizer." A horrid stench flooded the air. "What is that rank smell?" Roger asked.

"Because of their size, the Allosauri are a constant eating machine. As soon as they eat they begin to excrete the previous meal and being meat eaters, their digestive tracts are rather foul as they secrete very unpleasant digestive gases due to digesting only meat. So at least they most likely won't come after us at least as they are dining and from there usually go for a lay down nap."

"Hang on," Roger smiled, "This is good; very good. That dinosaur gulped down the Draco in one bite. If it digests its food that fast, then it should, ah, release the Draco in a day or two. Probably with little or no damage to its equipment. I hope."

"Brilliant. It might work; all we have to do now is stay alive until its next meal and check its stool."

"Right. Why do I get the idea that I'm going to be the lucky volunteer that gets that delightful job?"

"I can't with my arm injured like this. Most likely to get infected."

"Somehow I'd thought you'd say that." He shook his head and stared down at Sparky, who just stared back at him with the stupid 'I'll go chase the ball' look he so often gave with his tongue dangling out. "Forget it, you'd probably drown in dino poo." He knew the dog would most likely roll around in the stuff as he'd caught him doing on more than one occasion and end up spending the next hour hosing down the mutt in the backyard.

Belle Glade, Florida

Rick Desmond didn't usually patrol this stretch of road. He never liked the swamp and tried staying as far away from it as possible, but after the two weird incidences of the last week, it meant that something was probably going on. He'd read the autopsy reports on the kids and the mauled construction workers. His superiors told him to make a once-a-day cruise along this section of highway in case whatever did the damage returns for no other reason than to ease mind of the taxpayers. Still, he didn't like it. He'd seen the movie Swamp Thing in his younger days and read all the comic books. Pictures of graphic mutilated bodies, and cars with gleaming scratches down their side. Headless corpses still haunted him after all of these years, especially after viewing the pictures from the coroner's office of what was left of the ones found.

A late model Chevy came weaving around the bend, crossing the dividing line nearly sideswiping him. Rick slammed on the brakes, flicked on the flashers and tore after the car. "Damn drunks," he cursed.

The creature rose from the swamp and staggered towards the sound of the sirens just around the bend.

Rick walked slowly up to the car, his hand resting on his gun. Its driver, a middle-aged man, slumped half over the steering wheel. The stink of alcohol rolled out the open window.

Johnny slammed the last gear and laughed as the throaty growl of the fours kicked in. "Fuck yeah!" He hooted before realizing he'd already traversed the bulk of the distance to the end of the stretch and was about to get off at the next exit and head back home. He released the throttle and hammered the clutch to the floor, the backfire of the headers, popping like gunshots, echoed in his ears like heavy metal music.

The drunk blinked barely able to see as he tried digging free his wallet. Rick wondered if he could even get out of his car, let alone walk in a straight line.

"Do you realize you crossed the yellow line back there and nearly hit me?"

"That's a fuck of a place to park your cruiser ossifer. In the middle of the road," he slurred through sour breath and looked up. Horror spread on his face as the horrific looking beast approached. "Holy mother of God."

Johnny slammed back another gear and punched it coming out of the bend. As long as there was no one there he'd be okay. "Shit." He spotted the two cars idling. His heart sank as the reds and blues reflected off his retinas. That sight more horrifying than the beast that raised its arm to swat at the offending car quickly approaching like it was about to attack.

"What the ..." Johnny stared in shock forgetting to dump the clutch and instead yanked the steering wheel hard to avoid the beast. A thud and he saw the monster get punched into the waters of the swamp with a splash.

Rick turned to catch the plate number of the Mustang as it swerved by them, nearly slamming into his cruiser.

"Christ, is everyone around here nuts?" He pulled the keys from the drunk's car and ran back to his cruiser. "Sit here and don't move until I get back." He yelled as he sprinted back to his cruiser. "Officer requesting backup on Highway 98," he yelled into the mike, as he took off in pursuit of the plate-less Mustang.

Johnny went to punch the throttle again, only nothing happened as the pedal lay on the floor. The pin. He'd forgotten to put the cotter pin on the other end of the linkage. He pulled over as the throttle-less car slowed down, nearly sobbing.

Rick ran up to the Mustang, gun drawn.

Johnny jumped out of his car. "Jeesus, I just saw this horrible thing, a swamp creature of some kind. I hit it with my car." He blurted incoherently staring at the dent on his passenger side.

"Nice try kid. I've heard some wild stories in my time, that's one of the best. Get in back of the cruiser."

Half an hour later Rick Desmond looked up as the Mustang was being towed away. "Swamp thing. What a story." He laughed at the drunk, as he threw him beside the sobbing teenager. "A good night in the drunk tank will fix the lot of you up." Out the corner of his eye he caught four long gleaming scratches raking down the passenger side of the car and shivered as he caught sight of a broken claw hung dangling from the bodywork. He picked it off where it was imbedded and staggered back to his cruiser. In the gathering dark, another hideously four-inch-long talon lay twitching on the asphalt, bits of flesh attached to it, torn from whatever creature it once belonged to. "Crap! Maybe the kid was right. I don't think I'm going to sleep worth crap tonight either."

****

Two days later, Roger stood before a three-foot high mound pinching his nose in disgust. "How could something shit out that much at one time?"

"Just start digging before the dinosaurs come back." Sherida kept an eye open checking her perimeter sensors as Sparky sat down on his stomach wagging his tail, probably expecting some reward from the delicious smelling pile Roger was digging through.

Chapter Three

August Night, Fairbanks Air Force Base, Alaska

"What a load of crap, bleeding environmentalists. Getting to be a real pain, those bastards. What is it?" Captain Thomas McAbee of the US Air Force barked at whoever had knocked on his office door.

Sergeant Billings, one of his telecommunications officers, answered, "Permission to enter, Sir?"

McAbee noticed the slight quaver in Billings' voice. "Come in. And you can be at ease. Damn, it's hot out there today and my air conditioning isn't working worth a load of beans. What's the temp?"

"Ninety-eight. Sir. Quite unusual for here."

"Can you imagine? Some fucking scientists in this article," he shook the paper rather angrily "are trying to prove that Freon from our air conditioning machines will destroy the ozone layer, and when that happens they say we'll all begin to get skin cancer and our planet will start heating up. They call it the greenhouse effect. Apparently, there's already an ozone hole developing over Antarctica. Now isn't that a load of shit! What the fuck are we going to do without air conditioning?"

"Actually, Sir, they say it's just the CFC's that are causing the ozone destruction. Chlorine and bromine react to ozone and one atom of chlorine will destroy thousands of ozone atoms in a chain reaction."

"Billings! I said at ease. I didn't say to give me any backtalk. I read the article in the goddamn paper. A couple of scientists figured this out a few years back in the seventies when everyone in those flaky universities was tripping out on LSD. What I want to know if they stop using freon what the hell would they use to keep the tanks and our airplanes cool. Not to mention our buildings."

"Several options, Sir, including a number of HFC's." Billings stopped when McAbee gave him another look of tell-someone-who-gives-a-shit. "Actually Sir, I apologize for being off topic. I came in to give you this report."

"Okay let's have it."

Billings handed the communications report to his commanding officer. "It would appear that the Schuman resonance has increased to nine Hertz. Explains why our reconnaissance satellites are not responding properly."

McAbee stared at the report. His job was to make sure all the radio and communication signals were kept in link. "This doesn't make a whole lot of sense. Let's go have a chat with those clowns over in C building. But hang on for a minute while I give the boys over in the Fairbanks research center a call and see if they can verify this." McAbee put on his captain's hat. He'd worked hard to get his post, rising to the rank of captain faster than anyone from his division. "I got no use for fucking bleeding-hearts, Billings. All I care is that my job is done, quickly and effectively, Airforce style. I've only got three years before retiring. Now, did they recalibrate the equipment?"

"Just last week Sir."

"Then how is it possible that our signal strength is increasing? We've used the echo signal from the Schumann Resonance for decades. Seven-point-eight fucking Hertz, it's the one electromagnetic signal that our planet produces that doesn't change. It's been a constant signal for decades, as long as we have known it was there."

"Well, if I can add, Sir, the sun can affect the readings sometimes."

"Billings, don't you think I know that. That's why I had you ask them boys to check for sunspot activity and verify that our equipment is accurate. The fucking sun cannot increase the amount of the Schumann signal. Do you want me to explain how this thing works?"

"Yes, Sir, I would."

"You damn well oughta know this already. However, basically it's like this. The Earth's atmosphere carries an electrical charge. Within this electric charge electromagnetic waves are produced. They occur at certain frequencies and remain the same. Have been for decades, that's why we use them to co-ordinate and calibrate all of our satellites, airplanes and communications. The only way for the signal to be stimulated other than by the energy thrown off by the sun would be if- -"

"If our planet *was* actually heating up."

"Billings, you may make it into my chair someday, but it ain't going to be while I'm here. And if I find out you're one of them Greenpeace freaks, then I'll send a napalm bomb into your barracks. Should nuke the lot of them. Damn, its hot today," McAbee repeated, pulling at his collar and tie. He flicked through his old-fashioned rolodex and dialed a number.

"University of Alaska, Professor Nichols speaking."

"Nichols, Captain McAbee over at the Airforce base here. I've got a dilemma and wondered if you boys could verify something for me?"

"We'll give it our best shot."

"Our Schumann signal seems incorrect. Have you reported any unusual sun activity that might cause the Schumann to temporarily rise?"

"Nothing in the way of sun activity. The sunspots usually run in eleven-year cycles and we're in a quiet part of that right now. But we have also been observing that the Schumann signal strength is increasing and I haven't determined any aberrations that might cause that to happen."

"I don't give a rat's ass about aberrations. My job is to keep our communication satellites linked and in line with ground and air communication. I can't do that with a wavering signal strength! Damnit! I'll call the boys over at the Berkeley Research Center, maybe they'll be more help."

"But there's nothing I can do about it Sir. I can't change the signal. It's like the heartbeat of the Earth ..."

CLICK.

"... and it's like the heartbeat is speeding up." The professor finished his sentence into the suddenly dead receiver.

****

They shimmered back into Mrs. Millers garage, Roger holding Sparky in a vice-like grip. As soon as he set the dog down it took off in the direction of his home. "Sure, stir up all the trouble and take off as soon as we get home. That dog is worse than a kid, I tell you." Roger shook his head.

"First thing I have to do is get rid of this equipment in the garage," Sherida said as she looked around.

"What do you mean, 'get rid of'?"

"I mean I have to destroy every sign of illegal alien evidence on this planet. One of my underlying directives. Especially as he's now long deceased." Sherida frowned as she checked her scanner. "So far no signs of anyone following us."

Roger smiled at her. "I get it, wouldn't be cool if she goes looking for her overdue rent money and finds rotting dinosaur carcasses and, worse ,if she got zapped back in time like we did."

"Yes, or if anyone finds out about him being here." Sherida pulled up her sleeves. "Now I've work to do so stand back."

"Oh, poor Mrs. Miller. There goes her money for this garage. The dino dude was renting it from her. At least until Sparky began to drag his bones home. That dog got me into a shit-load of trouble for the last few days... Few days? Oh man. Beth's going to kill me! How am I going to be able to explain this one?"

"Take a close look at your watch."

"What?"

"Check the time," she said as she hurried about working at speeds Roger thought impossible, slowing down only for the moments it took to talk to him. The rest of the time she was a blur.

"You are amazing, wish I had one of those gizmos. Housework would be a blast." He stole a glance at his watch. "Yeah, so it's seven minutes later than when I went to go get Sparky, on the..." he clicked the date function on his watch, "...on the same day?" Roger stood there, numb for a moment, a feeling he was not liking but beginning to get used to. "Is this possible?"

"Time is something you humans use in the third dimension to manage your affairs." She slowed down to talk to him.

"But weren't we in the third dimension, just in the past?"

"Yes, but the Draconians use fourth dimensionality to jump between time frames and so in essence no time has passed since we left."

"Cool! Hey, you sure you want to wreck that thing?"

"Yes. Human greed is exactly why it must be destroyed. Could you imagine what would happen if this fell into the wrong hands? Okay, done. Now we must leave."

"Hell, I simply thought a couple of well-placed stock purchases wouldn't hurt."

"Actually, it wouldn't, and that would be contrary to that which your science fiction writers have written. You can't reshape the present by changing the past. The past is the past, it is immobile. But the future, now that is an unwritten thing, altogether different."

"Well that's a drag. I just thought- -"

"Damn!" Sherida yelled as she stared down at her arm. "They've tracked me down again."

"Tracked you? Who tracked you?" Roger heard the sound of a vehicle coming up the alleyway as they stepped out of the garage.

"No time to explain. Let's just say my mission is in danger. Out the front, quick."

They ran to the front yard. More headlights turned the corner at the end of the block. "More, right?"

"Yes," she hissed, closing her eyes and gripping Roger in obvious pain.

"You okay?"

"I'd forgotten how much an injury actually hurt. My sensors block most of the pain out. I need some time to heal though."

"What about the first batch?"

"Don't worry about them, I'll take care of two things at once." He heard a car door slam and feet running to the direction of the garage. A silent whump and the garage door popped open. "There's three, two now are inside the garage."

Roger watched the second vehicle slow, pull over and wait.

"They're waiting to make sure the first ones get us, no, I mean me. They don't know about you and nor can they find out. Come on, we've got to divert them away from here."

"How?"

"Simple. As soon as this garage goes up, they come after us... er... me. Now stay back." She snapped as she tore off at an amazing speed.

Sherida raced past the garage and punched her fist into the window of the car in the alley, snapping the neck of the person sitting there before he even saw her.

"Well, that was simple and direct. Remind me to never piss you off," he whispered, after she nodded for him to proceed towards her. She closed her eyes, a brief flash of light up the garage. She glanced around and closed her eyes again as Roger joined. He watched as the blood flow stopped and a coating of skin formed over the cut. Sherida nodded again and the garage thumped from an explosion within. Smoke billowed up through the rafters. Roger knew fire would be right behind it. "But all that equipment? Won't someone suspect something, with dino carcasses in there?"

"That first flash I sent our friends and the internal contents of the building back into the same time zone we just left."

"Nice. I've got some enemies I could use that on."

Instantly lights from both ends of the alley came to life. "Oh damn! More. Why didn't my sensors pick them up? They're blocking me somehow. Jump in and keep down. This is going to get rough. What kind of vehicle is this?"

"Looks like a Mazda Three with a standard transmission," Roger dove into the backseat as she shoved the lifeless body over to the passenger side of the car, jumped into the driver's seat and hit the accelerator pedal.

"They shouldn't have been able to find me. I removed all signaling devices that are designed to be able to trace me. Unless—"

"Unless they're tracking you directly through your equipment. That gizmo under your skin."

"The symbiont. That's it. Somehow, they've gotten access to that. How is that possible?"

Shots rang out as they skidded around the car partially blocking the alley. She geared down the vehicle and punched it into the street. Sherida rammed the stick shift forward and Roger lurched again remembering the times he was first learning to drive a car with his friends 1967 VW Beetle with a standard. They had many a good laugh over that.

"Not sure if you've driven many cars with a standard transmission."

"I can say this is much more responsive then the other kinds. I can see why your professional racing drivers use these." She smiled and put them into a skid around the corner.

"Wow! You're quite the driver. How many hours you have in one of these?" As it donned on him that she must have been here quite a while and had obviously driven some kind of car before.

"This would be the first."

"First?" Roger's eyes widened.

He felt his guts heaving as she nailed it around another corner. "Fast learner. One of the things I've been trained to do, most of the standard earth mechanisms are in my download circuits, including motor vehicle operation and handling."

"I've lost one of them, only two left." They sped down into the industrial part of town taking them away from Roger's neighborhood and hopefully people as well. "But I fear there will be more. Once we were back it didn't take them long to find me. I've got to get you back home and me away from here. So, you need to keep low."

They sped around a corner and Sherida slammed on the brakes coming to a screeching stop with burnt rubber erupting around then. She opened the passenger door and pushed the dead man outside behind an industrial dumpster. "Now get behind the wheel and drive."

"What?"

"Just do it."

As Sherida slip over to the passenger seat, Roger clambered over the front seat and into the driver's seat. He quickly buckled-up as he thought this could be a wild ride, whilst Sherida pulled out her laser pistol from somewhere. Roger wondered from where, exactly, but brushed the thought aside.

"Okay, step on it. You drive and I shoot. Can't do both with accuracy." She rolled down her window.

"I preferred the lying low bit." Roger punched the gas pedal and downshifted just as another car came around the corner headlights out.

"Then keep as low as possible and go around to their right."

Roger did and, as they passed the car, four red blasts seared into the window coming from where Sherida sat. The vehicle went careening out of control. "Holy! Do you ever miss?"

"Rarely; my neuro targeting mechanisms are also built in to take over."

"Okay, let's head out of here. The other car is about one minute behind yet."

Roger glanced down as they entered the nearly empty street and a red light came on the dash. "Damn! She's over-heating. Something must have punctured the rad," he said, as steam began to curl out from under the hood and the rank-but-sweet smell of antifreeze flooded into the car.

"Can we make it home?" Sherida asked.

"I'll try."

They drove for another minute until something popped and a sudden spurt of steam vented. "Crap! Can't see anything."

"Watch out; there's another car there."

Roger slammed on the brakes, too late, as they smashed into the vehicle crossing the lights. Both cars twisted sideways before coming to grinding halt. Roger felt the seat belt stop him from flying forward and the air being knocked out of his lungs as the airbags exploded and shoved him back into the seat. Pain flared up his left side as he pressed hard against the belt. He hoped he hadn't cracked anything. Sherida wasn't so lucky as she hurtled against the exploding windshield, there wasn't a passenger side air bag in this vehicle. Roger tried to open the door but it was jammed. Acrid smoke and fire poured out from under the hood of the other vehicle.

Sherida hammered her door open with her shoulder and fell onto the ground. Picking herself up off the ground pulling pieces of glass from her face and arms and ran back over to the car. Her one arm hung limp but with the other she heaved the door open and pulled Roger out of the Mazda.

"Thanks." He gasped looking at her arm, hanging useless. "Is it..."

"Broken? Not sure." She gritted her teeth shutting down the pain receptors inside her.

"The driver of the other car?"

"A young couple. I don't think we can save them." She closed her eyes scanning the two in the car. "We can't save them. He's dead and she's nearly in cardiac arrest, only has seconds to live," she said. "As we will soon be if we don't move it. The other car is only blocks away and closing in on us."

Sherida stared at the body of the lady in the car. She was blonde, nearly her size. The idea slammed into her head as dozens of possibilities spun back and forward from her programming.

It would work; it would have to, but she had to be quick. She could pick up their thoughts, knew they would be here in mere moments.

Roger was already rushing forward, trying to reach the woman who was slumped over in the burning vehicle. She scanned the woman's vital signs again.

"It's too late, there's no chance of saving her. She's dying." Sherida thought for a quick moment. "I've got an idea, but we haven't much time. They're tracking me somehow, either through the symbiont or my brainwaves, which are altered by the symbiont. I have to fool them into thinking I'm dead, otherwise we both will be. There's five more coming, in moments they'll be here."

Sherida moaned, her self-repairing circuits were already starting to kick in and shut down the rest of her body so she could rebuild herself. She flicked at what looked like a mole and a small flap of skin lifted on her neck. Sherida pulled at the flap, stripping it from her.

"Grab this and pull."

"What? I can't strip your flesh," Roger said, horrified.

"Do it now or we both die. I can't do it; the symbiont won't allow me to. I'll explain later, this isn't my real skin, it's an implant."

"Can't we just kill its power source?"

"I am its power source."

"Oh." Roger pulled hard on the piece of skin. It ripped further away from her body. Little metallic/fiber optic wires thinner than hair pulled from her body and she screamed. They were interwoven into her, grown into her, like stitches. Or roots. He shuddered, watching them wriggle under her flesh. They were translucent, nearly invisible, like some kind of ghostly threads of fiber optic strands. Some were several inches long, others over a foot in length. He pulled again and watched the strands sliding under her skin, along her arm, her neck, and eventually the whatever-it-was left Sherida's body and a sharp, shrill, scream psychically filled his head; it was crying out in pain. It looked like skin, yet had metallic-like roots, but whatever it was, it was alive. There was no mistaking that, it was some sort of living robot.

"Don't let it touch you or it will try to attach itself to you. Throw it on the arm of the female." With that she blinked and slumped over unconscious.

Roger ran to the car and as he was about to fling the piece of alien life into the burning wreckage, whatever it was flipped over and touched him. "Oh, God!" Roger screamed, his mind exploding under a barrage of images and thoughts. Pain seared itself into him. "Too much, this is too much." He struggled to shut it down. So much was happening around him, was this what Sherida lived with every moment of her life?

It told him of the approaching car. *There were five heading this way to make sure the others had finished their job. They were a block away; one of them wasn't human. The female is nearly dead. My former host, Sherida, her pulse is dropping.* He knew it, he knew it all and more as it flashed into his head.

"Another Alpha Draconis. This is bad." Roger grabbed a shard of broken glass and hacked at the thing, quickly cutting it away before it could take a proper hold. It was moving, throbbing, dying, he knew. Shrill screams shattered his mind. In that brief moment he knew what it felt like to be gifted beyond belief, what it felt like to be her, to be in touch with God. To be God.

"No, this isn't right." This, he knew wasn't natural, it was unnatural, ungodly.

The fire was intense. Roger covered his face with his other hand and flung the creature against the arm dangling from the car window. It attached itself to her, instantly dissolving its way inside her and began the herculean task of trying to rebuild her, doing whatever was needed to stay alive. Only the damage would be too great. She and it were both dead.

Roger slung Sherida over his shoulder. She was lighter than he had expected. With a Herculean effort, he managed to jog to the second house away, each step a race to stay conscious, and slumped behind some thick lilac bushes. Sherida was out for the count and with her arm mangled like that, probably would be for a while.

A car came screeching around the corner and five goons ejected themselves from the vehicle. They milled around the two cars, pointing guns and something that looked like a bizarre radio transmitter. One of them scanned the woman in the car with a weird-looking device. Police and fire truck sirens sounded in the distance. They knew they had to be quick.

Zolnar glanced at his scanner. The DNA matched those of a female Pleiadian with traces of symbiont attached to her body. He smiled, "Good, we've got one, boys. A job well done."

There were only four left to get, although this one had proven to be the hardest to track down so far and more than likely the one agent that had been responsible for the triggering of the ZPEC earlier this week. Which meant the Galactic Council would be watching this planet closer now. "Why don't we stop at the place with the Golden Arches for a celebration meal and I'll pay you the bonuses." *And wipe out your memories*, he thought to himself. They cheered as they piled into the van. He tried not to gag on the scent of the meat eaters. Meat - it was funny that they had McDonalds on this world like several others. *At least I could eat one of those,* he thought, *no real meat there, probably just Vesuvian Bean Curd.*

Roger watched the one with the transmitter throw something onto the burning vehicle and it erupted into a ball of fire. The men cheered and clapped themselves on the back as the police sirens came closer. They jumped back into the mini-van and disappeared. Roger sighed with relief.

Sherida moaned and he looked at her face and stroked her platinum blonde hair as she shivered in the cold. "I guess it's my turn to be the guardian angel now." He smiled, feeling the events of the past few hours catching up with him.

"Rest. I need rest."

He knew he did too but first he had to get them a bit further away. Roger picked her up and went down the street before they both collapsed into a clump of trees, well hidden. He set the timer on his watch, aiming to sleep too, realizing that anyway it would be better to wait until the cops cleaned up the mess before trying to make it home.

As she slept he watched as the few more thin tendrils of silver fiber oozed its way out of her body, like little silver worms. Worms that had grown into every muscle, tendon, organ and probably even her brain. Roger gagged.

How many aspire to be closer to God. For a brief moment, he had a taste of what she lived and breathed. And as unnatural as it seemed at the time, it was such an incredible feeling.

****

"Thanks for looking after me the other night," Sherida said, looking up at him. She tried to rise but couldn't. Tears welled up in her eyes.

"You're welcome."

"Sorry. My emotions are running amuck with me. They've been turned off for so long. So hard to control them or deny them." Tears streamed down her face onto the pillow. "I feel so helpless and so disconnected here. Is it always like this?"

"Like what?"

"So alone in this world."

"Not sure what you're talking about."

"Part of our training and culture is about the connection to the rest of the universe and our environment, much like what your First Nations peoples believe in."

"How do you know about that?"

"We study and get downloaded into our brains much history, current culture and beliefs in case we need such kind of information."

"Like knowing how to drive a car without getting behind the wheel."

"Exactly. Only I feel so cut off from everything; never thought I'd ever feel this way." She shivered. "Can you hold me? I'm so fragile, so weak in this form now." Roger sat on the bed and took her into his arms. This was such a change from the confident, take-charge person he'd met earlier. Yet at the same time there was a part of him, that male protector role, that found her softness, her weakness, arousing. The want to protect, to hold to ...

He stroked her hair, trying to sooth her like you would a frightened cat, tender like the sweetness of morning's breath crying in the mists of dawn. Her body, the warmth pressing against his, the crush of her against him.

Her breasts, naked under the tee-shirt rubbing against her chest, sent an electrifying buzz through him. Nipples hardening, desires stirring.

Did she also feel the arousal? Was the part of her that was sexual returning to her body?

"Roger?" She looked up at him. Cravings floated in her eyes, the hunger of seething passions simmering walked on hushed feet. He felt his response, stirring up from within. Need, sexual desires too long denied. Too strong.

Her hands slid across his chest. "I want to thank you, somehow, for saving me." Need, trembling hungers, surging within her touch, the soft caress of her hands. Touching him.

"I - we - shouldn't be. I'm married. I've a wife."

"I know. I just have to experience this once in this dimension. There are beings, seventh dimensional beings that live off energy. They feed on the sheer energy given off by humans when they make love. In the mixing of male, female, yin yang and both culminating in the release of a third energy. The power of creation, the energy of love is the greatest power in the universe."

As she talked her hands ran down his body. Her chest pressed harder against him. Her pelvis tilted forward rubbing against him, strong in her need. "So powerful, these emotions of arousal, of needing to connect."

Roger's response was immediate. Blood throbbed in his desire to possess her.

To be united, to release his energy. Knowing that there were others out there, voyeurs of the enigmatic sort, watching, feeding off the energy they were creating between them.

Esoteric watchers. Voyeurs of erotic needs from dimensions above.

Words fell away as need replaced rational thought. As her lips touched his chest, hands reached under his shirt and brushed against his nipples. Fluttering over him like feathers.

"No I can't, I'm ..."

Yet the truth sunk in, it had been too long. He'd wanted her before, desired her, now was his chance.

He sighed, he needed her, needed release from the damning urges filling his limbs.

Roger fell into the pleasure of her.

Of desire beyond desire. Intense exploding hungers. Passions building, surging, levels of arousal cascading higher into another, unbelieving that the next moved into sheer ecstasy of the moment. Blown away by the present, torn into the immediate fabric of the now. So intense he didn't, couldn't think.

Her breath gasped in his ear, sighs of her building needs. Groans, whose?

He opened his eyes for a moment as brilliance filled the room and saw light exploding from them, from her. Light like wings billowing from her back as she reached that edge. That angelic edge.

Mesmerizing him until ...

Release, the explosion leaving him hanging in the timelessness of null space, floating on the pinnacle of joy of sweet peace.

Floating like a feather falls to the ground, as reason slowly filtered back to his mind. Replacing the sheer pleasure of his emotions. What had transpired was wrong, yet the pleasure still tingled in retreating waves of tenderness like the ocean washing away.

Receding in shudders that shook his body, hers.

All wrong, and all so right, in the same breath.

He closed his eyes.

Sherida rolled over and grabbed him by the shoulders. "Wake up Roger. Wake up."

Only the sound of her voice wasn't right. She sounded like ... "Roger, tell me what the hell is going on here."

Beth.

Roger opened his eyes as the angel began to shove him.

"What...? What's happening?" Roger stared not into the face of an angel, but the face of his very angry wife. Beth was home. He'd fallen asleep after he'd managed to sneak away from the accident scene with Sherida. All he remembered was flopping into his bed after laying Sherida down in the spare room completely exhausted. Beth must have come home sometime after that.

"Give me some explanation of what's going on here. And it better be good. You look like hell, like you've been through a car accident or something, all scratched up."

Darn, he'd fallen fast asleep, Roger had wanted to shower and get dressed before she arrived.

"And there's some young blonde in our guest bed, lying there nearly naked, who looks in the same state as you. She's in shock, trauma or some kind of drug withdrawal. Tell me! What the hell is going on!"

Roger stared at his wife. "I don't know where to begin. Do you remember the incident on our honeymoon, where the metal detectors went off at the airport?"

"Yes." A faint glimmer of a smile haunted her lips. "This better be good!"

"That, and that giant bone that Sparky dragged home, is where this all started." Roger explained as briefly as possible, babbling from exhaustion, quickly explaining the events that had precipitated having Sherida here in their spare room. The only thing he didn't mention was digging up Mike's body. He'd sworn to secrecy with the guys on that one. "And it started last night with her burning down Mrs. Millers garage."

Beth sat there quietly through it all. "So let me get this straight. You're trying to tell me there's an alien girl, who looks just like an Earth girl, a beautiful near-naked Earth girl, lying in our spare room, you and Sparky were battling dinosaurs and a bunch of your buddies all had pieces of alien metal in them. Oh, and this alien woman can't go back to where she came from, which is who knows how many million miles away, because they, some kind of alien reptilian race is trying to kill her. You burnt Mrs. Miller's garage to the ground, got involved in a car chase and ended up being involved in a car crash with a stolen car."

"That's pretty well it in a nutshell." Roger smiled. He didn't like the funny look on Beth's face, it didn't spell humor.

She burst out laughing. "That's the worst load of crap I've ever heard. Why don't you just tell me the truth. You picked up this girl last night. You were having a good time in the van when you got in an accident."

"I didn't get in an accident."

"You fucking bastard!" Beth exploded. "Screwing around and we're only married a few months. You've probably been seeing her for a while. Angel my ass! More like angel escort service, I'll bet. This is complete and utter bullshit."

"But it's..."

"Don't go there. Don't say another bloody word. Aliens, saving the world, dinosaurs in Mrs. Miller's garage. Give me a fucking break. Tell you what, when you decide to tell me the truth, call me. I'll be at Mom's with the kids. The fucking nerve of some men."

Roger stood in the front door to his house an hour later watching Beth's taillights head towards her mother's. "Now what do I do?" This had all gone way too far. There were things happening here that were not only dangerous but beyond his level of understanding.

The soft pad of footsteps alerted him that someone was behind him.

"Overwhelming, isn't it?"

Roger turned and saw Sherida framed in the sunlight cascading down the hallway. He saw the naked outline of her under the thin white cotton of his long tee shirt. The curve of her hips. "God." He shook his head remembering his dream. She looked incredibly good. No better than good, delicious. Her beautiful platinum sparkled in the light from behind her, adding a near halo, almost as if she had wings. White wings radiating out behind her. Now he understood how people could mistake them for angels.

Jeepers, he shouldn't be thinking like this. It was a good thing she couldn't read his mind anymore.

"I'm sorry, I heard her voice sounding very upset and tried to get up," she gasped before collapsing, clutching her one arm that could barely move. Roger rushed forward and grabbed her before she hit the ground. She wasn't wearing anything under the tee shirt. He felt the softness of her breasts rub against his chest as he pulled her up. Why couldn't she look like Helga of the first division Nazi SS storm troopers. "Weak, this is harder than I thought it would be," she gasped.

"Back to bed for the likes of you, missy." He scolded trying to regain some humor, some sanity, when the only thing he could think of was the crush of those breasts and the fresh smell of her skin. Why did she have to be so gorgeous? No wonder his wife was upset, he would be too given the reverse of the circumstances.

"But first I need a hand with something," she said innocently.

As he lay her back on the bed Roger noticed red spots forming lower down on the tee shirt.

"You're bleeding!"

"I'm okay, but that's not what I need a hand with. My menstrual cycle is starting again. I haven't had these since I became a messenger. The bio implants suppress any unnecessary female functions and without them one obviously couldn't get pregnant as well."

"I guess I understand. You don't want to be a billion miles away from home and having your period start. Makes sense. Brutal, but understandable." Roger got up and headed for the bathroom.

"What are these? There are no instructions on the package," she queried, staring innocently at him after he returned with Beth's supply of tampons.

"Hmm, they obviously don't use tampons in the Pleiades. Great." Roger knew the next few minutes were going to be very interesting.

****

A figure shimmered into view beside the charred asphalt on the road. Trimus spun around, ready for anything with his pulse weapon built into his palm at the ready. He was dressed in this period's clothes to blend in without drawing attention, hoody, baggy pants. All the world looking like some punk on the street.

A sigh of relief, it was late, no traffic to be seen. The ominous smell of burnt metal, plastic and flesh struck his acute sensory nostrils. *Not how I pictured my first breath of this planet would be like.* He gagged and switched off the high intensity olfactory sensory neuron feeds designed to provide detailed chemosensory inputs.

Sherida's last known location before she disconnected or disappeared or... Or so he hoped. He walked around the charred remains, all evidence had already been removed by the local authorities, only blackened stains left. The odors of other chemicals told him they'd scrubbed the ground and sanitized it.

A crash? Collision? Or explosion? Turning on his remote olfactory sensors again, he sniffed deeper. A death. Someone had died here. Activating his Neutron Activation Analysis protocols, he scanned for any remaining particles of DNA, and it told him it was most likely human and not Pleiadian.

A quick sigh of relief and he inhaled some more. The traces told him female, Caucasian, with blonde hair. *Not Pleiadian confirmed.*

He walked back and forth, puzzled, until he got a sniff of Arconium and bent over to study the tiny silver wire. Only two inches of it remained a few feet away, missed in the cleanup. *Doesn't make any sense.*

Okay time to run the fourth dimensional time relapse device and let's see what really happened here. He stepped back three steps, being careful not to get caught in the vortex and looked around again making sure no one was about. He knew some agents had got sucked into events and never returned. No one knew for sure why. It was theorized that going back takes your DNA back in time as well. Others that unless protected, the memory of future events fades from the mind. Without certain protective sensors, he wasn't prepared to go directly back in time.

A shimmering flash and time spun backwards until he saw the motorized vehicle get slammed into another one. It exploded into a fireball. Sherida and a male. He stopped the replay and walked around the unmoving figures.

Human, identified as Roger Harrison, Caucasian male, her case study. *The one most likely to succeed at this point in her mission.*

Trimus let the scene continue, watching the events unfold once again. He watched them limp off, the human caring her and was about to stop it to walk to the location where he took her as another vehicle screamed to a halt.

He watched some more and caught the satisfied smirk on the human's face that quickly shifted into a Draconian's image. It hit him hard. He stopped and ran his analyzer over the scene. Draconian, definitely in disguise. *They are here and …. Rumors are true. Killing off our angels. That's why I was sent here, to confirm.*

He rewound the scene again and expanded his ocular sensor increasing the magnification. Catching Roger pull the implant from her body at the precise time home world received the signal. Roger struggling to not let it enter him, knowing it was about to die, and tossed it on the human female. He knew they had received garbled signals and that explained why before the symbiont died while trying to bring the female human back to life but couldn't as another explosion killed the woman and engulfed the car in flames.

He watched the reptile being enter a strand into some kind of detector. *She is alive then and being hunted by them. Only now he can't trace her. Brilliant thinking on Sherida's part. Only how did he get that technology to track her and probably the others? With the bigger question; how do I track her now?*

So how did they track her and probably the others? Trimus sent a signal to headquarters confirming their suspicions and scanned his databanks. The Draconians had been the race to be contracted to build the trackers. *Of course, Damn! Now they've stabbed us in the back and using the trackers or something hidden from us inside them against us.*

He thought hard. Memory banks calling up all known agents that were involved in that equipment's development. One name came searing to him to him. Vessno'ar.

He was the closest one, his tracers picking up his Draconian traces not only here on this planet, but in this city. Probably in disguise like this one was when he first showed up.

Time to go, but I need to find Sherida to see if she is safe and begin the next process. As he began to vanish his outfit in disguise faded away first exposing the dark exoskeleton armor and his shoulder length white hair with elongated eyes of emerald blue and long pointed ears. *I hope Sherida is safe, being an agent is one thing but being attracted to another is something else.*

****

The fourteen-year-old boy stared up from where he'd been watching all of this from behind the dumpster. It was a scene akin to those in a science fiction movie, and it had happened a few times now. The vision of the white-haired alien creature with spook-like eyes vanishing into nothing was the last straw.

He puked up what remained in his stomach and grabbed his burner phone. "Mom, I want to come home, I can't do these drugs anymore. I'm seeing bizarre aliens in hoodies and weird flashback shit like an accident with more strange beings with tentacles and weird equipment. Please come pick me up. I'm at the dumpster. You know where." He hung up and dropped the phone. He hit his head a few times with the heel of his and puked again; this time nothing but bile.

The sight of the car exploding and the weird reptilian being staring around would haunt him for many years. Not to mention the blonde woman pulling silver wriggling wires out of her body. He puked more bile, convinced he'd puke his innards up.

If that was what overdosing does, they can keep it. He shook as tremors went through him, knowing quitting wouldn't be easy, but after what he just saw, he would get through it. He tossed the small bag of crack cocaine down the sewer and huddled himself rocking back and forth, awaiting his ride to a better future.

****

Sherida absentmindedly pulled at a silver thread sticking out from her shoulder as they sat around the dinner table. "Keep shedding these things."

Roger just stared as she yanked the silvery thread from her body, watching it wheedle away under her skin.

"And thanks for cutting my hair. It was very distinctive and eye-catching and I need to be as inconspicuous as possible."

He'd cut her hair to near shoulder length, trying to make it look as even as possible. "Yeah, I'm not much of a barber, but it looks alright." The implant must have grown into every major organ, as far as he could tell. It was unnerving. She'd slept most of the day, as did he, dozing off here and there. He'd tried to call Beth but she refused to talk to him. Probably better if he let her cool off for a few days. He called work and let them know he wasn't going to be coming in all week. Fortunately, most of his work could be done at home if needed.

He sat down with her that night. He couldn't get over her amazement of food. Roger had made a simple meal of spaghetti with tomato sauce. In all of his years of being single, before he met Beth, he'd enjoyed cooking and had become quite good at it. Roger often cooked many of the meals. Still; it was better than doing the dishes.

He didn't cook any meat, as Sherida had told him that she didn't eat animal matter and actually usually ate nothing at all. The bio implant allowed her to synthesize sunlight in much the same way as plants do for energy and sustenance.

"So is this something other aliens do?"

"Yes. Most evolved forms do not naturally eat anything. Eating other creatures is unnatural and unhealthy," she told him. "Eating slows down the body and decreases lifespan. Many higher evolved races drink a high-energy liquid that supplies all major nutrients and shed any unwanted matter through the pores of the skin. The even higher evolved life forms subsist off the energy of the universe," she told him. "Most of us have a hard time walking around here on this planet, as we find the body odors of meat eaters, including humans, very offensive."

"Makes sense," Theodore had told him one time that when the aliens were discovered in the crashed spaceship near Rosewell in 1947, reports stated that there were no organs visible for waste elimination. Until now he thought he'd had one beer too many.

"So now what? How do I help a stranded alien a bizillion miles from home?" Roger sat in his living room, talking to himself. Sherida was still asleep in bed and he knew he had at some point try to talk to Beth. Not that she'd even remotely believe him.

Roger grabbed the phone and dialed Theodore's number, the one person that would believe him, and, hopefully, help. "Hi Theodore, do you remember when I said I wouldn't believe all this stuff until I saw a real live Pleiadian standing in front of me?"

"Yeah."

"Guess what! Well, she's not standing in front of me, but she's sleeping in my guest bedroom."

"What? I think you've had one beer too many, or some of that green tobacco."

"No, I'm not joking, Theodore. Our angel, the one that started all this, back at the summer camp, is passed out in my bedroom."

Click.

****

"Ah hello?" He tried dialing back but there was no response. "Damn! Didn't even get to tell him about the dinosaurs."

A couple of minutes later Roger heard the screech of tires and the thud of feet. He graciously opened the door as Theodore hand was raised to bang on the door. "You better not be joking about this."

"Trust me, I'm not. I'll prove it."

They opened the bedroom door a little and peaked into the room. Sherida still lay on the bed, unconscious.

"It *is* her! How...?" Theodore began to ask, before passing out himself. Roger caught him at the last second. "Great. Now I've got two to worry about."

****

The yelling and screaming set Sherida's senses on high alert and she spun around looking for the threat, but it was just small kids on swings and running on planks between small structures; a playground. Moms sat watching the kids or chatting to each other in what her empathic traits told her were 'mommy talk'.

So, the danger here wasn't obvious, but had to be deciphered. She shifted into clothes worn in the same style as the mothers and walked up. Her face blurred to an older dowdier mother type. *One of these is not as she seems.*

"Hi, I'm Sam. Nice day." Several smiled back. After several intros she made her farewells as she'd noted a single woman sitting further away, and she wandered over to her. The woman looked up at her from behind dark glasses as she slowly sipped on a beverage. Sherida cursed the glasses as she could not look into her eyes.

"You look sad, not like the others. Is your child here?"

"The world sucks. My world sucks." She reached out and offered her hand and the woman took it. Palm sensors went off analyzing data as she returned the handshake.

The woman told her of her life, husband dying, sorting out finances, rest of the older kids in summer school. Sherida's senses told her she was lying.

DNA unavailable. Blocked.

Her tracers responded. She had no idea of this world. No idea; that was the point, to be thrust blind into a scenario and have to puzzle your way out. *So, she's blocking me.*

Possible Ciscadiac DNAS.

Ciscadiac Dna, then I'm in the... Andromeda galaxy. Where and what was here that was a danger?

She ran through her training and knowledge base downloaded into her as she felt her knees go weak. *What the?*

'Infection detected, spreading rapidly.'

The woman smiled at her as faintness seeped through her. "You okay? You look weak."

"Ah, yes, just not used to the heat." Sherida wiped at sweat on her brow as bio-circuitry began to kick in, fighting the invading source.

"Let me introduce you to my daughter and make sure she's okay." As she rose the woman touched Sherida on her back.

'Further infection detected, source fifty percent stronger.'

Sherida could barely stay standing.

"I think she'd like you."

The words sent a shiver though Sherida as they walked, her knees wanting to buckle. *What type of germ infection is this?* There wasn't much known about this world and less about the creatures that inhabited it.

'Main agent detected, form of Apixaben, anti-coagulant. Also tricyclic.'

She thought a moment, blood thinners and sleeping agents, trying to keep herself rational as the symbiont flooded her with histamine and adrenaline. That's a similar tranquilizing agent used by Vampirine found on other worlds, so some type of blood sucking carnivore. A sophisticated method of seduction. She watched a young girl run into the woods with a boy. "That's her, my sweet angel." She yelled out, "Don't go there, it could be dangerous, Lemux are on the prowl."

"Let's hurry." Unable to resist the order Sherida complied. It was sapping her willpower as well. Making her helpless. Very clever. The woman reached up to touch Sherida again a third time. *Probably stronger dose again.* She gasped, trying to think, and ran off as best she could. "I see something." Everything around her began to spin. Vampirine seduce their prey through touch, sometimes hypnotically and ...

It hit her. Feed their prey to the children who have ravenous appetites. She spied the girl bent over the boy. His throat slashed and as he died she inhaled the vital soul essence that fed them above blood and meat. Their dessert, she suddenly remembered.

Vapors rose. Psychic witches or vampires of legend on many worlds.

She commanded the circuitry to begin bio-flushing the infection and pumping her with more adrenaline. Sherida's systems kicked in quickly as the girl looked up. Her teeth enlarged to long fangs and a mouth that doubled in size, eyes became mere slits. "Mommy said you looked delectable and she was right."

The girl spun around and leapt at her with a hungry snarl.

Sherida sidestepped, slamming her fist hard into the back of the girl's head. She transformed herself into her blackened body suit. Bio-circuitry kicked in, clearing her head. She couldn't let her touch her, this time the dose would be fatal.

Mother arrived and turned herself into the vile totally vampiristic creature she was, washing away her clothes and persona, dressed only in silks flowing over her naked body. Sherida knew they spun those from the skin of the dead their kids devoured as a means of protecting themselves if the children ever got too hungry and went after their parents.

She lunged at Sherida like a protective mother would, fangs and claws extended. Sherida flashed her built in palm lazar. Her midsection exploded backwards and she collapsed to the ground in agony.

The girl rose, sniffed at her mom and collapsed on top of her. The blood smells driving her into a rage. She tore aside the silken threads and in a fit of ravenous rage tore into her, devouring her mother as her incredible hunger took control of her.

Sherida signaled to leave but stopped. *No, she wasn't the object here. If I leave this child will attack and feed off the rest of the kids until satiated. Once the hunger feast began they couldn't control themselves.*

Sherida materialized a knife and grabbed the girl by the hair yanking her head back. The girl growled at her and attempted to sink her teeth into the Kevlar type of body armor. Bones broke under the incredible force of her jaws. They are known to have unknown strength in their rage yet the suit remained intact. With her free hand she sliced the child across the neck. Blood poured free as she collapsed to the ground. She growled gasping, her eyes returning to that of the young girl, full of innocent fun.

"Sorry, even the innocent are not so innocent, but sometimes more vile than the parents." A tear splattered the ground as she signaled the Agency to come get her as her hand numbed and repair systems began to kick in repairing the damage. She stroked the child's head. She knew this was a hard test, most failed falling for the innocence of the young, and having to kill something this young wasn't what she had expected she would ever have to do. But that was the point of these training exercises. Having to be prepared for any eventuality, or as someone once said on Earth world, "Always expect the unexpected."

Chapter Four

Earthweek: news story 1979.

The Japan Meteorological Agency announced that since August a hole in the ozone layer is growing. Observed over Antarctica, if it continues at its current rate of growth, it could expand to an estimated 75,000,000 square kilometers.

****

Theodore blinked and returned to consciousness quickly after Roger half-dragged him into the living room and deposited him on the couch. As he sipped at a reviving brandy, Roger filled him on the events of the last couple of days.

"Dinosaurs? What? And you claim an alien reptilian being was renting one of your next-door neighbor's garages to get dinosaur wall plaques?"

"Sure! People go hunting to get elk and deer trophies in our time, don't they?"

Theodore stared in disbelief as Sherida slowly walked into the living room and sat in the armchair, obviously still weak but somewhat revived, and he sat there with his jaw hanging open. "It's really her!"

"I sensed someone, wanted to check it out. Who is he?" she asked, closing her eyes, trying to recall why she faintly recognized him.

"A friend. Possibly the only one that I can trust to help us. Theodore, Sherida; Sherida, Theodore. You've both met once before at the summer camp a few years back."

"He's one of you; one of the people I implanted." She looked at him in a daze, sensing his intelligence but also taken aback by something in him. She smiled weakly at Roger. "I am needing the bathroom." Roger helped her wobble back to bed while Theodore sat on the couch, too shocked to move.

"God, she's alive and ah... gorgeous." Theodore smiled at Roger as he returned and sank down on the couch next to him. "And you say she's a Pleiadian?"

"Yes, yes and yes! True on all counts. And yes, gorgeous. I keep telling myself I'm a married man and I love my wife very much, but she is rather stunning," Roger replied, his voice too sharp for his own liking.

"Sorry. By the way, does Beth know about Sherida? About any of this?"

"Yes. She found her asleep in our spare room. Let's just say she hasn't taken to well to it." Roger quickly explained what happened the day before as Sherida staggered back into the living room. "Ah, I see our guest has returned. You're still not looking very good; how's the arm?"

"Throbbing. I may not have the implant but I think its residual side effects are still enhancing my healing time." She nodded to her hand in the sling Roger had made and wiggled her fingers. "Hello Theodore, sorry I'm not good company, I'm just so tired. It's really not like me at all. I'm beginning to dream again and they're so vivid. I think the dreams are keeping me from sleeping properly. I haven't dreamed since the implant was put into me."

"Implant?" Theodore looked puzzled.

"I forgot about the implant. She calls it a symbiont. I'll tell you later." Roger rose to help Sherida as she staggered a little from tiredness. "Now, back to bed before you collapse. You need more sleep to recover."

Theodore jumped up to help Roger with Sherida but she yanked herself out of Roger's grasp and stood there swaying, nearly out on her feet. "From my dreams, something... an event. No, a place. Calling me. You need to get me someplace. It's urgent."

"Someplace where?"

"Somewhere I keep dreaming of over and over, we call it the old Orion ascension transmitter. Images of it keep popping in my head. It's somewhere on this planet. The people called guardians of the Dogstar have knowledge of it, a key, I think, to start it up. Does that make any sense?" She moaned as she tried to move her injured arm. "I think it's a failsafe, some sort of implanted emergency backup measure should I ever get stranded." Roger glanced at Theodore obviously lost and looking for some kind of answer.

"What's an Orion transmitter and what does it look like?" Theodore asked.

"It was built by beings from the Orion system to enable other races to ascend to higher dimensions, and, among other things, used by the Mystery Schools to train adepts to connect with their Gods. It uses a ZPEC ..."

The two men looked blankly at her.

"Get me into the bed and I'll explain more. So weak at the moment." They did and as she lay there she explained further. "I mean a Zero-Point Energy Converter. It's an energy source and the guardians have something I need to re-power it. A key of some sort like I mentioned."

"Zero-point energy? That's only some scientific theory. So are you talking about ascending to the fourth dimension?" Theodore blurted out, as he rose and began to pace the room. Roger swore he could see smoke pouring from Theodore's ears. This was right up his alley; he was glad he called him.

"Yes, I think. My understanding of the ZPEC is it funnels the energy of the Earth, converting magnetic force, or ley line energy, into zero-point energy."

"Wow, that's amazing," Theodore uttered. "We've only begun to realize the existence of these energy fields and you're saying other races used it as an energy source?"

"For thousands of years."

"That's wild. I've read somewhere that someone plotted UFO sightings and noticed that they seemed to travel along certain lines. He thought that perhaps they were using certain energy lines of force that we know little about. I think he also mentioned something about energy centers and the pyramids. I'll have to check my notes." Theodore said excitedly as he paced unable stay still as his mind sought answers from so many questions coming to the fore.

"You guys are talking way over my head. It's the transmitter that worries me. How are we going to find some little transmitter device?" Roger added, thinking it was like the communication badges used in Star Trek.

"Little? From what I know I think it's actually a fair size, but maybe its true nature is just not obvious to you. Do you have a pen and paper? A vision of something is coming awake. I need to draw this out," she slumped back on the bed against Theodore as he grabbed a pad of paper from his pocket and pencil from his shirt that Roger knew he always had with him. He hesitantly put his arms around her and held her as she began to scribble.

"Sure." Roger watched Theodore cuddling Sherida in his arms. He had never been known to have a girlfriend and some of the others in the group wondered if he didn't lean the other way. He couldn't take his eyes off the way she moved into him or the way he tenderly stroked her hair. She probably hadn't had anyone show affection to her in a long time as well. There were definite sparks flying between the two of them. Which was good, as any sparks from her and Beth would sling Roger's balls up in a noose.

"Maybe you should get some rest first. We could do this later," Roger said.

"No. It is urgent that I get there. I must see the guardians first, they have the key," she grumbled, barely conscious, in a hypnotic state fighting to stay awake. She pushed away from Theodore slightly and sketched three triangular objects and a crude outline of a crouching figure. "Erected in a pattern to represent the Orion system as seen from Earth. It was built a long time ago, before any of your current civilizations were around. Its face would resemble a humanoid, the body a feline-like creature you call a ..."

"Lion! Oh my God! She's drawn the pyramids of Giza. That's right! They worshipped the stars of Orion's Belt. This is amazing!" Theodore's eyes widened. "And they were built in the pattern of that star system."

"Yeah, amazing. Well, that is a bit bigger than I thought. I guess they never heard of micro technology in those days," Roger said sarcastically. He hoped he wasn't about to be signed up for another adventure. "Nobody said becoming a gateway walker meant being Indiana Jones' apprentice." he muttered to himself.

The pencil fell from her fingers as she collapsed back into Theodore beginning to fade away. Theodore squinted as he nearly got poked in the eye by one of the silvery strands being rejected from her body. "What the hell is this stuff?"

"It's been coming out of her ever since I yanked out the symbiont implant."

"Her body's way of rejecting something I suppose. Probably part of why she's tired. From what I know the strands run bio-organically through her body so that it can perform whatever tasks are required."

Sherida mumbled as they wrapped her in blankets. "Keepers of the Dogstar, I must get there. They have the key."

"Dogstar, Dogstar. I don't know any..." Theodore muttered, as they closed the door after laying her down in the guest bedroom. "Wait a minute, do you have my computer disks here?"

"Yes, in the den."

"I think I know what she's after."

"But the pyramids?" They walked towards the den. "How do we know this isn't only some sort of lucid dream brought on by me yanking the implant out of her? If those silver threads could trigger some kind of physical reaction surely it could also mess up her head in some sort of psychotic way as well. I mean, 'Keepers of the Dogstar'? How could that have anything to do with that old pile of rocks? Zero-point transmitter? Ley lines? And what about the pyramids? I thought they were just some old pharaoh's tomb. This is all a little nuts, don't you think?"

"Nuts, yes. Implausible, no." Theodore replied as his mind raced away. "But there's been a few lesser-known studies that show the pyramids and the sphinx being here before 10,000 BC. Before the last great flood."

"What? That's contrary to everything in our history." Roger knew Theodore was going to launch into one of his alien theory of evolution rants that he'd heard more than once, only this time he was very interested.

"There's lots that goes against our established timelines of history. Did you know they've found many artifacts that don't fit into anything we believe to be 'quote' established history?"

"Like?" Roger indicated to Theordore to sit at his desk and start up the computer as he handed retrieved the box of discs which Theodore had given him over the years containing information about alien theories, most of which he hadn't watched, just accepted to appease his good friend.

"Well, from the top of my memory, a shoe print in 286-million-year-old rock, found in Kentucky, which we now know, after what you told me about being taken back in time, could possibly be yours." Theodore smirked showing a rare bit of humor. "They've a seashell in a two-million-year-old deposit in England, with a human face scratched on its surface. A human footprint found in 150-million-year-old material from Russia. An arrowhead found in the femur of an extinct Toxodon near Buenos Aires, in three- to five-million-year-old formations. Metal tubes discovered in 65–144-million-year-old chalk deposits from Saint Jean de Livet, France.

An iron pot, a section of block wall and a silver object found in 300-million-year-old deposits in Wilburt and Heavener, Oklahoma. A clay figurine found in two-million-year-old rock from Nampa, India. A metallic vase found in 600-million-year-old deposits in Dorchester, Massachusetts. That's all I recall but there's more in the file marked 'Trust Me, I Didn't Make This Shit Up!' There're many more objects found too that haven't been carbon dated, including human footprints next to dinosaur prints."

A shell-shocked Roger stood behind Theodore as he continued to search for the relevant files. "Whoa, slow down! Even I've heard of those, from the Discovery channel on TV," Roger replied thinking, hoping, he could wind him up and put away the soapbox or they would be here all night.

"People have found all sorts of iron nails, coins, silver and gold threads, encased within solid rock or coal and even in the center of quartz and geodes. My favorite though is a 2.8-billion-year-old metallic sphere with grooved markings located in Ottosdalin, South Africa. All oddities that don't fit into the accepted mainstream theory of evolution and so are quietly swept under the carpet. It's done by the scientific community all the time. The scientists that find these are ostracized by others and usually are shut up in order to keep their jobs and not be ridiculed."

"Jesus! Kinda like the ostrich sticking its head in the sand routine. And it's all on that disc?" Roger sat there, aghast.

"Yup."

"Man, you sure lead a different type of life. Obviously, I haven't looked at any of that, but will now that all of this has happened. That sphere is interesting, though. Do you think it looked anything like the pieces we pulled out of us?"

"Well, I'll have to pull up the pictures and take another look. I never thought of that. I think I have the book at home. What can I say, Roger? Some of us play baseball, some of us watch baseball and some of us study esoteric sciences. Just different interests I suppose. I've been like this ever since I can remember, ever since ..." Theodore looked down and swallowed.

"The camp?" Roger wondered why they hadn't picked Theodore to be the one that should be tested for this Ascension test.

"Yes, the camp. I think you may be right. That night has haunted me ever since. Now just wait until I show you the information I've gathered on those mere piles of rock. This is all beginning to make sense to me."

"Wonderful! Just wonderful! I'm glad it's making sense to someone. Maybe you'd like to fill me in a little, because frankly I'm lost here. Fascinated, but lost." He chopped a hand six inches over his head to illustrate his point.

"Okay, pull up a chair. I'll condense it as much as I can but listen up, there's lots here. The main pyramid contains two and a half million blocks of rock some weighing six hundred tons, sitting on thirteen acres cut from an Aswan quarry *six hundred* miles away, the total weight is estimated to be 5,955,000 tons or (metric) which when multiplied by one trillion is the estimated scientific weight of the Earth. Which is pretty amazing as there were no slaves known in the Old Kingdom, so you'd have to pay, house and feed these workers. If you take that number of blocks and built this structure in twenty years as claimed, you would have to cut and fit into the pyramid fourteen blocks every hour day and night seven days a week and that doesn't include all the efforts to ship them to the site. Here's the formula I created (2.500,000 divided by 7300 (365 X20) equals 342, divided by twenty-four hours, equals fourteen.) Using today's monetary values that would be a cost of somewhere around five billion dollars.

And it gets freakier, you take the height of the pyramid and multiply it by 43,200 you get the radius of the earth. If you take the base perimeter of the pyramid and multiply that by 43,200 you get the equatorial circumference of the earth. The number 43,200 is important because it is derived from the key motion of the earth called the precision of the earth's axis. The earth wobbles on its axis one degree every seventy-two years. 72 X 600 = 43,200."

Roger widened his eyes in shock. "And they didn't have anything remotely close to a computer."

"There's more. The square of the base of the Great Pyramid divided by twice the height equals 3.1416."

Theodore stopped a moment for Roger to let it sink in. "That's Pi isn't it?"

"Yes," he nodded and continued. "So apparently all of these 2 and a half million blocks of stone were floated up the river on barges. The weight of all of these blocks probably doesn't mean a lot until you consider it's heavier than all the cathedrals, churches and chapels built in England since the beginning of Christianity, and the tallest structure erected until the Eiffel Tower was built it 1889. The main pyramid was supposedly built by the pharaoh Khufu in twenty years which is a remarkable feat, considering the Egyptians lacked astronomical, geological and mathematical expertise. Although no records recorded anywhere by the Egyptians have shown any details on building, moving or assembling the blocks and the only details ever found inside the main pyramid was a cartouche found by Howard Vyse in 1837 and remains the only evidence that it was built by Khufu. What we know now is that this cartouche and a second was also discovered on the south ceiling towards the west end of Campbell's Chamber. The Khufu cartouche is part of a short inscription that reads Ḥwfw śmrw ꜥpr ("the gang, Companions of Khufu"), i.e. one of the gangs of workmen that constructed the chamber. Though the cartouche of Khufu is obscured by blocks or was cut off, this same gang name is also found several feet away on the last ceiling block. Vyse also depicts a partial Khufu cartouche on the North side of the chamber apparently trying to correct his spelling mistake.

A first, direct proof for fakery is the circumstance that Khufu is introduced by his Horus name first, not by his birth name inside a cartouche, as it was actually common at this time. And secondly, it mentions the goddess Isis, but her name does not verifiably occur before king (pharaoh) Nyuser-Rê of the 5th Dynasty and she never had the title "mistress of the pyramid(s)". In addition, the spelling of Khufu is incorrect, it today would actually read as Raufu and not Khufu.

Also it was written in a cursive writing which was not common in those days instead of more scholarly writing by highly trained scribes who had mastered it into a fine art form."

Theodore smiled at Roger before continuing. "Now the great pyramid itself was the tallest supposed man-made structure for over 3800 years. To build this grand edifice would require placing one block every two minutes. This doesn't even include cutting the stone, moving it and building the ramps needed to place them. Setting a mere twenty blocks a day would need 340 years just for the main pyramid to be finished."

"Wow! I never knew. Stuff like that is never mentioned on the PBS stations," Roger exclaimed, his mind blown away by the sheer numbers Theodore just showed him.

"Exactly!" Theodore answered, then continued, "Historians claimed that they were erected using an earthen ramp circling the pyramid. Engineering modern experts have said it is not possible to construct them to such precise dimensions in this manner. Also, that ramp would not be shallow enough to allow the huge blocks to be dragged up it. A ramp of a shallow enough gradient to allow this would have to have been 4,800 feet long - that's more than three times the length of the pyramid itself - and built out of stone. And if it were made of stone, where the hell are the remains? Nothing has ever been found to even suggest how all this was done and in addition where did the wood come from to roll these on as no trees grow in Egypt itself."

Theodore paused for breath and to let Roger take it all in.

"Okay. Now here's where the fun and real mind-blowing stuff starts. The precise nature of the pyramids is amazing. The difference in length of any of its sides is eight inches and it actually is eight sided with slight dents in each side. The twenty-two-inch thick plain it sits on is within one inch of dead level. Gaps between the casing stones measure just a fiftieth of an inch and the apex of the pyramid is located directly over the center with no deviance. The lower passageway is 350 feet long. It's straight to one fiftieth of an inch through the blocks they've laid, and straight within a quarter of an inch through 200 feet of solid bedrock and there are two channels going upwards from Chamber drilled absolutely straight to the stars."

"Wow, pretty amazing for copper tooling." Roger scratched his head. "That would be near impossible to do even with today's laser equipment, let alone with only copper tools and chisels."

"That's nothing, it gets better. The Meridian Building of the Greenwich Observatory in London was built to align with true north and even it is out by nine-sixtieths of a degree. The main pyramid is aligned to true north within one-twelfth of a degree. It sits exactly on thirty north parallel, that's an imaginary line one third the distance between the equator and the North Pole. Also, if a line is drawn along the longest land parallel on Earth and the longest land meridian the exact center is the apex of the main pyramid."

"How is it possible? Even an advanced civilization like the Egyptians couldn't have known some of this stuff way back then. In fact, one would have even been able to measure anything remotely like this."

"Ah, the disbelievers have been silenced. Don't worry, I thought the same thing once. Now the really weird shit. Calculations of the length of the King's Chamber and of the length of the pyramid divided by its height both equal pi. If a line is drawn through the apex of all three pyramids and another through the left shoulder and headdress of the sphinx then the entire Giza complex becomes a Golden Mean Spiral based on the Fibonacci spiral of numbers, which is a sacred set of numbers that govern all patterns and growth in nature."

Theodore winked by Roger who stared in utter shock. "And it doesn't stop there. Seashells and watermarks have been found about halfway up the pyramids which have been carbon dated to around 10,000 BC. These shells, along with a fourteen-foot layer of silt around the base of the pyramid, seem to indicate that there was flooding here at one time, a fact which could be further confirmed by the inch-thick sea salt crystals discovered inside the pyramids when they were first opened around 1200 AD. You're probably thinking 'how did that happen in the middle of the bleeding desert, but back in those times this area was a dense rain forest."

Roger half-rose from the chair.

"Where you going?"

"Actually I was thinking of taking a leak and checking on Sherida."

"Hang on, I'm nearly done. According to the Bible, and fossil records, the Giza area had a lush environment around 10,000 BC. This was also the time of the great flood. Erosion marks on the Sphinx, which is the largest limestone structure in the world today, show that it was subjected to rainstorms for thousands of years and is perhaps far older than the pyramids. Seashell growth on the Sphinx also indicates that it too was underwater at some time. Lastly, the alignment of the pyramids is the same as the three stars of Orion's Belt as they appeared from Earth in 10,500 BC. The two larger pyramids were originally encased in white limestone and the smaller in red to resemble the color of the three stars as seen in the night sky. Now this is a very important time in Egyptian history. They called it Zep Tepi, or 'the first time'.

The literal translation is the golden age when men lived in communication with the gods."

Theodore paused and Roger took his chance. "Okay. Now I'm going. I'll get some coffee as well, and see if I've got any spare brain cells lying around, because you just blew most of mine out of my head."

Theodore hit the button to print something and stood up. "Yeah, could use some coffee. I'll get that, you check Sherida and, err, whatever, and then I'll read you this about the fact that the Sphinx predates the Pyramids."

Theodore looked up from the paper he was intently reading as Roger came back into the den. He took his seat, grabbed the steaming mug from the desk, and resigned himself to some more facts.

"There's a structure called The Inventory Stele which is now locked inside a container to supposed protect it is a limestone tablet made by an unknown temple scribe during the reign of the 26th "Saite" Dynasty of Egypt's Late Period (664-332 B.C.E.) to showcase a temple inventory of precious statues. This was a time when a fragmented Egypt had been unified under Psammtik I and made independent rule from the Assyrian. The statues listed on the stele are those among others of: Horus, Thoth, Isis, Nephthys, Osiris, and the Great Sphinx, the last named both "statue" and "Horemakhet". The temple's origin is believed to be circa one thousand years older first built during the 18th Dynasty of Egypt's New Kingdom.

Inscribed into the Inventory Stele's frame, lowest register, and pedestal are a few lines of hieroglyphic text which have stirred controversy because they explicitly contradict the nowadays mainstream theory that Khufu's son Khafre constructed the Great Sphinx. The text has been independently translated by James Henry Breasted in 1906, by Georges Daressy in 1991 and Christiane Zivie-Coche in 1991. It is a detailed historical account of Khufu discovering and rebuilding an old temple, restoring its divine temple statues, building his pyramid and his wife Henutsen, repairing a worn and damaged Great Sphinx according to records of its prior image, and commemorating these activities on steles for the temple and the Sphinx.

This account clearly implies that the Great Sphinx predates the Giza pyramids and was already old then. Consequently, the current 'Khafre-Sphinx Theory' that his son Khafre built the Sphinx and the story told on the Inventory Stele cannot both be true. Hence probably why it is under lock and key."

Theodore sipped at his coffee enjoying the rather stunned look on Roger's face. "Oh, and one last point to blow your brains cells even further. The speed of light is calculated at 299792458 m / s. Guess what the GPS Coordinate of pyramid of Giza is 29.97924529°58'45"N 31°08'03". Not bad for dudes building with copper tools eh."

Roger shook his head wishing he had something a lot stronger than coffee.

"Very interesting. So I get that the stars of Orion's Belt are obviously important to the Egyptians." Roger scratched his head.

"Right. But the Egyptians weren't the only ones to build pyramids dedicated to Orion. Check out this picture from Xian, China. Same pyramids, different location and ones in Mexico, all on the same lines of latitude, and Nasa now claims they've discovered the same Orion alignment on, of all places, Mars."

"What? This is not possible. How could this have been built? In another part of the world?" Roger stared at the picture of the same looking three pyramids, with the four smaller ones beside them. "And the Keepers of the Dogstar? How does that fit in?" Roger asked.

Sherida came in just then and sank into the old couch next to Roger's desk.

"I think you need to see this as well. The Dogon of West Africa worship Sirius, or the Dogstar as it's better known."

"Dogon," Sherida interrupted. "That sounds familiar. I keep hearing words in my head every time I lay down and that's one of them. I think it's definitely some sort of failsafe buried in my memory. We must see these people and then go to the Orion transmitter. Somehow that is, how you say, 'my ticket home.'"

"Failsafe? You keep saying that." Roger scratched his head again.

"Backup mode in case of a catastrophic system crash. We use them in computers to keep data safe," Theodore interjected. "She has in her brain some kind of backup device running."

Roger looked more intently at the screen. "The Dogon? Aren't they that tribe in Africa I saw on the educational channel that knew about one of the constellations and the fact that it had, like, two stars, or something like that? How can they be some sort of failsafe to get Sherida to her people in the Pleiades?"

Theodore punched up the Dogon. "Well, if her enemies can go back in time and hunt dinosaurs, I reckon using a pile of rocks and some tucked away tribe in the middle of nowhere to return home wouldn't be too far out of the realm of possibility. You're close, Roger, on the Dogon, but there's more information about them than that. The Dogon said their gods, the Nommo, visited them from Sirius and told them some amazing facts. Now, back in the early 1920s when they were first discovered, it was dismissed as folklore. It was only recently that scientists noticed certain inexplicable changes in the rotation of the Dogstar and calculated that there must be a smaller but unseen star pulling on its orbit. The Dogon call this second star Po Tolo, which means the smallest seed. Po Tolo is a white dwarf star which we didn't actually discover until 1970. The Dogon legends said that it orbited Sirius A, Sothis, every fifty years. We've only just discovered, with all our technology that the orbit is in fact 49.9 years. It is said that the Nommo live there in a sixth dimensional state, watching over us and guiding us in our ascension. But it gets much deeper than that. The Dogon also said that there is a third star in the system, which they call Emme Ya. That star apparently ascended from the fourth dimension. Our astronomers did recently find some inconsistencies in the orbits of Sirius and Po Tolo but only in 1997, thanks to the Hubble telescope, were they able to discover that these were due to a third star in the system."

"Yes," Sherida said. "That is established fact from even my schooling. The second star is what you call a white dwarf and is extremely dense matter. A spoonful would weigh several tons."

They both looked at her in stunned silence.

"Now, if you read Zacheria Stichin, he says that one planet, Nebiru, was flung out of orbit by the arrival of Anu and captured by our sun that is supposed to follow an elliptical journey every 3,600 years between the two systems. Nebiru is supposed to be the home of the Annunaki, the gods that came here and originally altered humankind to help them mine for certain substances," Theodore remarked.

Sherida looked at Theodore quizzically. "Now that wasn't in our school orientation class."

Theodore and Roger stared at each other, then burst into snickers.

"This is definitely more than bizarre coincidence." Roger perked up. "Man, I feel so out of my league here it's like the inventor of the Model T watching a Corvette wiz by."

"Well, this we do know as established fact; the Dogon knew their stuff for thousands of years before we discovered them. Our men of intelligence do also believe that the Dogon are descended originally from Egypt and were displaced a long time ago." Theodore pulled up a star chart. "Now, the real freaky part. Draw a line from Sirius to Orion and continue in a straight line. What do you run into?"

Roger followed his finger on the screen. "Jesus! The Pleiades."

"Yes, indeed. Now it is imperative that I return home and find out who is behind this before they destroy all of the Council's plans for the ascension of Earth. The only way I know of doing this from the third dimension is using the ZPEC to re-power the pyramid."

"Power up the what?" Roger said aghast.

"No, get clarity here. She said 're-power the pyramid.'"

"Exactly."

"Makes sense now. Everyone through the ages thought the pyramids were just tombs to the pharaohs, large edifices for large egos. But they aren't, are they? They were a device to get closer to God, to connect with God. The zero-point energy," Theodore rambled.

Roger shook his head. "This is too much. I mean it's all not right. We've been told that the pyramids were built around 4,000 BC or something like that. Now you're saying they were built by some alien race possibly thousands of years before that."

Theodore looked at him blankly. "I can only tell you what information I've discovered. Remember the opening line from the X-files?"

"The truth is out there."

"And it's probably stranger than you two can even imagine," Sherida interrupted. "Maybe I should explain here. I can tell you this much since Theodore has already told you most of the truth. What you were told is wrong. The Orions built the pyramids around 13,000 BC with the help of your people from Atlantis. Your pharaohs merely cleaned them up around 2800 BC and reclaimed them as theirs."

"That explains why there was never any record inside the pyramid as to who originally erected them and the fact that the head of the sphinx looks smaller than the rest of the body, slightly out of proportion."

"Correct. They are built over the largest intersection of ley lines on this planet. The pyramids focus ley line energy and convert it to zero-point energy. This energy then creates an opening in the ozone layer to allow us to pass through." Roger sat stunned, trying to take everything in as all his beliefs came crashing down around him.

"Hang on here. Let me have a moment to digest some of this." Roger shook his head several times as he walked around the room. "Okay, most of this is sinking in except for a couple of things. Firstly, this zero-point energy. I still don't get what that is."

Theodore spoke up. "There is an energy source we've discovered even out in the vastness of interstellar space. It's very faint, but measurable, and it seems to connect everything. The scientists, for lack of better term, have called it zero-point energy as it measures barely above zero."

"Nice! Now, secondly, what's this about the ozone?"

"The ozone layer blocks the zero-point energy, preventing this planet from totally connecting to the rest of the universe," Sherida answered him.

"Okay. I think I'm getting it," Roger said. He paced further, trying to work it out in his head. "What you're saying is that you need to use this negligible energy source to get past the ozone barrier that keeps the Earth locked in by using a twelve-thousand-year-old pile of boulders as a sort of 'beam me up Scotty' contraption?"

"Yes! By Jove I think he's got it!" Theodore said, punching the air in triumph. "That's right, isn't it Sherida?" Suddenly uncertain, Theodore looked to Sherida for confirmation, and got it from a slight nod of her head.

"Oh man! I think this ride just went from sublime to ridiculous," Roger said and collapsed back on to the sofa his head spinning.

"Okay, now I've got a question then. The ozone layer is meant to keep us locked away, right?" Roger asked, "but isn't it dissipating? Isn't our pollution destroying it?"

"Yes, you're right," Theodore agreed. He turned to Sherida. "So now I'm getting lost too."

Sherida sighed weakly. "I'm so tired, but okay. I'd better explain it all. This is a closely guarded secret that normally I'm not allowed to reveal, but these are extraordinary times and unusual measures are called for. We need a way to judge a race's evolution in as unobtrusive a way as possible. We know from experience that all evolving races produce certain types of pollution once they have reached a technological stage in their evolution. These pollutants react with the ozone layer by breaking it down. As soon as we pick up on the depletion of a world's ozone layer in this way we know the inhabitants have reached one of the last steps needed for the ascension process to be able to begin."

"And it is the ascension process that your enemies are trying to stop," Theodore added.

"Yes. Keep Earthlings in the third dimension and they can use their world for whatever purpose they choose. However, there is another source of ozone dissipation. We also know that highly conscious beings live off sources of energy other than solid food."

"What?" queried Roger. "I'm still grasping the whole ozone-zero-point-ride-me-out-on-a-rainbow-to-the-stars-via-the-pyrmaid-stuff and now you're going to fry my head even more?"

"So, what I think Sherida is saying, is that awareness feeds off the ozone," answered Theodore.

"Yes. As the human race evolves and becomes, shall we say, enlightened - and I do mean that in more ways than one - it will also begin to feed off the ozone layer."

"That explains the stories I've read of the light beings; humans that claim they don't need to eat but use something else to keep themselves alive. They think they live off the sun's energy," Theodore added.

"Precisely. As more and more people become consciously aware they begin to need, and use, a higher form of energy to sustain themselves, the ozone layer. Once the egg sac is consumed, true ascension begins."

"Then what?"

"Welcome to the fourth dimension and the rest of the universe."

"To hell, for some, they say."

"To the heavens for others. We've already begun to experience some changes in Earth's magnetic field. It's collapsing."

"Yes, and at the same time the vibrational rate of the Earth will increase, causing global upheaval and—"

"Global warming." Theodore interrupted. Roger just shook his head.

"Yes, exactly. And as with everything in life the negative side of ascension and the equation is - -"

"Pole shift as the ice caps melt and Gaia, Mother Earth, begins to move."

"You have studied much I'll give you that."

"I think the term is called 'Christ consciousness' in its purest form."

"Yes."

"Okay, so say we get to the pyramids. What is it you want to do there exactly?"

"I can't explain it fully, but the Orions are very advanced in crystal technology and they used them to harness the Earth's energy fields."

This was so far over his head, but something Theodore said twigged at his memory about the crystals. Theodore was so obviously in the same league as he talked to Sherida. He just stood there, feeling like a fifth-grade student taking an advanced course in algebra taught by Albert Einstein. But there was something bugging him. Roger finally interjected, "Crystals! Hang on here. I recently did a trip to Sedona? I had the weirdest dream when I hiked into Boynton Canyon. Or at least I thought it was a dream, now I'm not so sure. I dreamt about finding some sort of cavern, filled with crystals. I thought it was real, only when I woke up, I tried to retrace my steps and there was nothing there, except the end of the box canyon."

"There is a legend regarding the existence of a crystal cavern under the canyon. People that are mystics, shamans, and others in tune sometimes talk of seeing it. Or at least in feeling its energy," Theodore added.

"But I've never been in tune with anything other than the NFL schedule. The weird thing was I met an old native man, in the washroom of all places, and he said some strange things about his people and their history. But before he left he called me something. Not sure what he meant, but he said I was a ... Gateway Walker. That was it."

The old native man's words began to play in Roger's head.

"Perhaps he's right. Not all of us awaken to our purpose in life early," Sherida said.

"Some of us get insights later in life and discover what we were really meant to be," Theodore added.

"Well, you've hooked me in now. None of this makes sense, yet it does. Somehow, I know it does." He stopped, realizing he'd just gotten married and thought he was quite happy. What if the whole honeymoon was just to get him to begin a new outlook on life? What if it leads into a whole new life? Too much to think about. "Okay, so if the pyramids were never built by us, what were they used for?"

"The original purpose I can't reveal, but they had several uses. People here would train in the old Mystery Schools and after several years of training and several levels of progression they would basically ascend into the fourth dimension. I can reveal that there are known to exist several crystal chambers or energy centers on Earth. They are all hooked together by ley lines of energy. The pyramids aren't the only ones," Sherida paused and sighed weakly. "I think you've heard enough for today, Roger, and I need to rest."

"Yeah, sure." Roger let her walk off to the bathroom to prepare for bed.

"She's amazing, Roger." Theodore said with a smile on his face. "And gorgeous."

"Yes, I know. I try not to think about that. This whole process, this testing thing. It's too much. So now what do we do?"

"Well, the way I look at it, we can just sit on our butts and leave her to get herself back home or we go along and try to help her. Only how do we get a Pleiadian out of the country?"

Sherida re-entered the lounge to say goodnight and Roger said, "We've decided to help, come with you, only how the hell do we get you a passport?"

"Easy." Sherida went into the bedroom and returned, holding up what looked for all the world like an American passport to the two bewildered men. "Will this work? There isn't much given to us agents when we go onto a planet's surface. But this is the most useful."

"Where the hell did you get that from," Theodore blurted, looking her over.

"Works, doesn't it. It's what we call a telepathic ID. When the immigration officer looks at this, he'll see what he expects to see and it is hidden in a place you don't want to know."

Theodore looked at her in shock.

"I know where your mind is going." Roger smiled, for once having the answer that the other and more importantly his smug genius friend didn't. "You don't watch Dr. Who then. It is the same as psychic paper. He holds it up to tell people he's some kind of authority or allowed into an establishment."

Sherida shook her head. "Some kind of information leakage. I wonder; did any of our agents sell information to humans?"

Roger shook his head. "I wonder if Skywalker ever had days like this." He remembered the line from one of the most watched Earth Series in several parts of the galaxy.

"Well, that is a much-loved show with sixteen trillion views on from your planet's video tube. If I remember last."

They both stared at her, mouths agape.

"And yes, just in case you think being isolated doesn't mean we can't see programs or products you've produced, forget it. I think there's another one that many found overly hilarious, based on a real being from Melmac, called Alf."

"Woah, Alf and Melmac are real?"

"Yeah, the character is pretty real in appearance. A sub-consciously planted memory."

"To get us used to aliens being out there." Theodore smiled while Roger just wondered if there was any end to the shocking news he had just heard today.

"Okay. I'll get on the blower and book three tickets to ... where did you say these Dogon lived?"

"Mali."

"Mali? Sounds like the middle of no place, definitely not in Tennessee. Okay I've connections in the travel business. I can get some pretty good rates and can get us on a plane pretty quick."

"Yup, good. Oh, and Roger, remember that suntan lotion you used in Sedona?"

"The SPF 645 stuff?"

"Yeah. Bring it, you'll be needing it. See ya now. I've some packing to do." He saw his friend to the door.

"This is not really happening, is it Theodore? I mean all this stuff; dinosaurs, aliens, and now pyramids. How am I going to explain this to Beth? Crap, how am I going to explain this stuff to myself?"

"You realize this all began when we put together the pieces of that metal puzzle don't you?"

"Yeah, that's what I thought you'd say. Sometimes a man's consequences can't be judged by his actions."

"That's pretty profound buddy."

"Yeah, well. I hate to admit it but I've always been fascinated with guys like Shakespeare and Da Vinci, now I'm becoming one of them." He said goodbye to Theodore and closed his door.

"Now what to tell Beth? She won't believe a word of it anyways," he muttered. "Not one fucking word. Not sure if I really do?"

****

Ten years ago, American Midwest

Kathy Stevens woke with a start. A blue pulsing light filled the room. A glance told her it was late, 2:33. Movement downstairs, shuffling sounds. "Dave, get up." Dave never budged. He was obviously out or, she realized with a gasp, they'd put some sort of spell over him. Steps in the hallway. Boards creaking.

How many times had this happened when she was a child? So long ago, the memories were nearly just vague nightmares. Why now? She'd just got married last week. The normal life, her life, a good man, big house, was all hers. He was supposed to protect her. She shook him again.

A blue light filled the hallway and seeped under the door. A normal life was something she'd never have ever again as three bodies materialized inside her room. Kathy tried to scream, but couldn't, just like in her nightmares. Only she knew this wasn't a nightmare, this was the curse of her reality. After all these years they'd found her once again.

The beings stood around four feet high, with spindly bodies and large heads. Their mouths and noses were mere thin slits, while their eyes filled nearly a quarter of their faces. Large, dark eyes, bearing no emotion.

One waved and she rose, her feet not touching the ground. Kathy passed out in horrified terror.

Something cold touched her and she opened her eyes struggling to move, unable. She wasn't in her room anymore, but in some sort of operating room. Sterile white walls and various equipment of shiny steel adorned the room. She tried to raise her head but couldn't, only knew she had no clothes on, a nightmare coming to reality. Her whole body felt paralyzed. Bands of glowing energy held her tight.

They gathered around her again and pulled an ominous looking machine, almost like a dentist's drill, close to her head. She'd seen the device before, as a child, and screamed. She knew what they were about to do.

Metal tentacles extended from the device, snakelike. A probe of some sort entered her nose and stung her like a bee.

Karen fought to free herself, but it was useless. She was helpless. Naked and helpless. One of the beings worked the controls to a bizarre machine that had several pointed ends on it, all of which, she realized, were to be used on her.

"No! You can't do this," she cried out loud. "You have no right." They continued working away. Just doing a job, like she was some lab rat in an experiment. One waved as she was about to scream again and Kathy's voice disappeared.

Then the machine moved to between her legs and entered her. She screamed a silent scream, remembering the cold touch of metal, once again, as it slid inside. Emotionless, hard steel.

****

Zolnar was awakened from his sleep by an incessant beep. He blinked twice and rose groggily, flicking on the ship's heat to quickly bring up the temperature of his cabin. He sat still, welcoming the warmth that was bringing him to life. He knew better than to try to move much until he'd warmed up. He was blessed with the hereditary cold blood that the majority of reptilian Draconians possessed. There were some that had the mammalian features of being warm blooded, but they weren't truly Draconius, they were half breeds, he sneered. Yet at times like this he'd wish he possessed the attributes of being warm blooded.

He read the coded message from his home world. "Damn," he swore. One of his main clients, Vessno'ar of Gloram, had died in an explosion at his base of operations on Earth. His estate, and in particular his wife, Bessnari, was offering a huge reward if Zolnar would track down his killer. Zolnar cringed; Bessnari was a typical Draconius female, sweet on the outside, but invade her domain and she became instant bitch. Kill her mate and she became unholy terror. There were reasons he'd never married, the volatile nature of their females figured in all of them. Most took the pill that kept them from devouring their mates when threatened or after giving birth. The advancements of technology.

Besides, why saddle yourself with a mate when you could reproduce with a simple egg insemination ceremony? He sent a reply that he would investigate when he was free. The reward would help make up for the fact that Vessno'ar would no longer be contributing to his fee for keeping Earth from being integrated.

"What the ..." He stared at the screen, at the coordinates of Vessno'ar's base of operations. It was the same city that he'd found and killed the angel code-named Sherida and not far away from where she'd pulled the home world device from herself. She'd proven to be one of the most elusive to hunt down so far. In fact, she'd been there at the time of the explosion. That was when his henchmen had originally picked up her signal.

"Something doesn't sit right here. Is it possible that she could have stumbled onto his operation base?" he sneered. "Or is there another angel involved." He flicked on the image transmitter and transformed himself into a typical white male human dressed in suit and tie and beamed himself from his ship back to Seattle. He'd do some cursory investigations, including talking to a Mrs. Miller, the owner of the property.

****

Roger was exhausted. He felt like he'd been through the wringer. He'd read somewhere that returning to a previous state of being after becoming conscious of a new thought or new way of looking at things led down the road to madness. After hearing about the pyramids and the Dogon he wasn't totally sure there was a path that led to sanity anymore.

He sat out on his porch sipping a glass of Sancerre, Beth's favorite wine, something that he'd got into the habit of doing with her after a hard day at work. She loved a glass or two in the evening, and although he was usually more of a beer type of guy, he had taken to sharing the more refined alcohol induced substance with her.

It is said that after the initial lust wears off true love begins. He realized that they had reached that stage already, and he really missed her company. He left Beth a message that he'd be gone for a few days and that it isn't what she thought. He had to help a friend in trouble and would explain later.

They'd lived together for two years before deciding to get married. Two great years, he smiled. It was the first time he'd ever met someone and when they were together it was like his soul was humming. Never felt that before. When they got back he'd send some flowers. Get back. That was a novel thought. Some semblance of normality? He didn't think he'd ever return to normal and perhaps there never was any going back. Roger sighed. *Why does it feel like my life has not only taken a sudden turn to the left but a swift kick up the backside.* He remembered the panic just before he went through the metal detector at the airport. *I knew I should have turned and ran away. At least Beth would be here enjoying the sun and wine beside me!*

****

Sherida relaxed on the porch chair next to Roger, taking in the heat of the sun. She'd been sleeping constantly, and it was nice to get outside for a change. He'd given her a glass of wine to try, saying it would relax her.

"I've had some bizarre dreams of meeting this old, rather, ancient being calling himself Hathor," Roger confided to her.

"That is not his name, he is from a race called Hathors and they are above naming themselves," she replied, speaking rather softly. "I must say this fermented Vinum drink made from the juice of the Uva is very good and the Vocatus content most relaxing. You're right, I can feel it relaxing me."

Roger shook his head and laughed slightly making him realize once again, that he wasn't really chatting with a human being. "Around here we call it grapes, wine and alcohol." He thought getting her outside for a bit of sun would be good for her.

Returning to the subject, she said, "The Hathor is, as you know, from another race; a race of great instructors and teachers. They are presented in your dream state to begin seeing if you are ready to begin the testing procedures."

"Did you have to do the same to become my.... ah... guardian angel?"

She giggled; it was nice to hear her laugh for once. "Yes, it is quite a testing procedure for us to become qualified to be Ascendant Guides, as we are called."

"Did you have to go through the Chakra tests as well?"

"Similar, but not in the same way." She closed her eyes letting the sun soak in and after a couple of seconds said, "One of my tests was involving using spiritualism on a remote planet, so somewhat similar."

"I know you can't tell me anything to help me, but can you tell me about that test? I'm curious."

"Sure! There was one time when I was being tested for my abilities to not use my strength or battle wits but my use of magic and spell casting."

"Strange?"

"Most of my training sessions were beyond strange, but I guess that was the idea to be ready for anything." She stopped and sipped the wine.

"I materialized on the surface of this one world and stared into my reflection of the water along the edge of the large lake I stood beside. Instead of my hardened battle armor coating a long silken gown covered my naked body and around my neck a necklace of lavender, sage, thyme. Dangling from it was a medallion of the sacredness of the four elements sacred to this world. I breathed in deeply allowing the earth to ground me through my bare feet and rise into my body becoming one as the planet's energy. The grass welcomed me. I realized very quickly that while on some worlds the plants are considered sentient this one was far more advanced than most along those lines. Not all life is of mammalian base, some creatures are plant based and highly intelligent on levels we don't understand."

Roger wanted to ask a couple of questions but thought better of it, allowing her to continue.

"I lifted my hands to the sky giving my blessings to the air as I breathed it deeply in. I bent over and scooped my hands in the water, allowing it to touch my lips and dribble down my body, blessing me for its touch. My toes sank gently into the soft soil and I gave my thanks to the earth. Behind me an alter with elements of sage, sweetgrass, cedar and oak sat in a small pile awaiting me. I rubbed my hands together and spoke the sacred phrase allowing it to smolder and begin a scented fire.

Before it was a long stick woven with branches together one around the other and a ruby crystal snuggled into its branches. That I knew was the only weapon I was allowed other than spells I'd learnt in our last testing program. I spoke a few words holding my hands cupped together and as I opened them the herbs began to smolder and ignite with a slow misty grace before catching fire. I moved forward and cupped the slowly rising smoke and allowed it to sink down along my body taking in the blessings of fire.

I lifted my wand and began to twirl it over my head erupting a high flame from the alter producing a soft wind to flow around it and myself allowing me to lift from the earth.

I floated along the caress of the wind thanking it as well until I spotted two women bathing at the edge of the lake's crystalline waters. I lowered myself down until I stood before them, only they were so engulfed with themselves they never noticed me. Both naked, breast to breast. One older mature woman with strong muscular arms had her one arm wrapped around the younger one kissing her as she stroked her between the legs. The younger one moaning in desire taking in the seductive mouth and tongue of the mature one pleasuring her and returning the sensual caress to the other. So intent in reaching their orgasmic states they never heard me walking up until a branch cracked underfoot.

They turned to face me. Blazing purple irises stared hard and long elven ears were flattened to the head, upset at being interrupted.

"Who are you?" growled the older one, "and what are you doing here in the Lake of The Mystics?"

"Sherida of the Pleiades."

"You are not one of us," the younger spat, trembling, so close to reaching her peak.

"It is forbidden to watch the high priestess initiating a new member into its maidenhood by anyone, especially a stranger."

By her words I knew I was on the planet called Allysiea. An Amazonian world ruled by women and full of powerful female mystics and many were known not to be of nice dispositions. They used males merely to do the hard work, menial tasks and for breeding.

"Even worse to see me naked unless I permit you to do so. For that you will pay."

She lifted one arm and a wand whisked through the air and into her hand. "For this outrage you will pay."

A bolt of energy cracked towards me as she pointed the wand towards me. I dove out of the way at the last second with my augmented bionic speed. I wanted to run towards her and tackle her but I knew the more I used my built in weaponry the more likely it was I would fail.

She thumped the ground with her foot, I was thrown backwards. The woman lifted her arm and a long ornately carved sword materialized. She twirled it with much well-rehearsed and used grace, having used it many times before most likely in battle.

I called on the wind's energy to fling itself at her. She lifted the one hand bearing the wand and laughed as it howled before her but stopped. "That is your best?" she laughed and turned her hand towards me. I was hammered to the ground by full gale winds, tumbling over and over, my silken gown shredding under the wind's onslaught.

Raising her sword, she ran towards me again to finish me off. Not wanting to tease me but finish off quickly and return to the younger woman awaiting her pleasures.

I slammed against a stone alter and held out my hand. Wishing my staff back to me. It flew into my hand. I summed the fury of the wind to abate before slamming it into the sanctuary of mother earth.

Earth exploded upwards in anger reacting like the wounded creature I knew it was. She fell into a gaping hole and the earth swallowed her up to her neck. She screamed in rage. I ran forward as I heard the thump of several feet towards us, knowing many more Amazonian female warriors were coming to her rescue. It had to end now. I patted the earth to allow it to harden and grabbed her by the back of her head. I jammed the end of my staff jammed hard against her neck. "Give me your wand or I take your life."

"You will not live either way and nor do you know how to use it."

A dozen heavily armored women ran towards us and two slung their long bows about to release their arrows. The wand rose from the earth and I grabbed it and broke it into two as the arrows whistled towards me, my mission complete as the arrows whisked through the clear space where I no longer remained."

Sherida sank into her chair. "Sorry that tale took a lot out of me, I need to get some more rest."

"And let me guess you have none of those spells with you now."

She nodded yes, "And they probably wouldn't work on this world, too much technological interference."

Roger rose and helped a very weary Sherida to bed; she was asleep before he could pull a sheet over her. He wished he could ask her more, but knew she had to rest up.

****

"I've some sort of flu. Feels bad so not sure when I'll be in, least a week I'm thinking. Sorry." Grimacing at having to fool work with the "I'm so sick" voice, Roger hung up and spent the day packing and making all the arrangements for the trip, including someone to look after the house and bring in the mail. Mrs. Miller was glad to do it; she was in a great mood, very happy that her garage had burnt to the ground as her insurance company was going to pay her twice the value of the place since her husband - 'bless his soul' - had well insured all his taxidermy equipment and stuffed models, that had been stored there. Roger recalled them with an inward grimace. He had found them sad and rather creepy.

Sherida was still asleep. Although Roger wanted to get moving, she'd barely been conscious enough to quickly eat and go back to bed, led alone travel, so they'd had to wait another night. "I've never known anyone sleep for nearly thirty hours at a stretch. Yet I'd hate to think what it would be like if someone yanked a chunk of my brain and soul out," Roger had remarked to her earlier.

He remembered the feelings that device had tried to give him. The awareness, being able to see and feel everything around him. Almost superhuman like in the comic books he used to read as a kid. Only she'd lived her whole life like that all of the time.

Relaxing on the porch with a beer, Roger stared up at the stars winking back at him. Orion, the Pleiades, Sirius.; he knew they were all up there somewhere, but he knew not where. The only star pattern he really knew was the Big Dipper.

Roger couldn't help but wonder if, someday, someone will find his footprints, along with Sparky's, from the past. Roger had smirked thinking of some archeologist discovering a human shoe and dog footprint next to a dinosaurs! So much had happened in the last few weeks, and he uncomfortably thought that it is just the beginning of an unraveling ball of wool. He'd not slept well last night either, dreams of being chased by darkness. By something in the dark.

He rose, scratching his head. He couldn't remember now, yet the dream seemed so vivid at the time. Roger walked past the mantel, and the picture of Beth and him with the Hopi's Creator God stared back at him. That whole Hopi and crystal canyon thing still freaked him out. Gateway walker? What the hell kind of gateways are they? He pulled the photo from its frame to take with him. He really missed Beth and wondered if, when all this was over, she'd take him back. If there was still a 'he' for her to take back, that is.

Chapter Five

Earth Science Week News, Four Days Previously

Measurements recorded over Antarctica have confirmed that the ozone hole was now a record 28,000,000 square kilometers in size. Reduction of the ozone layer allows harmful ultraviolet rays to reach the Earth's surface. Excessive UV radiation destroys tiny plants in the food chain and causes skin cancer.

Dust rose in swirling circles engulfing the old Toyota Land Cruiser jolting them along. "Bush taxi, the natives call this. I call it a bucking cast-iron jalopy. How can she sleep?" Roger asked, protecting his head as the vehicle lurched drunkenly around a pothole, narrowly missing several natives in flowing gowns. Sherida was asleep with her head in Theodore's lap as flipped through a French phrase book and conversed fairly fluently with a khaki-clad negro driver. "I'm nearly ready to hurl on some passing elephant." Roger held his stomach as they jostled again, feeling like a bodysurfer at a Green Day concert.

"Crap! I've forgotten most of the French I learned in grade school," Theodore complained. He glanced towards the cabbie and smiled at the cavity filled grin in the rearview mirror. Roger's Enence translator language app wasn't working, there wasn't any coverage out here in the middle of the Sahara Desert. Luckily Theodore had thought to bring along a phrase book.

"You're doing pretty good. Mine consists of 'parlez-vous French fries'. Friendly bunch though." Villagers, willowy Negroes, stared back at them and smiled as they passed. "How long before we get to ... what's it called ... Tireli?" Yesterday, after flying over the Atlantic to England, on to Senegal and finally Bamako, the capital of Mali, they'd arrived at the river port of Mopti. Roger glanced down at Sherida, still motionless, remembering the conversation they'd had on the airplane.

"Why is it that if you're so evolved you use physical objects, like these implants we pulled out of you?" he had asked her.

"Simple. This is a physical world and the third dimension is the most physical of all. The implants augment things like my natural strength and intuitive ability, help eliminate outside interference, like the strong electromagnetic fields in your civilization. We've learned to diminish these, so as not to damage the life cycle of living matter. This gives me greater focus for things like watching you, figuring out where you are and defending myself."

"You have these abilities naturally within you?" Theodore joined in.

"As do you."

"What?"

"I am a being of this galaxy, a spec, a microcosm of biological matter in a quantum universe. As are you. We are all interconnected and each speck holds all the information of the whole. Some races figure out how to expand into the realms beyond which you are familiar. Everything that exists in me, exists in you."

"Not possible."

"Yes, possible, but only if you believe so. Abilities are limited only by the cages of your mind."

"She may be right Rog. Don't forget, our scientists recognize the quantum universe, that's a start." Theodore replied.

"Possibilities are just that, and it's only impossible if you say it isn't. Reality is the greatest illusion."

"But this is my world, my truth," Roger stammered, figuring he might as well inject his thirteen cents worth.

"Which your parents, your teachers, your friends have shown you, taught you and reinforced in your mind. Only one percent of this universe is solid matter. The rest is, for lack of a better term, space or zero-point energy."

"You mean a void."

"No, not a void. A void denotes emptiness. Space is definitely full of life and other things."

"But if all I see and experience is one percent, and the rest is this zero-point energy as you call it, which as I understand from Theodore is merely a negligible energy source so weak it barely registers at all, then how much is out there that I don't see?"

"Everything else."

Roger shook his head, he wasn't going to get any change from this conversation, as the African sun beat down hot on them. That was the part of all of this he didn't understand: there wasn't anything else.

"How much further?" He stared up at the dwellings cut into the walls of the canyon they entered. "I take it we're entering the main Dogon area called the Cliffs of Bugaboo." They were following the Niger River and walls of canyon towered up all around them, reminding Roger of the American Southwest and the Grand Canyon.

Elegantly flowing canyon walls of red sandstone sculptured by nature's hands and nestled into the rocks, barely discernable, the villages of the Anasazi. A gentleness emanated from these villages as well as the ones he's seen in the American Southwest. Man living in harmony with his environment and not on top of it, cementing himself from the earth.

"They're called the Cliffs of Bandiagara," Theodore said correcting him. He flipped through his phrase book and fired off a question to the driver and translated the answer. "Another few minutes or so. Time to wake up, Sherida, we're nearly there." He eyed Roger. "Even without the biotic implant her arm is recuperating at an accelerated rate. I don't think she'll need the sling after today. Probably why she's been sleeping so much."

"I guess after having wires growing into every inch of your body, being flung into a backwater world, getting stranded a kazillion miles from home, having some sort of godlike implant pulled from your system and nursing a broken arm, yeah, I'd be pretty beat too."

She looked so helpless, so in need of protection. Or was that just his natural male reaction? She'd done a pretty good job of taking care of them while they were stuck in two hundred million BC. Even Theodore had a hard time believing that story. Hell, so did he, but he promised to show him one of the dinosaur bones that his dog had dragged back from Mrs. Miller's place when they got back.

Sherida moaned and slipped into the coziness of Theodore's arms. She looked so naturally comfortable there.

"You okay?"

Her eyes flickered open. "Just so tired. I can't believe how intense life is on a third dimensional world. All the emotions flooding back into me. Guess I'll get used to it, eventually." With that she closed her eyes again and drifted off. The two men smiled at each other.

"My first wife was like this," he told Theodore. "Every time we'd go traveling, she'd be out like a light bulb."

Theodore watched the road go by.

"I never did ask; have you ever been married?" Roger grabbed tightly with both hands as the Jeep veered to the left.

"Only to this haunting of my soul, ever since we were kids. Scarred by the summer camp incident I never did find the time to settle down, as they say. Times I wish I had, though. Gets lonely being on your own. I think holding her has made me realize what I've been missing. When I get back there's a lady from the office that has asked me out before and I'll call her when I get home."

"Is she smart?" He knew Theodore worked in a computer firm designing programs.

"Highly. Just my type."

"I bet." Beth. He missed her and wondered if he wasn't better off staying at home instead of being the odd man out.

"Crazy, isn't it? One minute we're in the USA and the next we're bouncing around the back roads of some African country looking for clues to help an alien return home."

"Yeah, I'd say that's pretty mixed up." They laughed.

A few minutes later they came to a grinding halt before a group of dark brown, squarish mud huts, they all sported a grass-matting roof, except for one building that stood near the center of town. It was the only two-story structure land resembled an overgrown Shreddie tossed on its side, with conical shaped turrets running around its top. "I take it that's their church?"

"A Binu shrine. The Dogon have two main beliefs, the cult of Lebe the Earth God and of the Nommo who came to visit them from the heavens."

A lanky black man walked down from the veranda to meet them as they piled out of the bush taxi, Sherida leaning against Theodore, fighting to get conscious and awake. "Our guide, I presume. You must be Mahsoud Barengti."

"Po."

"Po?" Theodore flipped through his phrase book. "That's not French. He must speak the native tongue of Mali." He pulled another phrase book from his pocket. "Idres, ah, yulli ya hendan."

Mahsoud broke into an open smile, his white teeth so stark against his skin.

"What did you say to him?"

"I thought I asked him where the Hogon of the village was ..."

"Perhaps my English is better," Mahsoud laughed, trying to contain himself. "What you asked was if you could shine the shoes of our mules."

They all burst into laughter.

"I apologize profusely," Theodore said. "I meant no offense."

"None taken. Let me show you around our village. Then we will take a drive out to Bandiagara, one of our sacred sites. There you may ask the Hogon your question. Although I must say it is rare for him to meet with strangers without their earning his confidence first, and this may take many years. If he does see you, I do not think he will share much of the knowledge of our people with you. Be prepared that you may be turned down. However, effendi, if that is your wish, we will see what might be done."

****

Zolnar sat in his vehicle in the alley just behind Vessno'ar's burnt-out base of operations. He'd since talked to Bessnari on a secure line.

It appeared that Vessno'ar had been trophy hunting ancient reptilians. Very dangerous but very profitable. Small wonder the Draconian was so wealthy. He knew many Draconians loved having stuffed ancestors in their homes and paid very well to procure them as well, if they didn't go back in time to hunt those ancestors.

He'd talked to the old elderly human who owned the property. She'd been of no real assistance She should have been put down, like they do on Alpha Draconius. It was a little more humane than letting them get that decrepit. Humane. He laughed to himself. Now he was even thinking like a hairy one. The only humane thing to do would be put her to sleep.

Still, he'd managed to scan the wreckage with the time coordinates Bessnari had given him. There were indeed several different ancient reptile DNA types, which by his carbon dating spectro-analysis verified her claims of what Vessno'ar was doing on this planet. But along with the ancient DNA he found slight scatterings of the Pleiadian agent, some canine DNA and a male human. Either recent visitors or present when the sight went up in flames.

Zolnar stared at his screen. He realized something was wrong here. If Vessno'ar died in this building, why was there virtually no DNA of his to be found. He decided he had to travel back into the past and take a look to see what happened. He knew better than to go back in time to when the building went up. Even shielded, so that he remained invisible and unable to affect time, he'd notify the watchers and someone would be sent to investigate. Unshielded, as he knew, would be a death sentence and lead to automatic erasure of his life. The closer to the present the more closely he'd be watched. But not so with two hundred million BC.

Zolnar took a deep breath and phase-shifted into the past. Even being shielded and invisible he knew he could still smell the surroundings. He never liked going into the past, not like so many pleasure seekers that loved to view what had gone on before. What did Earthlings call them? Voyeurs. That was it.

Rich the air was, rich with life, primordial and ... stimulating. He could feel his excitement rising. The calling to primordial instincts. He gritted his teeth, biting his own tongue. Blood, the smell of freshly killed blood ran on the damp air. No wonder so many came here and why Vessno'ar was taking specimens for trophy hunters and memento hounds. Many of his people loved to research and collect rare specimens of their ancestors.

He gave himself a suppression shot and relaxed a moment allowing the chemicals to cool his cravings. He needed a logical brain here and couldn't lose himself in bloodlust.

He scanned the area but no one was around. He looked down and saw the curious shaped mound of erected rocks. Someone's here alright, but none of his ancestors would have done that, nor Vessno'ar.

The blood curdling yelp of a dog sent shivers through Zolnar. *What was it about canines that did that, setting his teeth on edge?* Canines had been eradicated on his world thousands of years ago. He ran through the brush and stopped dead in his tracks at the sight of two enormous carnivores devouring their dinner. Even though no one could see him he still stood behind a large tree and watched as Vessno'ar looked up and became dinner himself. Zolnar spotted a human male crouching over a female. His scanner verified the female was a Pleiadian. Sherida. So, he must be her charge. Why else would she risk being here? Of course, he probably entered the garage and unknowingly triggered Vessno'ar's security system sending him back in time and she came to find him.

Sherida looked up in his direction.

"Damn." He blinked twice and returned to the present. Hopefully she may only have sensed him and not had time to pick up his thoughts or mental imprints. *So close. Well at least I've got visual imprints. It'll help in tracking them down when they get back.*

****

"This is the Hogon's hut, and you are in luck, he is drinking his afternoon tea."

Sherida drew away from Theodore. Discarding the sling, she walked very confidently and energetically up to the fellow. "Now follow my lead and, whatever you do, do not stop me." Her voice changed pitch, sounding almost hypnotic again as if some internal command had come alight in her brain.

Theodore widened his eyes. "Wow! She sure does heal fast. Either that or some part of a suppressed conditioning regime just took over."

"Well, I knew she was a 'take charge' type of woman. But I think you're right."

"I'll say. Rather sexy actually."

"I offer myself in purity from my people of the light, the light that exists beyond the mysteries of the night sky, seeking answers of peace." With that she pulled off her hat revealing her pure white hair, drew out a black-handled knife and cut off a few strands. Then Sherida dropped to her knees and sliced the end of her finger, allowing her blood to drip on the ground before the Hogon.

Roger moved forward to stop her but Theodore grabbed him by the arm. "Don't. She knows what she's doing. I hope."

Then she offered the knife, handle first, to the silent Hogon. He stood in numb silence, his face turning ashen.

Theodore also fell to his knees and pulled Roger with him, giving him a curt glance as he whispered. "Follow her lead, remember?"

The Hogon shook as he held the offered knife and the length of hair. He dropped to his knees, flipped the knife over and handed it back to Sherida.

"Welcome, Oh Great Messenger of the Nommo. The Hogon you seek is called Agume, in the village of Songo. He is very old and one of our wisest. That which you seek, he knows of."

"Thank you, wise one." As she rose the Hogon stayed on his knees, shaking, head bowed before Sherida.

"This has been prophesied for many, many generations. I never expected it would be me that was blessed enough to receive you. You have my blessings, Oh Messenger of Nommo."

"Thank you, again," Sherida said to the Hogon as they walked out.

"What was that about? And where'd you get the knife from?" Roger stared aghast at the holy man kneeling before Sherida's feet as he walked out.

"I'm not sure, I just know something told me to buy the knife when I saw it at the marketplace in town as we were shown around."

As they walked out the Hogon remained on his knees praying intensely and moving back and forth.

"It must in part of our training implanted in us."

Theodore agreed. "I think that there would be a backup plan to continue either the ascension process or get an angel in trouble to safety once they are disconnected. They would be told that if they get into serious trouble or need assistance of any sort to come here, perform that ritual and utter that phrase to the Hogon of these people. They have the key needed to run the chamber of the pyramids. It is most likely that the Dogon gods were sent here by your race or had another race come here tens of thousands of years ago."

"Wait a minute. Is this like the Star Trek shows where other races weren't allowed to be interfered with until they were ready? Only if needed clues were left behind? And you knew this all along?" Roger asked.

Theodore thought a moment interrupting. "I believe so, if everything I've read is true. All of the ancient races talk about communication from gods from outer space. The Sumerians had Enlil, Enki, even the ancient Jews claimed of Gods from space their oldest definition of god meant gods from the stars, the Japanese, If we follow the *Kojiki,* Japan's oldest myths, Japanese gods are divided into three groups. One of these groups can mostly be considered part of the Shinto tradition. The first group of gods in this tradition is known as the *Zöka Sanshin* and is responsible for the creation of the universe. To the Chinese its Shangdi or Shang-ti, also called Di, who controlled victory in battle, weather and harvests. To the Indians, In the Hindu Dharma there is no such thing as mythology and nor do the Gods age. Stories are very similar to the ancient Peruvians They had Viracocha, Inti, and Pacha Mama among others."

Sherida stood quietly letting Theodore finish. "It was weird up until the moment I spotted the knife with the black handle in the marketplace; all I knew was that I had to get here. When I saw the knife, I knew what I had to perform with it and the words rang out in my head very strongly."

"Most curious, like some sort of implanted event instilled in a memory capsule. Might explain some of the tiredness also, dredging up buried memories. You do the one thing you are compelled to and only then know the next step. That way no one can find out the information should you fall into the wrong hands. Even more curious is the fact that there are three colors sacred to the Dogon," Theodore said as they left, and jumped back into the Land Cruiser. "White, which represents purity and light. Red, which represents peace and is the color of the Hogon blood, and black, which represents mystery and night."

"Obviously, we just discovered the reason for the sacredness of those colors," Sherida added.

"Even more fascinating is the fact that, after all these thousands of years, they knew her hair color." Theodore frowned.

"Ah, just strange coincidence." Roger blurted out, as they drove off and they laughed. *Only the coincidences get stranger and stranger,* Roger thought.

****

Zolnar strode into the wrecker's yard. "Can I see the two thousand and ten Dodge minivan that was towed in last week, Police file number 32-BB52854?" He flipped the Bio-inverto device open, which appeared to someone else as what they expected to see. The human dressed in oily smelling coveralls stared at it a second barely looked up from the papers he was shuffling.

"Yeah sure, officer, I think it's just out to the left, second row. Can't miss it, it's the one burnt to a crisp."

Zolnar strode out past the wreckage until he located the remains in question. He wasn't about to go back in time to view the incident involving either the garage torching or this vehicle. Too risky, he couldn't afford the equipment that the Federation possessed in doing so and they might be able to track him as well. But he had to double-check something that didn't quite fit.

Would the garage get torched just to hide her tracks and get rid of all of the evidence in it? And, if that was the case, then he had to make sure both the agent Sherida and her charge, whose identity he should know any minute, were both dead. His other contacts were working on getting that to him.

He glared around making sure there was no one about and scanned the wreckage. As expected, DNA of two persons. He stared at the screen, both female, both human with female blonde hairs and only minute traces, faintly Pleiadian, barely registered on his scanner. Not enough to warrant an entire body, so only human remains confirmed in the wreckage. "What?" he hissed. "Damn!"

His cell contact device began beeping in his ear. "Yes."

"I've got the information you've requested. His name is Roger Harrison, address 34527 Riverside Street, Seattle. And there's more information, meet me at the phone booth at McCallum and Hershey."

"Thank you, you've done well. I can make it there in about twenty minutes and I'll have your reward money." Zolnar clicked off the phone and thrust it into his pocket.

What was the expression they used here to show utter disgust and rage? Oh yes... "Fuck!" He'd been tricked.

Her charge was located on the same block as Vessno'ar's garage. Mere houses away. What was the likelihood? Zolnar shook his head. Vessno'ar had the worst of shit luck in the universe. She was obviously still alive, although disconnected from her bio-implants and unable to be tracked. And her charge was obviously also still alive. At least he knew who to look for.

****

The Dogon village of Songo was built adobe-style under a massive overhanging rock. Roger and Theodore stared incredulously as they waited at the gates. "These ruins and buildings, they are so much like those at Sedona and the Anasazi," Roger whispered to Theodore.

"Yes, you're right. It's amazing; I never realized the similarity."

Two unarmed guards stood on the road and stopped the vehicle. They talked very strongly to Mahsoud. He jabbered back at them, obviously upset.

"What are they saying?"

"I can't make it out, they're talking too fast for me."

Roger stared over at the village and watched the dancers strutting about. One, in particular caught his eye.

"Effendis; they will not see us today. It is the time of blessing and they are performing the Awa dances in honor of our gods. Very sacred. No strangers, and no white people allowed."

"Tell them we only wish to speak to the Hogon Agume. Then we will leave."

The guide did. Roger knew by the response that the answer was no.

"No. The Hogon is very sick and most likely will die before this week ends."

"Can you do the thing with your hair again?"

"Only the Hogon would recognize the meaning. The knowledge is one of their most closely guarded secrets. We will have to wait a week for this to end."

"They will not see you," the man said.

"Looks like this mission is over before it even starts. Damn! Mahsoud, turn the jeep around," Theodore said.

"No! There has to be a way. I must see this Hogon," Sherida burst out. Tears began to streak down her cheek. "Damn, I hate this emotional crap." She wiped the tears aside. "All I want to do is break down and cry. I can't think logically. Small wonder the implants block these feelings out. Females are more emotion-based than logic-based males of your species, hence they are more intuitive, but the emotions can get in the way of true logical thinking."

Theodore gently wiped her eyes with his thumbs and stared at her. The two were silent for a moment. Roger knew if he wasn't there this would have been one of those sappy first romantic kiss scenes.

Roger stared at the dancers as his two friends held each other. One dancer caught his eye again. "Hang on!" he yelled and jumped out of the Land Cruiser. He flung his suitcase to the ground and rummaged through it until he found the picture from his honeymoon that he brought along from the mantel place. At the time he thought it was someone dressed up in First Nations garb, now he wondered if indeed it wasn't something else. He had it on his phone, but he wanted to find the picture itself.

The two turned to watch him. "What are you doing?"

"The buildings! Can't you see it, Theodore? This is nuts but trust me."

"Yeah, they look like the Kachina dancers from the Anastasi villages in Arizona you visited. We've already established that. So what?"

"Don't know, but like Sherida said, it's the intuitive thing. Just got to trust my guts on this one. Here it is." He handed the picture to Mahsoud. "Give the guards this and tell them to show it to the Hogon."

"They will not, effendi."

"Tell them that I am a messenger of Nommo. I have danced with him and he will be upset if they dare turn me away," Roger said in a very loud and aggressive voice. He pointed to the two guards and to the ones dancing.

Mahsoud did, looking shocked at being talked to like that. The two looked at the picture and then at Roger and back at the dancers. They argued back and forth. Roger stood very indignant. They glanced at him unnerved. Finally one turned and ran off with the picture in his hand. The one glared at Roger. He glared back; they were like two angry dogs eyeing each other. He wasn't going to be the one to back down from this fight.

Theodore and Sherida both looked at Roger like he was out of his mind. "Just trust me on this one and follow my lead." Neither one spoke and just looked at him as they held each other. And I hope I don't get us all killed, he thought.

Minutes later the guard returned and bent to one knee. "The Hogon will see you most quickly. But you must don these robes and keep yourself covered. You are only allowed two minutes."

Sherida and Theodore stared at Roger as they silently donned the white robes.

As they entered the courtyard, several Dogon fell all around them, their long spears menacing, the click of rifle safeties and sabers pulling from sheltered sheaths, even more so. In the background the dancers still swayed and strutted.

"This better work, Roger, or I think we're going to be in serious trouble."

"Go sit in that building and wait for the Hogon."

They had to bend their heads low to enter the thatched building. "What is this place?" Roger asked the guide.

"This is the House of Words. It is where the wise men come and talk business," he replied, "and where the truth must be spoken only otherwise death entails."

Roger stared at the sticks holding up the walls. "Why are these carvings all disfigured?" The broad sticks had many intricate drawings all over them, but they been scratched up and chipped away.

"That is to prevent people from taking away and selling these representations of our race and the Creator," replied an old voice in broken English that shook in its age.

They turned as an old man shuffled in, helped by two others that looked like younger versions of the Hogon they met earlier.

They propped the elder up against one of the posts, who stood shakily and handed the picture back to Roger. The one that spoke earlier looked sharply at him. "Now, one who claims to be a messenger of the Nommo, you have your audience. Speak, but know that in this house only the truth can be spoken, there is no allowance here for deceit." He waved his hand and several warriors assembled around the outside perimeter of the building, their spears and guns drawn. "Even less for one who might defile our God with lies."

Roger gulped as he took back his picture. "Okay, Sherida. Do your thing."

As she shuffled forward Theodore whispered over to Roger. "What was that picture about?"

Roger gave it to Theodore. "That is of the Hopi Creator God Maasaw. Look at the figure dancing in the circle."

Theodore did. Dumbstruck, he said, "they're the same."

"Exactly."

"How is that possible?"

"Don't know. Good call. One up on me. Looks like I've got more researching to do." He nudged Roger.

"I think if we live we'll probably find out."

Sherida finished placing the knife and another lock of her hair before her on the ground, several drops of her blood stained the sands.

The old Hogon stared for long moments, he whispered what sounded like hushed prayers and gave a sorrow-filled moan. The dancers in the background stopped so the only sound that filled the air was the rattle of the guards' guns as they drew closer. Theodore clutched at Roger, "I don't think we're going to find out."

The wizen old man pulled at one of the assistants and whispered something into his ear. He rose on shaking knees and walked to the center of the House of Words. The younger Hogon shooed away the guards, jabbering excitedly, and in seconds the guards dispersed like the wind. Only the hot African air moved in heavy waves about them.

The old man muttered something and the other younger one interpreted. "Welcome, the supposed messenger from Nommo, our Creator. We have waited many lifetimes for his return. Or, as he prophesied, for the return of his messenger."

"The Nommo sends their greetings. I need your help in order to return to my people. I will let them know that the Dogon have been faithful to the teachings of Nommo and still honor his word. We will be generous in our rewards. But I have come in a time of need. I seek the key to the pyramids."

The older Hogon nodded to the younger one who spoke for him. "I will think about that you wish for, but first I must tell you the story of the Nommo's visit. Our gods came in a great ball of light and fire. They landed in the middle of the desert and made a large lake in which to float their vessel. Then they jumped into the water. They had half-human bodies, scaly lower halves, no feet. They taught us many things and traveled to other lands in order to spread the words of the Nommo. They taught us of the Sirius and the stars around it and travelled to other parts of our world."

"Well, it appears obvious that the Nommo traveled to Sedona and visited the Hopi. Perhaps Sumer and China also. Both civilizations have legends of ancient fishy or merman-type god-beings that are among their earliest gods," Theodore said. He turned to the elder. "Do you know what other realms they went to?" Their guide quickly interpreted Theodore's question.

"Yes," the old man said through the interpreter, and, with his cane, drew two triangles in the sand. "There are lines of energy, male and female, that must be harnessed in order to use the great power. This the Nommo said. Here, the land of the red-skinned ones that live near vast, deep cuts in the earth." He indicated one point of the triangle and drew crude figures around the others.

"Very interesting." Theodore studied the triangles. "These three represent male energy, and what are probable Lemurian sites; Sedona, Easter Island, Australia perhaps, while these three represent female energy and possible Atlantean sites. Stonehenge, Dogon and maybe India. Overlap them and you get the tetrahedron, the Merkaba, the sacred human energy field. All the old scripts say that from the center the mixture of the two produce a third energy, birth if you will."

Roger watched as the old Hogon continued and drew the two triangles over each other. "The star of David. Why didn't you say so? At least that I can recognize."

The Hogon pointed to the center of the star pattern. "Here, the center." He moved his old hand shaking over to a new location and held out his cane in his shaking hand to Sherida. "Show me."

Without hesitation she drew three pyramids in different sizes. "Here lies the center." She thumped the cane into the center one of the pyramids. The main one, like she knew.

The old Hogon rose as the assistant returned and handed him an ancient leather pouch which looked like it would crumble to dust at the next second. The Hogon pressed it into Sherida's hand.

Roger strained to listen. Sounds from the pouch... humming?

"Go now and give the Nommo our blessings." The old Hogon slumped over, obviously very weak now.

"You have done well and will be rewarded by the gods for keeping the ancient traditions alive." Sherida glanced at Roger. "We must leave quickly, he is in very bad shape. I fear this excitement might be too much for him and

I don't want to stick around to see what would happen if he decides to die here and now."

"I agree." As Roger rose, he heard the hum of the pouch again. "Do you hear that?"

Theodore helped Sherida as she got into the jeep. "Hear what?"

"Whatever's in there is humming, singing nearly."

"We must go. I'll tell you on the plane ride over to Cairo," Sherida replied. Slumping into Theodore. She knew only the gateway walkers could hear the singing.

****

"Damn! Careful, don't disturb anything." Zolnar scanned the interior of Roger's house as his agents went through it. They had already found blonde hairs and some tiny metallic wires in one of the bedrooms. The wires were of off world manufacture, he scanned them, Arconian and the DNA matched the traces found at the wrecking yard. He'd have someone wait and stake out the place. His cell phone beeped.

"I've found something."

"What is it?"

"Tapping into airlines passenger manifestos was a stroke of genius, sir. Departures at SeaTac airport confirm a 'Roger Harrison' of this address and two others. A Theodore Nelson, and a Sherida Henderson. They've have flown out of the country bound for Gatwick, with connecting flights to Mali and Egypt."

"Great. How long ago?"

"Four days."

"Thanks. Treat job." Zolnar turned and strode into the living room. "Make sure your men return everything to the way it was before, and I want someone posted outside to monitor the place twenty-four hours a day."

"Got it, sir," The scruffy biker replied. He yelled instructions to his men in the hallways.

Zolnar strode down the street to his vehicle. He sat in his car, a 1976 Corvette LT1 and started it up loving the rumble of the over-cammed 350 cid engine. *Gotta like what these humans call muscle cars. Love the shudders they gave off, not to mention the rumble. Like a Trankeunsaurus on the hunt. Two hundred tons of predator.* He loved the recording of the ancient beasts. The blood curdling roars sent shivers down to his Quiggli. *Ah the good ol' days of relaxing at home to the virtual recordings, drinking Haxsa, and feeling the ground rumble below, and all around him watching a Trankeunsaurus stalking down its prey.*

He wondered why Egypt and Mali. He knows for sure but was guessing possibly to find the old Orion transmitter. He pondered on Sherida's cleverness; somehow, without killing herself, she'd disconnected from the agent network, in effect making herself invisible to him. Somehow she must know it's there. Only what good would going there do? Unless. Why else? Well, this meant he had to set up something back on the home world just in case they got it working, and deal with Vessno'ar's widow. Zolnar cringed; it was the 'blessed little woman' part he didn't like, dealing with grieving Draconian females was like trying to take meat from a starving jungle cat. You didn't. You just had to try to lose as few extremities as possible.

****

"That humming you heard... " Sherida said to Roger as they flew to Cairo International Airport on the small two engine plane.

"Yeah, I thought I heard something coming from the pouch."

"If you did, you're one of a few. The pouch contains a powerful, once part of a larger ancient machine. This famous device was broken down and this crystal given to the Dogon to be entrusted with its care when they left Egypt."

"Broken down? Famous?" Theodore fidgeted, suddenly awake at the knowledge that there was something he didn't know anything about like a little kid before a new video game gifted to him.

Roger could almost see the steam streaming out from his ears as the internal gears of his brain began to whirl away.

"The only artifact that I can think of, that contained crystals in Egypt, would have been the original Ark of the Covenant. You're not saying..."

"You've done your research. This crystal was one of the four crystal cornerstones of that Ark."

Roger's eyes widened. "For real? The gizmo from the bible? And we're not talking Noah here with all of his animals." All he could picture was Indiana Jones in Raiders of the Lost Ark.

"Exactly. Another adorned the Holy Grail that your people searched so hard for in the Middle Ages. Where the other two are now, no one knows. The Ark was originally left behind to build things like the pyramids."

"It has been theorized to be an anti-gravity device?" Theodore guessed. Roger shook his head in disbelief and stared out the airplane window. Being involved in such overwhelming concepts: aliens, dinosaurs, pyramids, ancient religious devices, crystals ... hell, he hadn't even read the Bible, let alone believed in it.

"Much more powerful. The Ark funneled fourth-dimensional energy into this realm. In essence, it makes whatever you think of hard enough become reality. A powerful weapon or tool."

"And you're saying this all that's left of it?"

"Not sure. Many pieces were broken off but couldn't be melted down by any means on this world at that time. They were inserted into various other mechanisms, such as sorcerers' staffs and magicians' wands and the crystals probably cut smaller over the centuries. As the parts became smaller their power diminished and things like the Ark become the stuff of legends."

It was humbling, that's what it was, Roger thought, to be involved in such endeavors, leaving him feeling so very insignificant. The big-time thrill of watching the Super Bowl or the World Series would never be the same. He winced. "I can feel the energy of that thing. Almost like it keeps calling out. Is that weird?"

Sherida shrugged and pursed her lips for a moment. "There's a phrase on this world, and many others, that states 'power corrupts and absolute power corrupts absolutely.' Simply put, one's ego is never satisfied. It's called to many over the ages, seduced many more. Only certain people, though, can actually sense it and use it for what it was meant for. People with great psychic ability."

He regarded Theodore. "Can you hear the humming?"

"Can't say I do." He put his hand into Sherida's. "You must be more tune with that sort of stuff. All I've ever had the ability to do is study. Ever since the summer at our camp, I've been intrigued by alien beings because I believed I had seen one, and the more I studied the more intrigued I became."

So, he could do something that Theodore couldn't. Was that a good thing? He'd never had a spiritual bone in his body, or so he thought, and as the plane began to descend he spied, cutting up from the haze, three mountains of ancient cut rock, rising above the mass of humanity known as Cairo. A shiver ran through him. As quickly as the pyramids were there they vanished as the plane banked into the airport. Something enigmatic about them. He never dreamed he'd see them with his own eyes.

"So how are we going to do this? Is there some sort of secret stone concealing an entranceway that this crystal will reveal?" he asked.

"Romantic notions. No, we'll just walk right in, like tourists."

"So will this crystal power up the pyramid by us simply walking in, or do we need to do something else?" Theodore added.

"The pyramid is, as you would say, offline. This crystal will allow me to open another entranceway to hide us and use the initiation chamber. It doesn't have the power to reopen it again."

"Initiation chamber? Nothing like that's ever been discovered there. Do you mean the King's Chamber?" Theodore responded.

"I'll explain after we land. The less you know the better, for now. In case something happens and you get captured."

"Right," Theodore said. "Can't get information out of a stone, or, in this case, six million tons of rock."

Roger sank back into his seat as the airplane touched down. Sherida was right. There was an impulsive urge coming from that pouch. It wanted to be held by him and not her, but she had to finish the mission in order to save more than just her life.

Again. He closed his eyes as visions came to haunt him. Dreams of a past life?

His head hurt; this was all too much. On some level he wished he could be back home relaxing with a beer, of watching the NFL or hanging out with Beth in their backyard. Not dealing with offline pyramids, secret chambers, historic crystals and the far bigger question of what his part in all of this was.

****

The next day saw the three of them joining the lineup entering Khufu's pyramid, the largest of the three. "Stay back, let the others go first," Sherida cautioned as they walked along the corridor leading to the King's chamber.

She felt along the walls carefully, trying to be as inconspicuous as possible, like she knew or sensed something as she held the pouch in one hand. "This is the one," she whispered, and waited as the others disappeared around a bend. "Now, this is critical. Hold my hands and when I say so, breathe in deeply. Do not under any circumstances let go of me, no matter what happens. Your life depends on it." She pulled the crystal from the pouch. It now glowed with soft green light and she grasped it in her hand to hide it from sight.

As the guard turned to open the gate she hissed, "It's time. Now."

Roger felt coldness, as grit and rock scratched his face and body as if he was being yanked along between two layers of sandpaper. The incredible weight of stone, thousands of tons of stone, pressing down on him. Her hand held his tight. He wanted to scream and raise his hands to his face but couldn't. Knew it would be far worse if he did. A final tug and he fell to the floor, shivering, alongside Theodore. Dank stale air stole at his lungs.

"It's okay now, you can open your eyes," Sherida instructed as she gasped. They were in a small chamber, about eight feet square. He gasped for breath.

"Be quiet. The guards can't see us but they'll be able to hear us. We wait now until they leave and close down the pyramid for the night."

He stood and stared at the wall they'd just been pulled through. It was translucent so they could see everything going on in the chamber before them. "This is like one-way glass?"

"The priests would spy on the initiates, coming to their aid if needed."

"Wow! We slipped right through the rock," Theodore uttered as he stared around almost in shock, still scratching at himself like he had pebbles covering him. "Feels like I'm covered in insects crawling all over me."

She smiled, lifting the crystal above them to light the chamber more. "It will go away in a moment, I get the same convulsions. You simply have to understand that ninety-nine percent of all matter is space. It is the rest that's hard to deal with all packed in. We flowed through the portions of rock that weren't joined together."

The chamber glowed a dull green as Sherida set the crystal down on a raised stand set into the center of the chamber.

"That's quite the flashlight you've got there," Roger teased, and touched the stone, not sure how they had managed to travel through the minute 99% that seemed more like the 1% she said earlier. The crystal began to glow brighter, almost as if it was glad to be back in this place and with him, Roger sensed.

Sherida huddled into a corner. "I have to rest now, still exhausted from the disconnection of my symbiotic self. Using the crystal is exhausting as well. Now I must prepare myself for the initiation. When I awaken, just follow me. I'll be in a trancelike state. When we get into the King's Chamber I'll climb into the sarcophagus, and you'll need to put that black sheet over me."

She pointed to a box in the corner with no markings on it. "If everything goes well and I do leave, then Roger can use the crystal to take you back to this chamber until the next tourist group arrives."

"Why Roger?"

"Because he's the keeper of the crystal, a gateway walker. That's why he can sense it. That's why he knows intimately how to use it as the crystal calls to him." She yawned and closed her eyes sitting in the pose most practitioners of yoga performed, legs crossed under themselves.

He and Theodore stared at each other. "Keeper of the crystal? What the hell is that about?"

"I was recently called a gateway walker." He recounted the story to Theodore of his honeymoon and the conversation with the Maasaw. "But how did she know?"

"I get the sense there's much she isn't telling us."

"Too right, but that's but that's probably the best way."

Theodore yawned. "I'll grab some shut eye too, I guess." He went to huddle with Sherida, but she stirred and warned him away. "Ah, I guess this isn't one of those intimate moments." He sat in a corner of the chamber and closed his eyes. For some reason the chamber seemed to be warm and not freezing cold like he expected. *Was it the crystal generating this?*

Roger smiled and sat in the chamber, wide awake for the longest time. This whole thing was too much: crystals, arks, walking through walls. But more than that. He knew he'd held that crystal before, used it. Another lifetime before this one, a moment of reincarnation he was only now remembering. He closed his eyes and tried to return to when he held the crystal.

****

"I can't be pregnant." Kathy Stevens stared at her doctor.

"Well, I'm afraid you are. You appear to be a healthy seven weeks pregnant." Kathy staggered out of the room and made it to her car in a daze. She fumbled in her bag for the keys.

"Seven weeks?" Darren had taken off to work on the rigs for a month right about that time, she thought. Right after she'd had the bizarre nightmare again. The one she'd been having ever since she was a child. The one that she'd never mentioned to him or, in fact, to anybody. The nightmare where silver clad figures enter her room and take her away. Helpless. She was then and she is now. No one could protect her. Kathy began to cry, realizing they'd be back, somehow she knew it. They didn't want her though, they wanted what she could produce. "No!" she screamed, driving a fist into her stomach. Pain screamed through her. "Stop." Seared into her mind. She tried to punch herself again but couldn't. Something was stopping her.

"What is going on here?" Kathy leant against the car, its familiar metallic chill soothing her, grounding her.

That is until she felt a sharp stabbing pain in her nose. Confused, she touched the edge of her nose. Blood. An insect bite? No. The terrifying realization hit. She'd just signaled them, the ones from her nightmares. The aliens, if that's what they were. They'd be back tonight.

In the doctor's office she'd read that after seven weeks the fetus was fully formed and could virtually be successfully raised without the mother. Darren was back on the oil rigs on a two-week turn around.

Tears streamed down her face as she unlocked the door and slumped into the front seat. Not that it mattered. They'd take her anyway, Darren or no Darren. He'd just sleep, oblivious, like her parents used to. She started the car, thinking it would be so easy to hit the accelerator and drive into traffic.

Let someone hit her, put her out of her misery. But they'd probably stop that too.

"Darren. Why couldn't you be here tonight?" When she needed him to hold her. Needed someone, anyone.

Another sharp sting. They'd not allow it. Kathy steeled herself and put the car into gear. They didn't want her, never did. Tears rolled down her cheeks as she drove home to the big house with the perfect view and the perfect manicured gardens. A facade, it was all a phony facade. The image she was to everyone else. They'd come tonight, that was reality. They wanted what she could produce.

****

Roger watched in silence as the parade of tourists filed through, as the others, worn out by the earlier exertions, slept on. As the group thinned, a curious and rather astounding thing happened. A rather striking fiftyish Arabian looking lady walked straight up to the wall of stone he stared through. Putting both hands on the rock she stood there staring, seemingly at them and, more particularly, at him.

Roger rose and moved closer to the wall; her head jerked up like she knew he was in there. He caught sight of an elongated earlobe. Odd. He'd seen beings with earlobes like that in his dreams. Dreams. Wait, did he just dream of her?

She smiled, staring right at him through the rock, and nodded like she'd just read his mind.

Roger reached up and touched the stone, she did likewise, mirroring his movements exactly as they each ran their hands across the surface.

Images flooded in as sparks erupted from her forehead and she reached into her blouse and pulled out a dim green crystal and held it.

Pictures of armies at war, in tanks. The Israelites, battling the Egyptians. Another flash, time moving ever backwards. Tanks became chariots.

Great campaigns commenced of building monuments to the gods. Rituals, thousands of years of rituals, priests leading the initiates up the inside of the worn steps of the Great Pyramid. Climbing into the sarcophagus.

Lights filling the chamber, spreading into the heavens via the two shafts from the Kings Chamber.

Another flash, she smiled again. This time the plain supported much life, lush grasslands and fertile vegetation before the rains began. Hundreds, perhaps thousands of years of rains, tearing down the face of the Sphinx. Wearing away limestone flanks. Floods, seas seeping in, covering the bottom third of the more complete monuments. White limestone, weird writings covering them. Through it all the pyramids and the watchful Sphinx sat.

Silent effigies in eternal stone.

Waiting.

A flash of light and all was gone. The virgin plain of Giza, where only antelope grazed and palm trees towered above all. Starships from the stars appeared.

The plains thundered with their arrival and beings soon to be carved over and over in Eastern legends poured from the ships.

"The Orions." Roger gasped, pulling away his hand in shock.

She smiled at him then, snapped her fingers and walked on, secreting the crystal back under her clothes. He now knew it was one of the two that Sherida had mentioned were lost in time.

Roger's head drooped as sleep claimed his mind to nether realms once again.

He jerked himself awake. He stared into the darkness cast back by the greenish light of the crystal. On the other side of the wall only darkness. Roger stared at his hands and at the wall where he remembered the Arabian lady staring at him. He told himself it was just a dream, but he wasn't convinced!

Sherida woke up with a start and rose to her feet. Oblivious to Roger she walked towards the wall. "It is time. Grasp my hands if you wish to follow or stay here for the rest of your life." She stood hands held out, waiting, muttering words over and over.

"Theodore, wake up or you'll be sleeping here for a long time." He shook Theodore hard.

Sherida stood there wavering before them. Lips moving in a quiet, unearthly chant as she picked up the crystal.

Roger yanked Theodore to his feet. "Come on, before we're trapped here forever."

Theodore staggered to his feet rubbing his eyes. "What ... what's going on?"

"I believe the expression is 'Toto, we're not in Kansas anymore' and we're off to see the wizard, would be one way to explain it." Roger grabbed his hand hard and Sherida's. "Oh, and here comes granite and limestone breakfast. Keeps the teeth clean though no need for brushing."

In a sickening instant he was hurtled through rock, pores and all. Roger and Theodore both fell to the ground gagging. "God can't say I could ever get used to that," he spat out trying not to puke.

They were back in the corridor, where Sherida patiently waited her lips silently moving. Theodore was right, whatever she had done had entered her into some sort of trance. Her voice, even her bearing as she walked, had changed. This was not the same person he'd known before. She stood mesmerized like the initiates in his dream. The room was cast in the green glow emanating from the crystal, which now hung from the pouch around her neck. They both stood up and reached into their backpacks to pull out the flashlights they had bought and until now didn't need.

Sherida began to walk up the ramp-way.

The men followed, emerald glow of the crystal lighting the way. Phrases chanted over and over poured out of her. "Do you know what she's saying?" Roger asked.

"Sounds Arabic or Egyptian only archaic. Can't make it out. From what I read the initiates of the Mystery Schools would use certain phrases to prepare themselves by going into a trance-like state." He reached into his pocket and turned on his cell phone and hit the translator app. It just kept swirling unable to decipher.

Roger shook his head. "You think that phone is going to decipher an ancient language? Really?"

"Thought I'd give it a go." He put it back in his pocket.

"Mystery Schools?"

"The Ancient Egyptians had schools for their priesthoods and one was called the Mystery Schools. It was believed that they used the pyramids for a unique purpose, allegedly the final step of becoming a high priest."

"What sort of mysteries did they teach?"

"The mysteries of the Universe, of course."

They followed her through the Grand Gallery climbing up a ladder and then through a large, corbelled entranceway into the fabled King's Chamber. "It's always been wondered why, if this is the pharaoh's tomb, there weren't any inscriptions found, like in the tomb of King Tut and others," Theodore spoke, yawning himself awake. "No markings of any kind have ever been found inside the pyramids, other than the now proven forgery of the name Raufu, supposedly Khufu, perpetrated by Colonel Howard-Vyse back in 1837."

"I remember reading about his discovery. Didn't hear anything about it being a fake."

"Well, back in the early days of Egyptology, the only books Colonel Howard had access to were proven to be incorrect translations. It's another one of those things that is kept as hushed up as possible. By as much as anyone even the Egyptians."

"Because being the only known inscription found it would leave the whole who-really-did-build-this-thing wide open again."

"Exactly and put into a quandary all of the established early Egyptian dynasties." Theodore confirmed. They finally entered Sherida's goal, the King's Chamber.

"This sarcophagus is carved from one single solid piece of granite larger than the entranceway. In addition, it's been cut straight through the harder quartz, a feat that would be extremely hard to do even with our technology today."

Roger looked on the inside and ran his hands over the surface. Something about this sarcophagus felt scary and yet familiar. He closed his eyes and felt himself washing away, merging into the fabric of time and space. Roger jerked his hand back. Visions again, like in the chamber with dream of the strange Arabian lady. He'd been here spent time in this sarcophagus.

"Under magnification the marks on the inside surface show spiral grooves that suggest the ancients could only have used some sort of ultrasonic drill similar to our lazars. You okay?"

"Yeah, just had a bit of a freaky experience."

"Many do."

"Prepare the sarcophagus," Sherida said. "It needs to be in the exact center of the room."

"What do you mean, hasn't it always been here?" Roger asked looking back at the center of the room.

Theodore explained. "The Egyptians moved it after many tourists who lay in it reported strange experiences. Even Napolean himself came here. It was moved to one side to stop people from getting disturbing thoughts and make it appear that way to be just an old sarcophagus."

"*The* Napolean? The French dictator dude who tried to rule the world with one hand in his vest?"

"Yes. The story goes that Napolean was greatly interested in ancient Egypt. When he led his armies here and conquered Egypt. He ordered his men to leave him in it for the night laid down in the sarcophagus in the King's Chamber by himself. When he came out, he was very white and obviously shaken up. When asked, he merely said no one would ever believe what had happened to him. He took the secret of his encounter to the grave," Theodore told Roger. They wedged their shoulders against the granite block and grunted in vain.

"We can't move it at all, it must weigh tons," Roger groaned, his head swimming as his body fought to move the impossibly heavy stone casket before them.

Sherida reached over and grabbed their hands, the green glow from the crystal spread into them. Tingles of electricity ran through Roger. "Touch the sarcophagus again," Sherida instructed.

Roger and Theodore looked incredulously at each other. "Okay, let's do what she says." They broke hands with Sherida and touched the stone coffin. Ancient words began tumbling from her mouth.

The heavy block began to vibrate and rose up about a foot on a precarious angle. "Roger, go to the other end before we break this thing," Theodore said.

He did and the other end lifted. They just simply walked the incredibly heavy stone block into the center of the chamber. Looking down they noticed an area in roughly the same shape as the block that seemed to shine as light poured in from the moon overhead through the channels in the walls of the chamber designed for that very purpose. "This is how the ancients built this place," Theodore whispered. "It is rumored, and in fact documented in many ancient scrolls, that they had the ability to levitate the blocks into place."

They gently lowered the sarcophagus to its old familiar resting spot. "Makes sense if what you say about the number of blocks and time needed to put them into place is true."

Sherida, oblivious to everything, walked around the coffin several times, chanting, before climbing in as they stepped back.

Roger looked up glancing over both shoulders. A creepy feeling washed over him, like he was being watched. They stepped back as a low hum began to emanate from the sarcophagus as the moonlight began to seep into its sides.

While Theodore just stood staring in awe at the sarcophagus, Roger looked over his shoulder again, unable to shake the sense of eyes on his back. He walked along a portion of the wall and stopped before a section, staring intently into the grains. *Could it be? Her?*

Remembering Sherida's instructions, he turned back to help Theodore drape the black cloth over her. Almost immediately the low hum increased, until the room was swathed in the green glow from the crystal that Sherida held in hands folded on her chest. Light bounced off the walls and sung past them into the Grand Gallery, erupting into brilliant white light.

"I think we've just discovered why they built the chamber this way. It was meant to contain the light and let it build," Theodore told Roger, his eyes fixed on the sarcophagus. "A complex study of the harmonics of light and vibration has revealed that the entranceway and the Grand Gallery have been designed purely to amplify and focus energy, funneling it into the very spot in the sarcophagus where a person's head would lay. No wonder Napolean was so freaked!"

Roger gasped and squeezed his eyes tight to protect his retinas as much as possible while the light continued to intensify. He grabbed the star-struck Theodore's arm and dragged him towards the exit.

"You can congratulate whoever did the harmonics thing later with a sugar cookie if you like but right now, I think we're about to get fried. If you focus a magnifying glass on a bug, it burns really good and I for one don't want to be in the line of fire." They crawled down the ladder as the humming grew in intensity and the white light continued to pour into the King's Chamber.

A final burst of brilliance, smoke billowed from the room and darkness. Roger and Theodore clicked on their flashlights and scaled back into the chamber. Frantically they whipped back the steaming cloth, coughing. She was gone. Only the crystal remained, nestled in a pile of whitish dust. Theodore handed the crystal to Roger and scooped some of the white powder into a bag he had in his pocket. "Need to study this. I'll explain better later, but there were reports of white powder being found where bodies have been initiated. Jesus included." He folded the cloth and put it into his backpack, along with the bag containing the powder sample.

"What?"

"You know the Shroud of Turin? If what I think just happened has happened, we've created our own version."

Roger blinked in complete surprise as somewhere outside alarms were going off. "This just keeps getting more and more unbelievable." He picked up his backpack as the sirens came closer and vehicle could be heard approaching. "Wait! The sarcophagus."

Roger picked up the crystal and concentrated on moving the heavy block of stone. Theodore looked incredulously at him as a green glow spread down Roger's arms. As before, they effortlessly moved the block, back to its former place, marked by the smudges in the dust. "Should we try getting out?"

"NO. The initiation chamber, we'll hide in there."

They scuffed quickly at the marks left behind and scampered back down the corridor until they stood in front of the wall again.

Floodlights blazed to life on the other side, accompanied by the sound of heavy boots, harsh commands and guns clacking. "Can't say I like the sound of this," Roger said nervously.

"Me, neither, nor the feeling of rock toothpaste flowing through my mouth."

"I agree. This had better work again or we'll be in jail for a long time. Okay, big boy," Roger spoke in a high soprano, "time to hold your hand, but no getting fresh."

Tiyah materialized in the King's Chamber, just in front of the section of wall Roger had peered at. Walking several times around the room, it studied the sarcophagus and muttered a few phrases as the electric lights blazed to life and the dull thud of soldiers' boots echoed up the Grand Gallery. Done, she merged back into its hiding place and waited until the tourists would arrive again. She smiled, having lots of patience, as she had been waiting for a very long time.

****

Roger walked into the dark forest. Malevolent eyes studied him in the dark. He was being watched. The crunch of vegetation. Watched, like being back in the King's Chamber. Roger shivered.

Again. He spun around as something crunched again.

It was there! He followed the sound; entered a worn pathway and saw something slide back into the bushes. A dog. A large black dog.

As a child he'd been attacked by one very similar. It had barked at him, nipped at his heels. He'd been terrified. Was this some childhood fear manifesting itself? Or was it something darker, something more urgent.

He awoke in a sweat, still inside the chamber deep beneath the massive tonnage of rock. Theodore lay sleeping nearby. The crystal, which he'd clutched in his hand before falling asleep, still cast an eerie green glow. He held it to him and, before its light faded, he glanced up at the transparent wall. He swore some of the dark shadows moved on the other side. "Sherida said we'd be safe in here," he whispered, hoping she was right. "Only no-one can protect you from your own thoughts and fears," he muttered clutching the crystal to his chest slowly falling asleep.

Chapter Six

Science Fact

In 1976 the landing on Mars of the Viking Orbiters and the first published photos showing what appear to be a gigantic face and pyramids on Mars.

In The Same year began the sightings of Crop circles, which has only increased in complexity and number since then. There are around 10,000 currently sighted around the world.

Roger and Theodore simply waltzed out of the pyramid the next morning, joining a group of tourists. They couldn't but help notice the large number of armed guards patrolling nervously about.

Outside the brightness of the sun stung at their eyes as the dryness of the desert air sucked at their lungs. They returned to their hotel room and rested for the day, only venturing out to tour the market, sip strong Egyptian tea and relax.

"We're stuck here. I've booked the earliest flight back via England, three days from now." Theodore put down the phone. "Well, I reckon we might as well see something while we're stuck here," he said, glancing up from the pile of tourist brochures spread before him. Roger moaned, "How about tomorrow; I'm into doing nothing today, just R and R." He watched the news noting that the pyramids would be unexpectedly shut down for maintenance the next few days.

That afternoon Roger had the same dream, only this time the large black dog stepped out onto the trail and stared silently at him, eyes of cancerous red.

The look of hunger and want inside its hatred. The want of his blood on its teeth.

Roger fought to wake, shake the dream's hold, only he couldn't, and he sank back into it. Again, on the path. This time it took a step forward and began to follow him as he backed up. Fear screamed at him in all of its myriad forms of electrifying panic. *Run! Run now.*

And he did. He ran through the forest, yet it was forever there, behind him, getting closer. Branches slapping at his face. The faster he ran, the closer it got and he knew he could not outrun this beast. It had him. The silence from its slavering jaws screamed for his flesh down its throat. It existed for only one thing, to feel the crunch of his bones between its teeth and the pungent taste of his blood, wet on his tongue. It cared nothing in the way of civilization or consciousness, it only wanted to be fed and its thirst assuaged.

Eyes of blood red, filled with delight. It was gaining, it was winning.

"No!" He shot upright in bed.

Sweat poured from him. Roger shook. "Again." He got up to stare in the mirror. Sherida had been gone for two nights and each night he'd the same dream. What the hell is this about? He splashed water in his face. In the drips falling into the porcelain sink he heard it.

"Roger."

He turned, there was no one there.

"Roger," again whispered from the folds of the bath towel he held to dry himself. "Help me. Clues! Go to Dendar ..."

The voice.

Sherida?

Then it was gone, it was her, he was sure of it. She was in trouble. And if she was in trouble, how could he save her? He walked out onto the hotel room's balcony into the night air and stared up at the stars in the clear night sky. She was out there, as were the rest of the endless stars of the universe.

Billions upon untold billions.

American Midwest

Blue lights descending outside filled the acreage. The neighbors were a mile away, at times like this she hated living on an acreage on the prairies. Kathy hated to be in the congested city but doubted that having neighbors close by would do any good anyways. Powerless, she sank into the warmth of her bed, wanting to run, but there was no place to go. Only to wait for the inevitable.

Footsteps filled the lonely house, floorboards creaked. She cried, wanting to keep her baby more than anything. She hadn't been able to reach Darren. Hadn't been able to let him know he was going to be a daddy. She tried screaming, as footsteps resounded just outside her door, but nothing came out and grabbed a copy of the Holy Bible, the book she'd been reading. Hoping to find some solace, some redemption for what was about to happen.

The little men shifted through the walls, entering her room. She tried to fling the book at the unwanted visitors but her hand quivered in midair. Inside her head a voice told her to stop and put the book down. She obeyed and began sobbing uncontrollably as they lifted her from the bed. She floated on thin air as the little aliens with the huge cold eyes pulled her along the hallway.

Before she knew it she was outside and in front of the large circular alien ship. Lights pulsed in blue and red flashes. Kathy passed out as they all rose in a beam of light and entered the ship.

The table: she was on the table again. Aliens had gathered around her. In a tube to one side she caught the glimpse of a tiny body curled up inside a greenish liquid. She wanted to cry, but there were no tears left. Only an ache that a mother has when one of her babies has disappeared. Another alien entered, it appeared older than the others, in the sense it seemed to have more wrinkles. It smiled and offered to take her hand.

Kathy rose, surprised there was little pain from her stomach area. She took the alien's hand and let it lead her as they followed the container they put her baby in, before entering a huge cavernous room. Again, she recognized that she'd been here before. Thousands of containers filled with fetuses like hers lined the walls.

"Why?" she cried.

The older alien reached up and touched her head. Images flooded Kathy's mind. Dreamlike images of a race doomed to a dead-end genealogy. They'd bred emotions from them, once ruled by them. So much like us. Analytical beings that now knew they could advance no further in evolution, doomed to die off if something wasn't done. On other worlds the genes of the human babies would be spliced with the alien DNA, producing a new race, new hope for a proud old people.

"But similar DNA? Wouldn't that mean we're related?"

"This is one of the races we originally sprang from and seeded."

"How is that possible? And why cows then?" she thought. Why would they also need to mutilate cows? She'd seen the lights over their fields and neighbors and heard the reports over the country of similar mutilations.

"To harvest organelles, needed to grow the hybrids like yours."

Somewhere a 'thank you' whispered in her head, that alone a huge effort of emotion for the elder alien. As much emotion as she could ever hope to elicit from such a logical being.

Kathy smiled amid her tears as she sank into the confines of her down comforter. It was over. They only wanted one, she could keep the rest. Still, she cried in grief. For the fetus that wouldn't know her touch. The baby that wouldn't ever hear the sound of her voice or feel a mother's love. In that she knew they'd made a mistake. As her head touched the pillow she closed her eyes. "Mary. I'd have named her Mary."

****

"Well, we've got another day before our flight back what should we do?" Roger said as they sat sipping their morning Arabian coffee. Already the bustle of morning life, Arab males dressed in flowing white dishdashas and women in their black abayahs, camels protesting as they were lead down the streets, amid noisy cars and diesel trucks spewing toxic black smoke. Dust rose in dizzying spirals. Life as it had existed here for ages.

"We could visit the pyramids, only this time, you know, like just tourists."

"Can't," Roger replied. "Forgot to tell you. They're suddenly and mysteriously closed for renovations."

"Renovations?" Theodore said. "They've been standing for ten thousand years or so. What's to renovate?" They both knew that obviously someone was investigating what had happened the other day.

Theodore looked rather forlorn as he sipped at his coffee. "Think she's alright?"

The waiter approached to refill his cup. "Bass shokrann. No thank you." He smiled to the waiter and turned to Roger, "Do you think we'll ever see her again?"

"Hope so. You do miss her, don't you?" Roger smiled, feeling the buzz from strong Arabian coffee.

"Yes, unfortunately I was beginning to really like her. Which is not like me, I know." Theodore stopped as a tear rolled down his cheek. "There is something about her that really tears at my soul."

Roger smiled, knowing what he was talking about. "Sometimes you just know as soon as you lay eyes on them. I knew with Beth."

He let Theodore sit there for long moments before changing the subject. "I had several strange dreams last night. And in one I think she came back and was trying to warn me that she was in trouble."

"What?" Theodore jerked, nearly spilling his drink. "Why didn't you tell me this earlier? We've got to go rescue her."

"Whoa there big fella. You forget one slight detail. She's out there and we're here. Stuck on this world."

"But we can't just sit here. Did she mention anything? Give you a clue of some sort?" The waiter rushed over to see if everything was okay. Theodore waved him off.

"Yes, now that you mention it. I think she was trying to tell me something ... about clues? Yes, maybe the ancients left clues behind." Roger stopped for a minute. "We need to get somewhere. She was trying to tell me to go somewhere only I don't remember where."

"Go somewhere?" Theodore pulled half a dozen tourist maps from his pocket. Taking his seat again he quickly spread them out before them. "Okay, take your time and look through these, maybe it'll trigger something. No pressure, no hurry. We've just done the most spectacular thing in history by using an ancient, and obviously alien-made, device to not only move a ten-ton piece of stone, let them quasi-egypto-oligists talk about sliding blocks on palm trees to build the pyramids, oh and we just sent someone into another star system. Proven the pyramid is something like a real Stargate and destroyed about five thousand years of Egyptian history. The implications are astounding. Not to mention that the person we sent is a live, talking alien involved in the process of opening up our entire world to the rest of the known galaxy, and now it seems she's been captured or is in danger and our chance at joining the rest of the universe has quite possibly just been flushed down the drain. No, go ahead, take your time! All the time in the world." Theodore's voice rose slightly as he got up and paced around the table. Others in the restaurant began staring.

"Hey! Sit down and just relax will you. Man, when you freak out you freak out. Look, I'm sorry. If I'd known she was going to send me a message I'd have a recorder by my bed, or at least pen and paper." Roger glanced down at the map of Egypt and pointed. The area seemed to glow out at him. "What's here?"

"Dendara? Don't know much about it, I think it's one of the very oldest temples around."

The word stuck in his head like glue. "I think she said something beginning with Den or Ben or something like that. Could have been Dendara."

"I'm not sure, but I think it has an ancient temple dedicated to Hathor the Egyptian God of Love."

"Hathor?" Roger nearly fell off his chair as visions flooded in. "I've dreamt about him too."

"Okay. That's it. Finish your drink; off we go."

****

Late afternoon caught them sweating as they entered the Temple at Dendara. "Most of the faces were eradicated hundreds of years ago. But there is one near the back of the temple still intact," the Arabian guide said. "I could be persuaded to show you." He held out his hand, smiling.

Roger and Theodore whipped out a hundred dollars each. "Show us."

"Ah, Alsalamo-Alikom, peace be with you," he bowed and began walking them to the rear of the temple.

"Many of the inscriptions and figures have been chiseled and destroyed over time. But up there on this column is the face of Hathor the God of Love." He pointed up.

Roger stared at the image in shock. The elongated ears, the extended facial features. It was the same face, identical to his guide from the other night. A face he'd seen many times before in his dreams.

"Are you okay?" Theodore questioned.

"No. I've dreamt of this being. In fact, I think I know him very well. I can tell you more back at our hotel room." He stood in shock. Other times, other dreams began to creep into his mind. "How is that possible? Is there more you can show me?" What he really wanted to know was who was the bizarre Arabian woman that he saw studying him in the secret chamber before Sherida left them. Roger gasped.

"There is always more." He held out his hand. They both pumped more cash into his palm. "The guards will come soon so we need to be quick. But you can take photos." He led them to more inscriptions. Theodore gasped as a scene from a modern day battle; tanks, planes, ships, and another of a light emitting device.

"Many of the oldest East Indian manuscripts, thousands of pages, talk about the building, flying and maintenance of flying machines. There're also ancient texts written about the use of nuclear type weapons. Some of the oldest Indians sites have abnormally higher radiation counts." Theodore stared hard at the picture. "It looks like a speeder from Star Wars. This is too bizarre. I didn't know anything like this had been discovered in Egypt." Theodore gasped, "but I've never seen anything like this in Egyptian times. I believe this temple is over three thousand years old."

"I could show you one more, but it is getting late and we really shouldn't be here." The man scratched his beard. Roger and Theodore whipped out another hundred each.

"Now the last image." He walked to another room and shone his flashlight on a picture of a round ball.

"It's just a sphere," Roger muttered.

"Look closer, infidel."

"Oh my," Theodore gasped. The sphere had marks chiseled on its surface, like the continents, and from its side a line extended that ended in a ...

"It looks like an electrical plug. The world is unplugged in this picture, but from what?" Theodore uttered, as he clicked off several shots.

Roger stared and blinked. "How old is this place?"

"Over four thousand years old, effendi. One of the earliest structures built. Now we must go before the guards come."

The two Americans quietly walked out of the ancient complex into the heat of the African sun. Roger's mind was flowing with questions and strangely things were beginning to make sense. "I think I've seen enough for today. Time for a stiff one."

"Another Arab coffee?"

"No. More like a double whiskey, straight up."

****

"I have to plug it back in, somehow," Roger uttered, as they sat in the airport waiting for their connecting flight to London the next day. He grabbed his carry-on bag and flipped through the pictures on his phone that they had taken of their Dendara trip. This is what Sherida wanted him to see when she called out.

"Plug what back in?"

"The Earth. Plug it back in and get back to Sherida. This is crazy, but someone drew a picture of our reality knowing a person in the future, me, would view it and realize its meaning. That's what this is all about. That's why she was trying to tell me about Dendara." He stared at the picture he'd taken at the Dogon village. There, reflected in the Star of David and in the center, a four-sided image rising to a point, just as drawn on the sand by the old Hogon.

"Yes, that's it. The same way Sherida did. She unplugged herself from the higher realms, the Earth is the same. She told me she had been grounded here in a third dimensional state after she pulled the implant from herself. Don't know how I know this, but I have to shift it, the Earth, back into the fourth dimension. In order to save her, save us."

"Ah. Is it me or is there a lot of static in the air. I thought I just heard you say 'shift the Earth'. You're talking a whole planet here, you do realize. This isn't like, say, going to McDonald's and asking for a Big Mac before ten thirty in the am."

"Well, if not the whole Earth then I at least have to shift back the pyramids. Something needs to be shifted or at least make whatever powers to be out there realize that we're aware of what's happened. This is it, this is the Ascension of the human race." Roger glared; he was certain this is what Sherida wanted him to do.

"Nice theory, but you heard what Sherida said. This is going to happen anyways, is happening now."

"Not if whoever is after her has their way. In my dreams there were others that hope to stop this process and she talked about energy centers on earth being turned off." Roger realized he was starting to ramble verbally at the mouth now like Theodore did when talking about all of this what people would call woo-woo stuff. It actually felt good.

"Who? Who would try and stop this ascension process."

"Don't know. My guess? Probably the snakeheads that were after her and me in ten zillion BC before he got ate by his close relatives."

They entered the lineup for the metal detector. Roger shivered, remembering a similar device that had started all of this. God he missed Beth, his wife. He shook his head. No, what he really missed was his old life. He was beginning to think that space travel, hordes of aliens and be-bopping around the galaxy was normal. What he'd give just to relax in his backyard, have a cold beer and be scratching Sparky behind the ears, while Beth lay beside him sipping her wine.

There was a lot said for just being normal and living a peaceful life with blinders on. *Why do I get the distinct feeling that being a nine-to-five salesman with a typical family severely ended when the red light started beeping at the Seattle airport?*

Kentucky

"This here's getting a mite serious." Old Jeff Parker threw down his trapline in disgust and grabbed his gun. Every trap he'd set during the past couple weeks had been empty. "Come on ol' Jeb, we's gotta go hunting and find us some food for the young 'uns to eat." He cursed and took a slurp from the old moonshine flask that hung at his side. It was getting dark, the sun had set over Kentucky's Blue Mountains. Jessie-Mae and their nine kids were all asleep back at their mountain shack.

A snap of a branch startled Jeff and he spun around, clicking off the safety. Jeb, his trusty hound dog, growled, the hackles on his neck rising. "Flush him out, Jeb." The dog leaped forward, baying like a banshee.

A scream rent the darkening sky as a man staggered forward. Several cameras dangled around his neck, along with microphones and other electronic equipment. "Are you nuts? That dog of yours owes me a new pair of pants. Tilley's at that, ninety bucks a pair. Tore a chunk off them and nearly tore a chunk of flesh out of me. I'll be suing you for damages if you don't pay up."

"Sue? You're lucky I sent Jeb in, instead of peppering those bushes with buckshot, young fella. As it is I should just fill your hide with the stuff for snooping around my land."

"Your land! I beg your pardon, but I checked with the Kentucky Land Registry. This is government land." The red-headed stranger checked his various cameras, making sure each one looked okay.

"You didn't check with the right authorities, fella. Because this is Parker land, has been since my great-great-grandaddy got it in the civilian war. Now I don't take no cotton to city folk tramping around my neck of the woods. You'd best be explaining yourself and fast, 'cause I've a gun load of buckshot here with your name of it." Jeff watched the redness grow on the city slicker's face.

"I'm a reporter for the Examiner. There's been some unusual reports of things happening around here, weird lights in the sky, things flying around, suspected alien activity. You know, extraterrestrials and the like. I've been sent to investigate. Have you seen anything like that?" the reporter asked, staring at the end of Jeff's gun. Jeb growled from behind him. "Look, I don't mean any trouble. I just want to look around, take a few pictures."

"The only alien I've seen around here is you, trampling up my woods and scaring away the game. Food's been mighty scarce the last two weeks. I ain't even snared a rabbit. You're about the only thing I've flushed outta the bushes lately and I think ol' Jeb probably agrees you're looking mighty tasty from here."

The reporter's eyes bulged. "Now hold on. I was told to be careful, that the mountainfolk were crazy out here. Let's get one thing straight. They're not your woods. I've got documents showing that this is..."

"Not sure who's the crazy one. This here Smith 'n' Wesson says it's my land and it's the only 'dentification I need." Jeff aimed at a spot of dirt two feet in front of the adamant reporter and let go with both barrels. Gunshot rippled through the night, deafening the two of them. Dirt sprayed the intruder from head to toe.

"I ain't a patient man and buckshot gets pretty pricey these days. I think we just settled this here matter. Got any further questions?"

The reporter stood there, his legs trembling, a big stain spreading down the front of his Tilley's. "You ... you ... almost shot me."

"Mister, ever since I was six I could hit the tail clean off a rabbit at a hundred paces, so consider yourself lucky I feel a mite obliging today. I suggest you'd better make a light for other parts, before I reload and decide to turn you into wimmen folk and blow your coonskin off." Jeff had enough of the confounded city slicker and his talk of aliens. Even he knew there was no such thing. Mind you, there'd been some odd goings-on of late, including lights at night up by the old Macon mineshaft. He gritted his teeth. Maybe it was the Macons stirring up trouble, though it had been pretty quiet between the two families for a while since Cindy Lou Macon had married his uncle Jeb.

As Jeff broke his gun open and ejected two smoking shells, the reporter's mouth gaped and his eyes widened. Finding his legs wet but still working, he turned and ran off. Jeb barked twice.

"I think that city slicker has a good point there. We's best be checking out them there lights. Ever since they's showed up, game's been mighty scarce around these parts."

His old hunting partner looked up at him with his lazy coon-dog eyes, a sigh escaping his drooling lips. "Don't you get a mind to being lazy tonight, dog. Some of us haven't ate in two days and I've been known to munch on squirrel, horse, and even the odd canine if'n I got hungry enough," Jeff muttered to himself as he cut a trail towards the ridge that bordered Macon territory. "I can take a growl in my belly, but to watch the young 'uns cry is a damn harsh punishment for a feller. And 'sides, it's too dang far to walk to the town store, and I ain't got no skins, so I got no money and two less shells. Damn 'porters," he fumed, taking lengthy pulls from his flask as he plodded along towards the mine site. On the way he checked the last two traps. "All empty. Same as the rest." He threw them down, spluttering more curses.

****

Trimus shimmered into view at the base of the pyramid. He switched his outfit to the traditional long white robe that the camel drivers wore and walked towards the side with one of the airshafts. A lone camel stood chewing on its Cud with its mouth open. It's owner nowhere to be seen.

He had been alerted to the power transference that had happened two days ago. He also knew he couldn't replay the scene due to the trans-dimensional energies it contained within. Instead he reset the time portal and watched the twin shafts of light shooting out to the stars of Orion and Pleiades. "Okay, it really happened, and I know of only one person who would have the ability to pull this off; Sherida. At least I know she's still alive, now to track her down."

He hit the device on his arm and his robe fluttered to the sands of the Giza. The camel stood there licking its lips and spat on the ground as sirens went off and several army jeeps full of soldiers came screaming towards the pyramid once again.

****

"So what's the delay?" Roger asked, looking up from his chest. He'd fallen asleep while they waited for their connecting flight from London to the US.

"Well, it appears that as our plane was so delayed our connecting flight has already left and the next two flights out are all overbooked. The next available seats are on the one after that, in the wee hours of tomorrow morning. They've agreed to put us up for the night though at their expense," Theodore replied, "but we're stranded in London for the rest of the day."

"So, if you're suddenly stuck in England for the better part of a day unexpectedly what would you do? Visit the Queen for a spot of tea? Tackle the meanest fish and chips this side of the Atlantic?" Roger asked.

"How about sit at the nearest pub, drinking warm beer and screaming at Manchester United losing against Chelsea like the locals would? Or how about a typical Full English?"

Roger raised his eyebrows who pursed his lips as if to say, "what-in-hell-is-that?"

"We're talking, bacon, sausages, eggs, tomatoes, mushrooms, beans and fried bread, all on one plate!" Theodore explained.

Roger's eyes widened fully. "*Fried* bread? Man, these Brits will fry anything! We're talking six thousand calories and immediate heart attack for dessert."

"Damn! Did want to try that just once. Okay..." Theodore mulled it over in his head. "Remember the drawing of the stones by the old Hogon?"

"Stonehenge," they both whispered, like two little kids just discovering they found the codes to override the parental locks on the TV and the keys to the candy cabinet.

"Now we're talking. Hail a cab. I'll make sure our luggage gets sent to the hotel room."

Minutes later they were on their way heading to southwest England.

****

Theodore pointed to the triangular rock behind them on the pathway. "That is the Heel Stone. If you drew a line from the center of the circle through the Heel Stone it would point true north," Theodore explained, looking up at Roger as they stood on the path built around Stonehenge. Traffic zipped by on the A303 near to the sacred site. The ancient monument had been curiously deserted. Since no one was around he'd taken a chance and walked off the pathway, lining himself up with the center of the circle and a triangular tipped standing stone a couple of hundred feet outside the ring.

Roger barely heard a word as they got closer to Stonehenge in the rental car. It was hard to explain, but as they approached the background noise, like a buzz or humming that seemed to build, increasing in intensity.

"The sun rises up behind that tip on the summer solstice, or at least it did in ten thousand BC. And stranger is this. If you were a crow and flew straight along this line through the center in the opposite direction, you'd run smack dab into guess what?"

"Not sure," Roger replied, vaguely only half listening to Theodore's facts, trying to concentrate instead on the buzzing. "All I remember about Stonehenge is that it's an old stone circle. Don't remember a fence around everything though, I'm sure you used to be allowed to walk amongst the stones. Is it only me or can you hear noise in the background?"

"Noise? No, don't hear any noise. From the pictures I've seen of the place as far as I know the fence has only been recently erected. Too much vandalism, I guess. Now, as I was saying, this line will run you into the pyramids of Giza. Not only that, the angle between true north and this stone is fifty-one point fifty-one degrees."

"And that means what to me?" Roger stared quizzically; unsure what Theodore was getting at. He was the sort of person that not only liked to impress people with his knowledge but liked to leave them hanging as well. "Other than you've got a flare for the dramatic." He bent over and touched the ground. It was coming from down below, from under their feet.

Roger closed his eyes and imagined a river, a powerful river of energy flowing into the circle of stones.

"That, my friend, is the same angle that the walls of the Great Pyramid are built to. Hey, are you okay?"

"Yeah, I'm fine. You don't hear anything? Same angle? How is that possible? Hang on, the Dogon Hogon did mention that one of the sites their God visited had giant boulders." He turned, standing in line with the Heel Stone. "This is what he drew! Two horizontal lines and a triangular stone. But how could there be a connection between here and the pyramids? Is this more sheer coincidence and how in hell would the Dogon know about this. I don't think they sit there watching the Discovery Channel! In fact, I don't think I even saw one TV set there."

"I wouldn't be so sure! I'm thinking there's much more to all this than we've been led to believe," Theodore replied.

"My thoughts also. Maybe it's me, or maybe it's this crystal, but I can feel the energy here; the ley lines perhaps. It's so loud. A river of energy flowing underneath those stones." Roger looked up at the massive stones of the Sarsen Trilithon.

"You could well be right. I remember now, a study I once read on vibrations and noise harmonics. Researchers have discovered that certain noise levels do increase as they approach ancient sites like Stonehenge. The noise stops curiously when you enter the stone circles. Perhaps it is ley line energy that you're feeling. Didn't the old Hogon call you a gateway walker or something? Perhaps that would make you more in tune with these things. I think we need to get you in there."

As Theodore finished speaking Roger caught a movement in the shadows cast under the inner stone circle of bluestones. "Hey Theodore, I thought we were alone here."

He walked around the circle and spied a figure turning away from him. A female, a familiar looking female.

"Yeah, where'd she come from, no one's come up the path since we got here?"

"Theodore, run round the other side, flush her out and I'll go this way."

"Hey! Come back here!" Theodore yelled as the woman seemed to instinctively know what they were trying to do and took off. Roger ducked around one stone and she dodged around another. The trample of feet alerted him as a slender figure sped by. Roger grabbed her hand. "It's you... the lady..." he gasped staring into the wells of her eyes. Incredibly old and knowledgeable eyes of the lady from the hidden chamber of the pyramid. "What the ..."

A zap of electricity made him drop her hand. He stood there in shock as Theodore ran up.

"Tiyah." he whispered, rubbing his hand. He knew her name! How was that possible...?

Theodore came running up as she tore off towards the entrance. "It's her. The one that stood before the intuition chamber at the pyramid."

"It's her who?"

"Tiyah. While you and Sherida were asleep in that hidden room in the pyramid, I thought I was having a dream where I saw a woman approach the wall and touch it. I could have sworn she could see us or sense us inside the chamber. I've just seen her run past."

"Oh." Roger held his head in his hands. "Images flooding in. Tiyah, she's an Atlantean, the keeper of the crystals. When Sherida received the crystals from the Dogon, Tiyah was alerted and followed us into the Great Pyramid."

"What? Buddy, have you got to start sharing more. This is vital information and whoa! Did you say Atlantean? Now you're starting to blow my mind. That's impossible. That would make her at least, well, incredibly old?" Theodore said as they ran after her.

"She's sixty thousand years old. One of the last remaining Atlanteans. And if that's impossible, so is the fact that we could walk through stone and that these erected blocks are aligned with the pyramids. But we did, and they are, and she's here, and I think I'm going nuts. You remember what happened to Sherida with the event release stuff? The ritual with the Dogons? I think when she zapped me to release her like she did at the pyramid, she imparted information of some kind or awoke something that was always buried there. We must catch up with her. Hang on Tiyah!" Roger yelled after her, "I've got questions to ask you."

"You've got questions? I've got a bloody computer full of info to go over with her."

The two men ran after the woman, who had already made it through the tunnel under the road and into the parking lot on the other side.

"Damn she's fast," cursed Theodore, as they ducked into the tunnel, "For an old broad. I gotta take up jogging, I'm being outrun by a sixty-thousand-year-old woman. Reminds me of the quote 'our grandmother took up jogging when she was fifty-nine. Now she's seventy-one and we don't know where the hell she is.'" Theodore stopped gasping for breath as Roger smirked. "Where'd she go?"

Roger glanced around and caught sight of her running through the parking lot into the adjoining field.

"There she is, scooting across that field."

"Damn she's fast." They both puffed as they continued after her.

"Either that or we're out of shape. Too much bench-pressing potato chip boxes and beer cans I think," Theodore huffed.

"Speak for yourself! At least I go to the gym regularly."

"Yeah, like once a year!"

"No very religiously, after New Year's, for about six days." They laughed, dodging a tour bus pulling into the parking lot. They clambered over a fence before hoofing it across a small field before falling into a ditch in the neighboring field. Both wheezed loudly, gasping as they scrambled out and stopped in their tracks. In front of them was a wheat field with about a dozen people milling about and no sign of a geriatric overzealous sprinter.

"What the hell?"

The wheat appeared to be trampled down. Roger and Theodore carefully walked forward. They couldn't see the woman anywhere. "She's gone."

"No, she could be simply laying down. But what is this area?"

They both walked until they stood in the middle of a circular depression. A rush of energy washed over Roger. He grabbed his head, trying to fight off the swirling chaos of vertigo.

"What's wrong?"

"Don't you feel it? The dizziness? The energy is different here. I can't describe it." He walked until he stood in the center. "Here, the noise has stopped." Roger looked around his feet. "The crop is flattened, as if swirled or something."

"Actually, I've done some research into these as well."

"Why doesn't that surprise me? You probably led the research into discovering why there are no more blue Smarties too. Researched these what?" Roger glanced up and noticed an older gentleman approaching them.

"Crop circles. I'm guessing we're in a crop circle."

The elderly chap was dressed in a flat-cap and plaid jacket. Hanging around his neck was a pendant that Theodore stared at.

"That pendant! The engraving shows the Julia Circle."

"Right-o on both accounts," the chap slurred through a thick west-country accent. "F. Henry Everton, at your calling. The F stands for Finies, my parents' idea. Bless them. I prefer Henry. Who be you two?" He jabbed his hand out towards them.

They introduced themselves. He handed them a card, it read Crop Circle Expert.

"I'm the head of this county's croppies."

"I thought I read somewhere that these crop circles were all faked by a couple of guys with boards," Roger said.

"Yup, Doug Bower and Dave Chorley spun that yarn originally. Claimed a big reward. Although I've also heard there's other groups that go out and tackle them now. Doug and Dave claimed to do all the circles, only since their admission the circles have only gotten more and more complex every year, with many showing up on the same night. A total of over ten thousand now recorded."

"Wow!"

"I've also read that many of them have symbols of sacred geometry in them. Any ideas on what's causing them?" Theodore asked.

"Them blokes up there," Henry said, pointing up in the air. "Them folks, the green men I reckon, are trying to communicate with us."

"What's this one of? It's too big to see the whole image from down here." The old guy showed them a scribbled hand drawing.

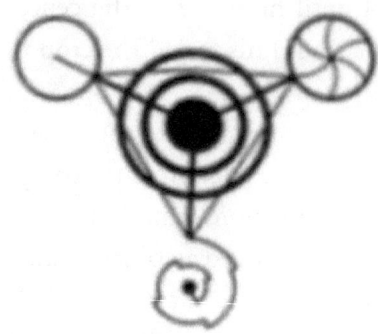

"One of our other guys flies over and takes pictures of the circles," he added. "I just had this right now, no real picture."

"Kinda looks like a pyramid with some circles attached to it. Not sure what it means." Theodore mused.

Roger stared at the picture. "That's it!"

"That's what?"

"Can I take a picture of this?" Roger asked as he got out his cellphone.

"Sure thing, matey."

"Thank you. You've been most helpful." Roger began to run back across the field.

"Roger? What the hell is going on here? Roger?" Theodore ran after Roger who was already stomping his way back to the parking area.

"I've got to go back into Stonehenge."

"Why?"

"Not sure. Just something, a feeling, hunch, intuition, not sure." Roger stopped to let Theodore catch up.

"What kind of hunch?" Theodore sputtered as Roger tore off again through the wheat field. "Actually, lunch would be a better idea."

"Later! I need answers," Roger yelled, as strode back towards the circle of stones.

"Roger! For crying out loud! Explain what the hell is going on here will you."

Roger kept quiet until he stood on the pathway before the ancient monoliths, pacing back and forth. "I don't know for sure. You mentioned the connections between Stonehenge and the pyramids. I've got to see if the energy waves I hear in my head stop in the center. It goes with what Sherida said." He stopped and showed the picture on his phone to Theodore. "It's so bloody obvious now. Tiyah led us to this on purpose."

"Sure! Thanks, Roger, for the information, but what is so bloody obvious? All I know is we've gone off chasing some sixty-thousand-year-old ad for Nike running shoes, met a crazy English chap who's seen one too many Sherlock Holmes movies and now we're ..." Theodore let out a major sneeze. "Shit! I knew it! My hay fever is acting up now."

"Sherida said in her dream the other night that I have to re-power the pyramid and you remember the pentagrams the old Hogon drew? This is one of those sites his God visited. The Hopi were another. When I was in the Hopi crystal cavern, I had the sense that they were merely turned off, sleeping. It just dawned on me that I have the same feeling when I'm standing here at the center of the Henge. These monoliths are the same. I think what Sherida means is that all of these sites have to be turned on in order to power up the pyramid."

"What?! That's insane. What do you mean 'all of these sites?'"

"No, it's not insane. You said yourself this structure points to the pyramids. It's a clue, the same people that built this, built others, all on ancient power centers. Maybe Tiyah's people, don't know, but I get these weird vibes since she zapped me. Remember the double pentagram that the Dogon drew? I'm betting there's at least twelve sites around the world that are all interconnected like the Earth is disconnected in that Dendara hieroglyph."

"Like an energy grid." Theodore thought for a moment. "Possibly?"

"Yes, like an energy grid."

"Wait; you may be on to something. In my research there was a fellow from New Zealand that theorized that all the UFO sights were concentrated on straight lines. He deduced that there was an energy grid with intersections that concentrated power. I think he calculated that there were ten or twelve of these centers."

"I'll bet it's twelve and I'll bet that if look you closely at that picture you'll see that Stonehenge and the pyramids are located on two of those centers."

"I'll check it out when we get back to our hotel room, I've got most of my research on my laptop. Now, I wonder if these energy lines are the same as ley lines." Theodore let out a sneeze and then another sneeze. "Damn! Roger, don't you think this is just plain bizarre? I mean, a woman that can see you through stone under the pyramid appears in England to show you a crop circle that just happens to give us the clue we need to reach Sherida."

"Not to mention the fact that she's old enough to be my great-great-great-great-..."

"Stop! I get it."

"...grandmother. Well, that isn't half as bizarre as the stuff you've already told me about Stonehenge and the pyramids."

"Yeah, you've got a point there. Okay, so the one-million-dollar question is this. If this is turned off, as you say, how do we turn it on?"

"Haven't a clue. But I do know I have to get into the center of those stones, and this crystal Sherida left us should open some kind of portal or doorway, like at the pyramid."

"And how are we supposed to get in there? It's fenced off, we're not allowed off the walkway."

"Didn't stop you earlier! Anyway, that fence isn't electrified and it's not that high either. I think after dark we just scale it and waltz right in." Roger started walking towards the exit.

Theodore shook his head, "I can see the newspaper headlines already, 'Two Americans arrested In Stonehenge, claims Atlanteans told them to do it.'"

"Well then, it's a damn good thing we're in the British good books after they helped us in Iraq." They both laughed.

"I'm getting hungry. I think we'll head down to the nearest pub as they do around here. Have a pint or two, a taste of the local fare, and come back later when it's shut."

"Jolly good idea," Roger uttered in his best English accent. "I always wanted to try a Steak and Guinness and pie."

****

Kentucky

Jeff slugged back another swill of whisky before he crossed the line of trees marking the boundary of his land. He knew he was stirring up a whole parcel of trouble by trespassing on the Macons' land. The Parkers and the Macons hadn't been feuding for the last ten years or so, and he was in no mind to start another ruckus. Still, some things a feller had to do and feeding his family was one of them.

He stomped over the ridge and stopped. "Get down, boy." Crouching low into the grass, he watched the beehive of activity before him. A large saucer-shaped object sat in the depression of the woods. Its lights were throbbing off and on as dozens of small bodies swarmed around it. Sparks flew from the tear in the hull of the vessel that they appeared to be working on. Several figures were coming and going in and out of the old mineshaft. "A mite peculiar, Jeb." Jeff studied them for a long time.

"Who knows, maybe this is some of them clone things they're making these days, like that ol' Henry next door keeps telling me about. Trying to feed the human race by making duplicates of stuff. I think Henry's gotta get himself a new woman, seeing as how he's watching too much TV and filling his head with 'toolectual garbage." Old Jeb just lay there, licking at his paws and staring at his master with a sorrowful expression on his old hound-dog face.

"You know, Jeb, all that talk about learning and stuff, that'll just get you in trouble, make ya want to do more thinking about things. Next thing you know, you want to make changes and go off to college and become one of them fancy-pants 'fessers. Nope, ol' Jeff Parker figgers he's plenty smart, and like the Good Book says, this here's the good life and the Lord always provides for those in his graces, so no sense in asking for any more, 'cause it just don't get any better."

Jeff's stomach grumbled. "Enough of the thinking, I'm gonna snare one or two of them critters. See if they's smart folk like us humans. Only they don't look too smart to me. They look like plucked chickens running about like that, just after their heads bin cut off." He snickered. "In fact they's even dressed up in the fancy tinfoil I've seen 'em wrap round that pre-barbequed stuff the lazy rich folk buy." He smacked his lips and pulled another drink from his flask.

Jeff stared a bit harder at the squat, grayish-white skinned beings with the large dark eyes. "I've a mind to go down there and raise a ruckus with them folk for disturbing my traplines. Only I don't think they's the reasoning kind. Nope, I think they's something else and there's only one other kind. You stay right here, Jeb, and guard my moonshine. This here's a job I best do alone and now's about the best time to be snooping around, since they're so darn busy. My pappy always told me, a man's gotta do what a man's gotta do, especially when the work of the Devil is involved." He unslung his flask, took off his jacket and drew out his trusty hunting knife and snare. "Yup, I'll be asking my own questions, Jeff Parker style."

****

Overhead the moon kept poking out from clouds as the two stared up at the ancient structures. "Well, that wasn't half as bad as I thought it would be. No guards, no dogs, and thankfully no electrified fence. These Brits are too darn trusting. Damn, it's chilly out tonight. So, now we're here, what do we do?" Theodore talked as he walked around the inner circle.

"Don't know, it's quiet, no background noise like at the crop circle. I do remember that when I was in Sedona the path to the cavern appeared to me when I sat down and meditated. All I can think of is trying that again." Roger stared skyward.

"Okay, you do it. I'm going to walk around here a bit. I've to take a leak anyways."

"You're not going to pee on these sacred stones."

"As if I wouldn't be the first. I'm sure some ancient Cro-Magnon man or old British peasant has done the same."

"I thought I was the sacrilegious one here." Roger shook his head in disbelief and quietly sat down with his back up against one of the bluestones. He placed the crystal that Sherida got from the Dogon on his lap and closed his eyes. "Oh boy, do I ever feel silly. Not sure how to do what I need to do. Okay, here goes. Ask for what you want, that's what you attract in the fourth dimension."

He forced his body to relax, put his head in his hands and slumped forward, trying to be as still as possible, the only thought repeating itself like a mantra, *show me the power center of these stones, show me the way to re-energize them.*

After a few minutes he opened his eyes and a trail of glowing crystals seemed to set a path before him to one of the downed stones. Theodore was nowhere to be found. He grabbed the crystal and walked along the glittering trail. He reached over to touch the large stone and tumbled down a short pathway set into the earth as it opened before him. Roger waited for his eyes to adjust to the dim light. He pulled the flashlight they'd brought earlier and began walking down the descending carved staircase.

After several minutes, it opened into a great chamber. Roger strode around; he was in a second semi-circular ring of monoliths, only these were not made of stone. The area was probably two hundred feet across and the monoliths were translucent, like ...

He reached up and touched the nearest one. It was cold and still, lifeless. Like crystals, he thought, giant crystals. Then he noticed the lights, changing like the aurora borealis he'd seen in Canada on his holidays one year. Only they weren't coming from above, it was light reflected from below swirling around the crystals like a river held at bay.

Only very little light flowed beneath him and the monoliths.

As he studied them he began to realize that the lights weren't in a disorganized pattern. They were a flowing river of energy. He walked to the focal point, which looked just like a crystal version of the Heel Stone above him, or at least should be above him; he assumed he was in the earth but somehow below Stonehenge or perhaps in some weird dimensional plane meant to represent the Henge.

He stopped as he reached the Heel Stone. These patterns of light, of energy. Were they the actual visible energy of the Ley lines? He walked around the Heel Stone. It was different in color to the rest, and below it the energy seemed to come up and virtually touch it. He glanced around the whole area. The Ley lines were converging on it, like a center.

The noise he heard was the flow of the lines, like a river increasing in volume. He walked towards the center into the silence where there was less or no flow. This area allowed the Ley line energy to converge and Roger stared upward into darkness. Overhead he could see the shadows of the rocks above him.

'Turned off', she said 'turned off, have to be re-powered'. Roger looked down again as he walked around. There was an area ninety degrees from the stone where the ground looked disturbed, almost like it had been moved some time ago.

"Okay, let's do it. If this crystal worked for Sherida, then if I really am a gateway walker or something, just maybe it will work for me."

Roger guessed that the crystal version of the Heel Stone should weigh several tons. As he put his hands to the rock the green light of the crystal flowed through him.

Scratching and grating as it moved easily along and the lights below bounced and shimmered in response. Roger grunted and moved it some more until finally it was in what he thought was its former position.

Part of the surrounding ethereal flow flooded into the Heel stone and funneled through it upwards connecting to the rock above.

"Well, this is closer to where it should be," he muttered, "but not quite right yet."

It wasn't connecting to the rest of the circle. Roger walked around the Heel stone studying it until he noticed a depression in the rock. It was about the shape of the crystal in his pocket. Roger pulled it out and remembered Sherida saying it was needed to open the flow or something, but he struggled to remember her exact words. All his instincts, though, were pointing at only one action so he set it into the groove.

Instantly the rock filled with the river of energy flowing through all the crystals in the cavern and warmth and pulsating lights shimmered everywhere. Roger stared upward. He could see the ground above him shimmering as well. It was like looking through a watery filter, and above that, stars that weren't there before flickered. The center of the energy complex somehow focused energy upward, connecting back to the universe.

He was done. He smiled and walked back up the pathway which vanished behind him like it never existed.

Theodore stood with his back to him, peeing.

"Wow! What a trip! How long was I gone?"

Theodore jumped, nearly spraying himself. "What do you mean, gone? You sat down, I went for a leak, and now you're sneaking up on me."

Roger explained what he'd just been through and as he did, he put his hand up against the imposing granite of one of the monoliths. It was as solid as it ever was. Everything was as it should be, solid and imposing. Yet, he could feel the slight vibration, like a gentle hum and, had he imagined it, or did the stone feel slightly warm to the touch now? "Do you hear that hum?"

"No."

"Does this rock feel warm to you?"

Theodore reached out. "Feels like cold stone should in the middle of England. You okay?"

"Just fine. I'll explain more on the ride back to the hotel."

Theodore glanced at his watch, "I guess this means you did what you needed to do."

"Yup, most definitely." He reached into his pocket and wasn't surprised to realize that the crystal was gone. "I've a better idea. Let's hit that local pub again and pull up a couple more pints of that Guinness first."

"Yeah, good idea. I could use another drink."

"You could use one? Wait 'til I tell you what happened, they'll be pouring us out the door after closing time and we'll miss our next flight as well."

"Well, there's no shortage of places to visit here, could hit Avebury next."

Roger shook his head, "could spend a decade checking out all the sites around this part of the world. I think after the last few days the only thing I want to check out is the bottom of my beer glass."

"Too right." Theodore tried in a pathetically poor English accent. They laughed and strode off.

Chapter Seven

Earth Science Week News

Scientists report the ozone hole is lasting longer this year. A leading expert for scientific study at the UN stated, "the ozone hole had begun to form over Antarctica in the 1980's and even though it fluctuates year to year. It has continued to grow in size every year. Usually reaching its maximum size in mid-September. This year, however, the hole has not shrunk in size like it normally has done in the past."

****

"So far you have been very quick to learn and understand, but the last three chakras are more challenging because they are not of things tangible."

"Not tangible?"

"They are of things your science can't put a definition to. This is why it is important to be clearly defined in the lower chakras, as the higher we climb now the more nebulous we become. The last chakra was the link between the more substantial chakras and these higher ones. The fifth chakra is of sound and vibration. Visuddha, this is the chakra of ether and spirit. Spirit is often called the fifth element."

I stare up into the bright blue of the sky. "When will I begin to see how knowledge of the chakras can be of any use?"

"When you need to use it."

"Thanks." I thought it might say something useless like that.

"Sound is the basis of life. This you must understand before you can continue. Everything, life itself, begins with sound, as do all foundations of communication. Sound, vibration, and hence self-expression, and from there to creativity. Communication focuses consciousness along the pathways of the chakras. The breeding ground of true creativity is the place where abstracted thought and manifested idea meet. That locale is where the physical plane begins. Order from chaos, the gateway." It hissed the last two words.

I said nothing and watched the fingers of mist reaching down to flow into the valley.

"Sound is not as fast as light, nor is light as fast as thought. Understand the secret of sound and uncover the key to the mysteries of the universe."

I turn and the Hathor is gone, only the bright blue of the sky remains. As I look down the ground too is gone. I am the mist and everything becomes a haze. I begin to panic, this is so disorientating. I feel my atoms dissipating, I'm dissolving, flowing.

Wait, flowing? There is flow here even in this vaporous state? No wonder the Hathor had given such a stern talk on this state. It would be so easy to melt away into the mist. Instead, I relished the freedom, the gentleness. Drifting effortlessly like water vapors rising up mountain slopes in the early morning.

Then from the mists a pulse of light appeared, and another. Drums began and, just as I was beginning to enjoy this state of ether, of non-being, I felt myself being pulled back to earth and a more corporeal shape.

The mist lifts and I am a dancer, one of many dancing wildly around a bonfire. I am in Africa, in some native village. The ebony of our skins shines with sweat and dirt encrusted from the stirred ground we are stamping on.

Drums, dozens of drums, pounding a beat that sends vibrations deep into me. Releasing all inhibitions I begin to gyrate like the others. I'd been here on nights like this many times before. Sparks of firelight crackle heavenward, flashes of spears, beads spinning away, headdresses of bird feathers and shells glitter. The sound of their clanging lost in the pounding of the drums and the voices of the people singing in some language I'd forgotten.

Each drumbeat now begins a resonance echoing inside. Pulsing, grinding.

Basic, earthy.

Booming.

Pulling at me.

I don't resist and become lost in the flashes of bonfire.

One flash I am here, in another I am on a dance floor. Techno beats pounding overhead. I am in some modern nightclub. Strobe lights begin and each flash puts me in another scene, on another dance floor, around ancient fires. People dancing to the throb of rhythm, of life. Becoming the player, the band. Sound and vibration, so basic.

Heavy bass thunders into me, allowing me to dissolve again, becoming the player, the singer and finally the music itself.

In another beat I open my eyes and stare at a canvas before me. It is blank. I have been staring at it for many days. Empty canvas, staring back.

Beside me an assortment of oils and colored pigments dabbled haphazardly on a palette board.

I pick up the brush, dabble in the colors and put a few swirls of paint on the canvas.

Not right. Try again. I wipe away the paint.

I stop, asking not what it is I want to paint, but instead what image is locked within the weave of the canvas. Only a true artist can release that which is contained already on the object inside.

I close my eyes, quiet the voice inside and stare from inside my mind at the paper, at the blankness. Then the whiteness begins to move, murky lines begin to erupt all around me as peels of music, soft and operatic, condense into rain falling in the background, revealing more hazy lines and I begin to move.

My brush doesn't hesitate, it knows what has to be done. Slowly at first, like the beginning of a waltz, and then as confidence grows and the images on the canvas solidify I let go, allowing the paint to speak and the brush to be the ears.

Brush dips in paint, scratches sing over the canvas; caressing hair on Bristol board. Mist swirls all around me and I become the arm, the hand, the brush, the paper and, finally, the hardening paint. Seeping into the spaces between the weave. Into the space between, becoming the void and watching the swirls of paint forming all around me in the darkness, like Aurora Borealis on Northern skies.

Green, reds flaring the gap between dimensions. The gateway.

I am there.

I moved to proceed and another voice calls.

The Hathor pulls me back, "You have done well, but not yet. There is more you need to know first."

I fall earthward into a deep sleep.

Kentucky

About three hours later Jeff was sitting before a crackling campfire. The smell of roasting meat filled the air. "Here, Jeb, take a chew on this shank." He cut a slice off the leg. Jeb took one sniff and bit into the meat. Bones crunching away, he quickly devoured the savoury-smelling morsel and licked his chops. "I ain't never seen you eat anythin' that fast, 'cept chicken." Jeff sliced off a small piece of flesh. "Smells mighty damn good." He popped it into his mouth and chewed real slow and cautious just like it was a fresh wad of tobacco. "Damn, tastes like chicken too, only more tender."

A sudden glare filled the night from behind the ridge he'd crossed earlier and rose into the sky. "Dang, look at that, ain't never seen a backwards meteor. Awfully dumb buggers they were, caught three of 'em in no time. Tried to ask a few questions, but all I got was a buzzing in my head like they was trying to talk to me or brainiac-wash me. Nope, I'm too smart for them buggers. What you figger about that hogwash about them aliens, Jeb?"

He scratched at himself between the legs. "I think that nosy reporter got it all wrong. No such thing as extat ... what'd he call 'em? Oh yeah, extatesticals. Nope, that's crazy talk. Besides, what would extatesticals want with us good Bible-fearing folk anyways. I ain't got a whole lot to offer 'em, other than you, ol' boy, and my whisky recipe granpappy handed down. Only them ain't getting the moonshine-makings from my hands, not as long as this here fella's a-breathing. Yup, God Almighty would have to pry the bottle from these cold dead fingers afore I'd do that." He snickered and took another swig before settling back with his head on Jeb's midsection. "Don't worry, ol' boy, they ain't taking you either, else what's I gonna use fer a pillow on nights like this?"

Jeff smiled as a stupor descended on him. Now that he'd found some grub to

feed the family, Jessie Mae'd be letting him back into their bedroom. He felt a familiar stirring between his legs. "Yup," he muttered as sleep tugged at his eyelids. "She'll be so happy I snared these extatestical chickens, I'll be working on the next young 'un, this time t'morrow night."

He burped and stared at the stars, watching one ship rising and vanishing into the

rest. "Way I figger it, it's a fair tradeoff. They's come and scare off my game, and I use them fer my stew."

Chapter Eight

There are those who dream and those who go out there,
those who only watch as a woman dances through firelight,
while rivers flow and turtles sleep
and a very few who rise to dance with the woman
before she has gone to where rivers go
until they cycle back to run again.
Robert James Waller

Salisbury Plain, Wiltshire, England

Edward Benwick stood in front of his farmhouse. A cool misty morning, typical for this part of England. He yawned. Last night he'd been disturbed by some strange noises. More disturbing were the pulsating lights that seemed to come from the south-west corner of his farm. He gripped the stock of his shotgun and scratched the head of his dog, Prince, a full-grown collie. "We'd better walk out there and make sure everything's okay." The collie growled, as if sensing his master's tension.

He'd been a farmer all his life. It paid the bills and gave him enough money to live comfortably, although the fiasco with Mad Cow Disease all those years ago had cost him many of his cows. "Daft buggers, feeding scrapie sheep to cows!" he muttered. Some of his neighbors had it worse. They'd lost their entire herds and ended up bankrupt. He'd be okay, though. He had the land as collateral to rebuild. It had been in his family for unknown generations. "Benwick land for as long as someone had seen fit to rule over us and take our tax money," he snorted and spat into the ground. No one, not even the Queen herself, could take it from his hands. "At least not as long as breath enters this Englishman's body." His family had not always been farmers; many of the men had served in the army and navy. Medals filled one of the stone walls of his house. "Brave lads, the works," he muttered and straightened up. Whatever was out here last night he'd face now, with that same stiff-upper-lip British determination and courage. The kind that had conquered many lands and formed the British Empire and ruled most of the known world.

Prince stopped and began to whimper as they walked through his field. Soon they were in the middle of one of his fields. "Come on boy." But the dog wouldn't budge. He began to growl. "Prince, you bugger. Let's go." But the collie had no intention of taking another step forward. Then the dog turned slowly and growled.

Edward cocked his gun and stared into his fields. They were on a bit of a rise and as the fog cleared, he began to notice what Prince was barking about. His field was covered in depressions. Swirls and sweeping pentangles everywhere. "Bloody hell." The same thing had happened to a couple of his neighbors. "Crop circles."

Overhead a part of the fog began to pulse. A whish of hot air blasted downward and transcribed another piece of the elaborate design he'd seen in the local paper. The same paper that had said his neighbors were crazy and making the circles themselves. Became a bloody zoo what with reporters and those quacks that claimed UFOs did it. "Aliens and the like. Bloody hell."

Edward backed up and retreated with Prince back to his farm buildings. Mounting his tractor, he realized his hands were shaking. It didn't get any easier this time or any of the others. He had to think this was probably the fifth time, but on none of the others had he seen what had created the circle, nor cared. "Well, aliens or whatever, no one's going to make a laughingstock of this family." He fired up the tractor and lifted the cultivator end before driving out to the field again. His dog stayed behind, not wanting to be anywhere near that field. Edward Hummed 'God save the Queen' and reciting the Lord's Prayer he began to cut down the grass, forever hiding the symbols carved in the flattened stalks.

****

Roger had checked for messages as soon as he walked in the door but there weren't any. They'd landed barely an hour ago. No word from Beth, although he could tell that she'd been here while he was gone as some of her things were missing from the living room. Not the wedding picture on the wall above the fireplace though, that she hadn't wanted to take. He sighed. He missed his wife; so much had happened and all he wanted to do was hug her, hold her and tell he loved her and explain everything that was going on.

He yawned, needing sleep. "Damn jetlag," he muttered, as he nearly tripped over a large bone on his way to the bedroom. "Oh yeah, I was going to take this to the museum." He flopped onto his bed, wanting oblivion but wanting to talk to Theodore first. He was going to the museum to leave samples of the dust that had been all that remained in the sarcophagus after Sherida had disappeared. Theodore knew the crew that carried out most of the studies on this kind of thing at the museum. Roger laughed to himself, he probably hung out there on his days off, checking out the latest corpse or pottery shard from some dig in Leduc, Alberta or some such place. He shook his head. He shouldn't be so cynical. One of the things he now realized about his friend was that he was very intelligent and usually right.

"Theodore here."

"Hey, it's me. Are you still going over to the museum?"

"Yes. I was just heading out the door."

"Could you come pick up this bone and take it with you as well? I promised to take it over to the curator for study. I'm going to hit the sack."

"Jet-lagged?"

"Yeah. Powering up ancient sites is tiring." He'd slept most of the way back.

"Is Beth home?"

"No, no messages left either."

"Sorry."

"Yeah, miss her, and the kids. It's going to be hard to explain this to her."

"Hey, I'll be there when you do, might help a lot."

"Ah, thanks Theodore. I'll probably need the support without Sherida to back me up."

"Anytime. What are friends for?"

Roger put the bone in a box and wrapped it up. He set it on the front step and crawled into bed. It felt better knowing Theodore was willing to talk to Beth. Perhaps she would believe him now. Roger smirked. Now if only he could believe it himself.

****

Trimus stared blankly at the message just received. Sherida did not return from the signal sent to us via the ZPEC device on Earth. He slammed his fist on the panel. *Now I have to figure out what happened to her and where she went.*

****

Two hours later Theodore stood with the curator before the Ceratosaurus skeleton. He'd agreed to test the ash, but it was the bone that really caught his attention.

"And you're saying your friend, Roger Harrison, found this bone?"

"Apparently."

"Well, I must say I vaguely remember having a conversation with a gentleman along those lines. He'd been here with his two bratty kids who nearly knocked the whole skeleton over. Indeed," the curator lifted the bone from the box. "It looks like one of the neck bones from this dinosaur. Only differences I can see are the fact your specimen is whiter and ..." he squinted closer. "It appears to have bits of meat attached to it."

"What can I say? I was going to give it to the lab for a DNA sample."

"Is this some sort of bizarre prank? This can't be a natural, un-fossilized dinosaur bone."

"No, I think you know me by now, didn't say it was, but, once you have the results back call me and I'll explain further how he came across it."

Theodore walked from the room leaving the flabbergasted curator standing there. He didn't know what else to say, only more questions to ask Roger.

"How is this possible?" the custodian muttered. The walls of insulated teachings and doctrines established Theories of Evolution and Darwinism banged in his eardrums. He put his hand in his pocket and turned to leave. He pulled the slip of paper from the gentleman that had showed up only yesterday from the FBI, insisting if anything unusual happened to give him a call. He remembered what had happened to the others, how ridiculed even great scientists had been when presented with outlandish theories and findings. "No, I'm in no mood for any of this." He frowned and pulled his cell phone from his pocket. He dialed the number to the rather distinguished agent, a Zolnar Grzyb. Rather unusual name must have been European descent, perhaps Romanian. No, possibly Polish, he thought.

****

Roger tossed in bed; he was on the trail again. Walking, slowly at first, behind him he could see nothing, yet he could sense something was there watching him, waiting. Bushes rustled as he walked, a crack not so far off. The moon ghosting along the trail. A howl. He sped up. Another, not as far away. He began to run, the thud of something behind him. Running, he glanced behind him and tripped.

Roger woke with a start. It was the middle of the night. He clicked on the nightlight and lay there wide awake. Fifteen minutes passed, twenty-five. "Damn. Can't sleep now, must be the time difference jet-lag thing."

He got up and plunked himself in front of the TV.

Beth was gone, he sighed. She'd taken off to live with her sister in Portland and had no intentions of coming back for a while. Roger had called his parents earlier in the day at their beach house in Alberta, Canada. With a month of summer holidays left, they were ecstatic to look after the kids. Canada always had a warm spot in his heart. How many summers had he spent up in Alberta, touring around? His dad was Canadian and had met his mom while on a business trip to the US. They'd chosen to live in Seattle, close enough to the border so it was easy to travel back and forth. Roger was glad he was born a US citizen, but sometimes he'd wish America was more like Canada, laid back and easy. But then it wouldn't be the good ol' US of A, now would it. So now what?

'Be open' Sherida had said in the pyramid. 'Listen to the voice inside, intuitions calling'.

"If it's calling why ain't I answering," he muttered, or was it because he wasn't listening.

The nightmare with the black dog was calling and had been since Sherida disappeared. What was that about, fears? Aimlessly flicking the channel changer, he came to a special on the west coast. Pictures flashed by images of temporal rainforest, huge incredibly huge trees and continued channel surfing.

"Wait." He stopped and backed up to the channel with the west coast splendor. Indescribable beauty. He'd been along the British Columbia coast and Vancouver Island, especially the west side. Huge cedars, empty beaches and images of large round eyes carved from wood stared back. All those ancient trees, somehow it was... grounding.

Beth had always loved native art and had several pieces on the living room wall. Including a drawing of a totem. Roger thought it was Haida He stared at the totem, wondering where it was from. Bella Colla, or the Queen Charlottes he couldn't quite remember. He was crap at American geography and worse with Canadian.

How many nights had he sat there staring at that pic like it was calling to him? Pulling at him. Asking questions from the three that sat on top like haunted beings watching over everything around them of everyone that had unsettled business.

During a commercial break, he walked over to the totem picture and stood before it once again, curious as to where it was from. As he turned the frame over in his hands he glanced up at the TV as it resumed its regular programming on First Nations sites along the BC west coast.

The same haunting image on TV of the same totem, only in its natural state. He stared at the totem in his hands and again at the one on the TV and placed the picture back on the wall. The same three men with what looked like top-hats, a birdlike being with large ovoid eyes, another holding a human upside down, and the bottom one with a long beak sticking straight out. The TV program continued and another picture, one of a lady whose head and ears had been deliberately elongated, a practice the Haida and other natives used to perform. He'd seen that woman before. Where? The ears; the Arabian woman from the pyramid and Stonehenge. She had elongated earlobes and the one from his dreams, the Hathor.

"The totems of Ninstints up in Haida Gwaii," the commentator on TV said.

The TV flickered in the background, and he just stared at the old totem on the wall. Ancient ovoid eyes stared back once again begging answers to questions he never had until now. "Okay call me nuts, but this is where the journey begins."

Intuition had called.

****

Zolnar walked out of the Museum, his body still hurt after dealing with Vessno'ar's widow Several claw marks still ached on his chest.

He put the package containing the bone in the trunk and making sure no one saw him; he flicked a switch on his arm and scanned the bone the curator gave him. It was indeed Ceratosaurus DNA and fresh, not fossilized.

The man named Theodore could only be one of the ones involved with her. How'd he get a dinosaur bone from the past? He hadn't been able to track down her or the other one called Roger, there was mention of some of the ancient technology that kept the user hidden from detection. He was tired of waiting to find out where the agent named Sherida was hiding as he couldn't track her location down. She, or whoever was with her, had the crystal he needed. He smiled. He knew just who to go after if he couldn't find her.

****

Roger sat at the window seat in the local Boston Pizza where so much of this had started. Theodore had called and wanted to meet for lunch. He wanted to give Roger the key to his safety deposit box that contained all his important research papers. "A little paranoid," he told him over the phone. Roger had told him about what he saw on the TV last night.

"Speaking of watching, I think you're being watched as well. I saw someone sitting outside in a black SUV when I left with the bone yesterday." Before it could sink in Theodore had started to babble about research involving natives; how the Haida language had no connection to the more than a hundred other languages along the North American coast, or those in British Columbia. "The Haida were not the only ones to insert labrets in their lips, elongate the women's heads by binding and wear heavy ornaments to lengthen the earlobes. To the Haida, Easter Islanders and Egyptians, long ears were considered holy born."

"Interesting. Now that I think about it both Tiyah and the weird dreams, I've been having regarding the spirit guide..."

"The Hathor you told me about."

"... yeah, both have elongated earlobes. Never really noticed that until now." Roger interrupted.

"Interesting," Theodore jotted it down on his notebook he always kept with him. "Statues found of Nefertiti and Akhenaten show the same bizarre deformities. Also, the fact that they were very tall, ten to fourteen feet, had long necks, protruding hips and round bellies."

"Akhenaten. Wasn't he the pharaoh that changed the religious beliefs of the people, made them worship only one God, the sun god, or something like that?" Roger visualized the being in his mind. There was something hauntingly familiar about it.

"Yes. He was sent here to do just that, break people from their beliefs on animalistic gods. He also formed the Mystery Schools, one of which was the Essenses."

"They were the early version of Christians and got wiped out at Masada by the Romans?"

Theodore nodded.

"And you're saying he was an alien?"

"If you look at these pictures and statues, does he or Nefertiti really look human? These long funnel shaped crowns were only there to hide their misshapen heads. There's even reports of two caskets found under Tel el Amarna, now reportedly in storage in Berlin, that bear skeletons matching these features. Coffins over ten feet in length."

"So, what did that have to do with crystals?" Roger interjected. "Tell me, then, is there anything like a crystal cavern hinted to in ancient oral stories around here."

"Hm. There are reports of Japanese coming over here and mining crystals and jade somewhere in the interior of BC, and there's even been ancient Japanese and Chinese coins found. But nothing else, although..."

Roger ended up cutting Theodore off after about twenty minutes of mind-scrambling overload, suggesting instead they meet for lunch. Roger did highly respect Theodore, the man knew his stuff, he just seemed to get on a particular discussion and if he got wound up there was no stopping his friend. He'd nearly fallen asleep on the phone listening to him ramble into the night.

Roger took another sip of his coffee and looked up, waiting for Theodore to arrive. He saw him parking his newer Accord across the street. Roger watched him begin to cross when the sound of screeching rubber turned his head. A black domestic SUV of some kind with darkened windows tore up the road. He'd forgotten what his friend had said, a black SUV was watching him at his house. Was it? He got up to warn him as the waitress came up.

"You ain't going anywhere without paying are you?"

The vision of what was about to happen flashed before his eyes. Roger leapt from his seat, throwing a twenty-dollar bill on the table, knowing it was already too late as the car careened down the road and slammed into Theodore and two others crossing the road. His friend was flung through the air and spun against the curbing like a rag doll. "No!"

The vehicle accelerated down the street without any hesitation. The sound of screeching tires disappeared into the traffic noise.

Roger ran as fast as he could. Theodore convulsed, his legs bent at obscene angles, white bone protruding and blood pouring in a gory river from his friend. A final squeal of rubber in the distance and the vehicle disappeared around a corner. Roger held his buddy in his arms.

"Hang on! I'll get an ambulance." Roger cried as Theodore's eyes fluttered, but before he could call, sirens sounded.

"I'm not going to make it," he moaned.

"The laptop, papers, money and credit cards are in my safety deposit box. In my pocket a key." He said, spitting up blood. "Fuck! It hurts. Number three thirty-eight at our bank." More blood gushed from his mouth. "Perhaps not so paranoid after all. Sherida, help her, get the bast..."

Theodore went limp in his arms as the ambulance pulled up and two paramedics jumped out. One hit him with a needle, Theodore moaned coming awake. "This will keep him going until we get to the hospital. Another ambulance is on the way. But we have to get him there quickly." They put him on a stretcher and bundled him in, leaving Roger sitting there in shock. "What hospital are you taking him?"

"UW General."

They tore off as another ambulance and a police car came screeching up. The second ambulance dealt with the two others.

A policeman came running up as Roger stood up wondering what kind of world this was, who could do such evil actions and why hadn't the first ambulance crew taken the two others? "Do you know him or any of the others?" the cop jabbered, as shock began to set in and a morbid crowd gathered. Some laughing and making motions like they were retarded with their arms splayed at bizarre angles. He spied a man walking a large black dog across the street, merely observing. He appeared to be chatting to a blue tooth device in his ear.

"Sir, do you know the gentleman," the policeman asked again.

Another, in dark glasses and dark clothes leaning against a post with what appeared to be a Bluetooth device in his ear as well. "No. No, just a bystander."

"I'll need to get your name and address. Everyone get back." The cop turned to push back the growing crowd of curiosity seekers and picture takers.

Roger calmly and quickly walked into the crowd of people. *Whoever did this may have been watching or even had someone in the crowd listening. Perhaps, as Theodore said with his last words, he hadn't been so paranoid after all, maybe he was being watched and possibly myself now as well.* He'd talk about the men in black, conspiracy theories, etc. Roger simply laughed, not believing a word. Mind you there wasn't much these days he didn't believe. After all he'd been through anything seemed plausible.

He tried not to look around, heart racing. He tried not to notice the man sitting in the car just in front of the pizza place reading the paper, nor the bum leaning against the building for support. Who had Theodore called since their return?

As far as he knew the only place would have been the museum. The museum!

"Shit!" If anyone was after him, they'd know it was probably him that originally had the bone. Or at least they would very quickly.

Roger walked briskly to his car, taking several unneeded turns to a gas station. As far as he could tell me wasn't being tailed. He grabbed his jogging clothes from the trunk and changed out of the blood splattered clothes. If he was being followed, they would know he'd probably go to the hospital and judging by the condition Theodore was in he didn't have much longer to live.

Instead, he drove straight to the bank and emptied Theodore's safety deposit box. Among other stuff there was a gold credit card, with the back unsigned, several thousand in cash and a small laptop. Maybe his friend hadn't been paranoid enough. Roger circled the block twice around his house. No one unusual, no removals vans or vehicles of any kind waited to unload their cargo of thugs nor spy on him.

Roger quietly parked in the garage and entered his house, shutting all the curtains. "Now what do I do next?" he muttered. Obviously calling the cops would be a complete waste of time, and probably be more trouble than help. As he sat down on his couch, he felt a wave of tiredness creep over him. Roger lay back and closed his eyes, tears streaming down his face. Theodore's bloody face staring at him.

"Roger! Danger. You must leave." A voice spoke inside his head. He'd fallen asleep.

"What?" A woman's voice, but it wasn't Sherida. He glanced at his watch. He'd been asleep for at least half an hour.

"Relax, I'm Tiyah, I can only speak like this to you if you are calm and your mind is open."

"And the world just got even weirder." He laid his head back, trying not to send his mind off racing.

"You are in grave danger and must leave your house as soon as possible." Her voice spoke inside his head.

"Tiyah? The woman from the pyramids? How do you know I live here?"

"Listen gateway walker, you must leave, and now. The crystal allows me to contact you."

"What?" He was stunned. Only Sherida, Theodore and perhaps Beth knew.

"There is at least one other that knows." She spoke to him again. "And others that want to do harm to you and this planet."

"I don't believe you."

"Do not be seen and look carefully outside your window. Now come to your bedroom."

He did and noticed a minivan with house renovations marked on its side parked across the street. It wasn't there when he sat down. Inside appeared four men appeared to be gathering equipment together, all had strange

Bluetooth-type devices in their ears. "Great! They know where I live, whoever they are."

Roger walked to the back of his house and opened the door to his bedroom. There on his bed sat the slender figure of a lady. An Arabian looking lady. "Holy!"

he gasped. It was Tiyah from the pyramid and Stonehenge.

"Now you believe."

"I-I, yes."

"You must hurry, they will be assembling more men shortly. Pack light. These are ruthless men and will stop at nothing to get their job done."

"Their job?"

"To kill you and stop this whole ascension process. I'll tell you more later. Hurry."

****

Roger drove north. He wanted to get out of the Seattle area, and the US, as soon as possible. With his vision of the place called Ninstints somewhere on the Canadian West Coast he figured that Vancouver Airport would be the best place to go to. Beside him sat a calm Tiyah.

"So tell me, how are you involved in any of this ascension process stuff? Are you also a Pleiadean then? One of the ones Sherida called an angel."

"No, I'm one of a few Atlantean's left, there are others, one you might meet on your journeys if you make it that far. I am merely the keeper of the crystals."

"Make it that far? Wait, Atlantean? That would make you very old, at least..."

"Yes, indeed, as I put into your mind at Stonehenge, sixty thousand years old. You'll find that as your soul evolves sometimes your consciousness realizes that looking after other soul's growth and guiding them is what you are meant to do."

"You're from the Mystery Schools then, a teacher I think."

"Yes, you are very observant. That was how I knew you three had entered the pyramid's secret chamber and had awoken the crystal."

"But if you could do that, why can't you turn these places on."

"I can't, it is not my place; I merely keep and protect. They exist where I can't travel."

"And I can, I suppose?"

"Yes. We all have our unique abilities."

"I was afraid you'd say something like that. So, you followed me to Stonehenge then?"

"Not really. I knew you were heading to the land of the English and that is one of my favorite places. I had the plane delayed and the thought implanted in your heads. Again, sorry about your friend Theodore."

"Why didn't you stop that?"

"There are some things I can't foretell. It was at what you now call Stonehenge that I was first entrusted with the sacred duty in the hyper-dimensional spiral ceremony and keeper of the crystals."

"But I never saw you on the airplane."

"There are other ways to travel, as you'll begin to soon realize." She smiled, "but I'm running out of time here, this is taking too much energy to maintain and have said too much already. There are things and sequences of events that you must experience in order to become what you are to be. I must go now. There are limits of what I'm allowed to do and say."

"Limits? Let me guess. I've got to learn this for myself. Hang on. Spiral? That rock I leaned against had a faint spiral. It looked like the Julia set pendant around that old English fellow at the crop circle."

"Yes, that's the place. I can't interfere much more, but you are on the path to have a teacher help to accelerate your training. Time is of the essence. But remember that teachers and students come in all shapes and forms. When one is needed, one will appear. I cannot interfere in the ascension process, but I can help your training. Oh, and one more thing." She reached into a pocket of her flowing abayah.

"Keep this after I leave," she said, and handed a crystal to Roger. "It is a more powerful version of the one Sherida used. But be careful, it's a very dangerous tool to use. Do not let it fall into anyone else's hands."

"Why give it to me?"

"We have no other choice. You haven't the skill to get into the pyramid so you must use the crystal, it is what I used. Go into the well, after you have done what it is you must do and from there you'll be able to enter the Halls of Amanti after you power up the pyramid."

"The what?"

With that she turned and stepped onto the curb, transposing herself right through the car at sixty miles an hour. Roger looked in panic in his rear-view mirror and watched her wave to him as she stood calmly on the roadside.

"God, I hate it when she does that." He could still feel the shivers as the three of them entered the chamber under the pyramid. The three of them, he smiled sadly. Now there was just one. As he pulled into the lineup for the border crossing, he phoned the city hospital wondering how Theodore was doing.

"No one of that name received here today. Can we ask who's calling?"

Roger hung up in case someone was recording the conversation and trying to track him. *Darn, now I'm paranoid of everyone. And with what just happened, I've every right to be.*

"Hey, wait a minute," he smiled as he pulled into the lineup. "She said we. Who the hell are we?"

Chapter Nine

Through all the days that eat away every breath that I take
All the words in truth that have been spoken
That the winds have blown away
For all those nights I have lain alone
In someone else's dream awake
Johnny Clegg

"Why did you stop me in that last dream?"

The Hathor stood calmly beside me as sparkles of stars slid by, flittering through the tiles of the dark hallway we stood in. "You were not ready. The threshold is a scary place to be, you reached it far more quickly than I thought you might. This is a good thing, but there are a few things to show you first. This chakra is about light. Light travels faster than sound and thought faster than light. Light is the connecting thread to the universe, to the Creator."

As he talked the flicks of light below began to speed up.

"As sound begins life, light connects and light spreads."

Beams of light began to lift from the tiles. Filling the corridor, until it seemed we walked only on a thin line of flooring amid the night sky of the galaxy. Paintings hung suspended from the stars as we walked. I stopped and stared at a painting of a sun simply shining above some mountains.

The sun sank behind the peaks capped with ice and snow. In an instant darkness swarmed over the sky and stars blinked into existence.

I lay awake, staring into the infinite night sky, or so it appears. The stars go on forever. I am only ten again. And beside me lies the Hathor pointing to various stars, telling me their names and which races live on the planets that orbit them. It has been going on for hours.

"The night sky isn't so dark after all. There are quadrillions of stars out there."

"Yes, quite right. One of the secrets of this dimension and the rest, I suppose, is that reality broken down is simply light. All matter is trapped light. Everything is light and light is."

"How is that possible?" We are suddenly in the hallway of pictures and standing before a painting of someone standing over a body. A healer, his hands are touching the still person on the table and his eyes are closed, concentrating on healing the one before him.

I step forward and not just I, but we, are in the body of the healer. Energy, a river of energy, is flowing from the space all around him into his hands, into the person he is touching. We shrink down and join the river, a swirling mass of light, of atoms bursting with energy, and of smaller particles. Like a biz-zillion fireflies, galaxies of brilliance awhirl. "These aren't atoms."

"You call them tachyons. Faster than the speed of light, they are tiny energy beings, like soldiers of light, they flow when called, to the healers that beckon."

Then the flow stops. "He is done." We returned to stand by the body. I notice a dark spot that the healer missed. I inadvertently reach out and, in a flash, I'm standing in a field of heartbeats and blood racing. Veins are pulsing with life, flowing back and forth, in and out as the heart beats before me. Lungs throb with a heavy basic pulse as intestines move like snakes gurgling away, as they process food. There, clinging to an area just behind the stomach, but pressed tightly to it like a Plecostomus catfish, I see it. A dark area, from within emanates another pulse. A hungry pulse. It breathes with an intensity like the fires of an out-of-control sun and begins to feed off its host, growing with each moment. The voracious appetite of the entity called Cancer is terrifying to watch as it readies itself to multiply and resume its mission, its need like every other living being to live. Only it lives in an insatiable state, like a vampiric cat set on a platter of simpering mice.

I reach out and showers of tachyons surround the area, with tens of thousands joining in. The battle is intense, swirls of lights exploding, colliding. Sparks of dying tachyons litter the area until finally the dark area begins to shrink in on itself. Compressing, condensing, increasing in mass until ignition point is reached. Exploding into a spray of light.

We are back on the hillside. "I see you are beginning to understand, even darkness has light," it whispers, and vanishes. I roll over and breathe the damp grass, wondering how one can understand anything when nothing makes sense.

"Son, it's your bedtime," my mom calls and I rise. The stars blink overhead, as they've been doing for longer than I've been born, for longer than this planet *has been born. The screen door slams behind me leaving the nagging question wafting to the winds, trees, sky and heavens.*

We sit in the hall with pictures again. I remember my summers as a child, spending many an evening staring up at the stars in the backyard of my grandparents' home. They lived in the country. Without the interference of city lights the stars were so bright and without end. I knew a couple of constellations; the Big Dipper and Orion and would catch the odd satellite skimming by. But on nights when the moon was absent, and no clouds interfered with the view, I'd see other things. Movements of lights that couldn't be explained. Almost like a haphazard skitter of bugs, fireflies, beams of light that turned at ninety-degree angles or sped up and slowed down. The comings and goings of vast armadas of alien ships, I'd dream. Me riding out there, like Buck Rogers or Luke Skywalker, off on some incredible journey to battle the most insidious of menaces. But the one thing I remembered the most was the nagging question left inside as the screen door slammed behind me and I retired to bed. What was life like out there? Really like?

"Again," the Hathor simply said without emotion, knowing that lessons and learnings sometimes take more than once to grasp, longer to master. It had more patience than I did.

We were standing on a sky of iridescent colors shimmering all around us while a erratic collage of energy patterns whizzed by. Over, around, below a crazy swirl of light with no set or measured rationality. Points of light stop, hover and explode into phantasms of fireworks.

"Energy is light, trapped in one form or another. All light, and conversely energy, is holographic in nature. Like a pebble dropped in a pond, each wave cascading outward contains all the knowledge of the event. Another pebble dropped contains all the knowledge of its event carried in each of the waves produced. When two or more lines intersect information can be exchanged inter-dimensionally producing a third dimensional image you call a hologram. Each bit of the image contains energy, each bit reproduces the whole.

"Since energy is light, all light is holographic." I struggle to understand.

"Depending on its coherency or wavelength," it responds, adding to the overloading stress on my brain. I know from my school days that incoherent light doesn't produce anything, that in the case of a laser beam all light is in one coherent direction producing a powerful beam.

I look around trying to adjust myself to the swirling madness. "Wait a minute, if all light is holographic then coherency is merely a viewpoint seen from the ability of the individual to comprehend, to organize."

The Hathor says nothing.

I begin after all of this time to finally understand. "Even in the depths of chaos and pandemonium, order and coherency are there." I focus on several specters of light flashing by. It, at least part of it, begins to make sense. "Everything, even in essence, must be connected. Holographically speaking. Order is a function of chaos."

The Hathor smiles. "The blue sparkles are fascinating to watch."

I study the shifting waves of light, watching the rising crescendos of fireworks flaring away. "I rather like the greens myself."

"You are learning well." It smiles and fades away as I wake in my room.

The musings of a child's mind, of my mind. Only now was I starting to know, to realize, as the child did, the changes unfolding out there and within. And in some ways the truth was more incredible than even I could have imagined as a child. That dream, or whatever is was. Astral traveling? That was the illusion, this was real. Or was it?

I lay there alone in the room and try to imagine myself floating out into space. But can't. "Ah, this is crap," I mutter and turn over, dragging covers over the warm bed. Yet, Sherida came from somewhere out there. I close my eyes and try falling asleep, hoping to dream of my wife Beth, whom I missed and not of aliens, starships nor black dogs a-prowl.

****

"Damn!" Zolnar cursed as he went through Roger's house. He'd gotten one of them, a man called Theodore, and held him in statis keeping him alive as long as possible to scan his mind and find out what he knew before he died. This human knew a lot. He knew much of the past involvement of outsiders into earth's past and alien intervention. The man was a true genius, too bad he had to die.

Zolnar also visited the Museum Curator's office, retrieved the dinosaur bone and wiped from his memory any knowledge of the incident and of himself. Before he alerted other authorities.

But it was apparent that someone had warned Roger. There were signs of her body tissues in the house, he was the one Sherida was guarding or helping her. It appeared he had allies, only who could he have for allies? Zolnar stared at his screen. Was there perhaps another angel in the area? Impossible; he only had three left to find.

His phone rang, "It appears that Roger Harrison may have left the country. His license plate is recorded entering Canada." One of his paid contacts said that was monitoring all recorded border activity.

"Damn! Okay try to put everything back together in case he comes back". Canada. Big place, too much open territory and not enough people, he'd wait, monitor the airlines and see if Roger moved anywhere from there before sending in a search team or going after him himself.

Chapter Ten

*Sometimes with the bones of the black sticks left when the fire
has gone out someone has written something new in the ashes
of your life. You are not leaving, you are arriving.*
David Whyte

Earth Science News Week: *Observers at the Western Wall of Jerusalem have
reported rivulets of water trickling down the face of the wall. Religious scholars
and scientists are rushing to the site to investigate. Many are already in
disagreement over the source and the possibility of the consequences.
Fundamentalists of both Christian and Jewish faiths believe that after the well
of Bethesda's waters, where Jesus worked many of his miracles, ran dry in the
ancient time of Rome's destruction of Jerusalem it would only spring forth water
again preceding the end of the world.*

Roger stepped off the floatplane onto the shore of the bay sheltering the once
native village of Ninstints. An elderly native gentleman leaning heavily on
his wooden cane waited to greet him. He peered out at Roger from under
his heavily pinned Toronto Blue Jays baseball cap. The cap and the blue jean
jacket and pants looked much like the native did, heavily creased, overworn
and probably washed about every season or so! He grinned at the old man.

"Hi, I'm Roger Harrison."

"I'm Charlie Stillwaters, your guide, the Watchman for this site. And I'm
glad you called me."

"I called you? I only booked this online. I didn't talk to anyone in
person." He'd tried to stay away from communicating with anyone as much
as possible after what happened to Theodore.

Charlie stared at him with a comical look on his face. "I guess that raises
a most important question. I'll have to jot it down with this pencil that once
belonged to Shakespeare."

Roger stared at the well-chewed pencil as Charlie scribbled on a small pad of paper.

"What makes you think that that stump of a pencil belonged to someone a couple of centuries ago."

The elder put it in his mouth, crunched it a couple of times and stared at it at length. "Well, I can't tell if it's 2b or not 2b."

Roger giggled relaxing his guard. "So, you're called a Watchman. I've seen the

trucks here bearing the decals and heard a little about them over here, what is it exactly?"

"I'm part of the Haida society of Watchmen, we simply watch over the old sites and educate people about our customs and ways. So, my job here is to watch, simply watch, and let others do other things with their lives. In the off-season I'm a Ska'ga, or what you might call a shaman - although shamans are originally what are called the magic people of the Mongols - and I've never visited Asia, although I sure do like Chinese food. I do manage to keep busy watching the Blue Jays on the tube." He looked Roger in the eyes as he talked, "And the nature of your visit?"

"A non-Mongolian shaman. Funny you'd say that. I've had a native elsewhere tell me something bizarre. A native American Hopi, I think. He'd be one of his people's ska-gas like you, I guess. He told me I was a gateway walker."

Charlie laughed. "Gateway-walker, eh?" Charlie lifted the end of his ball cap with his cane and stared up and down at Roger. "Well, I don't like many Americans, except for baseball players. You, I think, are okay though. Let's go for a walk. Besides, this plane is getting ready to take off and will return in a couple of hours with the next load of tourists."

They both stepped away from the shore and walked along the sands and the tall grass. "It's interesting what you say about gateways, we call our lands Xhaaydla Gwaayaay, the Islands On the Boundary between Worlds."

"Boundaries between worlds; that's interesting and quite a coincidence. You say you're a shaman. I'm not sure exactly what they do, but you'd probably know something about boundaries and other worlds." Roger watched the plane as it stirred to life, the engines revving to full throttle as it began coasting along the water and the background faded into the quiet of the day. Replaced by the saline smells of ocean decay, cedar forest and waves generated by the plane leaving in descending intensity rocked the shore. Roger studied them, mesmerized by the concentric circles, reminding him of a dream he had with the Hathor.

"Connections, each is separate, but connected. Like us."

Roger stared blankly at the old man, wondering if was that intuitive that he could pick up his thoughts.

Charlie squinted as he leaned on his cane. "Well, I know this much, something's happened lately. The boundaries have been changing in the last month or so."

"Changing? In what way?"

"Hmm. Well, they're not as solid as they once were. Almost as if certain edges are blurring."

"How long ago did this blurring happen?" Could this have been related to his putting together of the pieces, perhaps his first solid bit of evidence. Too bad Theodore wasn't here to hear this.

"Let's see. I remember watching the Blue Jays ballgame, between them and the Atlanta Braves. I'd taped it earlier that day. It was the last game I could watch before I came out here for a month. It's a good thing I have a VCR to tape the games while I'm away. Ahh, the marvels of modern technology."

"A month? You stay here for a month by yourself?" He didn't have the heart to tell him VCRs were already going the way of the dinosaur it was a wonder his still worked.

"Nah, I've my cane to keep me busy. We chat up quite the storm." He laughed and waved with what Roger saw was an Orca-headed cane. "I remember it now, because the next morning I was up doing some native cleansing rituals as a wave of nausea washed over me."

"A wave? Interesting." A month? Roger thought, how long ago had he put the pieces of the metal together? He made a mental note to check on his laptop when he got back to his room. So much had happened in the last month.

"So, describe this sensation, this blurring, I'm confused."

"Well, it wouldn't make any sense to you but as Yoda, a very old and wise American once quoted, 'I sense a disturbance in the force, young Jedi.'"

Roger smirked.

"So, my turn to ask something now." He leaned on his Orca-crested cane. "Never met a gateway walker before. I met a transvestite from San Francisco once with a bad attitude to life and great taste in clothes. Not quite the same thing I suspect."

They both laughed.

"But enough talk. The truth speaks from other places. Let me look into your eyes." Charlie stared long and hard. Roger wasn't sure if it was just his superstition or maybe this man was very perceptive, but he could sense the native man was looking past boundaries, past the walls of ego and image and into something few people dared to truly look; past even his heart, into his soul. Perhaps. He could be right. "How much time have you got?"

"Two hours before the float plane returns with another group of tourists. Why do you ask?"

"Because it's no mistake that we've been put together, here today, alone. Everything is done for a reason. So, virgin gateway walker on a mission, ready for one crash course in shamanic traveling?"

"Mission? I didn't say I was on a mission."

"Didn't have to. I read it in your eyes and your soul." He smiled, with a crazy far-off look on his face. "Let's go over to the totems, to the one with the three Watchmen on top."

Roger nodded and fell into a slow pace behind Charlie. His mood changed quickly as they walked, as if there were someone watching them, watching him. He just realized that they were alone on this tiny island, itself isolated from the main Queen Charlottes, which themselves were nearly a hundred miles from the mainland. Perhaps it was simply the isolation, or maybe apprehension. So like when he was standing at the airport waiting in line. The silent knowing that things, big things, were beginning to change. Again.

"You're awfully quiet back there."

"Just thinking."

"Well, as you probably know, the Haida were and still are the most powerful and feared of the natives on the West Coast. We'd hunt up and down the coast, as far as Oregon, sometimes taking slaves and raiding villages. Being an island nation, we need fresh blood sometimes to keep strong. Did you know how our name came to be?"

"Can't say I do really, thought it had something to do with a raven opening a clamshell or something."

"Nah, not that. When we'd go over to our neighbors, the Tsimshian, if their scouts spotted our large canoes, they'd take off running into the villages, yelling 'Hide Our Women.'" Charlie laughed.

It took Roger a second to realize Charlie had just caught him with a joke. He burst out laughing and finally realized that Charlie as wacky as he was, wasn't out to harm him. "You got me with that one." He did know, though, that the Haida were indeed at one time the most feared on the BC coast. "So, shamans, I mean Skagas, do they do things like astral travel? You probably read in my eyes that I've never astral traveled before."

"Didn't have to, you just told me, but I can usually sense when one isn't dimensionally challenged." He stopped and smiled out from under his cap.

"What?" This native was like nothing Roger had ever met before, he laughed, well and with a natural cutting sense of humor.

"Simple; you don't believe, so it doesn't exist. It ain't in any science book therefore it can't be real. Correct?"

"Well, yeah. If it truly existed, someone would have proven it by now."

"Yeah, I had that same attitude about fifty years ago. As I got older, I realized I knew a lot less than I thought and now I realize that as I've increased my awareness of things, I know jack shit." Now he knew trusting his intuition was way beyond correct. This insane First Nations Elder was who he needed to speak to and further him on his journey, even if he hadn't washed in a month or two. Which lead to another question, how had he managed to make a flight out here when all the others had cancelled other than himself. He remembered the pilot not caring as their deposits were non-refundable anyways. Another strange coincidence or had Ti-yah done something? "Then I must not know shit, is that what you're saying?"

"No," he laughed, "you don't even know Jack yet, let alone shit. That's a whole other conversation. One I haven't got time to go into today. Okay. The first major principle of traveling between dimensions is this. Before you take off, even for a brief trip, you must leave a safe place behind. One you can return to if you get lost or in trouble. I retreat to a couple of places, but one of my main ones is here under this totem with the three guardians, the three Watchmen." They stood under one of the remaining totems, leaning precariously to one side. Another lay on the ground beside them. Others like haunting mortuary stones in an abandoned graveyard stood silently around them. The totems of Ninstints. He shivered, remembering the faces from his living room painting staring at him for so many years and now he stood among them.

As for Charlie, he was an odd duck, he thought. Although he'd never met a native, nor a shaman, he'd never even heard of one with attitude that back talked to a white man. Maybe Canadian first nations were a whole lot different.

"So, tell me what you see when you stand here before this totem and stare around."

"Well, I see the aging totems, the trees of the forest, the bay before us."

Charlie poked him in the ribs with his Orca-headed walking stick.

"Hey!"

"Don't give me the tourist brochure crap. I ain't got the time. I want to know what you see when your eyes are closed. I want to know what you've sensed since you got here."

"But if I shut my eyes I can't see."

"Jeezus, I've only got two hours here, not a week. I think you need to ground. The eyes often overwhelm all the other senses. Okay, take off your shoes and socks, then I want you to clear your mind of all thoughts and reach out with one hand and touch this totem." Charlie stared up at the totem into the eyes of the Raven, "It's okay, my dear friends, he'll be gentle with him, this time."

Roger opened his eyes a little. Maybe this shaman was actually nuts. Wouldn't most people go bananas sitting out here a month at a time with no electricity or anyone to talk to, except maybe dead spirits. "You're not going to make me strip are you?" He had visions of a crazed native chasing him around the woods naked.

"No, dummy. I'm trying to establish a connection between you, earth and spirit. Besides you're not my type. I usually like them a little more buxom and this cane only swings one way." He smirked. "And with less attitude and more trust. I should have listened to my uncle he said the best thing in life is to chase fast whiskey and slow women. Instead, I picked slow women and fast baseball. So, we've just wasted fifteen minutes, so no more twenty questions and let's get on with the show, shall we? You'll simply have to trust that I am wise teacher and you are grasshopper the naive student."

"It's funny you'd say that, seeing without the eyes. The Hopi said that too."

"I see my southern cousins are wise indeed. Now tell me what you sense with all of your senses."

Roger took off his socks, the chill of the damp grass sent shivers through him. He tried to settle his thoughts down grounding his bare feet into the earth. The coolness of the earth eased his racing mind. Slowing, coalescing. The moss, a sponge that absorbed his matter and dispersed his energy into the world allowing him to connect to the earth, the planet itself.

"Good, that is good. Now reach over and put one hand against the totem and tell me what you hear, taste, smell and feel, with all of your senses. What are they telling you, right now."

"Strange, I hear the surf and the rustle of trees. Taste, I can only taste the wetness on my lips, dryness, I actually need some water. The air is rich with the tang of salt water and the clear crispness of pine and juniper. Sight? Yes, I see the shadows of the forest, and the glowing of the sun against my eyelids. I feel the roughness of the bark, and the lines. Yes, lines cut by the workers who created this totem." His hands ran steadily over the bark, smoothed by native artists hands nearly two hundred years ago, smoothed even further by time, rain and hail. "And... This is gonna sound silly."

"No judgment here. Just tell me whatever comes up."

"I can feel, sense, not sure what it is, but the fears, the anxiety of the carvers, wanting to make sure each chip taken away, each stroke, is revealing the being trapped inside. The pride as this totem is being created. No, not created, the being freed that this artist knew existed within."

"Good. I see there is potential there after all. Good potential. Now tell me about the other sense. You're strong there, just let go."

"Which other?"

"The one." Charlie's cane thumped into the ground like a person hitting a large gong sounding what was about to begin.

Roger moved as he felt the air rush, piling up behind him, warning him and Charlie's stick swatted only empty air. "Good, the sense is strong."

"How'd I know that?"

Charlie jabbed him in ribs.

"OW!"

"Because I let you and you picked up on it. Now silence and concentrate questioning does nothing but destroy serenity and put you into ego. You must stay in subconscious here. I haven't time to explain fully, but there are three levels of spirit in all of us. The conscious, the subconscious, and the superconscious. The superconscious is where people like me, and perhaps you if you stop asking questions, go. Now again. Tell me what you really see in your mind from your heart. Like when you began to talk about the carvers. Speak, as it comes to you, there is no right way here. Shut down the part that is asking questions and try to achieve silence and listen to the world around you."

Roger tried clearing his mind, again and again, but it wasn't easy. Time ticked slowly away. Air stirred up high, the plane was returning.

"Every time a question comes shove it aside, eventually you'll grow quiet."

After many long minutes in silence coolness began seeping into his feet. Grassy moss tickled his toes. Dew oozed its way to the ground, pulling at him. He let himself slip further into a quiet state, earth pulling away, rather enjoying the harmony of this moment. He took several deep grounding breaths like the Hathor told him.

"Good, it is beginning."

Air moved in soft waves on the breeze, tangents of smells, the ocean, salt decay mingling with the forest's freshness. Juniper and cedar, moving to the sway of the ocean's breath. Releasing cloying aromas, essences of their being.

In the grasp of smells other essences moved. Old graceful beings, like souls. Reaching out, he felt them. New souls and old souls like the ones in the totem milling about, touching him. Air, thick with them, it was obvious now.

Roughness of bark worked so many years ago into the images of the beings stored inside. Beings that still hung like mist in this place waiting to be found by those in the know.

Rustling, he sensed the rustling of birds, of eagles and ravens. Of great birds that moved before the dawn of time, avian beings of legend, that with one flap would send thunderclaps echoing over the hills.

Whispers.

Roger turned, allowing his ears to hear beneath the gentle wash of surf. Whispers from everywhere, arriving here, coming to him.

No, not arriving, they were here all the time, only he didn't hear them for they were talking through his hand attached to the totem. Voices of beings, that spoke without talking, in no language he knew. Beings that the carvers knew dwelled within the wood, beings they were in contact with and released. The voices of the wood itself calling to the carvers and to those who could hear.

Ovoid eyes talking from the depths of ancient carved cedar. Eyes that flickered and stared at him. Pulling him into their ancient souls. Tumbling into bowels of the wood.

"Holy! What was that?" Roger opened his eyes and instinctively pulled his hand away from the totem.

Charlie frowned.

"Sorry, I know, no questions. I got scared for a moment, like being on an edge and letting go."

"You were there. Now again, try again."

He closed his eyes, but it was of no use. Like wisps of mist, they were gone. He had too many questions disturbing his solitude. Finally, Roger opened his eyes. "It's no good. My mind is asking too many questions. Is this what shamans do?"

"Very similar, but I can see the session is over. You've done enough for today and besides the plane will be here early, so we might as well stop and go have some herbal tea I brewed while you were gone. You've done well, I think you have gifts, the Hopi man could be right."

"Gone? But weren't you here watching me the whole time? I mean, I could sense your presence, here watching me."

"What you sensed is what I wanted you to experience of myself while I made tea. But that is a matter of far greater difficulty and not something you will be ready to do yet. But you are good. Like I said, when you are traveling you must have a place solidly locked into your mind to return to. This can be your safe place if you so choose."

As they walked back to the hut Roger heard the drone of the approaching plane dimly in the background. "How'd you..."

"Oh, grasshopper, any master will not divulge all of his secrets right away."

"This super-consciousness, what exactly is it?"

"It's like the higher being, the seventh chakra as the Hindus say. Your connection to God and the energy of the universe, the energy that is always out there."

"But, those eyes that opened, what were they?"

"The soul of the wood, the beings the carvers knew lay inside. Who's to say the trees aren't alive in their own right?"

The rest of the time until the float plane landed and disgorged its passengers, Roger sat silently, thinking about what had just happened. Charlie let him be and greeted his new visitors. He merely smiled at Roger as he boarded the plane. But the look in the old Ska-ga's eyes were enough. "It begins," he whispered into Roger's head.

Roger shivered, and knew he was right.

****

Charlie walked back to the totems lining the beach as the last plane rose in the air and he was once again alone. He hadn't told Roger about the other things that had happened this last month, perhaps he should have. The voices and the strange visions.

"Ch-ar-lie." He turned at the calling of his name. He thought it was one of the German visitors at first, until he saw an indistinct image wavering before him on the beach. Hard to make out.

"Charlie." Much stronger than last time. The image solidified. Someone he recognized and visited in the other realms. A person he cared about more than anything else; Lucy. The only woman he ever loved, who died in his arms when he was twenty-one and too inexperienced to save her.

"How is this possible?" He walked towards her and as he reached out to touch her his arm blurred. Charlie looked down at himself, he was growing indistinct, fading.

"Charlie, my love, what is happening?"

"Don't know, transference between dimensions? This shouldn't be possible." The edges of boundaries dissipating. Pieces of him pulling away and parts of her were streaming towards him. Growing in mass. Dizziness swam in waves of nausea.

Charlie collapsed on the beach, the hollow echo of his wooden cane striking the rocks of the beach, reverberating in the background. The orca carved cane stared skyward at the watchmen staring back.

Charlie wasn't sure where he was as he solidified and opened his eyes, but he knew he wasn't on Earth anymore.

A native woman crying out filled the air as the Orca-headed cane stared up at the sky pleading. The watchmen? They did as they had for centuries, and simply watched.

****

The sound of the surf crashing against the rocks drifted on air with the sharp tang of salt through Roger's window at the Haida Windsong Bed and Breakfast. Located near the town of Massett, at the very top of Haida Gwaii, the surf crashing in as it had done for eternity, coming on currents from as far away as Japan. Endless thrumming until it became a dull white noise. He flicked on his laptop, well it was Theodore's laptop, and checked the date recorded on the camcorder when they connected the pieces of the alien metal against the Major League Baseball schedule. There was a baseball game between the Expos and the Braves earlier that day. How do you explain that one? How did Charlie know? And if an intuitive like him knew, did others? Roger tapped his thumb against the laptop. This also confirmed something else. They had released an energy burst, a signal, but to whom and what would be affected?

Man, did he miss Theodore and wished he were here now to talk to. He had the man's collected knowledge sitting on bytes before him, and even though he could ramble on like some delusional old man, it that wasn't the same as having a friend to bounce ideas off. To ask questions, like where to go from here.

Sedona was the next logical step. At least he knew what he had to do there. But that wasn't what was bugging him. He stared at the walls. Something else was bugging him, but what? He put on his shoes and left his room to walk along the beach.

What had Charlie done?

Roger walked through a stand of small windswept pines, one side bare from the constant buffeting of the ocean's wind.

Surf crashed, losing itself in the froth, the ocean's relentless pounding, eroding away at the walls of rock, trying to reach out. In the morning it would be scant molecules closer to him. In that there was something terrifying but there was more.

Charlie had begun something oddly familiar and yet arcane. Nothing he'd ever even remotely believed in his whole life.

Totems had reached out through the soul of the wood and actually tried to talk to him.

Tell him something. The something wasn't the problem though.

It was the fact that inside he understood what they were saying. Charlie said they spoke to him in ancient Haida, the only language they knew.

In the background surf crashed away. He knew that language, intimately. Had lived a lifetime, perhaps several in it.

Roger closed his eyes. This was nuts, all nuts and so had everything else been up to now.

What Charlie had done was open doors to places he'd never been, never knew existed. Yet lived there many lifetimes.

Begun the journey, the one that was always there, the new inner journey. The one he was born to live, that's what Charlie had done. Roger walked back to his room and started up the laptop again and booked tickets for Sedona.

Yes, they began a conversation in words he knew, and he knew they'd be back to continue what he'd started.

What had Charlie done? And how in the world did Tiyah know he'd open up doors for Roger to begin walking through.

Chapter Eleven

Science News, Washington

The Hubble telescope has recently spotted what appears to be an ancient planet or sun at the very center of our galaxy. It seems to be behind a permanent veil of cloudy matter. Calculations have determined that the age of the galactic core is around thirty billion years. Scientists have long theorized over what, if anything, exists at the galactic center.

Indian Hinduists have responded by saying that, according to their ancient texts, that is where God resides.

****

Dryness and heat greeted him as Roger squinted under the hot Arizona sun. Such a change from the lush dampness of Haida Gwaii. Scant greenery here; he wondered how people managed to survive out here and why, yet they did. The indomitable will of humanity. To live and flourish in such hostile environments. He wiped his brow, red dust clung to the back of his hand, reminding him of the red soil of Haida Gwaii. Only yesterday yet it seemed like a lifetime away.

The Enchantress Lodge was behind him, the memories of him and Beth so long ago. He'd searched all afternoon for the entranceway to the cavern in Boynton Canyon, marching up and down, only it wasn't there. Nothing was as he remembered it, in fact he hadn't paid much attention when he left last time in the dark, thinking he'd not be returning. Now not only did Sherida's life depend on it, but probably all of humanity's as well.

Mixed feelings welled up as he wiped away another streak of sweat. Memories of another time, being newlywed, faded into the confines of the ochre rock. He sighed as he sat down. He'd walked through the town earlier, even visited the same washroom that the old Hopi man had met him in, somehow hoping that he'd unexpectedly appear. Only there was no one, he knew this. The others had been taken away, now this trip he had to do on his own, he'd be alone.

The journey within doesn't come with traveling companions. He sighed alone, wishing Beth could be waiting back in his room at the lodge. They could make love again. It had been awhile, were people on spiritual journeys supposed to be celibate as well?

The sun's fire radiated up from the baked soil as Roger sat down in about the same area as last time.

Closing his eyes he grounded himself. What was it Charlie had said? Use a focal point somewhere to return to, a grounding anchor. He thought of the totems of Ninstints, their eyes wide open. The watchmen simply doing what they've done for eternity. As they've always done, simply watch and stare at him and at life going by, the universe unfolding. He'd use them as Charlie suggested, for an anchor, a safe place. For that was how he felt now, safe in their presence. He realized now that it was them, that they'd only been trying to establish contact with him earlier, in their own way. A way he'd begun to understand, somehow.

He sat for a long time letting himself relax, ground. Overhead an eagle cried, coolness seeped into the air, the sun setting. The universe unfolding and him just resting, grounding into the earth.

He was ready. Roger looked out not with his eyes, but his soul senses, Only, it hadn't worked, they'd deceived him with that which they couldn't see.

"Use the other senses and look in the places that exist where vision doesn't dwell." Charlie had said. "Look through them."

Scared, Roger took a deep breath, reached out to touch the Haida totem in his mind. The Tadn-skeel, Charlie called them. Under their conical hats, eyes wide open, they could see in all directions; north, east, south, west, up, down and inside or out.

Roger looked out with the other sense, as Charlie had called it, and the Hopi elder had eluded too. However, he'd done it last time, innately he'd found the entranceway this way.

"Let the illusion of perception wash away reality," whispered the Tadn-skeel as they watched from their lofty perches. He wondered if the shaman was behind all this? The sound of a cane tapping on the ground echoed. Who saw whom through another's eyes, Roger wondered. "Crafty devil," Roger smirked as a glistening pathway of crystals light up before him.

It had been there the whole time. Somewhere in his mind he heard the giggle of the shaman's voice.

He stood up and walked into the cave. Staring around Roger moved to the center of the room. The haphazard array of crystals glittered away.

Trust the sense, the shaman with the baseball fetish had told him.

He let the energy of the earth well up from below, it was already so strong here. Uncontaminated by man's machinations. Protection, everything here had been protected for a millennium. Unused. He turned, that was the link. That was what he had felt last time. Energy idling, certain combinations could produce such amazing results. Yet here was simply a rest. A place where potential needed a gathering point.

Roger circled the crystals and began to move them around until one set off an unearthly glow. He left that one in its new place. Roger continued to set the rest along the outside perimeter. When he was done, he took the last one and placed it in the center. A low hum began to fill the room as each crystal burst into a different colored spectrum of light, all exploding and mixing into a brilliant white light. The pure energy of the universe, he thought. Reconnected.

Done, he opened his eyes and stared into the stars of the clear Arizona night sky. Energy blazing back. Somewhere the coyotes howled, but he had no worries, for he knew they would not come for him tonight.

As he stood up the word Peru called from the eyes of the totems. Whispering repeatedly, over and over again.

"Thanks, Charlie, you're too much," he muttered as he walked towards the inn in the dark. But he'd done it, traversed the gateway.

****

Roger stood on the high plains; the city of Cusco in Peru spread out below. Not taking any chances he'd booked a flight here the moment he left Sedona using Theodore's credit card, only because he needed more cash. He'd also taking out as much cash as he could on the card and hoped it would pay for everything else along the way. Hoping to leave as little a trail as possible. Tiyah may have been right, someone or something could be after him.

Behind him the megalithic walls of Sacsayhuaman towered as they had for a millennium. Ricardo, the guide of the tour group he joined for this trip, pointed to the outlines of a depression in the rock. It looked vaguely like an upright snake.

"Ancient warriors who put their hands inside the snake's head were reputed to receive great powers. As you can see, my compass spins madly as I place it in the head of the snake."

Everyone in the group stared as the needles of his compass spun around and around. The young children rushed up to the depression and fought with each other as they tried to stick their hands in, just as quickly scampered away once they had. Several of the adults approached and withdrew their hands, rubbing them.

Roger waited, and when everyone else was done and had begun to wander away, stood before the depression. Without any thought he stuck his hand in.

Wind rushed away tugging on his breath. He gasped, silver ions of energy sparkled from his lips, wavered for a moment, then flashed zipping away on vacuous currents created all around him. He looked around, only blackness above him and earth below him. He was not here but, on a peak overlooking a desert rushing away into the distance. The ions of his breath left streaks of silver glisters of light as they zipped away to follow other lines of sparkles.

Energy, he was watching lines of energy pouring across the desert. A vortex, he was in the center of a vortex. No, he was the center.

The plains of the desert stretched away into the distance, a long way from this height. In certain areas other lines of energy flowed, coalescing as shapes swirled. Zipping off to other centers and others until a celestial grid sprawled vast below. Some centers glowed, bubbled and surged with life; others remained diffused in shadow.

"Not connected," he realized. A jab from his pocket, he pulled a green heart-shaped crystal free. The one Tiyah had given him.

He turned it over and stared all around him. This was what he was doing, hooking up the energy grid of the Earth. This was the grid and somehow this depression was a portal and he'd just ...

Walked.

Through a gateway.

Charlie and the Hopi were right. Roger looked down and spotted a cutout in the rock. Knowing what had to be done he bent over and placed the heart into the hole and stood back as this portion of the web began to explode in dancing pinpoints of light. Visions of Machu Picchu swam by, his next journey. He closed his hand and was back before the walls of Sacsahuaman.

Roger tucked the crystal into his pocket and hurried to catch the group.

Gateway walker. In the shift of things, he knew life would never be the same, nor could he ever return home. It was beginning to make sense. He'd just gone to Kansas on the yellow brick road.

And he liked it.

****

Back in the hotel in Cusco, Roger studied the energy lines on the grid Theodore had superimposed on a map of the world.

There was a center in the Caroline Islands at Nan Matol where ancient basalt remains had been found. No one knows who put them there, or how.

Roger glanced through Theodore's notes; there are twelve pentagram centers of energy on the Earth. He looks at the twelve markings and superimposed a map of ancient locations over it. Easter Island, Nan Matol, Sea of Japan, Machu Picchu, Pyramids, Zimbabwe, Indus Valley, Bermuda Triangle, Angkor Wat, Stonehenge, Hopi, Ularu, all line up, or at least very close.

Although with continental drift two centers were under the ocean, off the Sea of Japan and the Bermuda Triangle. *Well, that would explain all the bizarre happenings and airplane disappearances there.*

Roger knew where to go next. He'd already booked tickets on the train ride up to Machu Picchu. He cautiously began to think that this could be easier than he first thought.

A section caught his eye in Theodore's table of contents.

He stared at a picture of a statue found of the Egyptian female pharaoh Nefertiti. She was without her long Pharoah's crown. Her skull was long and misshapen, the ears elongated too, as well as her chin. A note next to the photo in Theodore's handwriting read "Odd; why would they make a statue of her like that? They wouldn't. Not unless she actually looked that way." In fact, carvings of the Pharoah Akhenaten and several of his children resembled her as well.

Roger scanned back through his friend's notes until he found the section on ancient Haida. Then he read the notes Theodore made on the tradition of elongating the misshaping the skulls of their females, as well as inserting labrets into their lips. People that did this were considered high born, godly. It was also funny that the Haida language was different, unrelated to any of the tribes around them.

And others, the natives of Easter Island, the Olmec, several African and Polynesian tribes. "Coincidence?" Theodore had written.

All of them, the Haida, the Moai statues of Easter Island, ovoid eyes staring into the heavens. Looking for something, or perhaps waiting.

"Staring at what?" Theodore wrote. "Waiting for what?"

"The spotting of the galactic center, of God. Ascension," Theodore theorized. "Signifying when the next seeding will take place when their Gods return. When it happens, your eyes begin to enlarge and glow a brilliant white." Roger sat stunned, how was this possible? Or was Theodore a little nuts from all of his research? Or could it be that is what happens when you begin to ascend into the fourth dimension, or your body transforms into energy?

He yawned. It was time to get some sleep. Vague connections. Roger shook his head, this man had studied his whole lifetime. Yet he was right about the Dogon. And their God turned out to look just like the ones at Sedona.

Coincidence? Roger shivered. He remembered the Easter Island story of the Rongo-Rongo boards. The ancient language they used, that complicated on such a remote island. A language that used ninety something characters from the oldest Indus Valley culture. A culture that reportedly had complete texts, thousands of pages, written on the use and maintenance of flying machines, like the ones inscribed on the walls of Dendara.

Coincidence? Had they flown there somehow from India?

Roger yawned and shut down the laptop. Was this all possible? What if there was some truth to this? Sherida had told him there were many races out there. Many had visited Earth in the past. Why? If all of this were true? Why do they keep returning to visit us again and again. What do they want of us?

****

"Got him!" Zolnar blinked at the screen. Someone had booked using a credit card under a Theodore Nelson, the same human that he'd ordered killed in Seattle. A flight to Arizona and now to Peru. "If he is going to Peru, there is only one place he'll end up at with no way out, and I intend to have people waiting there for him."

****

Roger tucked the laptop into his backpack as he got off the train. The air was thin; they were so high up here in Machu Picchu, and the dizziness caused by the mountain air struck him. How was it possible anyone could build anything up here? He could barely breathe. Someone in front of him stumbled. A lady. Roger helped her up.

"Are you okay?" he asked, not even knowing if she spoke English, especially as she was dark-skinned. Mexican or Middle Eastern, or ....

"Do not act as if you know me. You are in danger here."

Roger caught his breath, more from surprise than from lack of oxygen, as he saw a glimpse of her face under a shawl. "Tiy ...". He stopped. What was she doing here, of all places.

The rest of the group halted while he helped her up.

"Go ahead. We'll catch up, after I've helped this lady."

"No," she gasped. "I'm alright. If you don't mind me leaning on you, kind sir," she moaned loudly. "I just twisted my ankle."

Roger put his arm around her and the group continued down the trail to the ruins.

"Whatever you do, do not leave the group just yet. And don't look around, act as a tourist." They walked on. "There are three men in back, all white. I think as long as we stay in the group, we're okay for now. Get to

Intihuatana, The Hitching Post of the Sun. You'll need this." She pressed a small green crystal into his hand.

"Why there?" Roger lifted his camera and calmly took a picture of the mountain behind them. She was right. Three scruffy-looking white men lingered near the rear of the group trying not watch him.

"I see them," he whispered. "How do they know I'm here?'

"Not important. You must enter the gateway and find the Crystal Tower, leave by the gateway."

"Travel to somewhere else? But how do I do that?"

"These men will not let you return alive to the train. You are trapped here, there is no other way out. Find the Crystal Tower, use the gateway. There is no other choice."

The slightest slip-up meant his death and Tiyah seemed so calmly matter of fact about it. How did she know he was here unless she'd been watching him the whole time?

The group stopped and the tour guide spoke of several features. "The Hitching Post of the Sun is where?" Tiyah asked.

Then the group split in several directions.

"Shit. This is bad," Roger said, clutching at Tiyah as they joined up with the smaller group. The three men followed close behind. The clink of something metallic. His heart pounded; he was going to die here. He was sure of it. This was no longer fun, whoever or whatever was after him had already killed Theodore, possibly Sherida, and had the technology to track him.

"Go on," she whispered. "The Hitching Post of the Sun is just around the next corner."

Before he had a chance to defend her, Tiyah stumbled and gently pushed Roger ahead. He let her go, knowing the three men were not after her, or even knew she was here at all.

"Help me," she gasped, "the air can't breathe." She grabbed at the three men in passing. The three stopped for a moment to help her up.

In that split second, Roger sprinted around the bend and up the trail. He had mere seconds. Now what? he stood before the Hitching Post panting. Oxygen, scarce at this altitude, screamed to get into his lungs.

He stood before a large square of carved rock with a central piece sticking out of it. Archaeologists called it a sundial. Perhaps it was. In Theodore's notes it was rumored that a crystal tower once stood on this spot. Used like a tuning fork, the crystal tower allowed priests to channel energy and align themselves with other dimensions.

Tuning fork?

The rustle of voices behind him. "Search over there. I think he went this way." Click of guns drawn.

This better work. He jumped over the rope that partitioned off the area and sat down on the surface of the Hitching Post. He hit the portion of stone sticking up with the green crystal.

Reverberations rang out, shuddering through him, through the rock. Ripples of vibrations, ringing out like concentric circles in a pond. The crystal began to vibrate in tune with the ringing. He let himself relax, allowing the sound waves to vibrate through him, aligning himself in time to their essence. Pulling him away.

"No one here, damn he must have gone some other way." Shouts lost in the void. Tiyah was right.

He closed his eyes as the world spun away tumbling. Falling through space like being dropped off a cliff with no end in sight. "Safe place. My safe place. I'd forgotten." He fought back his panic thinking of Ninstints, the Watchmen. Instantly, he felt himself slammed onto the sandy shore of Anthony Island. Silent totems lined up watching him in morbid fascination. He gasped, trying to get his breath back. "God! What the hell was that?"

Roger knew if Charlie stood here now, he'd be laughing. "Still in training I see, virgin Gateway walker!"

Roger stood up and brushed himself off, spitting sand out of his mouth. *Next time it'll be safe place with a mattress to land on.* He took a deep breath and squatted beneath Charlie's totem. "Okay time to give this another try. Hope Tiyah's okay."

He knew she would be it was him they were after. "Besides, any chick that old could probably look after herself," he muttered, remembering how fast she could run and the jolt she'd given him at Stonehenge. Taking in a few deep breaths, he grounded himself before visualizing the image of the Hitching Post at Machu Picchu.

This time, instead of falling he felt the rush of cool air and the crisp smell of mountain breezes and opened his eyes. To his surprise he wasn't on the mountaintop at Machu Picchu but instead stood in a vast room. As he turned around, he realized he wasn't in a cavernous room but on a huge plain. In front of him floated a transparent map, made from some sort of translucent material. The figures he recognized he had seen a dozen times on TV before he saw them again in Theodore's notes, Nazca. He was on the plain above the Nazca lines. Whether this was some sort of astral projection or real he wasn't sure.

Only instead of seeing figures inscribed in sand and rock, they were etched in glowing lights. Crystals, hundreds and thousands of crystals everywhere, patterns interlaced. Roger stumbled around until he came to the one scientist had called the star. It looked more like a crystal growth if converted to a three-dimensional image. He counted the creatures on the map board that glowed, there were twelve main ones. Three of them glistened slightly more than the rest. So many learned professionals had tried to figure out what all of these markings represented. Roger stared at the map floating in front of him; somehow all of this was a ley line map. The whole plain, no, the entire planet. The lines radiated out, draining into the mountains. "Impossible," he said to himself, "impossible." He looked at the three that glowed more than the rest, and followed a single line down to the star, it should be the next one to energize or awaken, whatever Sherida had called it.

Sherida! He hoped she was okay. Roger touched his finger to the floating image of the star pattern and closed his eyes. He stood before a tall tower of white crystal. At the base several smaller crystals lay in a radiating pattern all around it. Intuitively he bent over and rearranged several until they more closely resembled the pattern on the ley map he'd seen at Nazca. As Roger laid the last crystal in place a hum and light began to flood up through the base as the entire crystal structure began to softly glow.

He was done.

Now the hard part. How to get out of here without ending up back at Machu Picchu. How to use the gateway.

He thought of the glowing map of the Nazca plain and was instantly there. Of course. Roger studied the floating map before him. The star pattern now glowed as brightly as the rest. Tiyah was right, she'd known about his map, but it was up to him to find it. This map showed him the patterns on the plain, it also showed him the ley lines. This map in itself was the gateway to travel between ley line convergence points. Unlocking the crystal tower had led him to here. He stood before the shimmering lights of the plain and laughed. The ley line map, the gateway between energy centers here, and eventually, when they are all aligned, probably the rest of the galaxy. From here, if he entered the energy grid, he should be able to travel via the gateway to the rest. Only he had to get out of Peru alive. Unscrupulous men had ways of finding him, especially in towns like this.

Roger closed his eyes and thought hard about his hotel room and found himself lying on his bed. *Well, that was easy.*

He stuffed his belongings into his suitcase and quickly bolted out the back entrance. Whoever was after him probably knew what hotel he was in also and would come looking as soon as they came down from Machu Picchu. He went further down the road and paid cash to get another room. In this country, as well as a lot of others, cash hid most tracks and left no traces.

He knew one thing, he couldn't go on outrunning these guys, they'd know where his next stop was. They'd been waiting here at Machu Picchu, so no online ticket bookings. They were tracking him through the tickets, probably credit cards. He booked two tickets, one to Easter Island and the other to Australia at the airport. Taking out as much cash as the cards would allow, he instead chartered a plane with cash from the next nearest airport.

If Theodore's notes were right the next logical step would be Easter Island, but the best place would be the next largest gatherings of ley lines, which was in Australia. Theodore called it the female center of the energy grids, like Egypt was the male center. This would hopefully throw off his pursuers and Australia was a big place to get lost in. From there he could use the gateway. He hoped, for Sherida's sake, and perhaps the entire planets. "Oh, why couldn't I just have booked a simple holiday in Hawaii instead of listening to Bill and going to Sedona. I'd probably be in bed with Beth right now," he moaned, feeling the urge hardening inside him. What he'd give to hold her right now and make love to her. "Damn." He turned off his light, exhaustion quickly pulled him into the warmth of the covers.

The trail. As soon as he closed his eyes Roger could sense it again. On the trail again. A crack in the bushes, the pungent smell of wet canine. This time he didn't have time to run, nor be pursued, it slid from the bushes and glared at him. A low growl and the black dog leapt for his throat.

Roger jumped up, "Shit," he muttered. Was this his subconscious fear? He propped a chair against the doorknob and tried going back to sleep. Each groan in the hallway, crack from something outside intensified. Murmurs from passing guests. It took a long time to fall asleep.

****

Roger dreamed of temples; ancient temples built to pay homage to the gods. Sumerian, Chinese, Thai, etcetera. Once grand civilizations. From the temple walls he stood looking out over the dark forest. That's when he spotted them. Small furtive figures hiding in the undergrowth. Their eyes glaring his way, curious. His crew had built this temple to protect themselves from the denizens and the carnivores of the planet.

They skulked around during the day, more brazen at night. They were like him, nearly. The earlobes weren't as long. But they were men, how was that? These were not the transplanted ones that they'd brought to this world.

Barbarian hordes in another time?

He stared at himself. He was human or at least human looking. He stared closer, noticing the subtle differences. These were the original inhabitants of this planet, crude and dirty natives, barely above the fire-making stage. They wore disheveled skins from animals they'd hunted. Yet already they'd showed no fear and quite a sense of intelligence. His race a millennia ago.

He studied them as they slept in the trees during the day, or as they ventured out on occasion as he wandered through the magnificent gardens his people had created in this world. A paradise, lush dense paradise set amongst towering temples.

The males ran away. But he began to study the females, cavorting as they played in the waters, enjoying themselves. They'd proved to be very socially able.

He noticed one in particular. He watched her for weeks. Every time he went to the gardens she was there. She studied him also and grew less fearful.

Until one day she stood before him. Nervous but unafraid. To her he was a god.

He smiled. she smiled back. There was so much he wanted to share with her, but couldn't, for his mission was nearly done here.

But she, he thought of her often. Her dark tanned skin, long flowing hair and her breasts, her naked breasts. The curve of her hips. The flatness of her belly.

He couldn't interfere, he knew this. No contact between us. Wasn't allowed to but did anyway.

Timidly, she began to respond, excited. And days before he had to go, they made love.

Releasing himself into her. Knowing this wasn't right but feeling the love inside. Knowing he'd never feel this again. The love of the universe.

They made love all of that last week. Then he had to go.

He knew his seed inside her had begun to grow, should have stopped it, it was forbidden. But didn't, what born of love was wrong?

She would bear his offspring. His DNA would spread and change these people. He only wanted to be with her, tears fell as he stared out into the window as their vessel climbed into the vast reaches of space and he was going home.

She was not like the women of his kind. She was dark, dusky, primal. That's how she made him feel. Alive, and earthy, just like this world. She'd shriek, bite at him as they made love.

So, unlike the cool sophistication of home. His kind were intelligent, regal, cultured, boring.

He realized, too late as his ship left Earth's orbit, he was leaving home never to return.

Chapter Twelve

Earthweek Science News

Report from the Mayo Clinic verifies the findings of other clinics, that most children tested under the age of twelve have not one pair of DNA strands, but two, three or higher. "This corresponds with us entering the photon belt," stated Tom Arnold, a well-known psychic and astronomer. With the speed up of the vibrational field of earth comes new patterns of growth and changes in Earth's magnetic field and all living creatures that exist in that field. Other scientists have debunked his findings as rubbish.

****

Mist, heavy and oppressive, hangs in the air. The stink of death permeates up through the soil. I stare at crumbling stone. An old graveyard. Edifices to forgotten lives lean at obscene angles. Moss, with its slow vociferous touch obliterates humanity's struggles with nature's relentlessly obscuring hands. It claims back entire generations, past loves, broken dreams, and fulfilled lives. Dew covers the grass in the dim sunlight, dawn or dusk, I can't tell which.

Gravel crunches behind me and I turn, my heart catching in my throat. The Hathor, sliding from behind one of the obelisks that bears a figure in its image. I step closer but can't read the language on the marbled surface. Perhaps I'm not even on Earth. "This is you?"

"I left my body many lifetimes ago. This realm of the fourth chakra that you enter next is of the heart."

I smell the dankness, the must of earth, raw decaying earth. Fetid dampness with the decomposing remains of what once was alive and vibrant in another age. "What heart is there in death?" And, I wonder, in this being that seems so drab and unassumingly boring.

The Hathor appears to ignore my question. "Breath is the connection between the lower body chakras and the mind or the higher chakras and comes from the heart. The heart is where everything comes together and begins to form into the higher spiritual forms."

"There is only death, decay, and rotting memories here. I don't get it."

"Hm, you've worked hard and well to come this far. I'd hate to have to begin again."

I stare into the shifting mist. "I guess I'm not quite ready for this learning. I don't see the connection I can only see finality and death."

"Ah, perhaps that is the problem, awareness?"

"Well, I ..." My answer is crucial. I blink, and in the flicker between the shutter of eyelids, the brush of mist, the cool of night air caresses me. "There is more here. I have let the eyes become my consciousness again."

The Hathor smiles. "They are the doorways of illusion."

"Like blinders, they show the easy road before me. I haven't truly tried to perceive what exists beyond vision. Just like there is much existence beyond death." As I speak blurred images shift by. Vague thoughts creep in.

"Then you have learned much more than you realize. So, close the doorways and be still, listen. Allow your other senses to enter and be heard for they are already trying to speak."

Nearly the exact words that Charlie had said to me. "Have you ever dealt with a native shaman from the west coast of my world?"

"Orca cane, sardonic humor, intuitive beyond his own good?"

"That sums him up."

"Can't say I have." It smiles and I laugh.

There is much heart, more than I realized in this austere being called Hathor. I close my eyes and begin the hard process of washing away thoughts, blocking them as they enter, until only my heartbeat pounds in my ears. Another gift of learning from Charlie, I wondered if I'd ever get the chance to thank him.

"Breathe, listen only to your own breath as you go inside, not your thoughts, to where the fourth chakra dwells."

Soon all I hear is the sound of air entering, air leaving, keeping me alive. Oxygen entering the bloodstream, rushing back and forth to a soothing rhythmic throb. Beating, no stress, a body at peace, in harmony with itself and its environment.

Then I hear another's beat, rapid and small, weak. I open my eyes and cry out. The voice of a newborn? A woman's tear-streaked face. She smiles, the joy emanating from her eyes overwhelming. I want to cry, to hold her, only I can't. My arms are too weak, I can barely lift them. The constant burble of liquid and the steady thump of the heart that sustains my life is replaced by audible voices and the odd cooling sensation of moisture evaporating from my skin, air, drying me for the first time. This is what it is like to be born? From somewhere I hear a snip and her heartbeat is gone. My heartbeat thumps hard, accelerating as it begins seeking to begin its lifelong task. I'm on my own, my life has begun without the life-support of my mother. All that I know, my sustenance, my security is gone. Now it is up to me to begin the life she started. Somewhere on a blank stage my heart pounds and begins to memorize this new life.

I'm wrapped in bedding and snuggle up next to her. She hugs me, places a kiss on my forehead and places me next to her breast. Her familiar heartbeat, my old life returns, but it is so different now, in the background. I've experienced so much since I've heard it last. Air on my skin, roughness of blanket cuddling me, hands touching. Voices talking in the background, once mere reverberations and the smell of musky skin against me.

The compulsion to suckle is strong so I latch on and warm nourishment enters my body. I smile up at her, milk dribbling from my lips as her life essence enters me again. I close my eyes content.

I stared down at my child, my first. She is so helpless, so tiny. No one said they were so tiny. I want to cry, from jubilation and fear. So much I have to do for her now. How could I possibly look after her and raise ... my God! Life takes on a terrifying slant.

Still, this is my creation, my child, my charge. Happiness sings to my soul as I clasp her to my breast and close my eyes to tears of joy.

In the next breath I watch the young playing in my yard. "Come in my dears, I've a fresh batch of cookies for you," I call to my grandchildren. My hand shakes withered and feeble.

They scream in delight and chase each other around, such energy to expend while I struggle just to get out of bed every morning. "You're the best, Granny," one yells, and the rest agree. They gobble down the cookies and juice, wiggle in their chairs, push each other, jiggle about and go running off.

Not a word of thanks but the look on their faces is enough.

I breathe again and hear the sound of a very old heart, a struggle just to beat. My hands are unable to lift, and I have trouble focusing more than a few feet away.

"She hasn't much longer," someone says from the gray haze around me. Each inrush of oxygen a struggle, no longer counted as millions, but one of a handful,

on fingers stiff and shriveled. Life has already ebbed from the extremities, and I can no longer feel them. Heavy, so heavy, an effort to breathe, even to keep myself beating. Arteries sag as the time between surges diminish. I struggle to find the strength to take the next breath, knowing death's hand is near, fearing the touch.

At a moment's grace I stop, fighting and let go. Only air rushing back and forth and soon that is gone and I am left with solitude. The physical pain of an old shell is no more. I am released from my confinement.

Silence. For the longest time, if time could be measured at all, only silence. I swirl in mists, sensing a pulling, a funneling, another beginning and another breath. Warmth flows around me and gurgles fill my ears. I listen to a heartbeat issuing life into my soul once again.

A thump and eyes open awaiting a smack to begin the process all over again. My hands are weak and I can barely make out anything around me.

But I am back in the graveyard staring at the words written in stone. "Gone from us. The gentlest mother, the kindest grandmother we have ever known. You, who brought so much joy to our hearts, leave a void never to be filled except with the love you left behind."

A tear streaks my cheek as I understand a bit more wake up.

Chapter Thirteen

Science News

Resolute Bay, Nunavut, Canada

In the tiny village of Resolute Bay, which is so far north that between November and February the sun disappears, there is a strange light in the sky. The residents say that about five years ago the nights were no longer dark. It used to be pitch black in the winter. Now a thin strip of red and blue lights edges the horizon. Scientists theorize that this is possibly an effect from global warming causing air inversions or the beginning signs of a pole shift. One asked what to make of it one village elder remarked, "it's the second coming."

****

Zolnar slammed his fist in anger. They'd failed, again. Were his agents, his human agents, that inept at catching someone or...

Or perhaps he was very smart, which would explain the reason the Galactic angel Sherida was elected to watch this one.

Or he had help. But from who? There was no one off world that was here, he knew that. His men reported a lady interfered allowing this American named Roger to escape. She nor Roger were on the train ride back down, nor the next one and other than walking miles through dense impenetrable jungle there was no other way out. So how could he?

And now this, he's booked tickets to not one but two merkaba centers. The one is where the last angel still managed to elude him. An angel that he couldn't find. But it seemed perhaps Roger had. "Good. Perhaps we'll take out two Barnari seeds at one go."

He smiled and asked his computer program to search any references to the land called Australia. As usual he would download all data into himself, before landing there.

"Never enter an area without proper preparations," he muttered. His diligence to details had got him where he was today. "Besides, even Barnari can reach out and bite you if you're not careful," Zolnar sneered, and he'd eaten a lot of seeds in his time.

****

As soon as he got off the plane in Adelaide Roger heard it. A light droning almost like singing, or chanting. He wasn't sure where the low tones were coming from, he hadn't heard them in Sydney while he paid cash to switch planes.

But this wasn't any kind of band he was familiar with, it was similar to African chanting, yet more subtle, and it seemed to flow more without stopping. Lower, bassier, he'd heard strains of it before, but where?

Roger gathered his bags and walked outside. The shuttle took him to the rental place he'd been directed to. He wasn't exactly sure where he was heading, only that Australia was a big place, nearly the size of America and mostly desert. Renting a car wouldn't be too smart in this heat. A motorhome seemed the best idea, no hotel to register in and leave records.

As he got off the shuttle bus he heard the music again, calling. He shivered, remembering his last experience at SeaTac airport, months ago that felt like years. So much had happened, so much. "I hear you have some small motorhomes to rent."

"Heading to the outback, mate?" The white man at the desk asked in a thick Australian accent.

"Yeah, Alice Springs, hear it's a good thousand miles, about a three-day journey." He didn't want to mention where he was really going just in case whoever was after him showed up.

"Too right, mate." The guy showed him a couple of motorhomes.

Roger noticed a dark-skinned, nearly black boy with scruffy blond hair, washing a vehicle down. Roger stared at him, and the chanting stopped. "Who's that?" he asked out of curiosity.

"Oh him, he's a abo hangs out here and washes my vehicles, smart little cuss, but unreliable, like all of his kind. They show up whenever and disappear like the wind, usually after payday. Probably to pick up a few pints, would be my guess, although he's pretty sharp that one. And you're probably going to ask about the hair. Must have had some Vikings come down and do a few of his ancestors I say, there's quite a few with blond hair." The rental guy laughed.

Roger didn't care for the white man at the desk. Only there weren't many that would take cash and not ask questions.

"Hey boy, get over here and check all the fluid levels on this one."

Roger felt sorry for the kid, working at such a young age, he seemed only about twelve or so. "How come his parents let him work like this?"

"Can't say he's got any folks, usually sleeps most nights under one of my motorhomes with the guard dogs. Says he likes connecting to the stars. Most of them don't like being indoors, cuts them off they say."

"From what?"

"Don't know, never asked. A bit daft if you ask me."

Roger walked into the rental building and signed all the papers.

"Well, g'day then mate. But I gotta warn ya, watch out for the 'roos, I don't recommend driving after dark, that's when they come out. And if you see one then just speed up and plow right through them."

"What? Why?" Not only didn't he like him, the rental man, was also cruel.

"Cause they don't move, rather stupid animals."

"Why wouldn't you go around them?"

The rental guy looked at him like he was a stone age caveman just presented with the theory of relativity.

"Sorry I asked."

"Obviously not from around here, are ya. Just get the keys from the kid. And have a good trip mate. And if you pick up any good looking Sheilas I just had the bed reinforced. There's a drive thru up the street, has most everything you can ask for, including twenty-nine imported brews."

"Drive thru supermarket?"

The chanting began again.

"No, beer store. For food you'll have to park and go walkabout mate."

Roger walked out liking the man even less. As he approached the boy the chanting stopped again. "The man inside says you've the keys to this one."

"Yeah, right here." The lad handed him keys without looking up. He'd obviously been very browbeaten in his time and learned his place below the white man's glare.

"Thanks," Roger said as he got the keys. The lad slowly raised his head and stared at him with long eyes. Such innocence, yet...

There was something there that was missing from the eyes of the rental guy. It was the same feeling that he got when he stared at Charlie. The heavens and the Earth. Connection. Odd.

"Wungiana, where you headed to mister." He spoke in a lyrical voice.

The slight accent caught Roger, he'd heard that tone before, familiar but where from? "Not sure, thought I'd drive to Ayers Rock. Looking for an ancient sight that might have a crystal cavern in it." He didn't know why he blurted that out. For all Roger knew the kid could be one of the people after him. Actually, he did know, he knew he could trust this one.

"Wuna wunaia wuniingu Uluru. I'm sorry, my English is not very good. Very sacred, that place, but that's not the place you seek."

"That's okay, I could stand to use a few words of aborigine. How do you know that is not the place?"

"I just know. You are a what we call a karadji, a holy man, or a dreamtime traveler. Very rare, never met a karadji amerjig looking for gubbera in narkindie. But that would be a good place to start. I hear there's a town near there that has many UFO sightings. Might be the place you want. I've been to Uluru, no gubbera there. But good place to do walkabout." The lad winked with an affable toothed smile.

Roger stared into his eyes rather gob-smacked. "How did you..."

"Know, just do. One of the things most amerjigs don't know or sense."

Over the radio Roger heard the sounds of rhythmic chanting, as he started the motorhome, like he kept hearing in his head.

Low, steady and droning. Almost like breathing.

"This is crazy, I hear singing in my head, ever since I got here and it's very much like that music on the radio. What is that?"

"Didge music mate."

"Didge? What's a didge?"

"You're not from here, are you?"

"No from across the way."

"The didgeridoo is probably the oldest musical instrument in the world. Originally made from tree limbs hollowed out by termites, it is cut to about five feet in length and is said to represent the sound of the Earth when heard from space," the boy explained. "It produces a low droning sound and we use it in songs and dances. To make it work you purse your lips together basically and blow between them, making a raspberry sound."

"Kinda like a farting sound." Roger smiled.

"Yes, only it's done in a continuous breath."

Roger thought for a moment. Hadn't the Hathors breathed in a continuous breath?

"Our people never used to travel by car. We'd use the songlines across the land. When the song is over, we are at our destination."

"Really. Never heard of songlines." No, but he heard of studies on ley line sights and the old stone circles in places like Avebury and Stonehenge. Where they discovered that radio waves increase in volume as you approach these places, yet once in the circle they stop completely. Could the songlines be the same?

"Use them songlines, they will lead you to your destination. Never heard of any mutants looking for gubbera nor being able to hear the lines. You are most unusual, Mutant from across the way. I think I will help you. Care for a passenger, a guide?"

"Did I hear the chap inside say you've no parents?"

"No, I have parents, but I was taken from them and put into an orphanage."

"What? Why?"

"Government policy. Take all the aboriginal kids away and make them into good little white kids." He winked. "They only got as far as the hair on this one."

Roger smirked, liking his humor. "How cruel. Sure, jump in then, something tells me I'll need a native guide around these parts, not that I've haven't had one before. What about your boss?"

"Nah, he just expects me to work whenever. I better live up to his expectations then." The boy smiled for the first time, and yelled out the window, "Farewell! See ya in a couple of weeks. Kalyan ungune lewin."

"Farewell? Hey what the hell? Damn unreliable abo's."

"Wangeganimba, name? I'm Stan Nurrumbunguttia or just Stan the black bastard as the rest of the amerjigs call me."

"Wow that's quite the last name. I'm Roger Harrison. I'd never say that to you though. I mean the last bit. I'll just call you Stan if that's okay. What does your name stand for? I read somewhere that usually you're named after your dreaming or your totem animal or something like that."

"Old spirit. It means old spirit and you're right, most often one is named after their totem animal. Don't know why I was named that, never met my parents."

"Sorry about that. I know we may be a technically advanced culture, but I'm coming to realize we're very backwards in many ways. Spiritually for one." Roger stared into Stan's eyes as he talked. "And I sense you're exactly that."

"See, I told you. You are a karadji, a holy man, or at least a wirinun, medicine man."

They both laughed as Roger gunned the motorhome down the highway. The kid spoke and thought with more intelligence than the salesman gave him credit for. Or was he dumbing down on purpose?

****

Mauna Kea, Hawaii

In the observatory in Mauna Kea, Hawaii, Richard Sutton sat in stunned silence. After years of waiting, he'd finally been granted a month to use this telescope, with nearly the same power as the Hubble, to focus on the anomaly again.

He'd found it nearly a decade earlier when he had access to the Hubble, and no matter how many times he'd done so, it came out the same way. There it was, positioned just inside the Venus orbit, a black area of space approximately ten miles across. Virtually invisible unless you nearly ran into it. Which is how he found it or should say rediscovered it. A researcher back in the fifties had dismissed it as a blur in his readings. Yet it was there, in nearly the same area, only in the past three weeks he'd trained the space telescope on it and incredibly it had changed positions. Moving against the rotation of the sun and even shifting its orbit slightly. Moving, as if of its own propulsion.

Richard sat quietly, pondering what to do next. Would he be laughed out of his position and ridiculed like some of his fellow peers for making such ludicrous claims? Or the bigger question, how could this have gone unnoticed for over fifty years? Or he thumped the papers before him, what if it was there for even longer? There are ancient reports of such objects spotted in the skies. Or if this wasn't alien, was this a nascent black hole forming?

He'd been involved with US government studies since the forties involving Foo fighters and other UFO's. The craft they'd seen couldn't have been big enough or powerful enough to travel between solar systems. They were small two to four person ships. There had to have been something bigger, with some yet-to-be-discovered technology that could do just that. Something, he sat down and twisted his ancient slide rule, a device his counterparts laughed at him for using, something that size could easily hold hundreds of UFO's and an estimated - he gasped and stared at the blackened image again - hundred thousand people aboard.

****

As they drove neither talked very much at first. Stan seemed happy enough just to be away from the city. He brightened up as they drove past the Mount Lofty ranges and through the thinning forest and lush countryside. The lad explained to him the towns and native features as they drove. Before Roger knew they were driving into the beginnings of the outback. Sparse desert-like land with reddish soil, in ways reminding him of Arizona and the Hopi lands. Stan seemed more relaxed in a home environment as they traveled through the outback. By the second day the lad began to chat up a storm. In another day they'd reach Uluru.

They stopped by a waterhole for the night, a billabong, the lad called it. The two sat around the fire staring into the stars. Both nights the lad had slept outside under the motorhome, refusing Roger's pleas to come in. The harsh desert night cold didn't seem to bother him. "Your hair is most unusual."

"Common for my kind, I hear."

"I met a person once who had stark white hair like yours. She's the reason I'm on this trip."

"Was she from Maya-mayi?"

"Maya-mayi? Can't say I've heard of the place. Where is that?"

The lad stood up and pointed to the stars in the night sky. "Follow a line along from Amayworra and you find the seven stars of the Maya-mayi."

Roger sat stunned. He hadn't expected a star system for an answer. "Just a second, are you saying you are from out there?"

"So I was told in dreamtime. But that was a long time ago."

He grabbed Theodore's laptop and flipped it up. He wasn't sure but had to check. He stared blankly at the screen. The boy was pointing to Orion's Belt and the Pleiades. "You don't have any parents, do you?"

"None. I'm what the mutants call an orphan. Although being connected to this land I can't see how I'm ever an orphan."

"Mutant? I've heard you use that expression before."

"You amerjigs are different than us. There are many things you cannot do, see or feel."

To hear the songlines are one, to hear each other in our heads, like this, is another.

Roger turned around. "What the? Did you just do that?"

"Yes, but only abo's should be able to hear me. You are indeed not an ordinary mutant, perhaps you are not a mutant after all. Nor an amerjig. There is an expression we use 'Illa booker mer ley urrie urrie'. 'The soul will not die'. When you are being born among my people we stand around and chant 'we love you and support you on the journey'. When a person is laying on their deathbed we chant 'we love you and support you on the journey'. Thus, when a person enters this world and leaves, they hear the same words, for we believe the soul never dies and that this realm is but part of the journey of your soul's growth."

Roger pondered for a moment. "Then Dreamtime is part of the other dimensions that aborigines have access to and that us amerjigs do not."

"I believe so. And I believe you have access to those realms, Roger the amerjig wirinun."

"It's funny that you would say that. I met a native shaman." Roger told Stan about his experience with Charlie.

"Sha-man?"

"Like your wirinuns. And he told me the same thing, that I had access to other realms."

"He is right. That is why you were chosen on this quest."

"I suppose, only it's so overwhelming at times. I'm not sure I can handle all of this." Roger put his head down. He wished he could simply go home, back to his former life. "What I'd give just to be able to hold my wife Beth again, take my stupid dog for a walk. Crap, I'd even walk him in the rain."

"Ah, to a umbacoora, a how you call infant. Even focusing on a mother's teat and holding to her breast is hard. To a wise wirinun, focusing on all the stars in the heavens is hard. It is a matter of viewpoint, perception. Yet inside you know instinctively it is the right thing to do."

"The right thing to do. Yes, I know. This whole journey, as much as I've denied doing it, feels that way." Roger pursed his lips. He was beginning to realize that this was no poor aboriginal child. The lad was very bright and highly intelligent. "I guess I just never saw myself as anything but average."

"Barrdarrgindo boomari."

"What's that?"

"An expression. Do you hear the wind? It is saying Warrawee, come here."

"Yes, as much as I deny it, I know. I must do what I must. It's just a lot sometimes."

"So is life, my amerjig friend. So is life. I shall sleep now."

"Before you fall asleep can I ask, can you read my mind all the time?"

"Only if you want me to, but it is against tribal law to do that unless invited, so I don't."

Roger pondered. "You said that earlier Uluru was very sacred but not the place I seek."

Stan sat quiet for a moment. "There are some that wish to stop you in your quest. They are coming. The place you seek I sense is near Uluru. It is there that we shall lead them."

"Great, I thought I lost them. Do you know where to go from Uluru?"

"No, but you do."

"I do? Why did I know you'd say something like that. Good night."

With that Stan closed his eyes and curled up in a ball under the blanket Roger had given him from the motorhome.

He went inside and turned Theodore's laptop again. He read in Theodore's notes previously regarding ancient Earth history that was channeled to someone, supposedly that humans had their DNA cut back to only two strands. Perhaps that was what Stan meant by mutant? The bulk of humanity had been altered. Maybe telepathy was something that we'd been able to do once. He'd read that the average human only uses five percent of their entire brain capacity during their lifetime.

Aborigines had lived here for eons, perhaps because they were isolated, maybe they weren't altered. Perhaps they were in touch with other dimensions, dreamtime. Maybe so was he or at least reconnected? It would explain his feeling the ley lines, or songlines as Stan called them. Interesting thought. Roger yawned. What was it he'd read in Theodore's notes? A quote about the more you know the more you realize you don't know. He smiled to himself, remembering the 'Jackshit' line Charlie used.

He shut down the computer and stared out at the stars and at the sleeping figure of Stan. So much of this made sense and so much of this was just a chaotic mess. Roger breathed deeply.

And, oddly put as Stan had said, so much of this was strangely familiar.

All part of the journey, only to where?

And how to get there?

Chapter Fourteen

Earthweek

Data collected from satellites suggests that the Earth's midsection has been getting fatter in the last two years, whereas it had previously been growing slimmer and more elongated. Scientists are scrambling to determine the cause, although some blame it on post ice age glacial rebound, others on the collapsing magnetic field.

****

It was almost dark as they got near to Uluru. The sun setting on the giant red rock was spectacular. It was like when Theodore and himself drove to Stonehenge, the feeling of being watched and not the watcher was strong, as was the humming in his ears.

Roger had driven slowly so he wouldn't hit too many kangaroos, which were numerous. As the ignorant white man at the rental place had stated, if they were on the road they wouldn't move, perhaps no inbred fears of predators. Just stood there mesmerized by the lights. He had to go around several times. Which made Stan very happy.

"They are coming. The ones that want to stop you," he suddenly blurted out. "We must abandon this vehicle. Pull into the ditch just past that dead kangaroo." Roger did as Stan suggested, backing up and hitting the brakes to leave skid marks, making it look like he swerved to go around the 'roo. He slid the motorhome into the soft dirt of the ditch.

"Use the spare petrol and soak the front of the vehicle."

"What."

"Iterra, be quick. Somehow, they have blocked me out and are closer than I realized. Grab your backpack and the machine with the knowledge." Stan sounded very alarmed. "We are in trouble soon. They bring pandappure, guns."

Roger did and Stan threw a match on the fuel, causing a huge ball of fire to go up in flames.

"Great. Now what do we do?"

"Now we walk." Stan says.

"Into the desert?"

"I do not see a taxi waiting for hire. Let us go."

"But this is madness, we've no water, food."

"We have the desert. It shall provide."

"I was afraid you'd say that."

They tore off into the desert, early evening had begun to cast its lengthening shadows and the heat of the day had lifted. To be replaced, he knew from being out in the desert in Sedona, by the frigidness of the desert night.

After about two hundred feet Stan stopped and turned around. He gripped a bush and tore it loose. Running back, he brushed over their footsteps, all except for a few new steps he made leading away from the motorhome across the road into the desert on the other side. He scampered back and they'd barely gotten far enough into the desert when lights pulled up behind the motorhome. Several men swarmed out.

"Now we walk away from Uluru first after it gets darker and then towards it. The rest is up to you."

"Me? Why did I know you'd say that also." Roger shrugged.

Someone yelled in the semi-gloom. "We found tracks on the other side. They've gone into the desert."

One of the men scratched his head.

"Quite stupid I would think. They're as good as dead."

He waved some sort of device around the area. "Fuck! Not necessarily. One is the young bushie the boss is after. He could survive out there without difficulty. I'll radio the boss. We can't follow them out there, not without supplies. This will cost us a day while we drive back to Alice Springs. Damn."

The motley crew of men jumped back in the van and burnt a u turn on the road. As they picked up speed a kangaroo stood in the middle of the road, they punted it into the bushes. It quivered for a moment and then lay still.

****

As Roger walked around the massive outcropping known as Uluru, or Ayers Rock to the whites, he realized Stan was right. There was no crystal cavern here. Still, the silence and the deep sense of sacredness allowed him to relax and not worry about the men after him. He pulled out a map. "Let me try something. I keep hearing this song or notes in my head as we walk around here. This is a ley line center, like Stonehenge. If what you're saying about dreamlines is true, then by tracing this map. I did it in Egypt, maybe I can find where I need to go."

The boy smiled. "We have our ways of locating where we are going, you obviously need to find yours. Simply trust that you are indeed wise amerjig."

Roger closed his eyes and began to trace his fingers in a circular pattern radiating out from Uluru.

Rhythms of music appeared, the drones of didge music. Flowing like water over rocks, fields of grasses rustling in the gentle breeze of the Earth. Roger got lost in the sensations, so ethereal, so natural, so peaceful. Finally, it stopped. Roger ran his fingers away from the spot and the music started up again. He returned to the silent area. Only the whistle of etheric wind on stillness. He opened his eyes. "That is where I must go."

"Very sacred site," the boy said. They both laughed.

"I'll bet every bush and," he thought for a moment, "malleee around here is 'VERY SACRED'."

"You know, for a mutant you're getting pretty smart."

They laughed again.

****

Arizona University

A keen Jason Brand pulled open a long-closed drawer full of artifacts marked Hopi and dusted off the pieces within. A member of Arizona University's newly formed group involved with the returning of important artifacts to native cultures, the student of archeology stared at a few, lifted them and set them back in their cataloged positions.

He squinted at a chunk of rock, with ancient pictography on it. "This appears to be broken off from a larger section." He studied the note attached. The section in his hand looked familiar, he'd seen it before, or at least he'd seen photos of some sort of important stone of the Hopi's before. "Possible Fire Clan fragment" was marked on a small piece of paper attached to the stone. If it is what he thinks it is, the missing piece is from one of their oldest documents.

He smiled and put it carefully into a small box before packing it with several others. "They shall be so excited over this find." He smiled to himself.

****

Roger and Stan walked for two days across the desert. Roger had brought his canteen with water, laptop in his backpack and virtually little else. Yet it didn't seem to matter. The boy knew where to dig to release water from the ground, the certain roots of shrubs to eat. Even where grubs lived. He was hesitant to eat at first, although when you're starving, you'll eat anything He discovered they tasted like chicken.

Not only did Stan know where food and water was, he knew when they'd cross it. It was like he had a built-in divining rod sense that could scan for kilometers around them. No wonder the aborigines thrived out here in the desert when a white man, or mutant, would have starved. As they approached a small canyon of reddish rock the music he'd been hearing in his head, which had slowly increased, stopped. "This is the place."

As they entered a pathway between rocky crags Roger looked up. The sky began to invert. Turning colors of the desert into flowing clouds of ochre and sand while the walls shifted into shades of blue and cotton. Stan smiled. "This is very sacred. I've never been here, but it is a Bullima, a spirit land. Part of dreamtime."

Roger didn't need Stan to tell him that they'd entered another ley center, only in this one dwelled many nurrumbunguttia, old spirits.

As they walked everything around them began to change. The same sensations as when he entered some of the other ley line centers. A subtle, almost imperceptible shifting, from one realm of existence to another. He was walking the gateways, aware that things were harmonizing, morphing, into what possibly Stan called dreamtime.

Perhaps Stan was a gateway walker also. "It is just ahead," he said. How he knew this he wasn't sure, but he knew. He also got glimpses of conversation in his head. *There were elders ahead.* Stan had been talking to his elders at the meeting place. In this place Roger could pick up those snatches of conversation, much to the boy's surprise, and although Stan had taught him some of his language, a lot of the conversation was still lost on him.

Boulders like those at Uluru surrounded them as they walked along the small pathway between them. It was deceiving, and so it was meant to be, Stan told him. Illusions are only for those who use their eyes. They walked for hours through what appeared to only be a small rock outcropping.

"That was the trick, wasn't it?" Roger asked. "We depend too much on our eyes, when true sight comes from within."

The aborigines understood mutants and knew used their dependence on their eyes to create the illusion. "There were many such sites on this land," Stan told him.

Along the path as they walked, he began to see figures drawn on the rock. Some he recognized as horses, dingoes and emus. They were drawn over other ones, older ones. Extinct creatures, thousands, maybe tens of thousands of years old. Maybe older, as he studied a very badly faded drawing, men perhaps, and what appeared to be a giant reptile of some sort.

The ghost faces, white with round eyes, staring at him as he walked by them. Ancestors, he sensed. The one thing he knew from Theodore's notes was that the aborigines were the oldest known culture on Earth. Unchanged for over sixty thousand years. They simply trust that the Earth will provide for them every day and if it didn't, it was time to pass on. They were like this, egoless, before the dawn of Atlantis, perhaps descended from ancient Lemuria.

He continued until he came to an opening in the walls. He glanced into the opening and saw a large dark cavern, in the center a fire-pit crackled to life. Around it were what he thought were rocks at first, but as Roger focused his eyes he realized the still objects were aborigines, very old aborigines.

"Sacred elders of the dreamtime." Stan stood on the edge of the path. "You go into the opening. I will wait here and keep guard. This is your place and not mine. I shall watch for those that pursue you and I think they may pursue someone else as well. Roger the amerjig, it has been a great journey." He smiled at Roger and said nothing else walking back the way they came.

Roger smiled wondering what he meant by that as he walked along the canyon. On the far side of the canyon Roger spotted the glitter of crystals coming from yet another pathway in the canyon.

"You have come far in this dreamtime." One of the elders rose and spoke into Roger's mind. "You come alone?"

"I was guided here by a young one of yours, called Stan Nurrumbunguttia."

"Only aborigines are allowed in, and of course those known to walk between the gateways. The other is not one of ours."

"He is one of the twelve sent to watch us by the great gods of the dreamtime," another spoke. "For the gathering."

"What do you mean?"

"Sit and we shall tell you as you prepare to enter the last crystal cavern between us and the great stone building that sits like a spear-tip on the Earth."

Roger sat, and the elder continued, "The original signs of awakening began with the release of the great powerful seed that blossoms into a terrifying cloud of mushroom dust to destroy all with its hot touch. We are all connected and the impact of that blast on thousands of worlds in dreamtime was horrible."

'The atom bomb,' Roger thought. Now that he thought of it, it was just after the first atomic weapons were tested that the first foo fighters were spotted and events like Roswell happened.

"The trigger to release the ones you have called angels came with the return of parts from the big rock that hangs in the night sky. The viewing of the ancients on the planet of the red, like us, began the release of the mystical symbols all around the other great center of the square stones of the circle."

"Stonehenge. You must mean the crop circles. But why? What are crop circles doing?"

"They begin the preparations for the end of this cycle. Solidifying the energy centers on this plane. The last phase involved the decrease of the air particles that keep us in suspension from dreamtime."

"The ozone layer. Then it is true. All of this is true. Another cycle draws near and if I fail, does it start all over again, until finally one of us completes the ... what? The next ascension process."

"Life on this planet is about seasons, when one ends, another begins. That is the way. When one cycle ends another begins."

"And what about Stan, the one from the stars we call the Pleiades, you the maya-mayi. What becomes of him?"

"He is in grave danger, as are the rest that are still alive."

"I know. But he has no special powers, not like the other one that was my guide, Sherida."

"Different guides for different people, one like her would stand out like a Binburra tree on the great desert. Eventually wilting away."

"I see."

"You are one of the last signals before reality ends and dreamtime seeps in."

"The black rain," they hiss together into his head. "When that comes the end is near."

"If you know of the other angels, then maybe I can contact them, help them before it is too late."

"That is not your place to decide. And for most it is already too late, they have disappeared. They dwell not in this place."

"The ones that choose to end your quest were close to discovering him when you took him on the journey with you."

"I saved his life?"

"And he yours."

The karma thing Roger thought, what you put out in life you get back. He thought of Stan's sudden vision that those that were chasing him were close and he made them burn the motorhome. It was that ability that probably kept the lad alive this whole time. He must remember to ask the boy if he'd earlier visions and not told Roger. "How do you know so much?"

"Dreamtime. It is all dreamtime, and when one stops the pursuit of ego, one can rest and ponder the existence of this dreamtime and all possibilities."

One rises and begins to paint a picture of a white man with a necklace of green crystal around his neck.

"The crystal Tiyah gave me. Who'd you know? Unless this, all of this, is the hall of records for this area, the female side of the equation, like the Dogon said, isn't it?"

No one replies, but he knows the answer.

"Even rarer than me are the ones that watch over all that is, the recorders, the watchers like the Haida Watchmen and the Moai of Easter Island. That is you, for this area you are the watchers, the recorders of this cycle's history."

"Yes, our brothers, you know of them. You are very aware, Roger the amerjig. Now we must prepare you for the next journey."

They strip him down until he is naked and paint him all over with little balls of white paint.

"Now go. There is still much to do."

Roger steps into an opening between the ring of flames, ignoring the hot coals. One of the elders rises and sprinkles something from a bag. Flames erupt several feet and Roger finds himself standing in a great stone enclosure.

The heat is intense, even though it is near dark. Great stone walls reach over thirty feet high. On the other side of the walls, even before he heard the bellow of lions, he knew he was in another land. A dreamtime of a more primordial base.

"I am in Africa. Then this must be the enclosure of Great Zimbabwe." He walked around the three hundred feet across yard, past several lower walls, into the treed area where the great conical tower sat, as it had for over a thousand of our known years. He knew from Theodore's notes that no one knew who really built these ruins. They left no written language and built it puzzlingly enough near several rivers but not actually on the shore of any. Stuck in the middle of nowhere on the huge plains. Some believed it was built to worship Mwari, the Creator.

He strode through the ruins and walked around the base of the great tower. No opening was ever found, no purpose ever discovered. Roger smiled and, holding the green crystal of Tiyah's, he closed his eyes and walked past the barrier of stone into the tower's interior. A well similar to the one under the Great Pyramid sat dark and silent. Around its perimeter several large crystals lay scattered, knocked on their sides. He picked them up and carefully set them down in the dusty depressions they once dwelled in. As he set the last in place a hum and a gentle swirling of light. Tendrils of light began to fill the complex.

Roger smiled and stepped down into the well. Energy coursed all around as he climbed down and soon found another opening.

He looked around and knew instantly he wasn't in Africa anymore as he stared up at the mountain before him. The smells, the air, so distinct from the African continent. Only he knew it wasn't a natural part of the earth. The shape was too perfect, he realized as he walked along its side. It was so ancient; someone had covered it in earth and he stared at the regular spacing of the large trees covering its flanks.

They'd covered it over, attempted to make this edifice look like a mountain, but it was obvious he stood before a huge pyramid. Roger craned his neck upward; it must have been nearly three hundred feet high. Where was he?

He closed his eyes and breathed the essence of this land into his nostrils. Old cultures, gentle people, and a land of inscrutabilities.

He began to walk along another side of the pyramid and stopped when he saw the red star painted onto the side of the military vehicle parked on the road just below him. China. He was in communist China.

He slowly crawled back the way he'd come. Even naked, painted in white, they'd still probably shoot first and ask questions later, he thought. And other than Chow Mein, he knew no Chinese in any of its dozen dialects.

This then must have been one of the nearly hundred pyramids found in the great plains of Southern China, near Xianyang. He looked up, this is the largest one, the white pyramid.

Of course, Theodore's notes had mentioned it and the fact that it, like the Giza complex, was aligned with the stars of Orion's Belt in 10,500 BC. An exact replica of the Giza complex, or was this the precursor? Who knew? What did it matter? Roger clutched the green crystal and closed his eyes. He entered a hallway that had seen no human eyes in over ten thousand years, perhaps never.

He let in a tentative breath of air. There must have been airshafts here like at Giza. The air was crisp and clean. Before him stood an altar bearing two human sized metallic hands. Above it was a golden rod with a red crystal in its end, cradled within them was a four-inch crystal ball. Roger gasped "just like the fellow from Theodore's notes, what was his name? Ray Brown. A diver exploring in the waters near Bimini located in the Bermuda Triangle. He discovered an underwater pyramid and within it a very similar looking crystal, hands and all."

Roger gently clutched the round smoky crystal and began walking down a familiar sloping hallway. As he did dim light glowed on his approach. "Amazing, why can't we make light bulbs like that." He gasped as he strode into a room the exact copy of the King's Chamber in Giza. There in the center of the room was a sarcophagus, its lid intact standing beside it, on the portion that had been broken away on the Giza pyramid was carved a depression the same size as the crystal. Not a mark nor hieroglyph anywhere.

"This must have been a backup to the Giza Pyramid; if destroyed it could also be used. Or simply another zero-point energy converter to contain part of the Earth's energy fields. He smiled and placed the crystal into the depression on the sarcophagus' lid and stepped back as light began to flood the room and the entire complex surged to life.

Roger smiled and began to leave the chamber. "At least I know now, if I have to, there's possibly more than one way to go home."

Roger quickly strode down the hallway. He wasn't sure if the soldiers below had heard the pyramid start up or not, nor was he planning on finding out. Once outside he grasped the green crystal around his neck and closed his eyes.

When he opened his eyes, he stared into the eyes of several giant stone faces carved into the very walls of an abandoned city on huge, corbelled arches towering over him. Humidity assailed him, moisture surged forward to cling to him, like everything it touched with its cloying caress.

"In the jungle again. This must be Angkor Wat."

He didn't know much about the lost city in Cambodia from Theodore's notes, other than it was rediscovered in 1860 by a French explorer, Henri Mahout, and was built by the Khmer people around 980AD.

"So why am I here?" Roger studied the intricate carved walls, so like many pictures of Hindu sites in India. Unless it was built over a ley line center, or something even older. As he walked Roger could feel the hum under the ground and knew he was in an area of very strong energy. Roger simply walked until the hum stopped and stood before a large carved image of Vishnu. He didn't walk around it, knowing that there was no door.

"Charlie would be proud of me." He laughed and walked through the stone wall, "I think I'm getting the hang of this gateway stuff."

Another crystal chamber lay inside. Roger rearranged the crystals until they began a now familiar hum. He walked outside and closed his eyes again. "Yes, definitely getting good at this hocus-pocus stuff."

Hiding behind an ornately carved wall of figures, a young boy gasps and begins praying to Buddha. The sight of a painted man with a green crystal will haunt his memories.

Crisp ocean breezes whistled across his skin as he stared up into the wide-eyed stare of a row of stone figures staring out into space. The moai were carved from volcanic stone, some adorned with pukao, round topknots carved from red scoria, sat silent as they had for millennia on their ahu shrines. Gazing with eyes open, as if waiting, or perhaps simply watching, like the Watchmen of Haida Gwaii. Who knew. Roger had read the notes on Theodore's computer regarding amazing Easter Island, located over fifteen hundred miles to the next nearest land mass.

The natives even had a war amongst themselves, between the long ears and the short ears. When the whites came here, they enslaved and killed off the vast majority of the population. Roger groaned. "So much slaughter. Why do we go around destroying everything that is alien to us? It is no wonder that we are kept in isolation."

He knew the history of his own country and the dealings with their natives wasn't any nicer. Although it could have been, he knew the early Americans had made an effort to establish reservations and live peacefully with the natives. He remembered reading from even his school days about the five civilized native tribes in the eastern states that even had their own banks, newspapers, courts, churches and schools. Virtual statehood, modeled on the American Federal Government. In fact, they even owned their own black slaves. Until we took it all away in the 1830's and moved them out of their own lands and reservations to east of the Mississippi.

He shook his head. Why do we fear the unknown? Perhaps the aliens out there were right in trying to slowly reveal themselves to us. After all our track record didn't prove we were very accepting of different cultures and peoples.

Perhaps what he was doing wasn't right, and perhaps based on past actions we didn't deserve to continue with this ascension. But the past is past, he thought, and it has got us here to where we are today. Perhaps it would have been far easier if we'd saved some of the old texts instead of burning them and perhaps had more of an open mind to seeing the information left behind instead of using blinders and trying to justify our own egos.

He thought of the Rongo-rongo boards of the original Easter Island peoples with their bizarre written language that had a hundred characters, many nearly identical to the language of the oldest peoples of India, the Indus valley culture. Both languages are undecipherable. Maybe Theodore was right, and high-and-mighty scholars simply overlooked the odd facts that didn't fit into their perfect idea of how this world, and evolution, supposedly worked. Of course, the whole theory of evolution may be just that, a theory which in reality hadn't been proven to work.

Roger closed his eyes and tried to visualize what was needed to set this ley center back online. The pukao, topknots, were on backwards. He smiled and touched the base of the statues. With a dry scrape one after another the pukao slowly began to rotate and as they aligned themselves properly a familiar hum filled the statues. Roger smiled as the white of their eyes began to glow. Reconnected to the flow of Earth and the universe.

Done, he let go and slumped to the ground. Tired; he was so tired. He needed some reconnection to food, sleep and himself. But there was still one more site to go to before returning to the aborigines.

Roger clutched the crystal and opened his eyes again. A wall of basalt rock towered over him. He walked along the boundary between two buildings. He knew from Theodore's notes that the structures at Nan Madol and Nan Matol, on Pohnpei island in the Carolines composed an area of over twenty-five square miles and the stone complexes were built over ninety islets, all connected by shallow canals. Archaeologists still haven't figured out how the natives, maybe numbering twenty-five thousand moved, transported or erected the walls, some nearly fifty feet high out of blocks as heavy as fifty tons. Roger smiled as he walked into the center of the area called Nan Douwas. He knew the crystal guided him on these trips but hadn't asked himself how he intimately knew how to set each ley center back online. If entire past lifetimes are stored in each person's DNA then the memory of how he returned the centers back to operation was simple. He must have been part of the ones that took them apart somewhere in the distant past.

That was a question he had to ask the Hathor. Although he reckoned, he wasn't naked and covered in balls of white paint then. Roger laughed and stopped as part of the darkness hiding under the walls moved. For a brief moment, he thought it was the black dog of his dreams, but the Mangrove monitor lizard scuttled off into hiding. He breathed a sigh of relief and continued walking to a platform area near the center.

There he grasped the crystal and felt himself sink into the core of the island. To a vault with numerous coffins and a light dimly cast by other green crystals housed in the walls. Ancient kings of Lemuria, he knew before it ended its cycle. In a daze he walked to a small circle of crystals and quietly rearranged them into a pentagram. As he set the last one down a now familiar hum filled the cavern and white light flooded everywhere.

Now he could go home, or at least back to the men of dreamtime.

****

Zolnar cursed. He'd lost the last Pleiadian left alive on the planet and the human named Roger somewhere east of the large red rock. The boy's signal was very faint to start with, almost like he wasn't truly here in this realm or something was trying to filter it. Now they'd vanished and all of his screens were going crazy as one energy center after another began to light up. If this was the human's doing, how was he doing it? And who was helping him?

"By Holy Sagribs!" he cursed again. Another signal, this one from the Pleiadian mothership hidden in orbit near Venus. It had released a dozen shuttlecrafts. "No doubt scouts to investigate the increase in the energy flux." They'd probably pick up his signal once they entered Earth orbit. "Time to leave."

Zolnar punched in some buttons and stared at the blue planet below. "It doesn't matter. I know where the human is going and once I have him, I have the ZPEC." He laughed as he phased out.

****

Night had fallen when Roger stepped out from the crystal cavern. The fire was out, the ashes cold. He shivered as he stared up at the wall the elder was painting on earlier. He saw himself, the white man with a large green crystal around his neck and behind him he saw a triangular shaped building. In the distance he caught the streaks of black rain and the figure of a little native boy with white hair.

Roger smiled. In the picture he noticed one other thing, a crudely painted jagged line. "What would that be? A break in the ground, some sort of fissure perhaps." He looked closer. It actually stood before him and the pyramid, with the cavern behind him. "The well? Gateway walker? This was the only cavern that had a well, so much like the one at the pyramids. Could it be?"

Roger walked back into the crystal cavern and glared down into the well. The darkness was gone, it now glowed with a soft brilliance around its edge. "Why hadn't I seen that earlier?" He picked up a small, long and thin rock and let it fall. Waited and waited, before realizing it would be forever before he'd ever hear the sound of it touching bottom.

Taking a deep breath Roger climbed down inside the edge and began to make his way down. He'd done this before in the sessions with the Hathor and failed each time.

The further he went down, the dimmer the light above became, until everything was black again.

"Trust your intuition," he murmured and closed his eyes. "Let go of the one sense that will not do any good here." He let his mind drift as he slowly scrambled down, focusing on the glow of the crystal. Thinking of Egypt, the pyramids, Tiyah and Beth. This was the lesson of the dark hole under the water all over again, he knew. The one lesson he never quite got. He understood what the Hathor meant, but to do it and trust was another matter. He climbed for what seemed like forever, perhaps it was.

"Trust, don't let your fear rule you," the voice of the Hathor spoke inside his head. How many times had the teacher said that? He looked up and gripped the rock tightly as the oppressiveness of tons of rock and eternal darkness, thundered in veins. Only rock and inky blackness appeared as far as the glow of the crystal penetrated in either direction.

"Let go and simply trust." He closed his eyes again and kept climbing down through the dark over craggy surface, until only the sound of his breathing and the occasional rock tumbling away into the dark could be heard. His hands were soon aching, fingers sore, perhaps raw.

After what seemed like hours the scrape of something against his back jolted Roger from his trancelike state of climbing. He pushed back against the interfering object. Solid.

He turned around on the rocky surface and felt all over and over in a circle. Rock everywhere. The tunnel had narrowed. Funneling down until he was in the heart of the spigot.

The tunnel had shrunk down just like the hole below the temple of Dendara with the alligators swimming overhead; they'd prepared him well. He swallowed down his fear and kept going lower and lower into the darkness, scraping against rock. Hoping that at any moment he wouldn't get stuck, or worse have rocks tumbling down on him. He squeezed his way down now into the constricting hole.

Claustrophobia's claws sunk in hard as he felt the rock press his chest. It was no good the cavity was too tight. This was too much he'd die here trapped between the pincer-like walls of this tunnel. As Roger struggled to climb his way back up, his feet gave way, unable to find purchase. He scrambled to get another foothold, feeling himself slipping into the tightness of the hole.

Quelling the panic threatening to take over Roger lifted his hands and clung to the face of the tunnel over his head. His feet dangled. "How long can I hang here like this?" He cried, his heart thumping away. "Trust." Whispered into his head.

"No, I can't."

Yet he had to keep going, had to believe.

There was no water here to leech at his lungs like at Dendara. He would not die here like he did there, over and over again. He swallowed down the overwhelming feeling of panic. Taking several deeps breaths he slowly opened his eyes and could barely make out a dimness somewhere below him. Light. Perhaps an end?

Unable to tell how far down, Roger closed his eyes and let go.

Scrapping rock on skin he fell several feet and collapsed to the hard packed ground below. He'd been so close to success. If he'd stopped back then.

Roger fell to his knees and sobbed. This was hard, so hard, but there was no going back now. Looking around he could see there was what appeared to be an exit in the distance.

Plunk.

"What?" Roger staggered and looked up as a rock hit him on the head. Moving aside he was prepared for more to fall in case he'd dislodged some on the way down.

When none came, he rubbed at the already rising welt and stared at the small rock on the ground. It looked like the one he'd tossed in so many long hours ago.

"What's this, some cosmic joke?" He put the pencil thin rock in his pocket, "Oh, I can hear an old ball-capped shaman laughing his ass off."

He looked around and spied carvings on the dimly lit walls. This room, this passageway, he'd been here before; in his dreams.

The halls of Amenti where the Akashic records were stored, the entire history of human activity on Earth. Somehow, he was very deep below the earth.

He walked along the tunnel, passing several rooms. Holographic images came to life in each room, various periods of time. Walls filled with books, knowledge, history. Awe, utter awe flooded him. He stared at the enormity of the knowledge towering all around him. Memories of ancient cultures, entire civilizations, Atlantis, Mu. Entire cycles of life. Why would someone store that here? And more, he knew he'd been here before. Why? He continued to walk in humble respect like a second grader would stroll the halls of the Library of Congress. Knowing enough to understand what he'd stumbled on, but unable to truly grasp the volume of knowledge, sheer brilliance of learning and comprehension contained within the endless volumes all around him.

He didn't stop, knowing he could, but the enticement of scholarly pursuit would swallow him up and stop him from his mission. He'd return another day. "Even too much of a good thing was bad," he muttered and kept going to the end of the corridor where another tunnel and another well leading back up beckoned.

"Scholarly pursuits? I must be turning into a geek." He laughed and stopped staring at the vast knowledge, wanting to know so many things. "Or could it be that I'm evolving?" Roger kept walking. "I have been here before, with the Hathor."

How he knew this, he didn't know, but Roger kept climbing again, this time up and before long as he reached his hand up and he felt a ledge. Roger looked up over the edge of the well's lip. Rock surrounded him, he could feel the pressure of tons of stone above him. He was here, not sure how he got here, but that he was back here. A very familiar chamber.

Roger pulled himself up out of the well and stared at the section of wall where he, Theodore and Sherida had stayed. From the confines of the sacred chamber Roger saw a glow begin. He peered up trying not to reveal too much of himself. The glow grew in strength until it burst from the rock and a figure walked through. "You've arrived," Tiyah spoke like she'd been waiting long. "Wasn't sure if you'd make it."

"It wasn't easy, I nearly turned around and went back up. Didn't trust myself to get through. How long have you been waiting?"

"Does it matter to a being who's been here already a few thousand years?"

"Right. Silly question," he gasped as she pulled him from the well.

"You must be tired. But we have no time to spare, the lights will come on in less than an hour. We must hurry." She began walking towards the tunnel that sloped upwards. A green crystal in her hand lighting the way.

"Well, it's been quite a trip so far. Old Jules Verne thought he was doing incredibly well going around the world in eighty days. I've done it in one. But let me guess, fatigue is simply a gift of illusion's graces."

"No, physical bodies do run down on occasion." She smiled, and pulled a wand from her pocket, the end housed a large crystal. He felt all the tiredness seep from his body as she touched him. "A piece of the Ark of the Covenant. A magician's wand you'd call it."

"Like Urim and Thummin, I read about in Theodore's notes. All part of the Ark?"

"Naturally," she replied, "you are learning fast. Crystals are solidified light, the energy of the universe. I wish I had more students like you in the days of the Mystery Schools, you would have excelled and probably become one of the teachers."

"Ah, just courtesy of Microsoft, Apple and the net." He felt honored as they virtually ran up the hallway.

"I don't recognize the names of these teachers, or were they students of some other Mystery School?"

"To some I guess." He laughed as they entered the King's chamber, his breath hoarse from the running.

Tiyah smiled as he crawled into the sarcophagus. "Nice paint job by the way." Staring at the circles drawn on him by the aborigines.

"Early Cro-magnum, heard it was the rage in 200,000 BC."

As he lay prone and crossed his hands over his chest, she smiled. The first smile he recalled ever seeing on her face. Tiyah planted a green crystal over his chest. "I think you could be right on that one."

Crap, he thought and laughed. She'd actually know for sure.

Chapter Fifteen

As a man who throughout his life served the most rational of sciences, namely the investigation of matter, I am surely free of the suspicion of being taken for a fanatic. So, I say this to you after my research into the atom, there is no matter as such. All matter originates and exists only through a force which sets the atomic particles oscillating and holds them together to form the minute solar system of the atom. But as there is neither an intelligent nor an infinite force in the whole universe, we must assume a conscious intelligent mind behind this force. This mind is the fundamental basis of all matter.

Max Planck

1918 Nobel Prize winner for Quantum Theory in Physics

"For a third dimensional being to enter the fourth dimension he must overcome his fears. The last chakra is about thought." The Hathor spoke as they walked into a temple complex. "All of these temples are part of the initiation. To train individuals to be ready for the experience of the fourth dimension."

Light streamed in from an opening in the roof of the complex, shining behind a wall that stood in a large pool of water.

"You must get to the other side of an identical wall and stand on a platform like this one."

I walked out to the platform that stood away from the water and looked around, "But there's no way around this wall. Except…"

"And what did this have to do with thought?" I asked. The being that called itself Hathor had vanished. I was alone. I stared at the wall. "No way over, it's twenty feet high. So, the only way is to go under." I stripped off everything except my shorts, took several deep breaths saturating my lungs and dove under the water.

As I descended, I noticed a dim light and swam towards it. The wall didn't connect to the floor of the pool. There was a gap of about two feet. As I swam under the wall the light increased from above, light and movement in the water. I swam up to the top and gasped for breath. Dark objects that appeared to be logs floated in the water. I gulped in air and blinked, trying to get the water out of *my eyes. In front of me was another wall, an intense beam of light cast above it, and another identical platform to the one I started at.*

This seems easier than I thought.

A current of cooler water suddenly welled up as something moved below disturbing the stillness. I heard a splash behind me and flinched as a log to my right opened its eyes. They weren't logs. Another splash as something large entered the pool. Crocodiles! I was in the middle of a pool of live crocodiles. Something rough brushed against my feet and I watched a large shape move below me.

Panic seized me in its frigid arms. I had only one chance. Either stay here and die or make for the platform. I gulped, staying still would probably not give away my location. The second I moved I knew the crocs would be on me. I wanted to strike out and swim with everything I had. I knew I couldn't stay where I was. My heart raced, as I slowly filled my lungs with air and allowed myself to float on the top. With slow measured undulations I eased towards the platform. Trying to be as still as possible, sliding across the waters like the crocs did. Trying to become one of them. About ten feet away my hand slipped and made an audible splash. Instantly the crocs around me opened their eyes and some dove under the water.

Move your arms, *I screamed at myself.*

My heart threatened to explode as I swam with everything I had. My hand grasped the edge of the platform. I began to pull myself out of the water and stopped. Something wasn't right. The Hathor said I had to stand on another platform like the first one, on the other side of a second wall. Not before it.

I gulped; the wall was about twenty feet away.

No, *I wracked my mind, this wasn't the right platform. Even if it was bathed in light. I turned and took a deep breath as the crocs moved through the water. None appeared to be really heading in his direction. They appeared to be aimlessly swimming about, nearly in contentment or idle laziness.*

I swallowed and gripped my fear like a knife dove under the water. Down into the darkness of the pool. Only there was no opening, no light and the wall extended all the way to the pool's bottom. There was no way under it. Light shone above me. No, my intuition, called. There had to be an opening. I raced along the wall, frantic as my lungs began to ache.

Near the center of the wall, I spied a darker area and swam closer. A large croc swam just above me. There was an opening into the wall, a dark opening. I stared into it. Blackness stared back at me. A square area barely larger than my shoulders.

What if I got stuck? What if I ran out of air? I couldn't turn around in that tunnel.

I swallowed. This had to be the way it had to be. Trust the intuition. Blood pounded in my temples as I forced myself into the tunnel. Trust yourself.

I woke up.

We stood in a long unending corridor, full of books towering in shelves up into the darkness. "I ... I know this place."

"The last chakra is about thought."

"I know, you've told me this before. A long time ago."

"Yes, you failed last time."

"The fact that I remember this conversation tells me that."

"Then perhaps you have not failed after all."

I turn stunned, overwhelmed by what is before me. I don't want to breath, the thought of everything contained here is mind blowing beyond the wildest dreams. It has been written that in our current history there were several events that forever changed our view on life and the past, that destroyed so much of what we knew once. The sacking and burning of the libraries of Alexandria, Egypt and Nalanda, India among others and the ordered burning of over 700,000 texts at Tenochtitlan and Texcoco.

Hundreds of thousands of books, some dating from as far back as the ancient realms of Atlantis, Lemuria, even ancient Mu. I turn in awe, utter awe.

"Does this place actually exist?'

"Yes, on Earth, below the ancient Seer of Sirius you call the Sphinx."

"On Earth?"

"Yes, your fellow being called Edgar Cayce was right, below the right paw is the entrance to this. The Akashic records, the hall of records."

"The sum total of mankind's knowledge. All here. Do I have time?"

"That is an irrelevant question. Time is irrelevant."

"Yes, right. So how do I?"

"Just think it."

"Jesus, where do I begin?"

"Ah, a good place."

Images of a woman being struck by light from a bright star overhead. Her son being born, growing up, long walks by himself and deep reflections. He begins his studies early, travels to all the holiest of places, India, Egypt, China and learns as much as possible. His understanding and perceptions immense, he walks on water, a dark Arabian man that radiated love and put his hands on people, gave life and hope to those suffering. His love of Mary, their children smuggled away to Massada by the Essenes. Trapped there by the Romans after his death, suicides. Mary dead, their son escaped to modern day France. He himself died a lonely, silent monk in the hills of Kashmir. "Shocking, this is wild."

"This is the real truth contained within these texts, not the versions you'd be led to believe by certain authorities that are in power at the time and altered by men of power to suit their needs."

I let go of the book and touched another. Michelangelo, dabbling away on his back painting the Sistine chapel, year after painstaking year. Another, the sack of Peking by the Mongols. The firebombing of Dresdan, human bodies igniting from the heat of the firestorm. The tens of thousands killed by the hands of despots, Adi Amin, Saddam Hussein, Pol Pot.

"So much violence." *I shake my head trying to contain my tears.*

"Then shift your thoughts to something else. The choice is yours."

"I don't understand."

Einstein plugging away on a chalk board. A young Indian named Gandhi staring up at the heavens. I blink and see myself as a child staring up at the stars.

"The pyramids. Tell me about the pyramids."

"Ah, for that we need to go to another room." *We walk into a larger room.*

"This is older, isn't it?"

"Yes. This is the entire history of the last cycle of Atlantis."

"Last cycle? I remember the Hopi and the Dogon stating that we were in a fifth cycle. Does that mean that there were four previous cycles of Atlantis?"

"Yes, as a matter of fact that is correct. The place you come from is the current reincarnation."

"America?" *I sit stunned for a moment before staring at the date of the last cycle, it is nearly twenty-six thousand years ago. I watch as remnants of Atlantis mystics move them with the power of crystals.*

"They were later rebuilt by your pharaoh, Khufu around 4,000 BC."

I see flying ships in the Indus Valley. "Explains the thousands of ancient texts found in the oldest of Indian ruins regarding how to fly and maintain flying craft." I wonder why they'd need these.

Visions of mining activity on the moon, crystal structures towering over a mile high. The Face on Mars and entire cities there. "Wow."

Another room, even older. "From the time of Lemuria." The Hathor answers the question fermenting in my mind. I see the destruction of the fifth planet in our system, Maldek.

"Our asteroid belt now," I gasp.

Another room, so very old, "Mu," it whispers in reverence. "My ancestors lived here then."

"Why? I don't understand. Why do we save this? I've been studying my friend's notes, the Hopi talk about cycles as do the Mayans and many very old cultures."

"When all of this knowledge is stored, it empowers the pyramids, the ley lines of energy that emanate from here."

"Ley line energy from books?"

"Our knowledge encircles the globe, superconscious energy. Everything converts to energy. Different building blocks, for different kinds of energy. All of this for a reason."

We walked into the long endless corridor. "I know everything is energy and energy converts to light. But why? I still don't understand the why."

"You will at some point. But not yet. This Orion transmitter was built for several reasons, one of which is to withstand the photon belt we have recently entered."

"To survive what?"

"The photon belt, the energy source that culminates as we end this cycle and begin the next." The Hathor began to shimmer, preparing to leave I knew.

"If everything is trapped light, everything converts to light. I've been told that light is the Creator. This photon belt energy comes from the center of the galaxy, doesn't it?"

"Light is the connection to God, the Creator. Perhaps you understand more than you know." With that it disappeared in a flash, and I woke up.

Or had I?

"The last Chakra is about thought."
"I know you've told me this before. A long time ago."
"Yes, you failed last time as well."

****

An aborigine lays his head down. He has come to Uluru to listen to the dreams of his people. Singing his way here all day, he knew the moment of arrival would be around nightfall. That was how the songline went. He had watched with benevolence as the last of the whites came down from the sacred rock they called Ayer's, sweating and cursing. Trespassing over one of his people's most sacred sites. How little did they know. His darkness blending into the shadows, he approached, finding the one outcropping he sought. Crawling into the fissure, he huddled. Hieroglyphics older than most civilizations had been etched by his ancestors upon the cave walls. The mutants, the whites, had never seen these, never lessened their magic by the poison of their sight.

He lets the warmth of the rock surround him and comfort him as the temperature plummets with the sunset. Lizards skitter into their night crevices, the dirge of wind whistling like dried bone scraped over sunbaked wood, the voices of his ancestors lost somewhere, whispering to him. Closing his eyes, he dreams of blood-red moons and white desert sands. Howls of dingoes and the chuckle of kangaroos. Didgeridoos droning.

Eternal callings.

Calling.

Sweat forms on his black forehead, creasing the dust-baked brow as the rain begins. In the heavens the stars disappear as the patters become a torrent. A foul torrent. Dark as coal dust, covering everything, smothering everything in the absence of light. A night without stars, a rain of black water. Obliterating all light, ending existence.

When he awakes, he sees the stars overhead and cries. His ancestors still whisper in his ears, as does the haunting throb of a didgeridoo. As foretold, the end begins. One cycle ends; another will start.

He cries again and drifts back to sleep, the black rain continuing to fall.

****

The lights of the pyramid flooded in, and Roger closed his eyes, unsure what to expect. He'd been through so much already. He wanted to hold Beth again, feel her in his arms. Laugh with the kids, curse his dog for being out in the rain, shake his head at Mrs. Miller's deafness. What he'd give to swap crystals, crop circles and enlightenment for cold beer, NFL on the TV and normality.

To return to normal, only he wasn't sure what was normal anyway; he hadn't been it in such a long time. Maybe normal had ended the night at the lake when the aliens implanted them. Or is this normal now, and all of his past life illusion?

Visions floated by: Theodore pacing the room in consternation over discovering Sherida and her mission, Sherida on her knees before the Dogon Hogon, Bill standing in his living room staring at the alien metal, spouting "in-frigging-credible" over and over again repeatedly. Where were they now?

The Hathor appeared, smiling, and beside it, affable black Stan winking from under his mop of unruly platinum hair pronouncing, "Very sacred, this site."

He was in some sort of dream state. Or another gateway. Had to be.

Even old native Charlie, leaning on his Orca-headed cane, showed up. Only he wasn't smiling like the rest. "Remember what I told you, virgin gateway walker, Remember," he warned.

He vanished. They all vanished as a long powerful arm slammed him to the ground, knocking his breath from him.

****

"No! It cannot be!" Peter White Smoke Frederick felt the color of his skin drain away until he was as white as a Bahanna. His hands shook as he set down the parcel from Arizona University and picked up the phone. "Gather the elders for a meeting tonight." He rewrapped the triangular piece of stone and eased it into his backpack.

On the cold floor of the cave near the hills of Oraibi his grandson held the lantern over his head as Peter withdrew the stone tablet, given to his people nearly a thousand years ago. He didn't have to compare the piece to the power stone of the Fire Clan to know it would fit exactly into the place it was broken from.

"Grandpa, you told me that when the missing piece is returned to the Fire Clan's power stone, the fifth cycle will begin. So, what do we do now?"

"We take both pieces to the elders' meeting tonight. They will know what to do."

Sadness weighed his heart as he put both pieces into his backpack then rose and sighed, tears streaking his face. As they emerged from the cave's dim recesses, he placed his weathered hand on his grandson's shoulder. "And one other thing we do."

The boy looked up with the innocent eyes of an unfulfilled youth.

"We pray."

****

Roger struggled to rise but couldn't, held helpless in the grip of the beam of light flooding up from underneath him. Everything else was foggy. He blinked several times, letting the mists fade from his eyes. Beside him, Sherida was lying limp on a metal slab, probably similar to his, her chest rising and falling slowly, eyes glazed. "You're alive," he rasped. He'd done it, he'd actually done it. He'd found her.

Roger fought to rise again but couldn't and gave up. Only what had he got himself into? As he lay there his vision cleared further until he squinted at a figure nearby. He gasped. An Alpha-Draconian, a facsimile of the one the dinosaurs had eaten, stood before him grinning like a lizard sunning on a desert boulder. He was beginning to hate these creatures with the sort of inbred antagonism cats had for dogs and vice versa. "You'd be the bastard who's been chasing me." It was so hard to even speak. "What have you done to Sherida?"

"Zolnar is the last name you need to remember. But you needn't worry about your friend here, we never meant to kill her. At least not yet," the Alpha-Draconian hissing like he wanted his prehensile tongue to be treading where his hand was as he ran it over the cover of Sherida's breasts.

He moved towards Roger with the same grace as snakes slither through grass. "Rather ironic though. We knew of her mission, and the eleven other angels released from the moon's surface to test this planet's inhabitants. Locating and dealing with the angels was a simple matter. Finding their contacts proved harder."

His lips pulled back in a thin curl, revealing an array of teeth dulled to hide their natural razor sharpness, the teeth of a true carnosaur, capped in glittering gold. "Until now, and now we have you."

It was a trap, all of this was a trap to lure him in. Roger stared into the unblinking, yellow, slitted eyes of the reptile. So alien and cold-blooded.

"And you might like to know I also have the ancient ZPEC working. Thanks to you. A weapon rumored to exist that has eluded so many of us over millennia. A prize that will keep even the Council at bay. And I dare say, will make me very rich and powerful. An unexpected bonus. One of those rare fringe benefits." A translucent membrane shielded one of his eyes in what Roger presumed was a wink.

Sherida had said the tool could perform incredible feats, but in the wrong hands it could perform unimaginable destruction. He shivered. The room was becoming so cold, hard to think, as if he were being put to sleep ... no, drained.

"As the stasis beam pulls the life from your bodies, you and your angel will die. Shame though," he said as he ran his scaled hand over her breast and cupped it. "No point in keeping evidence around. I'd tasted what you call your burgers and Big Macs. Hadn't had meat in such a long time. I can see why my ancestors devoured meat once. Such powerful ancient cravings. Perhaps I might freeze her for a midnight snack later." The reptile's flickered out catching the dribble from his mouth.

He glanced back at Roger. "Do know this, hu-man from Gaia. You will not be alone. With control of the ZPEC the whole Gaia experiment will cease and as for the hu-man race? I'm sure it'll make a nice, although rather short footnote in some reference book written about forgotten races. I suppose we should be grateful to you for helping us so very much. You really have no concept of what you've done. Amazingly stupid and naïve creatures you warm bloods are. But enough of this. I have a bowl of Elysian blood worms waiting and they get rather tough if they're too agitated." He flicked a switch and left.

Instantly Roger sagged. The energy to resist evaporated. Coldness seeped into his bones. He tried to scream but couldn't even struggle as his body numbed. Only his brain functioned. Was this what had Sherida had been going through until his arrival?

Fringes of frost splintered and cracked across his mind. Spreading, growing, multiplying and finally engulfing him. Time, he'd run out of time, only had time to die a slow, agonizing death.

Then a voice. No, someone breathing. He looked around, hoping it was Sherida, or Tiyah, or Stan, anyone ... no, it was something he'd heard before. From the place in his mind that held no room for forgiveness, the place where everything he kept hidden from everyone else dwelled. From the darkness of his soul came a loping figure he knew all too well. The creature that in his dreams had attacked and killed him several times. The black dog had returned, to finish him off. He could taste his own flesh tearing. Feel its teeth razoring, ripping into him like they had done so many times before.

It moved closer. Roger cringed and backed into a wall of thickening cold. Ice, groaning, fissuring across the dark, cutting off all escape. Coldness, flesh sticking to ice, he pulled away, frost's frigid bite stinging at his flesh. Shapes formed around him. Columns of ice. Pillars?

The teachings of the Mystery Schools, of Hathor. What good could that do now when he had only time to die?

The dog drew nearer, eyes of blood-fire, jaws slavering.

"Well, this'll be the last time, then, won't it?" To his own ears, his laugh sounded insane. Madness, it all ended here, but wasn't laughter the best medicine in the moment of his demise. He felt a twinge in his left hand.

He opened his palm and found the sliver of rock, like a toothpick compared to...

Illusion.

What had Charlie said? So hard to think. He coughed, seeing his breath. Illusion ... how many times had he heard that the eyes were the deceivers of illusion. This time he laughed louder. A shudder rang through the ice sheet that was rapidly engulfing everything around him. The cracking, thunder of ice straining. The dog, still loping towards him, growling. Everything repeating itself in slow motion.

You are my greatest fear, one I've been running from since I was a child, when that black dog nearly attacked me. The soul is eternal, the Hathor taught me that. And the light of life will always conquer darkness. So, in essence I have nothing to fear except life itself and I am life, will always be life.

The growls grew angrier, louder. Roger leaned back. *It begins to make sense: my greatest fear, my subconscious, my demons all rolled into one. The me I keep denying, a higher self. I know now.* The beast was nearly on him. The Hathor had said that no one can fight anything until they become conscious of what isn't working. "You chasing me isn't working. Me denying the truth isn't working. But this is!" He held up the sliver of rock. It burst into blue flame, engulfing his hand and expanding into the mercuric gleam of a silver blade. "Ah, the brilliance of Illusion."

The dog snapped at him, its eyes narrowing in the fear usually mirrored in Roger's own eyes. How he knew this Roger wasn't sure, he just knew fear had shifted from one place to another, like rats in an abandoned house when a cat sets up residence. He hefted the heavy handle of the sword and the canine's growl reduced to a whimper.

He held the blade in front of him. The Hathor had done this. Given him the sword of consciousness, of awareness. Had set him on the right path.

The dog stopped in front of him, barked. *Oh yes, you're just an illusion. Fear is merely an emotion, its flip side excitement.* Roger waved the sword of awareness before him. "Ah, the bitter throes of madness. There's a time for everything, isn't there Poochy? Including a time to die." The dog howled and leaped for his throat.

He ripped the sword upward, tearing into the canine's chest, staring into its eyes as the sword gutted the dog, spraying the crushing ice and Roger in a spray of red and intestines. The light faded from its dark sight. "I say begone with the likes of you." *I have no need of you, no room for fear now. The time for change is begun. He knew this, it was the lesson the Hathor had tried to instill into his thick head, time and again.*

Inside, walls collapsing, doors opening, others swinging shut. Everything he'd been shown and taught had finally begun to make sense. Gateways awaited to be walked.

He dragged the sword downwards, splattering himself and the ice with the ruby stains of blood and entrails. The dog fell to a heap by his feet, one cold eye staring at him from the congealing pile of once-great terror.

When you know this, you will have succeeded, the Hathor had said.

Roger turned. No escape. The ice had closed all around. He slashed at it; it exploded and a few shards fell away, only to regenerate. Groaning, it kept growing inward. His breath came shivering on icy currents. Thoughts slowing down. The dog's blood and entrails congealed into frozen iced parts.

"Illusion, this is all illusion." *No escape, not this way. Time for the greatest illusion of them all. Time to surrender all that this mortal body contains.* He stood over the remains of the dog. *If am to die here then I will stand over the corpse of my fears, anchor myself with this sword and wait for the wall of ice, of death to claim me. For I know it cannot. Beth, wherever you are, I love you.*

The ice surged forth to sear him with its final embrace. Congealing thoughts, solidifying memories. Roger thrust the sword, punching it straight through the corpse and dove into the remains. "I've become my greatest fear."

The ground collapsed, plunging him into an unending pit. Everything fading, going blank, tumbling into frozen nothingness.

Becoming nothing but infinitesimal substance dissipating into the ether until only one cell, one single speck of himself, remained.

No running, no fighting, only eternal peace. He should have feared what was now happening; instead he surrendered to the blackness.

The Hathor had said that the end of all illusion is the reality of illusion. There were no senses here. Only stillness. Was this death? Or was this truth, stripped of all his preconceptions, all his fears, the absolute reality. A single cell of life floating on the cosmic soup. So hard to think. His mind slowed down, evaporating into the void.

All he had to do was trust.

Simply trust.

And that faded,

until nothing remained,

not even a single cell of memory.

Chapter Sixteen

om

OM

OM

Tonal vibrations sweep the dark, beginning a rhythmic dance answering the call. A single cell fluttered. Trembling's. An egg thumped with its first heartbeat.

OM

Life beginning. Darkness, floating in darkness. He was but one cell. How was it possible that he could think? Comprehend?

An urge came from within as the tones ringing through the shell he was encased in reverberated again. He shuddered through his entire being.

The need to pull. Overloading pressure, growing at a phenomenal rate, until it became too great. Intense constrictions, the need to pull out, away from pain. He felt himself twisting in two directions. Until finally he split. Anchored together, himself, yet two.

He floated on the warmth of a black ether. How long had he lain asleep? Hadn't he read that some believe that all of your entire history, past experiences and lifetimes, resides in your DNA, in each cell? It was obviously true. Was this place the fourth dimension then?

Wind borne on cosmic currents began to moan by; dormant sparkles stirred, sprinkling the heavens with a glittering light. The awe of wind sighing like angels humming and fairies breathing. Surf, gentle surf moved through him, and the drumbeats returned. Inside a compulsion formed again as the pressure grew.

The need, the time to split. And another surge, like birthing, now he was no longer two but four, again, now eight.

He shuddered, the joy within, love flowing through every part of his being. The drone of Buddhist monks on their long, low, bassy, and tonerous horns.

Again, the surge, the need to pull and he divided again. It was quickening now. From within, warmth poured up from below, filling him with the white light of pure love, swelling the root chakra, filling the next as it rose, a bowl running over with water. Fishnets brimming over with fish.

Again, he divided.

White light surged upward, igniting the next chakra, he shuddered in response. The surge began again, and again. A flow of erupting life, cells replicating and duplicating themselves.

Again and again. Unto the next, until it reached his brow, the crown chakra. Splitting, growing life beginning? The clutches of becoming alive, the merest chance that this was what it was like for the first conscious cells, so many millions of years ago?

Let me breathe, let me open my eyes and walk?

Warmth flooded him as the song of the interstellar currents rushed by. Music from somewhere. A soft hum of violins and mothers singing babies asleep. The dirge of Celtic monks. Drums, the measured rhythms of drums. Vedic verses on Indian lips, haunting melodies of Hindu holy men praying, while Indian sitars sang to the heavens.

The deep throb of Australian aborigines and their didgeridoos, calling. Calling him into dreamtime. Everything exploding in orchestrated uprisings as an urge to speak, to utter a single powerful word craves its way over his lips.

OM

He was told within the harmonics of that note resides the voice of God. Completing the circle started, releasing back to the darkness the essence of beginnings.

Celtic chants and the rambling patter of Welsh, Gaelic mutters in time to beats of soul. He knows now that he could never die, not today, not ever. Druidic rituals flowed over ancient stone on henge. Chanting. Black gospel singers belting out heart and soul. African drums and natives dancing to keep away the hyenas lurking nearby. Chanting.

Vastness of space fills with a volume of awe. Scottish bagpipes playing Amazing Grace. Choirs of Christian and Catholic voices raised in great cathedrals. Millions of Muslims flowing in circular tempo during the pilgrimage of hajj. Around and around the sacred rock of Kaaba at Mecca. Praying in salat, one voice.

West Coast natives in longhouses, smoke curling through cedar roofs, calling in ancestral beings in shrill wailings on deep bass drums. Pounding on sinew and hide stretched over cedar and pine.

Spirits being blessed on Hopi ceremonies. Incense burners carrying away the deep droning murmurs of Buddhist monks and in the sunlight reflection of their shaved heads are cast the prayers to Amaterasu of Shinto followers. Kami energies rise up through mountain slopes, mixing with the tread of footsteps traversing Mt. Fuji. Russian dervishes swirling as a Mayan priest slices down through bone and muscle until he holds a pulsing heart to the heavens.

A single child singing to itself as it plays.

OM

Silence like Jews praying in reverence before the wailing wall while vibrations pull at him and like the horn of Jericho the very air collapses all around. Vacuum inhales and expels. No longer a prisoner, no longer separate, no longer one.

No longer...

And he knows.

Ascension, true ascension. Brilliant white light floods him from above, as above is defined from below in a void, funneling into a beam. Entering his head flooding the seventh chakra. And the light that has been there all this time flows downward in a spiraling flashflood, absorbing and spinning into alignment the other chakras one after another until...

Silence.

The long cry of a wolf on a full moon night cut the void.

Enough, eyes grow heavy, and he fades into a blissful sleep, cuddled in darkness. Floating on the nether of space. Curling into a ball, finding solace in sucking on his thumb.

Done, for now.

Roger awoke in dark stillness. He turned and saw a thin blur in the distance denoting a horizon. Gentle swaying of waters or at least some viscous substance of similarity. The sense of a great ocean at night, resting, calm.

Moving, he realized he was in a membrane thin capsule encircling him. He reached up, feeling the edges of his enclosure. Naked, trapped in a jelly-like cocoon. Drifting alone on a vast ocean. A serene calmness sung home to his senses, averting fears.

Was this what a baby felt like within its mother?

He turned carefully, fearing rupturing the thin protection that kept him from falling into the dark waters.

Warmth welled up from below, like the up welling of volcanic vents or the breath of a large creature. Something below stirred, shifting him in his light compartment. Sending him bobbing along like jetsam.

A spot of light, then several moving up from the abysmal depths. Luminous greens and blues, surging, flowing directly to him. Roger waited as something approached.

The lights grew until they reached nearly human sized proportions and hovered below him. They formed a circle around him. Lights surging changing in color, pulsing in a rhythmic pattern. Flowing as if they were talking to each other, using light and colors to communicate between themselves, studying him.

Rising they broke the surface of the water hovered over him. Gelatinous, indistinct shapes in the dark. With many long flowing finlike members, elegant angels with lionfish-like appendages. Fluttering in the air, they watched him until a surge of white light burst suddenly from all of them.

As if panicked they flowed upwards to disappear into the heavens becoming pinpricks of lights, like stars winking overhead, then gone.

What had scared them?

It began, an upwelling from the depths again. Only far larger. Water swirled.

Something very large, from a great distance below was coming. Heated water from the deep pumped upwards, the surface heaved in tsunami like undulations, tossing Roger on the waters. Clinging to his sac of fluid praying to his luck that it hadn't ruptured yet or would.

Lights approaching. Huge pools of brightness from each side of him, illuminating everything above and below him. Massive, on a scale beyond comprehension, crossing the gulfs of dark oceans, moving up and him directly in its path.

So large he realized there were just two groupings of lights approaching. He wanted to swim out of the way but was afraid of wrecking the safety of his capsule. Only to realize there was no escape as whatever was coming continued to grow in size until the two lights filled the entire ocean and he knew that whatever this was that was coming, it was still very far away.

Galaxies away.

The sensation of being a gnat on the back of a flea on a dog, was how he felt as it slowly advanced. From the center of both lights, atoms swirled like pulsars and whole solar systems turned on their axis. Merging in the center of the two lights forming a heavier area, darker, like ... he hesitated ... like two iris. Whirlpools of black holes lost in their depths.

He was in awe, total awe.

This entity, the matter of all creation.

The all that is.

Moments of eternity spent focusing on him.

A being of timelessness, who'd seen the beginning of the universe, for it was the cause.

It was the universe and it ...

STARED
AT
HIM.

At the far end of his vision he caught the subtle flicker of movement, like the lifting of an eyelash. Approval and love, overwhelming love flooded him. The true essence of this being.

Pure, unadulterated love.

Then it pulled itself back to where it came from, the center of the universe. Creations roost. Dark waters of space swirled in quieting eddies cast by its retreat.

Roger trembled. To be the focus of something so overwhelmingly massive. So inspiring. So, the thought clung to him, denying comprehension, so godlike. He wept, his tears filling the capsule, and fell into a deep calm sleep.

How long he'd slept Roger had no idea.

Only that he was floating on an unending ocean of warm darkness. He sensed there was more to become later, more to learn, in other lifetimes. He knew he would return to Earth, to his wife, his former life. Only this journey wasn't quite finished yet.

He had an angel to rescue first.

Mist streamed away from his eyes as he smiled and in the corner of his iris a world resided, into there he blinked, flooding himself with light.

Brilliance overpowering. He closed his eyes and let the white light enter his head, focusing it, allowing it seep down through him. Shifting from white, pure consciousness, to a deep purple, fading to a dark blue. He took a deep breath allowing the blue to fade to a vibrant green, which burnt away to a surreal yellow, slowly cooling away into orange and then red. A dark grounded red.

The teachings of the Hathor had again been correct. He opened his eyes and looked down, realizing he'd hands again and wiggling his toes, feet. Looking around he was back in the cell. Everything shimmered translucent around him, as if he wasn't really here, but immaterial, like a ghost.

He closed his eyes and slipped from the bonds of the confinement cage the Draconian had put him in. Concentrating harder he pulled himself back into this reality and watched the room grow silvery as the dimensions solidified around him until he stood newborn naked on the floor.

How was he doing this? Had he died and ascended or was he somehow drawing on the power of the ZPEC he'd started up? Did it matter? He was back.

Cold stone on his feet assailed his nerves. Dank air trapped in underground stone chambers for centuries clung at his nostrils. Hair bristled as he ran his hand over his chest, noting the pliability of his skin, so comforting to experience physical sensations again.

Roger walked over to where Sherida lay, still and cold. Was he too late? He reached over and touched her. Universal life energy flowed through him, like he'd seen the shaman perform and through her. Warmth flooded her, filling her with the ultimate power in the universe. Love.

Tachyons or whatever science called them, didn't matter as the light flowed through him into Sherida.

The ZPEC wasn't meant to be used as a weapon, that would be wrong. The Hathor and Tiyah both said that. Now he was beginning to understand why.

The click of weaponry, as guards flooded into the room. Somehow, they'd been alerted.

Sherida gasped, regaining consciousness.

Zolnar strode in. "How did you?"

A wave of Roger's hand and weapons blazed into intense light, melting, transforming into flowers. Stonewalls melted around them, starlight flooded in as the roof vanished. Granite reconfigured into wood and soon a forest of trees stood around them.

The Draconians stood stunned as body armor transformed into billowing dresses. Terrified, they ran fleeing through a mountain meadow of alpine flowers, raising clouds of multi-colored butterflies. Zolnar stood in stunned submission, cradling a bouquet of flowers in his arm, instead of his gun.

Sherida smiled, struggling to get up. A cascade of rainbows flowed from her lips and stars stole from her eyes as she soaked out the retreating tachyon energies. Roger grabbed her and held her up.

"Thank you," she weakly whispered.

Slowly currents of brightly colored butterflies began to swirl around them.

Zolnar stood aghast, helpless. Roger lifted his hand towards him. "No, don't kill me. Please." He sank to one knee.

Roger moved his fingers and painted a happy face on the being's forehead. "Sorry, I'm not big on killing things and we gotta go."

Zolnar glared at him. "How did you know how to use the ZPEC?"

"Simple brother. Peace and Love," Roger uttered remembering the words of John Lennon, lifting on interstellar currents created by the thousands of winged insects, swirling around them. The energy of life, of the universe, of God and love flooding him. Long, slender ethereal wings sprouted, translucent shimmering with each slow stroke, spilling glints of starlight, they rose through the nether. Entering into what was once called the void of space, the thinnest most undetectable matter, holding everything together; Zero-point energy, the Creator's milk. Swimming in the vastness of the universe's lifeblood.

****

Trimus shimmered into view as Sherida and Roger vanished into the stars. He'd finally had a lock on Zolnar's ship. Spinning around he stood looking perplexed as Zolnar sat on his knees, shaking. All around were flowers and drawn on his face a funny smiling face. "Well this is interesting." He was ready for a hard-fought battle. It was obvious that the human study Sherida was in charge of now controlled the ZPEC and perhaps much of reality. A flick from his controls on his arm shimmered around the reptilian and held him in a frozen mist. *Time to bring you to justice and bring you before the council.*

****

In a blur they approached a pattern of stars Roger recognized, the Pleiades.

"That is home for me, but not where we need to go. The Galactic Council is meeting on Sirius." Sherida said.

He held her under his arm and together they beat as one entity. Moments later they circled a large green and blue planet many times the size of Earth. Sherida drew them down into a city with towers of large crystalline-like structures. They landed and walked up to a towering wall of crystal.

"There is a code in order to enter."

Without hesitating Roger studied the hundreds of pictographs scrawled on the opaque surface and reached up to touch several. Each light up as he did, he'd done this before on the crystal tower at Machu Picchu. "The symbols of the seven chakras."

Sherida smiled as invisible lines appeared in the crystal and the massive door slid back. They enter a cavernous room, full of thousands of beings that sat, floated and swam in contained waters: Hathors, some Alpha Draconians, thin large-headed Zeta Reticuli, feral cat-like beings, several dolphin-like beings, and even a few Avian species that twittered back and forth like budgies. Many in fact most were humanoid type species in different colors, verging on the end of the blackest Negroid types to deep blues, even greens and reds to albino white, in sizes of squat to nearly ten feet in height. There were also many wispy beings of energy. He knew it was a struggle for them to even hold their shape in order to be here.

"Welcome. The Galactic Council shall begin this session with the first human from Gaia in the Sol system to call."

Sherida lifted her head. "But first I must speak. Your honors, there is treachery here. We must stop the Alpha Draconian named Zolnar. He has attempted to destroy the ascension process, has knowingly hunted down, killed my fellow angels and is in control of the ancient ZPEC device installed on Gaia."

"We know, have known all along." Many smiled. "He is now detained by one known as Trimus."

With that Trimus shimmered into view, Zolnar held in a frozen mist.

"That one will be dealt with later and we salute you for this great victory, Trimus."

The council moved Zolnar to a compound as Trimus bent to one knee in respect to the thousands of representatives gathered. "It was not I, but the human called Roger who defeated this creature, by unleashing the ZPEC. I merely followed his trail via the energy of the ZPEC he opened and arrested him."

Roger watched near tears forming in Sherida's face as she stared at Trimus, realizing he was alive. She obviously had very strong feelings for this fellow agent, probably more pronounced now that her emotions were free once again.

"You knew?" Confusion crossed her face before anger bit in, turning to the council. "You let them die? All of them?"

"Of course," Roger groaned, as Sherida looked bewildered. Anger raging inside, *how could they?* Roger read her thoughts. There were costs sometimes greatly in lives to succeed. Costs that could never be rectified, yet had to be paid to achieve the needed results. "It was part of the process. All of this was a test. Wasn't it?"

"We did not know which person nor agent would succeed. Nor the undermining of the process done by Zolnar. Yet, you three still managed to succeed."

After that a flood of telepathic information welcoming him entered his head from the many worlds gathered.

"Bastards!" They both thought loudly to each other.

"You will now be returned to Earth in your human form. We, the council thank you for everything you have done, Roger, our distinguished Gateway Walker."

Roger looked blankly at them and at Sherida, not quite fully understanding, but knowing they were right.

"First of all, there will be one needed to show them what is about to happen, and you are after all simply the gateway walker that solved this process. True Ascension awaits you when you are ready. As you have seen and gone through the process. You will be now returned to your planet."

"But... No time for goodbyes then..." Before he could reply any further Roger vanished before everyone.

Epilogue

Earthweek: Science News

Scientists in California, by way of the Hubble Telescope, have begun to notice slight differences in the positions of several stars. After studying distances, they have determined that the big bang theory may have to be revisited as it appears that the universe is no longer expanding but has stopped and it would appear several stars are apparently contracting. They are running more tests on another sector of space to further verify the data so far received.

Reaction from Hinduists in India upon hearing the news. They refer to the oldest scriptures that say that the universe is merely the breath of Brahma. Like any being that breathes, eventually the out-breath stops, and the in-breath begins. So does the process of life go on. That God breathes out all of creation and eventually breaths it all back in again.

Machu Picchu

Roger stared high into the night sky. Standing on a hillside overlooking Machu Picchu, he hugged Beth. Below them in the ancient town thousands of people stood and waited. No one had called them, but they all knew psychically what was about to happen and like the movie, Close Encounters, were waiting perhaps for the song 'Play the Five Tones' to begin awakening the heavens, calling to the arrival of those somewhere overhead. Only the silence of the night called out.

Watching as the stars shimmered away and what appeared earlier in the night to be a new light source began to form in the center of the darkness. That light kept expanding until it filled a moon-sized portion of the heavens. The protective layer of ozone above them had begun to dissipate, being dissolved away by the funnel of light. "The essence of God flowing in," Roger told Beth. It was flooding them with an overpowering feeling of love.

One pinprick of light in the sky began to shift. Then another, then several, until hundreds began to dance and converge.

"They're coming, aren't they?" Beth asked, as he held her in his arms. It had taken awhile to convince her, but once he touched her forehead and flooded her head with everything he had experienced in the couple of weeks, Beth believed him. The one gift he found out he could transfer to her and others, was what he had experienced at a mere touch to the forehead. He silently thanked the council for that, it had saved his marriage and the love of his life. Maybe their way of repaying him for everything he went through, as a thanks, knowing otherwise he would never be respected and possibly scorned.

"Yes, after thousands of years. Daniken, Sitchin, and all of those telepathic people that had information channeled to them are about to be proven correct."

"Is this what happens when ET phones home?" Beth asked.

"Apparently, but there's other funnels forming over ancient energy centers like Stonehenge and the pyramids as well." Sherida smiled directing him to what was happening and beside her stood Trimus. He knew after she got back to her home-world she was granted the rare honor of retiring, along with Trimus as her mate. Roger could see the joy in their eyes when they looked at each other and a touch of sadness remembering how Theodore was love-struck by her. Since he got back he hadn't had a chance to pay his last respects to his deceased friend.

The wormhole continued forming above them, growing brighter, as they reconnected. Light suddenly flooded down from the sky, flowing onto the mountaintop they stood on. Roger turned away for a moment and saw several of the people in the crowd begin to glow, first through their eyes which seemed to enlarge with the energy flow that was beginning, until they were coated in a soft sheen of white energy. Then they poured themselves out through their eyes, becoming beings of white energy, and lifted upward, shaking themselves free of the old material bodies. At first a few, then thousands of beams of light flowed up into the cosmos dancing all around them.

Roger was reminded of the Sumerian and Egyptian drawings, the Easter Island statues, the Haida and other native totems across North America and the Pacific with the statues of large luminous eyes. "Somehow they knew all along this was going to happen and their jobs are done here aren't they?"

"Yes, these are the Lightworkers, that have either come to be here to experience this event or to help others. Some may have already begun to ascend, others just visiting, as tourists. Others here to help new initiates like yourself, to understand the journey they must now take as they reach the higher dimensions and continue their soul's growth."

Roger turned around and watched as several spacecraft ejected from the core of the white light.

"The Visitors from the rest of the galaxy, I presume."

"Yes, you'll finally get to meet all of those that like your yourselves have joined the rest of the cosmos. But there's more. Watch, the next wave of coming teachers to help us."

Roger stared as several figures materialized in the center of the square. Oddly enough he recognized many of the people and somehow knew who the others were: Judaism's the Messiah, the Hindu's Kalki Avatar, the Moslem's Imam Mahdi, the Buddhist's Maitreya Buddha, Shiva, Osirus, Muhammad, Odin, Zeus, Vishnu, the Dogon's Nommo, Omo and Maasaw, Quesiquatal and one he knew very well. A tall figure in white robes, bearded so like all the holy pictures he'd seen drawn over the last two centuries smiled at him as he walked by. "So, the age of Christ consciousness truly begins. Not quite like the great book states?"

"Ah, I wouldn't say I was that important." A familiar voice broke the stunned silence.

A man walked free of the light transporting the lightworkers. Dressed not in white shimmering robes like many of the others but in the last clothes he remembered Theodore in, smiled with a large grin on his face.

"Theodore?" Roger gasped as he ran over to hug the friend, he thought was long dead.

He clasped his friend, hugging him tight.

Static electrical waves surged through him like hugging an energy beam as the ZPEC energies slowly dispelled from Theodore.

"How...?"

"Didn't I say there were things out there we'll never understand?"

"Understand, but I saw you die. Flattened by a car."

"Yes, but after all you have discovered, you must realize that the soul is eternal and this is but one plane of existence. I took a similar journey to the one you needed to take to start all of this. I've not only studied past earth history and alien involvement on our planet, but esoteric matters like fourth dimensionality, and ascended beings. I knew that once my spirit was forced to leave my body I had to go and find Sherida or at least check out what the Pleiades were really all about and the next level of ascension.

I managed to run into Trimus or him to me, didn't matter. He helped me and got me to join the academy of light workers where I volunteered to help civilizations to evolve and hopefully be a part of this one."

Trimus interrupted, "I replayed the scene where he died and knew who had done it to him. So I searched for not only Zolnar, but Theodore's spirit."

"But I thought maybe Sherida and you would you know... get together."

"I think what he actually meant was shag your brains out." Came from one of the others, emerging from the light.

At the sound of a footstep behind him and the beginning swish of air, Roger ducked, pulling Beth down with him. "Trouble just arrived."

The Orca-headed cane sang only to empty air as he spun around and in slow motion kicked the staff from Charlie's hand.

"Damn smart-ass gateway walkers," Charlie said as he bent over to retrieve his Orca-headed walking stick.

"Beth, meet one of the other ones I told you about."

She smiled, "This would be Charlie, no doubt."

Roger looked at him puzzled. "Hey, what are you doing here? I heard the last train for Clarksville left a few seconds ago. Taking most of the enlightened and those nuts either plain or of the salted variety as well."

"Not all teachers are sane, nor come in holier than thou outfits, you know," and in the blink of a fly's wing Charlie spun around as he picked up his cane and jammed it between Roger's legs sending him sprawling, repeating the same lesson he taught him when they first met. "Nor are all gateway walkers that bloody smart or aware."

Roger, Beth, Theodore, Trimus and Sherida all laughed as Charlie helped him up.

"So, I'm beginning to realize." Roger said dusting himself off.

"Time to go." Charlie looked into Roger's eyes. "However, you have learned well. Thank you, you helped inadvertently save my life and reconnect me to my heart, my twin flame also."

"Really, didn't know you had a significant other." Roger was afraid to say lady, he wasn't quite sure what Charlie fancied. Hell, it coulda been a squirrel for all he knew and nor would be surprised.

"Yes, a native woman, my childhood sweetheart Lucy. She'd died many years ago and after you left something strange began to happen to me. I knew I'd been called into the area to investigate some bizarre energy fluctuations. Only once you were gone, I began to discorporate right there on the beach and somehow Lucy began to shift into this realm. It was like we were shifting our place in dimensions, soul transference. In the end I managed to end up back here with her."

"Sounds wild, must have been a tough journey." Theodore added, "Or do I sense another book we haven't the time to get into right about now."

They all laughed. "It wasn't the Iliad, more like Zombie Attack on Bomb Beach, but in the end it was all worth it." Charlie smiled with a wink and tinkle in his eyes that Roger had never seen before. He wasn't sure if that wasn't more from finding the love of his life again, more than Ascension or the fact that he could still pull one up on Roger. With that the elder sauntered off to join the others leaving, his eyes aglow.

"To answer your earlier questions about Sherida. Before our First Nations guest interrupted. I didn't realize how much I enjoyed this journey of mine along with helping others. Besides I found out the guy she really liked." Theodore pointed at Trimus. "And him to her. Hence why he risked his life to find her."

A familiar dark-skinned boy with a blonde head of hair emerged from the light. Stan Nurrumbunguttia smiled at him. "I told you were very wise Roger the amerjig."

"The hair," he stared at Sherida and Trimus. "Why didn't I guess by the hair that you were possibly one of them? A Pleiadean?"

Stan smiled back at him and replied to them. "Ah, your mind was on other matters at the time, amerjig." Behind him came Tiyah as Trimus spoke.

Trimus replied. "Yes, he's from one of the other worlds in our system, an older version of us that remained on earth when the last phase of ascension failed, along with Tiyah who's from Atlantia. Both of them along with others can now ascend."

Roger looked even more stunned. "He's sixty thousand years old as well?"

"Not all teachers appear as old as they look." Tiyah replied emerging from the others. "And for some of us, we are now allowed to return to our home worlds."

With that she and Stan moved into the light and were swept upwards.

A tear fell down Roger's face, not even being able to comprehend what it would be like to have to wait that long to return home. *But if I did nothing else, that alone was worth everything I went through.*

"Yes, the next few years are going to be chaotic as this system will begin to join the others as it begins the journey back to normalcy with the rest of the universe. Leaving one realm and joining another." Theodore said.

"I keep thinking, all of what we did really matter?" Roger asked.

Sherida looked at him puzzled.

"This ascension stuff would have happened anyways, wouldn't it?"

"Not really. This one had failed before, hence why Tiyah and Stan were stuck here along many others. The planet would have begun another phase, that's true. But without humanity's ascension and no help from the other races. There are some worlds that have never ascended and won't and others that took a few tries, like this one before they made it."

"Why?"

"Non-interference."

"I don't understand?"

"You cracked the code; you allowed Earthlings to be acknowledged by the other races and the Federation. The alignment of energies on this planet has allowed the zero-point wormhole to form. It will Allow us to come to your aid and help rebuild your world for the next cycle."

"But many will die if you didn't. A lot of our civilizations will be destroyed. You would be doing nothing to stop that?"

"Can't, don't you remember they, the others, did nothing to stop all of those who died in order for you and me to allow this above us to happen. The termination of this cycle, this circle of life. In the past, in other cycles, some races tried to stop this process and were destroyed or, worse, caused the destruction of Ley line centers which in turn formed such dangerous anomalies as the Bermuda Triangle to emerge."

"Yes, I read that in the chronicles in the Halls of Amenti. Among them, Lemuria and Atlantis."

"The destruction destroyed not only their civilization but the one on Mars, and the fifth planet Maldek, which created your asteroid belt and many other worlds out there. A seed world exists only for one thing."

"To sprout and feed those who planted the seeds."

"To germinate, yes, feed the one that has planted the seeds originally, but also to spread its seeds. Enhance its genetic structure. The strong survive and in so doing strengthen the species. There can't be any cheating."

"But all those souls, those that are sacrificed? Are they then, the weak, not meant to live?"

"No one is sacrificed. This process has been going on for billions of years. This is the flow of life in the universe, by doing what your society is currently doing, you are weakening your species and not allowing the soul within to move on."

"Like our seasons, only consider the Great astrological year of 25,920 years as one season or cycle as the ancients did and you can begin to look at things in the bigger picture of the universe."

Sherida interjected. "The soul never dies. It is merely transferred from one state to another. Theodore is proof of that. This way of existing ceases, and yes, creates chaos at first. A new greater one will begin when order is established."

"When it happens, some are ready, others are not. Some ascend to higher purposes. Others stay here for further lessons. Part of the pattern of life."

"So many will be earthbound in that circle thing you're probably going to say."

He stood, feeling heat pouring into his eyes and knew he was about to join the others, to do what he'd dreamed about since he was a child, out there in the stars. Tears streaked his face as he clutched Beth's hand and watched her eyes begin to glow as well. "So, in the scheme of things, I'm not all that important, am I?"

"Important enough to be one of the few us messengers we were sent to watch. You just happened to be the one that cracked the code."

Shudders continued to ripple through the world. "The rebirthing process is never easy, is it?"

Roger stopped for a moment and looked into Beth's eyes before he answered. "From what I learned that the universe is a far vaster and stranger place than we can possibly conceptualize. That I am truly a connected part of this universe, part of life and God isn't just out there in any form but is within me. Knowing that, I and we can never be alone. Most important thing I learned through all of this was to love myself, my wife and my world. It's really a pretty cool place. But I believe it's time to get off my soapbox."

"So, enjoy the New Earth's Spring. The planet's harmonics are aligned now, humanity can now ascend and join the other worlds. Thanks to you. Part of the process is to get Earth ready for the next seeding after the destruction of this one. The humans that live can tell the tale of this day. Form their own legends, their own Gods."

Roger smiled. All is as it should be, as it was meant to be.

****

In Roger's mind he saw a young boy dreaming of spaceships racing across interstellar skies, his hands buried in the long, wet grass of his youth and beside him a gangly young girl. Him and his first love, Susan, when they were seven years old. They laughed, giggling long into the night.

To See The World In A Grain Of Sand

And Heaven In A Wildflower
To Hold Infinity In The Palm Of Your Hand
And Eternity In An Hour
We Are Led To Believe A Lie
When We See With And Not Through The Eye
That Was Born In A Night,
To Perish In A Night.
When The Soul Slept In Beams Of Light
William Blake

And Above All Else

To my wife Jenny; who does all of my corrections, grammar and proper punctuation before the rest of the world, and any editor, gets to see it, along with putting up with all of my sh*t.

This novel and all of my others wouldn't be possible without all of her background work.

PS. And she still loves me unconditionally (also she just edited this over my shoulder!).

If you really enjoyed this novel,
please feel free to leave a review.

The author will highly appreciate it
And will help my rankings on Amazon
Thank You!

Novels Under the Pseudonym
Felicity Talisman

Two heart-wrenching tragedies in the same week served as a stark reminder of the brevity of life. It was time for Leanne to free herself from the humdrum world of real estate and fulfill her heart's desire. The need to achieve her dream became even more poignant when she discovered her mother had carried the same dream of wanting to paint, but self-doubt had prevented her from even trying.

Leanne embarked on a road-trip to Banff, a town nestled in the heart of the magnificent Rocky Mountains, surrounded by the most perfect of nature's beauty. Since this was where her parents had fallen in love, it felt crucial to achieve their shared dream there. However, unbeknownst to Leanne, her run-of-the-mill road-trip turns into anything but and her journey to fulfillment becomes even stranger than fiction.

Shuttered Seductions Romance Novel

She only wanted Not to fall in love with him.
He only wanted to steal her company. Roy only wanted to
seduce Julia-Rae and convince her to sell him her company.
Julia-Rae wanted to shut him out of her heart like
every other man that ever got close. Only what do you do
when you fall in madly in love with the enemy
and the enemy with you. Will the dark secrets they hold
tear them apart or bring them closer together?

Autumn's Summer

Written in his wife's hand a beautiful leather-bound diary is delivered a year after her passing which contains many secrets. Showing how his lonely empty-nester wife's life changed profoundly after a purely-by-chance meeting in, of all places, a mundane, corner grocery store. She embarks on a voyage of discovery with the spiritualist, Summer, to find new meaning to her life, that, once commenced, transports her to realms and dimensions she never knew existed.

A contemporary literary romance novel mixed with a suspense-filled mystery thriller. The writer combines magical realism and paranormal urban fantasy on a profoundly spiritual level unlike any novel you have ever, or will ever, read.

Reviews

I thought I'd have a quick peek at Autumn's Summer and then finish the book I was currently reading! I was entranced and spellbound from that moment, my current read neglected! Couldn't put it down, read it in one day. Yes, the love scenes were intense, passion blossoms in many forms! I enjoyed this immensely!

Shelley W.

Run, don't walk to your nearest bookseller and pick up a copy of Felicity Talisman's Autumn's Summer. I didn't know what to expect from the book, but I was immediately drawn into the world the author has created. It has everything a reader could want, real characters in a fantasy world while bridging the gap between fantasy and reality.

Great job by this Canadian author!

Greenhill

5.0 out of 5 stars <u>**Five Star Review**</u>[1]

"Autumn's Summer" is very complex, and readers will begin to develop feelings for the characters as if they were real people you could become friends with. Each character is multi-faceted, and the storyline is completely believable. The intertwining of Celtic beliefs and legends throughout the story offers readers a wonderful way to get to know Celtic history while reading along. The author even offered an additional section called Celtic Facts, Legends and History if you are so inclined to want to learn more about Celtic history and practices.

Overall, "Autumn's Summer" by Felicity Talisman is rich in details, especially in Celtic legends and traditions. The characters will enchant you and the story will entertain any reader who appreciates great characters. It's well worth looking into!

Life had seemed to be unfulfilled for Autumn for quite a few years, but she never completely realized it until she saw an ad in the local grocery store for someone offering yoga classes, meditations, and spiritual readings in "Autumn's Summer" by Felicity Talisman. Something about this ad offered by a woman named Summer caught her eye and intrigued her. While reading the ad, someone off in the near distance began watching Autumn without her knowing it. Summer just so happened to be in the store at the same time and couldn't help but approach Autumn. Both women felt a stirring inside themselves but didn't quite know what fate had in store for the both of them. They became fast friends, and this led to them having an affair together even though Autumn was married to Richard.

A fun fact explained in the back of the book is that the author's name, Felicity Talisman, is a collaboration between Frank and his wife, Jenny Talaber. How wonderful to learn that a husband and wife team worked on creating such an entertaining story!

Reviewed by Diana Coyle for Reader Views

---

1.   https://www.amazon.ca/gp/customer-reviews/R1Y9GW1AMUDAOX/
ref=cm_cr_dp_d_rvw_ttl?ie=UTF8&ASIN=1738658376

Afterword

Writing As Felicity Talisman

He was once told by a woman that most guys don't know how to romance let alone write it. Hence the pseudonym 'Felicity Talisman' in his more romantic ventures.

Frank's Bio

Born on the wild Canadian prairies but tired of the winter months in Edmonton, Frank immigrated to the more temperate cedar forests of coastal British Columbia. Yes, they get snow in Chilliwack during the winter months, and on that odd occasion Frank is forced to search out the snow shovel, dust off the cobwebs and have a go. At the snow, not the cobwebs.

His run-of-the-mill day job of auto technician/service advisor seems at odds with being an inspired, off-the-wall, author, but his zest for life, the environment, and the little muses that won't let his pencil stay still, spring from his mother's Hungarian ancestry. It's the Gypsy blood, he says, which pounds through his veins with wild abandon, driving him to the realms of fantasy.

This is the muse inside, the essence of Frank Talaber.

People who have read Frank's books describe him as a natural storyteller who writes like his soul is on fire and his pencil is his voice. They go further to say that they find his books grabbingly intense and hilarious at times, screaming everyday life from such a realistic viewpoint you're drawn into his world, hook, line and plum bob, unable to stop; almost cursing that they can't set the book down, page after page. Frank takes great pride in the realism of his work, painstakingly visiting most of the locations, (obviously, only the "real-life" ones!) and he is so thorough that many readers have remarked that they can hear, taste, visualize, smell and feel the essence of the place. "It really is like being there" one remarked. There isn't a greater compliment to be made.

His tagline is Canada's Foremost Off-beat Author (also the name of his YouTube channel; check it out for his witty and informative videos) who writes in urban fantasy, science fiction, crime, spiritual, romance, erotica and comedy genres. Well, anything that comes to him, basically! Except westerns. Although he does like to ride Gangnam style; does that count?

Literature written almost beyond genres, whose compelling thoughts are freed from the depths of the heart and subconscious before being poured onto the page. Or, as he often says, "you don't have to be mad to be a writer, but it sure helps".

Other Novels by Frank Talaber
Stillwater Runs Deep Series

Book One: Raven's Lament
(based on a true incident)

A madman cuts down a rare tree in protest of logging, releasing something he didn't intend to. Reporter Brooke Grant investigates the story, finds the love of his life, only to lose her to said being. Enlisting the aid of a deranged shaman he has to save his love and stop the world from being changed forever.

Reviews

WHISTLER INDEPENDENT BOOK AWARDS Fiction Evaluation 2023

Easy to follow and immerse oneself into this well-told story. The pace unfolds so naturally, I forgot that I was reading - which is essential to achieving this result. Loved the narrative voice that brought Characters to life through vivid descriptions and unforced dialogue. Time and place are masterfully captured through poetic and beautiful imagery. The writing style is wonderful, a celebration of words, both visual and imaginative. This story has depth, the themes are heartfelt and lingered long after I finished reading it. The pulse of energy - otherworldly, Raven's Lament is a classic in waiting with dream-like narration. I loved every inch of it.

[Thanks Frank & good luck!] Molly Harrison WiBA Coordination

I was touched when I sensed the author's profound reverence for trees; especially when I read his descriptions of the 'sobbing trees' as they were axed down. This novel has the ring of an epic "Lord of the Rings" journey -this is one journey that I'll always remember!

This is one of these books that you don't want to lay down until it's finished. Great stuff!

Stephanie A. Bridgeman

"After being stranded twenty kilometers from the nearest road at the tip of Rose Spit, Haida Gwaii, and having to push Frank's spanking new SUV a few kilometers along the beach before the tide came in and we ran out of booze, my first reaction on being asked to write a back cover blurb was, "over my dead body." Some people will do anything to get an endorsement."

Susan Musgrave/Cargo of Orchids/Given

On The west Coast, a journalist investigates a killing linked to destruction of old growth forest on First Nations land, and finds a spirit war as well as a real-work environmental struggle. He also finds love and meaning. It's a lovely, timely story line, and the outcome is arrived at in a surprising confluence of plot and subplot which makes the book ultimately charming and moving.

Candas Jane Dorsey

Stillwater Runs Deep
Book Two: The Lure

Ever go out drinking and don't remember what you did? What if there was a bar where spirits use your body for whatever they want until you sober up? What if the city's mayor has been murdered, his family missing, no clues and a witch has been released from her centuries old imprisonment? A deranged shaman shows up leaving clues and vanishes. So begins police detective, Carol Ainsworth's first big detective case.

Here is the film pitch to the novel. I've had a request to do a possible Netflix film on this novel. (Turn up the volume.) From My YouTube Channel, Let's Be Frank, Canada's Foremost Off Beat Author.

https://youtu.be/pa_-l2WejjA

Reviews

Your book kept my attention riveted from beginning to end. I liked the way you presented the female character being in control of the outcome and the fact the story was based on local settings. i.e. Victoria, B.C. Canada. Riveting Work .....

Linda Low

A refreshing change from the usual and all too familiar cast of deities and spirits. Talaber pulls his characters from the vast and untapped riches of aboriginal myth and legend, bringing to life their intricate stories largely unfamiliar to wider audiences. He intertwines their ancient tales with the dark, gritty and dangerous under belly of contemporary urban life. The whole makes for an interesting and compelling read with an ending that's impossible to predict.

Robert Winslow

Damn Frank—this writing is as tactile as a 1955 T-Bird. Very nice descriptions, good dialogue, a thinking man's book but one that can be read entirely for pleasure. Good work.

Michael Arkin/Judicial Indiscretion

Paranormal fantasy, mystery thriller rolled into one. The Lure is a well-crafted story that builds suspense through flowing narrative, life-like characters, and believable dialogue. If you're a fan of any of the above mentioned genres, or if you're just looking for a page turner to get lost in, The Lure will not disappoint.

Cris Pasqueralle/Destiny Revealed

A gritty book flavored with primitive urges and mysticism. As I followed Carol's foray into the realm of shamanism, I realized that it took a special touch to pull off a complicated plot the way you did. Your prose was concise, powerfully descriptive, the dialogue lively, and your photographic mastery of the fixtures and streets in Vancouver's hub, in clear evidence.

Kenneth Edward Lim/The North Korean

Carol, the head detective, has to solve several murder cases: with many twists and turns. There's Shamans, Animal Spirits, and "The Lure" thrown in for good measure. No wonder, Carol wanted to resign! Yes, this novel is a roller-coaster ride, with the author cleverly hinting along the way, ending with a roller coaster ride! Read this book. It is different. It's as if Elmore Leonard has risen as a shaman, to guide others to write about Indian lore.

Nancy Bridgeman

Your book was a rollercoaster ride thorough my emotions which, when I got off, left me stunned and breathless.

Your portrayal of sociopaths and the criminal mind in the pursuit of the sexually willing was so disturbing I had nightmares and had to set the novel aside for days. But the writing was so compelling I had to finish it, and I'm glad I persevered.

I literally cheered "go get them!" when Charlie used his protectors to deal rather uniquely with the antagonists.

I was enlightened to the Native spiritual culture which pleased me for which I now have a greater understanding and respect.

Carol G.

I want the author to take me to their world. I love the adrenaline rush I get from reading a book that scares the crap out of me. You know, the ones that have you screaming to the characters in your head or out loud. It tells me that the author did his or her job by getting me emotionally involved. I give up on books if I don't feel something. This book isn't one of those.

April Wolfgong

Stillwater Runs Deep,
Book Three: The Awakening

Its Ghostbusters teamed up with a female Mickey Spillane who has a Native Shaman sidekick nuttier than a squirrels winter stash as a side kick.

Agatha Christie, roll over in your grave, new sleuths on the prowl. A deranged shaman breaks his way into jail to stop all hell from breaking free while police detective Carol Ainsworth has to bring justice to a forest being's murdered mother.

How angry would a mythical god be if he found himself beginning to awake inside a mortal after centuries? The duo are determined to find out who killed the previous native elder before all lightning and thunder breaks loose. They encounter deranged inmates, mystical beings, ancient serpents, wood sprites and someone who should have been dead long ago.

Not your usual crime/mystery!

Not your usual criminal investigators!

You thought Jack Nicholson was mad in The Shining...

Wait until you meet Charlie Stillwaters in the Sweat lodge.

Reviews

There are many aspects true to First Nation's beliefs. For example the transformation of animals and anomalies within our realm. Frank Talaber's writing is clear and concise, leaving no grey areas. But his true talent as a writer is not only a sense of time, history and capturing First Nation's humor, but going from the real to the surreal and the supernatural. A gift he plies very well.

Tom Patterson Nuu-Cha-Nulth Artist and Master Carver

I've read and reread his previous series, Stillwaters Run Deep, several times. Frank's writing is original and compelling. You run into characters and situations totally unexpected. Keeps you on the edge of your seat and your heart.

Greta Olsson

Just when I was beginning to wonder where the next great Canadian story teller would emerge from, Frank Talaber has written a modern crime mystery with a twist. In "The Awakening" Talaber weaves the richness of Canada's west coast aboriginal spirituality into the science of modern forensics. CSI comes to Haida Gwaii as the shaman and the detective conduct an investigation that will take them and the reader on a journey to a place where murder, redemption and ancient mysticism intersect.

Michael G. de Jong, QC, Minister of Finance, Government House Leader,
Province of British Columbia

The Ainsworth Chronicles, Book One: The Joining

Welcome to Victoria in Beautiful British Columbia, the most haunted city in North America, and to Detective Carol Ainsworth's first day undercover at the very grand old lady, The Fairmont Empress Hotel. Ready to deal with the two Italian families flying in for a wedding to unite them, she did not bargain for the ghosts, the FBI agent or the ancient curses that come along too. Add to that the very wonderful and mysterious psychic lady claiming you've invited her, the young boys disappearing, and the weird things happening to the unfortunates looking for their next fix trapped alongside spirits in the sewers, Carol found her first undercover assignment way more challenging than she could have imagined.

The one saving grace was the great Empress High Tea that Agnes introduced her to and the fabulous scones that are to die for. Literally.

Reviews

I hate you! My wife, who is off on medical leave, won't get out of the bathroom. Can't put your book down. LOL.

Bruce W.

The ghosts of Victoria, BC are restless. The Joining is a riveting read for crime fiction lovers and those fascinated by tales of hauntings. Talaber expertly draws you into a multi-leveled world of local history, crime, and the supernatural, where a blue fairy, comprised of two sorrowful creatures, is more powerful than it knows. A perfect read for those foggy West Coast nights.

Melanie Cossey, A Peculiar Curiosity

I bought four of his novels, all right up my alley, urban Fantasy and Paranormal thrillers. But as we were leaving my girlfriend opened up the copy of The Joining, I had purchased and said, "Stop! You gotta go back I have to buy this book." Frank had hooked her in the first three pages. Well Done.

Joyce Nicholls

I've read and reread his previous series, Stillwaters Run Deep, several times. Frank's writing is original and compelling. You run into characters and situations totally unexpected. Keeps you on the edge of your seat and your heart.

Greta Olsson

On my YouTube Channel
Let's Be Frank, Canada's Foremost Off-Beat Author
Link to The Joining Movie Trailer
https://youtu.be/5oHtLOA4DQI

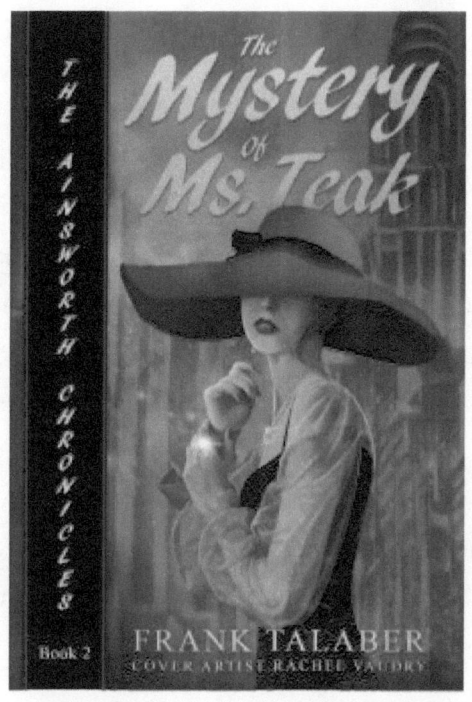

The Ainsworth Chronicles, Book Two: The Mystery of Ms. Teak

Agnes at her craziest best. Only what secret does she have to hide from herself and the one she thought dead? How does one psychic stop another from hunting her down, especially when the other hires the services of a mystical being long thought perished! As for Carol, she has her hands full with pissed-off Russians, the reborn builder of much of Victorian Victoria (yes, *the* Sir Francis Rattenbury), a young girl claiming to be our aforementioned psychic, and, to top it all off, there's something very wrong with Nathan, her nephew that they saved from death. But in traditional English fashion High Tea is *of course* still being served.

Reviews

I hate you, I can't put this book down. Every page gets more interesting, suspicious, wondering what is going to happen next. I sit down to only read one more chapter but end up having to read two more, because I need to know what happened in the past. Each chapter keeps you wanting more and now I hate it even more since I can't get to it before Long weekend coming up. I just read the last six chapters, clinging to every word, every sentence thinking I know what is going to happen next. Oh no, you take me in a completely different direction. Great book.

Sandy Strebe

Fasten your seatbelt as Frank Talaber takes you on a multi-dimensional trek through time where history comes alive to reveal buried secrets and tortured souls. From the stately tea salons of old Victoria to the haunting desolation of British Columbia's rugged West coast waters, The Mystery of Ms. Teak will both entertain and invite you to confront the demons that live within us all.

Michael de Jong
Provincial BC Liberal Minister

The Mystery of Ms. Teak

Do not read this book! Seriously, do not read this book - unless you are prepared to deal with a rift on your personal timeline. You will find that this book causes you to postpone activities that you would otherwise be doing.

You will be transported into a world of history and mystery, crime and grime, Spirits and other worldly time travel, with the delectable Detective Carol Ainsworth.

An amazing tale, which I thoroughly enjoyed.

Paddy Kopieczek

As a weaver of books you're beyond compare.

Greta Olsson

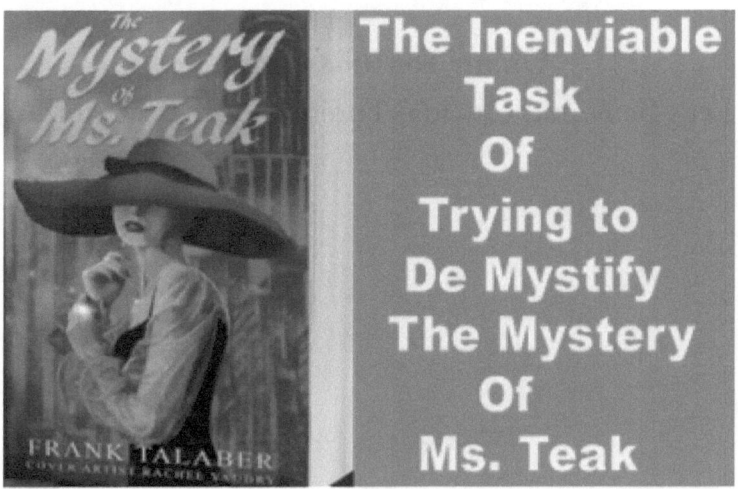

If you are into Videos, check out my Youtube video.
Trying To De Mystify The Mystery of Ms. Teak
https://youtu.be/TQKXOrJlpgw

On my YouTube Channel
Let's Be Frank, Canada's Foremost Off-Beat Author

Seeds Of Ascension Book One: Spirits Awakening

In a normal relationship a man gets married and has the time of his life on a memorable honeymoon in Hawaii. A small dilemma begins for Roger Harrison when normality ceases existing with the discovery of metallic alien metal planted in his body.

Roger is thrust onto a path he never dreamed his life would ever take as one of the chosen few to start something that philosophers and spiritualists have discussed for centuries; the Ascension of humanity.

Only this isn't how the human race's next level of evolution was supposed to happen, and nor did Roger think he was the guy that would pull it off.

Toss in a guardian angel, alien hunters and Roger soon begins to realize his life's perfection ends with the understanding that memories are the illusion to which reality is draped and all is rarely as it seems in the journeys of a soul's growth. Especially when he doesn't even know how to spell chakra, let alone deal with having to master the seven levels in order to attain ascension.

Nor can time, as he knows it, be measured in heartbeats or lifespans and a heavy price must be exacted in order to stand in the gateway between memory and knowing, reality and illusion.

Especially when that effort means stopping those who would doom humanity's next phase of evolution.

Short Story Anthology Volume One:
What I'd Say To Buddha If I Met Him In The Pub

(Includes Sylvia's Sun-catchers, voted #1 by the readers in
Rejected Manuscripts Anthology)

Enter the literary world of Frank Talaber, Canada's Foremost
Off-Beat Author

A natural storyteller, whose compelling thoughts are freed
from the depths of the heart and the subconscious before being
poured onto the page.

Literature written beyond the realms of genre he is known
to grab readers; kicking, screaming, laughing or crying, and drag
them into his novels.

Short Story Anthology Volume Two:

What I'd Say To Einstein If I met Him On The Dance Floor
(Includes Sylvia's Sun-catchers, voted #1 by the readers in
Rejected Manuscripts Anthology)
Enter the literary world of Frank Talaber, Canada's Foremost
Off-Beat Author
A natural storyteller, whose compelling thoughts are freed
from the depths of the heart and the subconscious before
being poured onto the page.
Literature written beyond the realms of genre he is known to
grab readers; kicking, screaming, laughing or crying, and
drag them into his novels.

Also, If You Are Interested In Hearing My Newest News

Send A Request To Join My Author's Newsletter
At <u>franktalaber58@gmail.com</u>
Or <u>twosoulmates@shaw.ca</u>
And in the subject line just state 'I'm In'.
And I'm Always Open To Chatting As Well.

Social Media Links

Visit Frank Talaber's Published Author page on Facebook at: https://www.facebook.com/FrankTalaber/

(If you want to join his fans' newsletter to hear about his latest ventures, send him a request to his email at twosoulmates@shaw.ca

Website:

<u>https://franktalaberpublishedauthor.wordpress.com/</u>

Facebook Short Stories Page:

<u>https://www.facebook.com/franktalaberpublishedauthor/</u>

Twitter:

@FrankTalaber https://about.me/ftalaber

Linkedin:

https://www.linkedin.com/feed/

My novels on Amazon.

https://www.amazon.com/stores/Frank-Talaber/author/B00UC407R0

https://www.amazon.ca/Autumns-Summer-Felicity-Talisman/dp/1738658376

My Youtube Channel.

https://www.youtube.com/channel/UCx5ki4gpdokN-9KAIZzu53w

Instagram

https://www.instagram.com/franktalaber

Goodreads

https://www.goodreads.com/author/show/8092362.Frank_Talaber

Ebooks on Smashwords:

https://www.smashwords.com/profile/view/Frank38

Instagram

https://www.instagram.com/franktalaber58

tictoc

https://www.tiktok.com/@franktalaber [1]

Ko-gi Funding Page

https://ko-fi.com/franktalaber?ref=onboarding_email_founderwelcome

Medium Site

https://medium.com/we-paw-bloggers/the-doctor-to-the-rescue-byline-frank-talaber-b5aa29203065

---

1.   https://www.tiktok.com/@franktalaber

Don't miss out!

Visit the website below and you can sign up to receive emails whenever Frank Talaber publishes a new book. There's no charge and no obligation.

https://books2read.com/r/B-A-FCHU-MRSKF

BOOKS 2 READ

Connecting independent readers to independent writers.

About the Author

Frank Talaber lives in Chilliwack, BC. He currently has twelve novels released, most set in BC, including Victoria, Haida Gwaii, Vancouver, and Prince George. He's written in many genres: Urban Fantasy, Science Fiction, Spiritual, comedy, Erotica, and Romance. Well, anything that calls to him, basically! As well as the novels, he can boast over eighty published short stories, articles, over sixty blogs and ten live interviews.

Frank is also published by The Wild Rose Press, one of the largest traditional Publishing houses in the world, with "his other half" Felicity Talisman.

People who have read Frank's books describe him as a natural storyteller who writes like his soul is on fire and his pencil is his voice crying out. They go further to say that they find his books grabbingly intense and hilarious at times, screaming everyday life from such a realistic viewpoint you're drawn into his world, unable to stop; almost cursing that they can't set the book down, page after page. Frank takes great pride in the realism of his work, painstakingly visiting most of the locations, (obviously, only the "real-life" ones!) and he is so thorough that many readers have remarked that they can hear, taste, visualize, smell and feel the essence of the place. "It really is like being there" one remarked. There isn't a greater compliment to be made.

Literature written almost beyond genres, whose compelling thoughts are freed from the depths of the heart and subconscious before being poured onto the page. Or, as he often says, "you don't have to be mad to be a writer, but it sure helps".

He writes in urban fantasy, science fiction, crime, spiritual, romance, erotica and comedy genres. Well, anything that calls to him, basically!

"To be honest, I loved to write novels, like a rock star that loves to thrill an audience and get that cheering response. That I've moved them, made them laugh, cry, scream and dream. But overall entertain them in a way they have never been entertained before."

Read more at https://franktalaberpublishedauthor.wordpress.com/.